FATAL AUGUST

⟪ In memory of Corin, for his patience and encouragement many years ago.

Certainly my affections to you are so unchanged that hostility itself cannot violate my friendship to your person, but I must be true to the cause wherein I serve. Where my conscience is interested, all other obligations are swallowed up. I should most gladly wait on you according to your desire, but that I look upon you as you are engaged in that party beyond a possibility of retreat. That great God, which is the searcher of my heart, knows with what a sad sense I go upon this service and with what a perfect hatred I detest this war without an enemy. We are both upon the stage and must act those parts assigned to us in this tragedy. Let us do it in a way of honour and without personal animosities, whatsoever the issue be.

Extract from a letter written by Sir William Waller, the Parliamentary Commander, to Sir Ralph Hopton, commanding the Royalist forces, before the Battle of Lansdowne July 1643.

Fatal August

SUE BODDINGTON

Privately printed for
Sue Boddington
Dacia, 99 Poulshot Road, Poulshot, Devizes, Wilts SN10 1RX
sue.boddington@virgin.net

by The Hobnob Press
8 Lock Warehouse, Severn Road, Gloucester GL1 2GA

Design and typesetting by John Chandler. The text is set in 14 point Doves Type, leaded 2 points. Doves Type is a digital facsimile, created by Robert Green, of the celebrated face made by Edward Prince in 1899 for the Doves Press, based on Jenson's 15th-century Venetian type.

ISBN 978-1-914407-35-2

Born and bred in Wiltshire Sue Boddington graduated from Bristol University in History, English, Theology and Philosophy. After flirting with teaching, acting and singing, she joined Wiltshire Library Service, holding the posts of Senior Librarian Adult Learning for the county and Community Librarian for the Calne area. Now retired, she still lives in Wiltshire and is the voluntary curator of Calne Heritage Centre.

Front cover design by Freda Jackson.

CHAPTER ONE

Sunrise was long past, but it was more like late evening. When Will Barry walked through the gate in the dry stone wall that encompassed the front garden and stepped into the pasture, he was in the habit of pausing to gaze at the cluster of cottages dotted irregularly down the valley and could see the elaborate chimney pots of Wanley Hall , almost in to Bromham. To the left he would have a view of Heddington and the undulating downs beyond, but this morning the mist was so thick nothing was visible as he turned to take the short cut through the edge of the copse towards the school house.

The mist hung over the tops of the trees, damp and swirling. It eased its way between the sere leaves that still clung to the branches of late October and encircled the trunks until they were nothing but elongated shapes lost in a grey oblivion. Somewhere a thrush was singing, but even that piercing, optimistic song was choked and muffled by the fog. Will Barry looked up in a vain attempt to see the defiant bird, whose song spluttered through the mist again and then drifted away.

It was not until he left the house that he had really noticed the dismal weather. He had been delayed by Mark Smart asking his advice on the best treatment for a sick goat, but he was grateful for the delay. It gave him more time to work out how he was going to express all the things he had been turning over in his mind, complicated issues that had no easy solutions.

He had promised to explain to his class of fifteen children why the country was in such an uproar, why Parliament was at the King's throat, why contention was boiling up everywhere. These children had heard their parents talk of war and they wanted to know if it was coming. They fully believed that Will could make it all clear to them and flattered as he was by their trust in him, he knew it was an impossible task and felt a twist of despair.

The vision of these country children, farmers' and labourers' sons and daughters, was black and white. They looked at the world with practical eyes and minds that attempted to bring all things down to simple, incontrovertible essentials. They knew of good and bad, but not of the subtle moral distinctions and strange contradictions that formed England in 1641.

They would ask Master Will if the King was a bad man and consequently did bad things. If he was bad, did this mean that the men in Parliament were good. They would demand positive, clear cut answers and he could not provide them with such answers. He was aware of all the strands in the argument, strands interwoven into an intricate mesh that he could not break through himself, let alone make clear to others.

He took a deep breath, which developed into a sigh as he struggled to formulate some of his ideas into words which they might understand. He was trying to anticipate some of their questions when his train of thought was broken by the sound of laughter, which hung suspended in the fog and seemed far distant. He walked on in what he felt sure was the direction of the sound, yet when he heard it again it was just as faint and far away. The fog was playing tricks on him, for when he bent down to step under two low branches, intertwined like an archway, there was a scuffling, a whisper and a shape loomed up in front of him. As he stared at it, the shape materialised into a shaggy, half-grown boy, who grinned at Will, declaring,

"Oh, tis you Master Will. You fair scared I. I thought twere Squire Wanley's new gamekeeper. He's not easy like old Catchpole used to be. He do prowl about these woods at all hours of the day and night."

The boy was talking fast and uneasily, pulling at his string belt and clawing at his matted hair with his fingers as if he were trying to comb it. Will laughed.

"Why should you worry about the gamekeeper Phillip? You haven't been poaching already this morning surely?"

"Poaching," Phillip Long, the wheelwright's son repeated the word as if it came from some strange, alien language. "Oh Lord no master, whatever makes you say that?"

"Well you have been up to something or you would not be late for school. That will be the third time this week. I admit that I am late myself this morning, but I have a good excuse in the form of a sick goat. What's yours?"

Phillip glanced over his shoulder, gave his hair another yank with his fingers and was about to say something when the tree at his elbow appeared to give a convulsive, half-stifled sneeze. Will swung around the trunk of the tree in time to see a flurry of skirts and heard that laugh again, as a girl darted away through the wood, her escape route revealed far into the distance by the cracking of dry twigs. Will raised his eyebrows at Phillip, but he was clearly amused. The boy coughed, then ventured with a weak bravado,

"Different kind of poaching Master Will."

"Yes, very pretty laugh for a pheasant."

"Well sir, this Jessie-"

"Alright, I do not need to know who she is, as long as you do. The fact remains that you should be at school. You are one of my senior pupils now Phil. This is your last year. When I am not there, you should be helping my sister, making sure the little ones are doing something constructive, not swinging from the rafters. Look, I tell you what, if you can get there a full five minutes before I can and get things organised, I will forget you were ever late. On the other hand, if I beat you to it, you are for it my lad. Fair enough?"

Phillip's face brightened. That seemed more than fair to him.

"Well, be off then."

The boy set his square shoulders and crashed into the mist, Will calling after him,

"I warn you, I know these woods pretty well myself."

Once Phillip had disappeared however Will made no attempt to hurry. He knew his sister Lucy would have the situation at the school in hand. He knew also that the wheelwright's son would be there long before him. The children from the tiny Wiltshire village of Sandy Barrow knew the woods and fields as well as the animals that inhabited them. They were kin to these creatures with their instinctive reactions and motivation. He knew that whatever he laboured to teach them, the power of their environment to mould them was too strong to be broken altogether, even by his enlightened humanism. He was eager to teach them the basic skills of reading, writing and arithmetic and to offer them the chance to widen their outlook with further reading, but he did not wish to alienate them from their environment. Most of them were destined to continue working beside their parents on the land and he was careful not to sow the seeds of discontent by suggesting that it was an inferior occupation. He did stress though that the development of the imagination by reading could make their lives much richer and hoped that now and then an exceptionally bright pupil might come along whom he could help to make a mark on the wider world.

He strolled on with his lithe, elegant walk. His movements were casual, almost lazy, yet he gave the impression that he could accomplish most physical tasks with consummate ease. He was a good height with a straight back and long limbs. His clothes suggested that he had no taste for extravagant display, but they were good quality and well cut. He did not have the cramped, threadbare look of the typical village school master, existing on the fringes of poverty. Yet village school master he was by choice and at no time was he more aware of it than now as he applied himself once more to the perplexed question of explaining the political, religious and social turmoil of England to his pupils.

The problem occupied him until he came out of the trees and reached the school house ensconced comfortably in a hollow between two ridges at the side of the valley with ploughed land stretching down beyond it. Built of grey flint, it was a modest building on one level, but every time he saw it, Will Barry was filled with pleasure, not because it was an architectural triumph- it was hardly that-but because four years past, when the twenty year old Will came back from Cambridge loaded with academic honours to his family's country farmhouse in Sandy Barrow there was no school, only the hard school of experience in which the children rough and tumbled as best they could.

Half the villagers were illiterate, or at best could just scrawl their names and pick out a word or two from the proclamations which the parochial and church officers pinned up on the church door in Calne or Bromham. Those who were fortunate to be literate could not lay their hands on any books. The church libraries were for clerics and scholars only. A vast number of cheap pamphlets were being printed but for the labourer even a penny was a price he could not readily afford.

Will's father had often expressed a wish to improve the education of the village children, but it had never got beyond a vague exchange of ideas.

Ralph Barry was a busy man. He had inherited a fine farmhouse and a hundred acres of land from his yeoman ancestors who had come up in the world, but he also ran a business importing teasels and dyes from the Continent to supply the local fulling mills. He was often away from home overseeing the unloading of goods at various ports and his ideas on education took a back seat.

He died when Will was sixteen. Sir Roger Wanley owned all the land around Sandy Barrow adjacent to the Barry's one hundred acres. Most of the villagers were Wanley's tenants. Sir Roger had been a close friend of Ralph Barry and when he died, took it upon himself to support his family. He employed a reliable agent to keep the import business going on their behalf, which safeguarded their income.

Will Barry declared himself quite capable of running the farm, but Sir Roger knew that Ralph wished his son to attend university and made sure Will had the leisure to go up to Cambridge the following year.

People in high places forecast a brilliant career for William Barry. He had been offered several attractive, lucrative posts, one a secretaryship with a high ranking minister of state. He had only come home for a short holiday, but it was long enough to tell him where his vocation lay. He could not turn his thoughts to affairs at court when people in the village where he grew up could not read or write and often lived in poverty and squalor. He was sure that his father would have approved of what he chose to do, although it was a great disappointment to Roger Wanley.

Will had heard tales told by the older villagers of a knight, Sir Thomas Mountfield, a scholar and adventurer, who fifty years or more past had opened a school in one of the small settlements near the road that ran from Chippenham to Devizes. He had led a colourful life by all accounts, sailing to the Americas and returning with an exotic native wife, who was the subject of much local gossip. He had built a house deep in Chippenham Forest where he ran a timber business. Some of the villagers reckoned that he and his wife were alive, though very old and living in the house still with one of their three children. Others insisted he had died long past. However they all agreed that the school had been shut down after about ten years because the religious authorities considered the syllabus was too unorthodox, going far beyond basic literacy skills and bible study.

The story intrigued Will. He had travelled along the Chippenham /Devizes Road, turning off towards Lacock and eventually found the settlement where the school had been. He was shown the cottage that Sir Thomas had converted into a school and was now home for two families. He even spoke to a man who admitted that his grandfather had worked for Sir Thomas for many years and when he died Mountfield had paid for his funeral, but he was not willing to reveal the location of the house- said he did not know the way or if Sir Thomas was still alive.

Will did not believe him. The man was evasive, almost hostile. All the villagers were suspicious of a stranger asking questions. It was clear that the memory of

Sir Thomas was revered and they were ready to protect his privacy from prying folk who might be up to mischief.

Will rode into the forest hoping to find the house, trying a number of paths, but they were all dead ends. He was disappointed because he longed to talk to what sounded like an exceptional, enlightened man about his experience of setting up a village school. If he had indeed died, perhaps his children would be willing to share their memories of him.

He went back three days running searching for the house with no success and began to wonder if it was just a legend. True or not the story strengthened his determination to set up a school. There were no empty cottages in Sandy Barrow suitable for conversion, so he decided to have one built. He had drawn up the plans, financed its construction and watched it grow. In the four years that followed he had built up a library, housed in the school, with a stock of books that reflected his wide-ranging, eclectic tastes and also his desire to give the little community of Sandy Barrow as comprehensive a selection of literature as possible.

That morning, as he grew closer to the school, he could he could hear the buzz of children's voices. The wooden shutters on the windows were closed against the fog and the rush lights still burned. When he reached the first window he eased the shutters open a crack. The wavering beams of the rushes were ineffectual and the children were sitting in patches of dark shadow. They were straining to see as they scratched away on their slates with charcoal, their heads bent low over their desks. At the head of the class, sprawled across the front desk, his brown face a strange parchment yellow in the light of the lamp at his elbow, was Phillip Long. He was giving the class a spelling test. Will smiled to himself and pulled the shutters together with deliberate care before he passed through a doorway with a rounded arch into the room that was library and study combined.

His entry caused a flurry in the long, narrow room. In the far corner a girl was rummaging in his desk. At the opening of the door, she sprang back like a cat, knocking a whole bundle of papers and slates to the floor with a clatter. She dropped to her knees, her cheeks flushed, as she gathered up the scattered papers into an untidy heap. Will strolled over to help her, but she pushed his hand away.

"Don't do that Master Will," she said sharply, not looking up at him, but still snatching at the papers as if her life depended on it. "I knocked them down, so I'll gather them up. Father told me t'other day I hadn't learned no gracefulness at this school."

Will eased himself into the oak chair that stood behind his desk and sat back to study her.

"There are many kinds of grace Hannah," he murmured.

"Aye and I don't have none on 'em."

She was on her feet now and dumping the bundle on the desk, turned to go.

"Wait a moment. You are in a bad mood this morning Hannah Moss. Is anything wrong at home?"

"No."

She turned her back on him, tossing her hair back over her shoulders. The two thick ropes of silver blonde hair looked as if they had been plaited a fortnight before and had not been touched since. Everything about her was untidy. She was clean and so was her russet dress, but it was patched and threadbare around the bodice. It was also a size too small for her, strained at the shoulders and across her full breast. The strings of the apron she wore at her waist trailed awkwardly behind her. Beneath the folds of her skirt her shoes were ill-fitting and clopped when she took a step forward.

Yet she was a pretty girl despite her incongruous appearance, tall and supple with a well-shaped figure. There was vitality and health in her movements, in the tanned skin and the jade green eyes that now gazed down at her feet and refused to look Will Barry in the face. He was used to a more direct approach from Hannah.

"Then you are feeling guilty about something. Were you ransacking my desk when I came in?"

For the first time that morning she looked at him fully, but she closed her mouth tight, refusing to answer.

"Your silence is answer enough. What were you looking for? If you had waited to ask me I might have saved you a great deal of bother."

"You'd laugh at me," she blurted out.

"Well, I don't do that very often. Try me and see."

She hesitated for a moment, running her hands down her skirt self-consciously, as if his steady gaze made her aware of her untidiness. Yet there was something about Will Barry that always encouraged her to tell the truth. At the same time as those serious dark eyes made her feel her inadequacies, they also gave her confidence. She often puzzled over the conflicting emotions he drew from her. He was leaning back in his chair now with a complete lack of impatience, yet giving the impression that the answer was important to him.

"It were a picture," she confessed in that same abrupt way.

"A picture?"

"One of them drawings of yourn. Catherine Hollis said that when I were with Mistress Lucy helping the little ones to sew, you were drawing my picture. I wanted to see it, that's all."

"Oh, I see. Well for once Catherine proved an accurate source of information, I was sketching you. You were so intent on your work, I took the opportunity while you were still for a moment or two. You are never still for very long."

He paused, watching as she tried to disguise the pleasure that brightened her face. "It was only a very rough sketch, but you are welcome to see it if you really want to."

He opened a drawer in the desk, pulling out a sheaf of papers wrapped in a leather cover, then he took the top sheet out and offered it to Hannah. She held out her hand gingerly, taking it with the tips of her fingers, eager to look but frightened that the drawing would reveal how Will really saw her and that it would not be the way she wanted him to see her.

"Oh Master Will!"

He could not interpret the loud exclamation immediately.

"Come, it's not that bad surely?" he queried, laughing.

"Bad! " Her whole face was a smile, "Tis a marvel. Tis the image of me, down to the very lines at my mouth."

She ran her hands over the corners of her mouth and then over those on the drawing as if she expected them to feel the same.

"Your fingers be blessed Will Barry, my mother always says so. Oh tis me right enough."

She held the sketch out at arms- length and danced a little with it. All her self-consciousness was gone now and she was the Hannah he knew.

"Well if you like it that much," he said, thumbing carelessly through the other sketches that filled his leather binder, "You had better keep it. I promise to do a better one in the near future, if you can keep still long enough."

"Can I really keep it?

"Of course."

"Thank you. Father and Mother will be fair amazed to see this."

She was still dancing and marvelling her way to the door, when she stopped suddenly, a troubled expression crossing her face.

"Oh, I near forgot, he's here, in the guest room with Mistress Lucy."

"Hannah, who is 'he'?

"Richard Wanley, Mistress Lucy sent me to see if you were in yet. That's why I come in the first place."

Will sighed. "Then why didn't you tell me right away? No never mind why. Is there a fire in the guest room?"

She shook her head.

"Then bring him in here for heaven's sake, he must be frozen."

He glanced across the room to the grate, where a log fire crackled and roared. It must have been burning for some time because the whole room was warmed. The girl was already closing the door behind her, when he called, "Hannah, did you light the fire in here this morning?"

"Yes Master Will."

"Thank you."

Her reply was to close the door. He listened to her footsteps echoing down the passageway, a light tap as the ball of her foot touched the floor and then a clop as the heels of the oversized shoes came down of their own accord. He could never mistake Hannah's footsteps; she only had that solitary pair of shoes.

Hannah was an intelligent girl, quick to learn and with a gift for passing on what she had learned to younger children in a way they could easily understand. Will and Lucy agreed that she was an excellent assistant in the classroom and with training and guidance could develop into a teacher, but they both knew that she did not have the time to spare to concentrate on the necessary study. Her brother Noah died five years past, when she was thirteen and from that time her father relied on her to fill his place, helping him to eke out his existence on his small plot of land. When the school was opened she was eager to attend and badgered her father relentlessly until he agreed she could spend two hours there in the mornings. "No more than two hours mind," he would shout after her. "That be more than enough. Your brother would have had no wish to waste his time learning stuff he would never need."

Noah Moss was six years older than his sister. Cheerful, confident, handsome with a wild streak in his nature which made him fearless, he was adored by his mother and was always keen to please her. Rumours of a few cases of plague in Calne had filtered out to Sandy Barrow early in 1637. Annie Moss' sister Sarah had married a weaver, Jabez Hart and lived in Calne in a cottage in Mill Street, one of a row of cottages occupied by weavers working for the Noyes family of clothiers. It was Annie's habit to visit her sister once a month, walking into Calne with a basket of fresh eggs to help supplement the Harts' meagre diet, but the talk of plague filled her with fear. She was worried about her sister but was afraid to venture into the town.

Noah volunteered to go, assuring her that the stories coming out of Calne were exaggerated. He was keen to meet up with his favourite drinking companion, Abel Cotton, who lived in the dingy, smelly top end of Church Street, known to the locals as Rotten Row, although he did not mention his ulterior motive to his mother. He had promised her faithfully never to get involved in any more ale house brawls and he had meant it at the time, but Noah always found it hard to keep his promises. His confidence that there was no real danger convinced his mother and he strolled off into Calne, whistling, with a dozen fresh eggs in basket. Annie Moss never saw her son again.

The plague was spreading and people were discouraged from entering and leaving the town. Fearful of bringing the dreaded disease to Sandy Barrow, the Moss family dare not go in search of Noah. They held on to the hope that he had decided to remain with his Aunt Sarah until it was safe to return home.

The outbreak which had begun with a few cases in the previous autumn, did not die down until July and by then it had claimed almost two hundred lives in Calne. In early August John Moss ventured into the town to visit his sister-in-law and discovered that Noah had not been staying with her for the last three months.

When he had knocked on her door back in late April, she had called out to him to leave the basket on the doorstep and go home as swiftly as he could, avoiding contact with anyone. She had assumed Noah had done just that. John, with a sinking feeling in the very pit of his stomach, went to the house of Benedict Browne, one of Calne's two Guild Stewards for that year, to ask where he might find any news of his son. Browne sent for the borough constables, employed by the burgesses to keep order in the town. Josiah Babcock had been a constable for ten years and was familiar with Noah Moss. On several occasions he had manhandled him out of local ale houses for brawling and sent him on his way back to Sandy Barrow. But he knew that although Noah was wild and handy with his fists when in his cups, he was a decent lad at heart and it saddened him to tell John that they had found his son, anxious and shivering, in the churchyard where he had slept overnight, his back against a gravestone.

Instead of taking his aunt's advice to go straight home he had risked a visit to Abel Cotton's flea-ridden dwelling first. He had told the constables with the horror of it reflected in his eyes, that he had found Abel's parents dead and Abel barely clinging on to life. His friend had grabbed hold of his sleeve before he could back away and begged him to stay. He was terrified of dying alone and Noah could not refuse him, sitting beside him until he died. After that he was not sure what to do, although he was determined not to take the risk of infection back to his family and decided to hide in the churchyard overnight.

The constables had no choice but to take him to the Pest House on the Alders, where folk displaying symptoms of plague, or who had been in close contact with victims were kept in isolation. The Alders was a broad expanse of common pasture land, south west of the town, held jointly by the burgesses, who regulated grazing use. The head of each household in Calne was entitled for a small fee to graze a limited number of cattle from May to mid-November. The mown grass was sold to the highest bidder and William Ingram, who lived on the edge of the pasture, was employed as hayward to oversee the mowing and the sale.

Ingram's dwelling seemed the obvious place for a pest house because the bodies could be buried in pits on the Alders, so William was offered one pound to leave his house and lodge nearby, his rent being paid by the burgesses. As he was their employee he could hardly refuse, even though he was expected to buy provisions for the occupants of the pest house out of that pound. He was also obliged to keep a record of those people who were buried in the pits and pass it on to the parish church officials to be entered in the burial register.

Josiah Babcock took John Moss to Ingram to check the record. It was there, scrawled in brownish ink- Noah Moss died of plague. Buried in plague pit on the Alders 6th May 1637. It was no comfort to John to be assured that it would be entered officially in the church register. He trudged back to Sandy Barrow feeling as if the life had been sucked out of him, not knowing how he would tell Annie.

She was desolate, blaming herself for not trying to prevent him from going into Calne that morning. Ever since there were times when overcome with guilt and grief, she was incapable of physical effort. She would sit staring ahead of her, rocking backwards and forwards in a trance-like state, sometimes for hours.

Hannah had to set aside her own sorrow over losing Noah, for although she often resented the favouritism shown to him by her parents, who would forgive him anything, she loved her brother deeply and missed his careless optimism. Expected to take his place beside her father, she was also required to do all her mother's tasks when Annie fell into her melancholy musing.

John Moss buried his pain deep inside himself. He never berated Annie, but there were times when an angry frustration spilled out of him and Hannah bore the brunt of it. She forgave her parents because she understood the bitterness of their loss, but it was not an easy life. The time spent helping at the school was her escape. Will and Lucy marvelled at her courage and spirit, her determination to squeeze in time at the school, amidst everything else that her father expected of her.

Will had turned over the piece of paper on the top of his binder and was sketching the fire and the wide, brick fireplace, when he heard more steps in the passage. These too were familiar, the springing walk of a confident man. Even before the echoes were swallowed up in the darkness at the top of the passage, Richard Wanley exploded into the room. There was no other way to describe his entrance. He never appeared to open a door and walk through it. There was always a great noise and there was Richard in the centre of the room, like a genii materializing from a bottle.

"Damn it, it's warmer in here Will," said Squire Wanley's eldest son, as he made for the fire, stretching his fingers out over the flames.

"I am sorry you were kept waiting in there so long. Lucy should have brought you straight in here. I don't know what she was thinking about."

"Ah now, we were having a fine, philosophical conversation, very profound," Richard explained, a mocking note in his voice. He was leaning against the fireplace now and began to scrape the mud from his knee-length boots with the poker. Will raised his eyebrows in a show of disbelief and Richard laughed. He had a cool, controlled laugh which did not blend with his vigorous manner.

"Don't look so scornful. You do not monopolize all the philosophy around here. Though I must admit my intellect is not quite as well developed as my appetites."

He stopped for a moment to flick a large clod of mud into the fire and watch it splutter, sending a vein of blue along the red glow of the flames, then turning to Will he said abruptly, "You were damn late this morning. Doing a spot of meditation on the way? That's what they do these Puritans don't they? Spend their days meditating on their own sin and unworthiness. Get up at five in the morning, have a damn good grovel and self-abasement, make a few apt comparisons between themselves and worms and they are ready to face the day with a sour but humble face."

"Richard, what are you talking about?"

Will was genuinely puzzled. There was a sharp edge to Wanley's mocking and Will felt that some accusation was levelled at him. He gazed at Richard in the few seconds silence that followed the question. Wanley's frame stood out in relief against the fire. It was a slight frame; he could not have been more than five and a half feet tall. The high wedge heels of his boots and the padded shoulders of his jerkin were intended to flatter his stature, but there was a strength in his sinewy body visible in the decisiveness of his movements. His hands were huge for so small a man. The fingers were thick and covered in a light red down. His hair and beard were a fierce, startling red and his face speckled with pale freckles.

"You know what I am talking about," he replied. " I thought you might have been contemplating the theories of your new found friend, Praying Isaac. More than one person has seen you in intimate conversation with him this past week. You have even been to his house, if you can call that dovecote a house. Damn it Will, a dissenting minister is not a person to know these days." The light had dawned on Will.

"Oh I see, you object to the company I keep. You think that a few conversations with Isaac Hewer will fire me with a zeal to pull down the fabric of the English church and batter in the gates of tradition, so all class distinction will be levelled and murder and rapine will engulf the land."

Will had left his chair now and was standing beside Richard at the fire. His remark was in the main good-humoured, but there was a trace of scorn in his eyes, an hauteur in the way his mouth with its full lower lip was set, that irritated Wanley.

"Don't you be clever with me Master Barry," Richard snapped, jabbing a hairy index finger into Will's shoulder.

" Well you began by trying to be clever with me. I think I am better at it than you, so let us be straight-forward about it shall we? I hope we have been friends far too long to have to goad one another."

Richard assured him that nothing would suit him better than straight-forwardness.

"Then you know full well that I shall not be led into sedition. Hewer is a fascinating man, with a powerful spirit that draws like a magnetic force. I don't agree with all he says, but discussions with him help me to finalise my own opinions. For years now I have felt that something was wrong with the Church. I used to think that it was only small, trifling things that could be easily remedied, but I have now come to see that it is something fundamental. All this hot air over vestments and ceremony is not what it is about. In the Anglican Church the relationship with God is wrong. Hewer's is right."

Wanley snorted like an impatient horse and swung his boot into mid-air as if he longed to kick something.

"Grovel and you will be saved- a grand religion for a man with spirit."

"That is typical of your massive simplifications."

Will was very earnest now. He was searching for the right words to explain his reactions to Puritanism, but found it difficult because he could not explain it to himself with any clarity. There were times when he cursed the eclecticism and breadth of vision that made him the tolerant man that he was. Richard Wanley was like the children of Sandy Barrow, an adherence to one point of view excluded all parts of the other. He too saw the world in black and white, but the black was that which offended him and the white that which gave him pleasure. The foundation of the division was not morality or logic, but his own will.

" I don't suggest that extreme Puritanism is the answer" Will Barry continued.

"Can you see me accepting the doctrine of predestination and all that it implies? 'Nothing can separate us from the love of God'- that's what I think predestination means, but that isn't what John Calvin thinks. I am not exactly an ascetic either am I? Without the vision of beauty God is only half a God. No, the point is, Hewer has his finger on that fibre of reality that reaches straight to God. I want to put my finger on it too and I want the Anglican Church to be bound with such fibres."

Richard had been opening and closing his fist mechanically as Will spoke, an expression of mounting impatience in his hazel eyes. He now stepped back, made a bow of sweeping acknowledgement and said loudly,

"Will my boy, you should have been an orator. You look so damn handsome when you throw your head back like that."

Will sighed and dropped into the rocking chair by the fire, where he rested his head against the high back and rocked himself gently.

"Oh Dick I thought we agreed to be serious about this. I just cannot make people understand. Mother and Lucy try so hard, but even they are puzzled, so how can I expect it of you?"

He looked disappointed and weary. A flash of remorse passed across Richard's face. He walked across to Will, putting his heavy hand on the one that rested on the arm of the chair.

"I'm sorry. I was only teasing- I didn't mean to hurt you. It's just that I do not want people to get the wrong impression of you, that's all. I know there's not a more reasonable man alive than you, but you must take care. It is the political implications. There isn't such a thing as religion without politics these days."

"Then there should be."

"Oh I dare say. I don't doubt that there is a lot wrong with the Church. I can't say I care much one way or the other, but it is up to the Church to reform itself, not to be insulted by upstarts like Hewer with their lunatic notions. I mean Laud was trying to restore the beauty of holiness and all that."

"Yes, he is courageous, but he is a fool. He went too far, too fast, underestimated the strength of feeling in the opposition and trying to impose the Book of Common Prayer on the Scottish Church was a disaster. But I can't condone his being held in the Tower as a traitor all these months. Parliament has no legal proof. That is why there is a reluctance to bring him to trial."

"Damn it!" Richard thumped his fist down on the arm of the chair and set it rocking so violently that Will almost slid off the seat. "There you go again, confusing me. It reached my father's ears what you said about Bishop Pakenham's monthly sermon last Sunday and he knows about the books you have in this library."

"He would know more about them if he used the library once in a while," Will replied quietly.

"Don't evade the issue. He knows you have Parliamentarian tracts in here. I wouldn't be surprised if you had leveller pamphlets here as well."

Will smiled at him in an enigmatic way that Dick could not interpret, then he went over to the shelves, taking down a handful of cloth-bound volumes. The paper was fragile and inferior quality, the text not printed but written in a bold hand in black ink. He offered these to Richard, who was watching him suspiciously.

"What are these?"

"Leveller pamphlets. They were written by a fellow named Gerard Winstanley, who I feel sure is going to make a name for himself someday. He has some very interesting ideas about property. You should read some of his writings, they-"

Before Will could finish Wanley snatched the pamphlets out of his hand and attempted to hurl them into the fire, but Will's reaction was faster. He caught hold of Richard's wrist and held the hand in mid-air.

"Oh no Dick, I cannot let you do that. There is much that is socially relevant to the people of Sandy Barrow in works like these and I am not going to let you destroy them."

Richard was breathing heavily between set teeth. His face muscles had tightened, but he did not attempt to free his wrist from Will's grasp.

"Now look here, this is not the sort of thing I would expect from you. After all, you are going to marry my sister."

Will stared at him, then he let go of his wrist.

"Yes," he murmured in a vague way, as if the thought was new and strange to him, "Yes, I suppose I am."

The change in his manner was not apparent to Richard who continued to fulminate about the dangers of allowing subversive, thick-headed farmers and labourers to read such inflammatory works. Will took the pamphlets from him and began to shelve them, still in that abstracted way. He was only half listening. He could see Maria

Wanley draw back with instinctive revulsion when he stopped to talk to his ploughman, on their walk back from Bromham church last Sunday. Later he had tried to share with her his plans for expanding the school, but she had laughed at him and turned the conversation into a channel of such studied inanity that he had made up a hurried excuse and left the company. He had seen her twice since, but could not be at ease with her. The incident had thrown up a barrier between them, at least he perceived it as a barrier. He doubted if she did. Perhaps it was his fault, always expecting too much. She was only nineteen and strongly influenced by her father's views on maintaining the social order. She had been brought up to believe the Wanleys were superior beings.

It had always been Sir Roger's wish that his elder daughter should marry Will Barry and unite the families even closer. Everyone took it for granted. He planned to find a wealthy heiress for Richard, but Dick had no intention of settling down yet. He liked variety and was inclined to spread his favours around. His father was willing to indulge him for a while and concentrate on getting Maria settled. She seemed perfectly happy with the idea of marrying Will Barry. For several years now Will had accepted the notion in a general way, but always saw it as something in the future rather than the present and now he was beginning to doubt that she had any deep affection for him.

He was gazing into the fire, running his hand over his unruly, shoulder-length hair, when he was suddenly aware of Richard saying, " Are you listening to me?"

"Yes, of course I am listening."

" Well, do you really think it safe to let people read stuff like this?"

"It would not be safe if they did not have anything else to read, but look at the shelf just above you." Richard instinctively looked up. "Just read off the names of some of those authors, Lancelot Andrews, Hooker's 'Ecclesiastical Polity', the writings of Matthew Parker- could you find anything more judicious and orthodox than that? Besides, I have a good collection of the early church fathers in those folio parchment volumes down on the bottom shelves. Would your father consider having me arrested for a potential papist if he knew about those? The villagers are entitled to as wide a range of thought as I can provide for them."

Richard was beaten. He had never come out of an argument with Will and felt the better man. It had been the same when they were children. He did not want to resent it- Will was his closest friend- yet he did resent it. The indomitability of Will's idealism rankled in him. He threw himself into the rocking chair that Will had vacated earlier and announced in an irritable voice, "I could do with a drink."

Will was relieved that an opportunity to relax the tension had presented itself.

"I'm afraid I can only offer you damson wine. I had a class in here last night for a few labourers who want to pick up the rudiments of reading and writing. They brought their own barley bread and peas, but they drank dry the barrel of ale I had stowed away in the cellar. I didn't realise that reading was such thirsty work."

As he spoke he fetched a decanter from the wall cupboard behind his desk. "I have no wine glasses here either, only tankards."

He poured the smooth, plum coloured liquid into a tankard, handing it to Richard, who was watching the firelight strike through the glass decanter and throw shafts of rainbow light on the ceiling. Wanley swirled the wine around in the tankard with a moody distaste, then unexpectedly, he laughed.

"That I should come to this- damson wine- God forgive me. Ah well, your health and mine."

He drained the cup in one draught.

"You are a fool about these people William, letting them drink your ale and monopolise your time. You could have been secretary to an important diplomat, a good writer or an even better artist instead of a yeoman farmer, doubling as a village school master. You know what the gospel says about pearls before swine."

Will did not answer as he poured himself a drink.

"You can't even be sure that they appreciate all you do for them. For instance I bet they thieve no end of these books."

Dick had his feet up on the fender and was wriggling his toes inside his boots to warm them. "Those folios ought to be chained. Show me a library in England where they fail to chain valuable folio works. The cathedral library in Salisbury does. Even that copy of Foxe's Book of Martyrs in Heddington Church is chained to the table."

"However could I, with all my advantages, so different from their circumstances, ever have formed any relationship with them, if I had not made it clear that I was willing to trust them completely? Besides, it's their library, not mine."Richard shrugged.

"If one or two books are stolen and I will admit, a few are, I am optimistic enough to believe that they read them at home and learn something."

Wanley let out a snort. "My God, your innocence amazes me sometimes. They do not steal them to read. They steal them to sell and if they can't sell them, they use the pages of St. Jerome and the agricultural wisdom of the ages to stuff bolsters and tie on sticks to scare the pigeons out of their patches of vetch. Don't sentimentalize them Will. How much do you think they really learn?"

Will shook his head. "It's hard to judge. Sometimes I think very little, but at others I see good general progress. But I do know I must keep on trying."

"Then there is no help for it is there? I have no argument to combat that. High-mindedness is too much for me. Thanks for the wine- tasted better than I imagined."

Dick stood up, shoving the tankard on to the desk and slapping his boot with a show of purpose.

"I must be off. I have to see about the horses. You will come to the race this afternoon?"

"What race?"

"Well would you believe it? I came here with the express purpose of telling you about it and I damn near forgot. Sir Gervaise Cleverdon, that pompous oaf from

Lacock, who keeps ogling Lucy in church, says he has a bay faster than my black Brimstone, so we are going to race it out- a circuit round our land, then across to Heddington Wick, up to Roundway and back. If we start promptly at three, we should finish before the light starts to fade. I am putting up pretty high stakes, so I hope he is as big a fool as he looks."

Richard was full of the race as he walked down the corridor with Will. He was back in good humour, their altercation seemingly forgotten. He was animated and laughing, the dashing Richard, who for all the difference in their temperaments, had always kept a hold on Will Barry's affections. He was so insistent, that Will agreed to come, although he made it clear he had another engagement in the early evening. He did not confess however that he was due to meet in Isaac Hewer's house to discuss the meaning of true religion. If he had, he doubted that Richard would have parted from him so cordially. He closed the

door on his friend, after watching him disappear into the fast thinning mist, dispersed by a pale, gilt sun. As he leaned with his back to the door he could hear the children sing-songing the lines of a poem, following the clear voice of his sister Lucy. The voices rang through his head. He felt depressed and sick as if there was something in front of him, some immensity that he could not control, some blackness that would engulf him. He could not explain such a sudden wave of emotion logically, but it was so intense that he began to shiver. He closed his eyes, trying to concentrate on something that would blot out this foreboding, this iciness that was like the shadow of death passing across him. He found himself picking out the voices of individual children amongst the drone. There was Philip Long's bellow –'The banks of flowers, the starry bowers, the woods so green and fine.' Will repeated the words in an effort to bring himself back to a stable frame of mind. Taking a deep breath, he forced himself to go into the classroom.

The children stopped their recitation and scrambled to their feet to chant, "Good morning Sir."

"Good morning." He faltered a little but was relieved that the words came. Lucy looked up at him, wondering if he was ill, for his face was as grey as the linen dress she wore.

"The mist has almost gone now," he said. "Phillip, open the shutters and let in some light and we can turn out the lamps."

The opening of the shutters seemed symbolic and helped him to clear away some of that dark shadow from his mind. As he talked to the children he became more like himself and Lucy's anxiety for her brother faded. She could not know, even as Will himself did not know, that in a brief moment, he may have seen reflected in his own anxieties, a presentiment of the spectre of war and misery that was soon to split England asunder.

CHAPTER TWO

The residents of Sandy Barrow were adamant that the dozen cottages and huddle of squatter dwellings, one of which was little more than a wind-break with canvas stretched over it, that made up their settlement should be called a village. Bromham folk laughed at their presumption and were inclined to consider it just an overspill from their own village. On the other hand the inhabitants of Heddington claimed it with equal confidence, while some of the workers on the Whetham estate were of the opinion that it should be regarded as part of Whetham.

Sandy Barrowites treated all these suggestions with distain. They admitted that they did not have a church like Bromham or Heddington, but they did have a school in a proper building, something none of their near neighbours possessed. They could boast that it was as good as any school in Calne or Devizes. Besides that the settlement was book-ended by two substantial houses.

At the top of the valley with its back to the narrow road that wound through the woodland of Sir John Ernle's Whetham estate down into Calne, stood the Barry family's farmhouse. Built in the previous century, the wattle and daub over its timber frame had been replaced early in the reign of James I with knapped flint and rubble, forming thick, sturdy walls. Four bays of mullioned windows ran across the front of the house, letting light into both the ground and upper floor. It was solid and unpretentious, but with an air of comfortable prosperity.

The front garden, enclosed by a dry-stone wall, was divided down the middle by a tiled path. On one side was a wealth of shrub roses, musk and eglantine still in their wild state mixed with more cultivated varieties, which in the summer bloomed white, pink and crimson, filling the air with their heady scent.

The other side was dedicated to herbs and vegetables planted around the red brick well with a pagoda-shaped wooden roof. The bucket attached to the winding mechanism sat on the well cover, for when not in use the well was always covered to prevent accidents.

Beyond the garden wall stood a row of open-fronted cattle stalls, divided and supported by round, stone columns. An impressive barn with two entrances, two small sheds, chicken coups and a weather-boarded granary, raised off the ground to deter rodents, completed the array of buildings in the yard. A duck pond, oval in shape and edged with chick weed and rushes lay where the yard merged into the pasture.

The building at the bottom of the valley was very different. At least five times the size of the Barrys' dwelling, Wanley Hall was a manor house of style and ambition. The original fifteenth century building had been transformed. Roger Wanley's ancestors would not have recognised it. Flanked by two four storey, square towers with castellated parapets, the main block of three storeys showed the Italianate influence made popular in England by the architect Inigo Jones. It was too free form to be purely classical, but the two fluted pillars either side of the steps leading up to the main door gave the impression of entering a Greek or Roman temple. Besides the numerous fancy chimney pots, there were scrolls and lozenges in abundance on appropriate parts of the structure, carved by skilled Flemish immigrants hired from London at great expense. Overall the building had a pleasing symmetry and sat well in the landscape.

Roger Wanley was aware that it did not compare with Bromham House. He wished that palatial edifice, where both the present King and his father had been guests, was farther away to make comparisons less likely. He had wished the owner, Edward Baynton in hell many a time, perhaps the farthest distance mankind could travel. The two landowners were frequently involved in angry disputes, but to be fair to Roger, the arrogant, litigious Baynton was at odds with most of his neighbours, his labourers and even members of his own family.

The houses at each end of Sandy Barrow kept the villagers employed ploughing, sowing, reaping, threshing and herding through most of the year. They preferred working for Will Barry because although he was not as wealthy as Wanley, he paid higher wages and treated them with respect. They could not afford to offend Squire Wanley because they were his tenants, but they did not like him.

The north paddock of Wanley's estate abutted on to the village common. He had put up a picket fence to keep the villagers' cows off his paddock and the creatures forever ranged restlessly up and down the fence, hoping to find a weak spot where they could push through.

Sir Roger considered the common an anomaly. It was a natural extension of the slopes of his north paddock, on his estate land and he was itching to enclose it. He had grazing rights on it of course, but so did his ploughman.

He resented the inclination of his labourers to hang on to every vestige of independence. He was once heard to remark that 'while every Tom, Dick and Harry can own a cow and rely on land to graze it, while he can still claim petty rights and talk about some meagre square of land just large enough for him to stand on as being his property, we will never have any progress in England.'

He believed in large scale enclosure on his own terms. He was willing to rent land, but the tenants' only security must be Roger's word and when it pleased him to turn them out, they must accept it. He had no overall vision of agricultural progress, although he used the concept as an excuse.

As he stood on the edge of the paddock, waiting for the competitors to assemble for the race, he was eyeing the expanse of common speculatively. His muscular arms were folded across his chest and he nodded his head from time to time, as a gaggle of parish officers, two members of the select vestry, plus the constable and overseer, all tried to impress their opinions on him. Whetham and Sandy Barrow were included in Calne Parish and whenever they had the opportunity the various parish officials danced attendance on the Wanley and Ernle families. Bromham was in a different parish and they were grateful to be free to steer clear of the unpredictable and often malicious Edward Baynton.

The Parish Constable, Jeremiah Jackson was clutching his white staff of office. He had just transported some malefactors to Devizes prison to await judgement at the Quarter Sessions. He always took his staff of office on such occasions; he felt it enhanced his authority. He was invariably pleased with himself when he had been on official business. The fact that the felons in question were two half-grown boys who were apprehended for plucking the tail feathers from some chickens hung up outside a butcher's shop in Calne to stuff some bedding, did nothing to lessen his feeling of self-importance. He was particularly loud in expressing his opinions and had cowed his more timid companions into a fidgety silence.

"If I were you Sir Roger- mind you I don't presume to know better than you- this is just my humble opinion you understand- if I were you, I would use my influence with the High Sheriff. He has got the ear of our representatives in Parliament. One or two well-chosen words and there's an enclosure bill gone through in no time. All these odd scraps of land can be gathered up. You could even deforest Brindley copse and get the cottagers' stinking pigs out of it."

The constable was a big man with a barrel chest and broad, heavy face, but his voice was thin and high-pitched. When he spoke at length his eyes would bulge as if his larynx was strained to breaking point. He saw himself as a man of some refinement and although he was born the illegitimate son of a Devizes merchant, who had set him up with a legacy in his will and he had never travelled far outside Wiltshire, he advertised himself as an urbane, cosmopolitan fellow, who knew the world. He tried to speak and act like his conception of a gentleman, but a persistent whim of his tongue to leave the letter 'h' off the beginnings of words and attach them to other words that it was never meant to proceed, was always a great sorrow to him. He thrust out his chest like a turkey cock when Sir Roger agreed that it might be a wise move to approach the High Sheriff.

"It would be such a pleasure to me to have this common enclosed," murmured the Squire, "Then we would not be obliged to witness this spectacle. There are so many damn folk on the common you can't distinguish them from the cattle."

There was indeed great activity on the common. News had spread that there was to be a race in the squire's paddock. There had been a hiring fair in Lacock that morning and a group of Bromham labourers who had been offering their services, hoping for good positions to help them survive the privations of the winter had drifted up to Sandy Barrow common on their way back to Bromham. Lean, brown, tousled men in smocks, lounged upon the grass talking over the happenings of the day. They wore the insignias of their calling, the usual practice at a hiring fair, so that they might be distinguished easily. The carters wore hanks of whipcord pinned to their shoulders or in their hats; the cowherds had strands of cow hair twisted about them in prominent positions.

Many of them had no luck at the fair. They had not been engaged and were wondering where they could find work that would bring in enough money to feed their children, but they did not look desperate. Some of them had indulged in a bit of illicit gambling at the fair and spent their winnings in the Lamb's Fleece on the way back. The name bestowed on the establishment by its patrons was an ironical one, suggesting to the uninitiated that it was a tavern. In fact it was a ramshackle barn attached to a squatter's dwelling at the end of the track that divided Whetham estate land from Abbot's Waste and Bowood Park beyond.

Andrew Clark had settled in a sheltered corner and his wife Hester brewed strong ale in the barn, serving customers from a hatch in the side window, charging a halfpenny a pint. To reach the barn villagers eager for a drink had to weave their way between a small flock of attentive sheep, who would accompany them right up to the serving hatch- no doubt why the name Lamb's Fleece had been chosen for the ale house.

There were no houses along this section of the road that turned down towards Lacock and on to Bath just before it reached Abbot's Waste. People from Sandy Barrow had started to call it Sandy Lane to establish a link with their own settlement, mainly to annoy their Bromham neighbours.

The wooded area known as Abbot's Waste was so called because before the dissolution and despoiling of the monasteries it had belonged to Lacock Abbey. It was granted to William Sharrington along with the Manor of Lacock in 1540 and William's great-niece, Olive still owned it. However it was rarely patrolled by any game keepers or forest wardens, so local villagers found it handy for poaching. Bowood Park was a different matter. Enclosed from Chippenham Forest on behalf of the crown just over twenty years past and furnished with several hunting lodges for the use of courtiers and royal guests, it was home to a herd of tempting deer. But unlike Abbot's Waste it was well guarded by wardens and the penalties for poaching on crown property were draconian. That very day the Bromham men heading for the Lamb's Fleece had dissuaded one of their company from trying his luck. The risk was too great.

Now sitting on the common, their throats washed by rough ale, they were talkative and high-spirited. The winter was coming, but they had survived other winters. Their resignation was based in hope. They were not yet degraded into a wage-earning mass, drained of pride and initiative. Although prey to the vagaries of the seasons, they still had reason to believe that their lives were their own, a matter between God and themselves. While they owned livestock and a piece of land, no matter how small, no one could deny it. They could hardly guess how men like Wanley were plotting to deprive them of their liberty.

At that moment the squire was eyeing them critically, wondering where they had all come from. "Many of these fellows don't work for me or for Will Barry. Who the devil are they?"

He was informed by the constable that they were labourers from Bromham and Jackson offered to move them on. Wanley shook his head.

"No, cause too much kerfuffle now. I can see Cleverdon and his party over there. Better get on with it or we will be too late to start."

He strode off with his entourage in close attendance.

Will Barry sitting against the trunk of an oak tree, his sketch pad on his knees was thinking how fine the labourers looked. He tried to capture some of the strength in their broad, seamed faces, many past generations reflected in their appearance and attitudes, but he was dissatisfied with his efforts. All the sketches turned out too rosy, too noble, the fruit without the thorn, which irritated him. He screwed the fourth sheet into a ball and tossed it at his feet with the other rejects. His border collie Flash, who had been skirmishing with two lurchers, pounced on the paper and began to throw it around with great energy and pleasure.

"That is all they are good for Flash," Will said, smiling at the dog's enthusiasm. "You lay into them."

The early mist had cleared by midday and left a pale sun to give the afternoon a wan, sad brightness, but the air was already sharpening as if for frost later. Every sound had a distinct clarity. The thrush, perhaps the very one that had sung for Will in the mist that morning, was no longer muffled. The notes vibrated in the ear like a lightning strike. The carriage wheels rumbling along the loose stone track at the edge of the common could be heard at a great distance and Will paused in his sketching to watch it draw closer. It had come from Wanley Hall and was one of the squire's carriages. Will was not surprised to see his mother and Lucy sitting with Ellen Wanley and her daughters. Galloping either side of the vehicle, yelling good-humoured imprecations at each other were Richard and his brother Edward.

Tucking his sketch pad under his arm, Will strolled over to meet the carriage with Flash at his heels. Caroline, a child of ten with long, gazelle-like legs that wanted to do things her voluminous skirts would not allow, was already running across to him. She made a fuss of Flash, stroking his ears, then Will took her hand and they walked to the carriage together. He acknowledged Lady Ellen and Maria, then stepped forward to help his mother down, kissing her on the cheek as he did so.

"I'm sorry that I did not come home for dinner mother."

Lucy had alighted with agile ease and Maria was the only one in the carriage now. Will offered his hand, but she did not take it. There was no hostility in her refusal, her eyes were smiling, but she continued to sit there surveying the scene as if it was all so fascinating that she had hardly noticed him. He was watching her intently, waiting for her to speak, but his attention was called from her by his mother, who was saying, "I think you might have come home with Lucy. Your dinner was ready for you."

"I was obliged to stay a little longer at the school to spend some time with Job Dilke. He is having such trouble with his figures. The sum of four and four has a whole range of possibilities in Job's mind. His father gets so impatient with him because he is a slow learner. The poor lad tries so hard, but that doesn't seem to count for anything with John Dilke. By the time we had finished

I realised that it was almost time for Richard's gallant display of horsemanship, so I came straight up here."

Richard, who was pointing something out to his sister, laughed and slapped Will on the shoulder.

" And I suppose you have not eaten anything since breakfast," his mother chided gently.

"Now there you do me wrong. I called in at Josh Carter's on the way and had a meal with the family, a good helping of bacon and turnips with freshly made rye bread, so I did well."

"So you didn't come straight up here" Olivia Barry observed, wondering how her son could prefer eating with the villagers to a meal with his family.

"Delicately permeated with the flavour of wood ash that rye bread no doubt," Richard threw in.

" It is a flavour that I have almost grown used to," Will reflected, but Richard was not impressed.

"It's a wonder they don't all die of slow poisoning, all that wood ash in the dough and then there is that vile concoction of barley bread diluted with lupins and vetch."

Richard was looking at Maria and laughing. There was that expression on her face again, the one that so troubled Will.

"Do you think they would eat it if they could afford anything better?"

He had not intended his words to sound so vehement, but the angry frustration that rose in him when he saw that expression on Maria's face, was reflected in his tone. Everyone stared at him for a moment.

"William dear, there was no need to say it in that

way," Olivia Barry's hand was on her son's arm. "Of course we know they have little choice. Richard was not condemning the Carters."

Will's eyes were fixed on Maria's face. He was hoping for a favourable sign, something to allay his fears and she was wise enough to give him what he wished to see, her sweetest, most endearing smile, which softened her oval face. He could not supress a sigh of relief. The effect did not escape her and from that moment she was all attention. She dropped the careless air, treating him with such tender, thoughtful charm that all the anxieties he felt concerning their relationship were soothed away for the time being.

As he walked across the paddock with Maria on one arm and his mother on the other, he could give his mind more easily to young Edward enthusing about the race, Caroline playing with Flash and Richard teasing Lucy about Sir Gervaise Cleverdon. He felt happier than he had all day. The impact of the strange emotion that had so shaken him that morning had left him feeling hollow and weary. Now he was beginning to feel himself again and was soon caught up in the preparations for the race.

Sir Gervaise, a vision of incongruity in an ill-assorted collection of fashionable fol-de-rolls, lace collar and cuffs, velveteen knee britches, a violent pink doublet that was almost luminous and a wealth of plumes in his hat, was arguing with Roger Wanley in the centre of the paddock. An assortment of retainers, grooms, jockeys, servants and the four inevitable parish officials were gathered around, while the horses fretted and stamped. Will had an overwhelming desire to laugh.

"Oh I wish I had time to draw that. It would make a magnificent illustration for a printed copy of a Ben Jonson satire."

"My God," exclaimed Richard suddenly, " I think father's going to knock the fellow on his back. Come on Ned, let's go and discover what's wrong."

The brothers dashed into the fray and another bout of arguing began. Sir Roger had been under the impression that the race was to be between Gervaise and his son, but Cleverdon had brought a horseman with him, 'a damn professional fellow' as Roger put it. At last it was decided that both competitors should enter two horses.

The crowd on the common was growing restive. They began to cat-call vociferously and offer advice. Some began to wander home, whilst one enterprising cowherd standing on a heap of stones, was taking bets on the outcome of the race. Hannah Moss with a basket of wet washing under her arm, was making her way up to the picket fence for a good view. She had been to the pond to do the family washing, but she could not resist the excitement of a horse race. Besides, Will Barry might be there.

As she pressed herself against the fence she could pick out his unruly, dark hair in the midst of the gathering in the paddock. It was a distinctive shade of rich, nut brown with auburn highlights. Hannah recalled that Will's father had hair the exact same colour. Lucy's hair was like her mother's, the colour of honey. Hannah envied Mistress Lucy's hair, so smooth with a warm glow that reminded her of summer. In comparison she felt her own curly, silver-blonde tresses were dull and lifeless.

She watched Will stroll over to the Wanley carriage and dipped her hand into her apron pocket to make sure the sketch he had given her was safe. When she felt the paper crinkle in her fingers she was satisfied. She contemplated staying to watch the race, risking her father's displeasure and another verbal tirade, but when she saw Maria Wanley descend from the carriage and link arms with Will, she decided she had best go home. Seeing that conceited, disdainful girl clinging on to his arm, looking up at him so appealingly filled her with jealousy. She hated the idea that he might marry Maria Wanley. She accepted the fact that he must marry one day, but not her, please God, not her. She adjusted her basket of washing and walked away briskly.

Still the preliminaries for the race dragged on. Wanley could not resist bating Sir Gervaise. He liked to see him ruffle up like some angry game bird.

"We must get started ," Richard shouted, above a particularly insulting verbal joust between his father and the Lacock knight, "It will be dark soon."

He was impatient and excited, clutching his riding whip and slapping it with a tetchy rhythm against his boot as he paced around . " The main point to be settled is who we are going to have as our second rider."

Edward clamoured for the distinction, but was told unceremoniously by his father that he was too hare-brained and did not know how to hold a horse back when it was needed. Will Barry was watching Edward take his disappointment with all the ill-grace of a seventeen year old eager to prove himself, humiliated by his father, when he heard Sir Roger say, "How about you William? What do you say to upholding the honour of the gentlemen of Sandy Barrow?"

He looked at the squire in vague surprise. This was something he had not expected. He felt that Wanley had been ignoring him; Richard's warning at the school house had given weight to that impression. Now Sir Roger, arms folded and an affable smile of encouragement on his face, was waiting for a reply.

"You mean ride for you sir?"

"Of course. Your father was the best horseman I ever met and am ever likely to. He could outride me any day of the week and I am not ashamed to admit it. He would never have thought twice about accepting a challenge. Let's see what you can do."

Wanley had a bass voice that carried without effort and commanded attention. Will was struck, not for the first time, by the impressiveness of his father's old friend. He himself was tall, but Wanley was at least two inches taller, with massive shoulders and forearms. He was growing fleshy now in his middle age, but was fit and active. His movements were rapid, decisive and surprisingly graceful for a man of his build.

Will realised that he wanted to please this man. He always did, despite the radical divergence in their ideals. The Wanleys were part of his childhood, part of the image of his father that was so important to him. He hardly dare admit to himself how painful it was to be at odds with them. Now Sir Roger's frank approach left him strangely flattered.

"Rather immodest for the village school master isn't it?" he said lightly, but knowing he was ready to do it.

"Nonsense," roared Richard, "We'll get first and second."

"Please Will," Maria murmured, close to his ear. "I would love to see you leave my braggart brother standing. He thinks he is invincible."

Her small fingers played on his arm and he checked an urge to kiss them. He could see encouragement on every face and he knew he could ride well.

He loved the moment when horse and rider became one, when muscles strained and throbbed in unison and a spontaneous joy thrilled through the frame of both. He had opened his mouth to say yes, when Roger Wanley reached inside his shirt and pulled out a medallion on a long chain. It was gold and cast in the shape of a book, the hinged front pierced like a grill. Roger opened it to reveal a watch face with one bold hour hand that had moved past the figure three.

"Not sure how accurate this damn contraption is," he said. "But I have wound it twice today and by the look of this hand it is well past three, a good half hour past I'd say. Richard is right. If we don't get on with it, we will lose the light."

Half past three Will murmured to himself. He had promised to be at Isaac Hewer's house by five o'clock. It would take him less than ten minutes to ride to Stockley, but he had to go home for his horse and he had promised to bring books and pamphlets for them to study, which meant calling at the school on the way. Even if he finished the race in time, he might get caught up in the aftermath- the celebrations or commiserations depending on the outcome and it would be harder to break away without revealing his destination. It was easier to go now. But he wanted to race. He stood there undecided, wishing it was not so important to him.

"What is the matter boy?" demanded the squire. "Don't you want to do it?".

"I am sorry sir, but I can't. I have an appointment. I almost forgot. I must go."

Wanley raised his thick grey eyebrows.

"Rather abrupt isn't it? If you do not want to ride, say so. There is no need to make up excuses."

"No, it is not an excuse, truly. It is an important appointment."

Richard threw his arm around Will's shoulder saying, "Now come on- some ploughman who wants to learn his ABC. Don't be so damn conscientious Will. Have some fun for once. You were never such a sober-sides before you went up to Cambridge. Well- tell us who is more important than us then."

He could not tell them and he hated his lack of courage. He pulled away from Richard's grasp and calling over his shoulder, "I shall be late. I really am sorry. I hope you win Dick," he began to sprint across the paddock.

"Will!" There was pained reproach in his mother's voice, but he did not hear it. He had already vaulted over the picket fence and was pushing through the thinning crowd, heading for his house.

"There is no need to worry Mother," Lucy assured. "Will knows what he is doing."

Roger Wanley was shaking his head. "I shall never understand that boy, never. The Lord knows what his father would make of him."

He threw a pointed glance at Olivia Barry, but Lucy squeezed her mother's hand and Olivia said nothing.

❄

The lantern, held so firmly, nosed its way through the darkness spreading a half circle of light. It was past eleven and a heavy frost had settled on the earth. The mud of the cart track had frozen solid and the horse's hooves crunched in the frosted grass on the edge of the track. Will Barry blew on his fingers to ease the pain, as the blood began to circulate in his numbed hands once more. The fingers throbbed and plunged as if they would burst. His companion, who held the lantern, was singing softly to himself as he trudged along, heedless of the cold.

He wore only a hessian jerkin and a pair of cloth trousers held up by rope. His shoes were leather, but the soles were worn so thin he must have felt the ridges of the cart track pressing on the bottoms of his feet. Yet he stepped out at a bold pace, his shoulders thrown back.

Will, leading his horse by the reins, thought of the warm fire that would greet him when he reached home, the glass of brandy and the comfortable bed. Samuel Selfe did not have such consolations ahead. He was going to a damp, thatched cottage with two rooms and a narrow truckle bed that he shared with his wife Keziah. His son and daughter slept on the floor. Yet he was the one who sang. Will wanted to feel sorry for him, but could feel only admiration instead.

"Are you not cold Sam? It is about time you had a new jerkin. You could make use of that one as a colander."

"Tis a bit worn I know," Samuel confessed cheerfully, "But there are more important things in the world than jerkins. My youngest needs a new smock before I start thinking about jerkins. Besides I bin out on colder nights than this one. I heard enough wholesome conversation this night to warm my blood for days to come."

He was holding the lantern close to his face and the light flickered on his earnestness. It was a square face. Everything about Samuel Selfe was square, his shoulders, his head, even his black hair was cut in a severe fringe like a Norman baron. He had high cheek bones and eyes that were almond shaped. His eyebrows slanted slightly upwards, which gave him a quizzical air, but the brown eyes were humorous and sympathetic. The unwavering way he held that lantern testified to his steadfastness.

"It does my heart good to know that so many folk, honest, steady sort of folk, are eager to come to know God as He really is and to bring true religion into this land. Did you not feel the devotion present in that room tonight Will?"

Will nodded, but he was not so certain as Sam; he had many reservations. Devotion was present certainly and none could doubt the sincerity of Isaac Hewer, but some of the people in that room wanted reform for far more selfish and materialistic reasons than the spread of true religion.

He thought of yeoman John Dilke, who was one of Wanley's more prosperous tenants. Dilke's greatest desire was to get himself a coat of arms and he thundered against the Church of England because he resented paying tithes and hated the Squire because he would never be able to match his standard of living. He was jealous of the Barry family because they owned their land and did not have to pay rent to Roger Wanley as he did.

Then there was Gabriel Bush, the miller's son from Heddington, an amoral opportunist, who saw in revolution the chance to strike at all authority and capitalise on the resulting anarchy. These men talked of religion and politics but thought only of themselves, just as men like Roger Wanley in espousing the cause of king and church were struggling to protect their way of life.

There was no hidden agenda in Samuel Selfe. All he knew was that Christ, not the state was head of the Church and that each individual Christian should be free to interpret the scriptures for himself- that nothing should stand between an individual and his God. For these few simple principles he was ready to die if such an extremity was asked of him. It was so clear to him, he failed to understand how others could doubt. Although he valued Will Barry's friendship above all others, the young man's equivocal attitude bothered him, often appearing to be an attempt to stand in both camps. He laboured with all his earnestness to convert Will, as he called it.

"Were you not convinced of the truth tonight?" he asked, as they left the cart track for the broader, softer pathway made by generations of livestock, that led directly to the Barry house. "Did you not feel your soul leap within you and be free? Will Barry I pray every night that you might feel this."

Will watched the clouds of breath drift over his shoulder as his horse snorted behind him. It seemed to freeze as it rose.

"I am glad someone prays for me," he murmured.

"Oh I do that right enough." Samuel spoke slowly and deliberately, weighing the effect of his words. "'Tis time you made your decision. You must stop going to church and denounce what she stands for. When the faithful up there in Parliament say to the king, 'Charles Stuart, you must do this for the good of the country and the furthering of God's purposes,' then you should say amen and let all know you have said it. Then you'll feel right within yourself."

Will laughed, but it was wistful.

"Will I Sam? I wish it was as easy for me as it is for you my old friend."

"Why 'tis easy, there is nothing to fear. The Lord will be your strength and support, just as he is mine."

It was just as impossible to explain to Sam as it was to his family and the Wanleys. Will felt trapped in a limbo of non-communication and longed for release. He could see the lights of the house ahead of them, wan gleams in the darkness and the dogs were already barking at their approach. He recognised the deep, reverberating bark of one of his own dogs, Baron. Sam was listening to it also, his head on one side and a troubled frown on his face.

"It sends a shiver through a man, that bark. Makes you feel what it would be like to be hunted."

"It's only old Baron. He's noisy, but you know he is not dangerous. It's this darkness that makes him sound so eery. He gets frustrated because he can't keep up with Flash, who is much too fast for the old boy."

In that instant a sleek shape sped out of the murk and Flash hurled himself at Will's legs in joyful greeting. It was several minutes before Baron appeared, pounding along in pursuit. Baron was a shepherd's dog from the French side of the Pyrenees Mountains. He was a giant, thirty two inches at the shoulder and weighing over eight stones. His thick coat was mainly white with tan patches down his flanks and along his back. His face was tan also, but a white streak ran up the middle of it between his eyes and on to his cranium. Despite his great size and formidable bark he was a placid, amiable creature with gentle amber eyes.

He pushed his head into Will, barging Flash out of the way, but the border collie dodged underneath him in an effort to be closest to his master. Will ran his hand along Baron's back.

"It's no good old fellow, you are never going to outrun Flash and he knows it. You were not built for speed. You were bred to protect the sheep from wolves up in those French mountains."

The dog gazed at him, listening intently. Will's father had bought him from a French sailor at Dover, a puppy hardly old enough to have left his mother. Ralph Barry loved dogs and knew his children would take good care of this vulnerable pup. Sam held the lantern so he could see Baron's face and smiled.

" I remember the very day your father brought him home. You and your sister showed him to me when I was out in the field – little bundle of fluff he was, small enough to hold in your hands. Who would have thought he could grow to such a monstrous size? He's a kindly soul though, not the least harm in him."

"True enough. A stranger up to no good is more likely to get a nip from Flash than be attacked by Baron. But his size is enough to discourage a malefactor," Will agreed.

He was thinking about that year his father came home with Baron. It was etched in his memory, for two months later Ralph Barry died. He developed a high fever that seemed to burn him up from inside and there was nothing the physician could do to save him. Sam knew what his young companion was thinking.

"Twas a sorrowful year for your family right enough. I have always believed your father caught that fever from one of them foreign sailors at the ports he visited in his trade. There must be all manner of strange maladies in foreign parts. I be content to bide in my own territory."

They were now crossing the farmyard and Will said, "You'll come inside to warm yourself and take a drink before you go home won't you Sam. I was thinking there are two of father's coats in a chest in my bedroom. They do not fit me, too short in the arms, but he was about your size."

"No thank you. I won't come in, though tis good of you to offer. I must be off to my bed. I must be up early in the morning to do some hunting before I start work, or there will be no food in the house."

Will winced. "You know you can help yourself to whatever is in the buttery right now."

"Bless you, but what sort of husband would I be if I could not provide for my own. I'll get Old Beauty out and fetch down a duck or two up by the pond."

He stopped, wondering why Will was laughing. Barry was thinking of Old Beauty, the matchlock musket, a relic from Elizabeth's reign, that was Sam's pride and joy.

"Is that contraption still working?" he asked.

"Of course she's working."

"I think it is high time you scrapped that gun before it blows up and I am being quite serious."

"If it were good enough for my grandfather when he fought with Leicester in the Netherlands, it's good enough for me now."

"My dear Sam," Will put his hand on his friend's shoulder. They had stopped outside the gate into the garden. "That was more than fifty years ago."

But Selfe was adamant. "Well they did make guns to last in them days, not fall to bits like they do now. With gentle handling Old Beauty will last me some time yet."

Will had to admit defeat. Samuel's steady persistence was always invincible.

"Very well, I concede, but if you happen to stray up by Scarwood Copse- and you might find a few decent pheasants in there- watch out for my bailiff, Crispin Collington. He cannot see the sense in my throwing open part of my land for use by the village to hunt for food. He thinks I am a little touched and tries to save me from my own folly. If he catches you, he might whisk you off before Constable Jackson without reporting it to me and you will be in Devizes jail in the wink of an eye and you know what a terrible fuss Jeremiah makes about people trying to undermine his authority. He nearly had apoplexy the last time I tried to get someone out of his clutches. I would rather it didn't happen at all."

Sam was nodding solemnly. "Sometimes I do feel sorry for Jeremiah Jackson and that's the truth on it. But don't you worry, I never bin caught yet. Now I must be away. I would not say no to them coats you mentioned if you truly have no use for them. I'll come and collect them later in the week. Call in and see the wife and littluns when you can. They be always pleased to see you. I will keep up the praying for you." and with that he was off with his determined trudge.

Will watched his lantern winking into the distance like a firefly, before he went to stable his horse. He was surprised to find an unfamiliar horse in the stables, lathered up and steaming as if it had been ridden hard through the frosty night. It was late for visitors. The lights still burned in the parlour and as he crossed the yard he could distinguish the silhouette of someone moving around just beyond the window. By the time he reached the end of the hall, dimly lit by candles in brass wall brackets, he could hear voices. One of them was his mother's cool, soothing tone, but another was Sir Roger Wanley's.

The door of the parlour was half open and a bar of light from inside the room fell across the end of the dark passage. Will could see the glow of the fire reflecting on the surface of his mother's dress as she sat in the chimney corner, stitching away at a piece of embroidery. Her hands were working steadily, but every now and then she would lift her eyes to look at someone on the opposite side of the fireplace, someone who was blocked from Will's vision by the door.

Sir Roger's voice was saying, "There are no reliable figures yet of course and you know how fanciful rumours can be, but I heard that thousands have been killed."

"Thousands have been killed where?" Will walked into the room without ceremony, Flash and Baron either side of him. It was indeed Sir Roger who stood the other side of the fireplace, his broad back against the mantlepiece. Sitting behind him in a wicker chair, entirely excluded from the warmth of the fire by the squire's huge frame, was Robert Seddon, the curate of Heddington.

Lucy was in the window seat, her hand on the brocade curtains as if she had been staring out into the night. Her hair was unfastened and hung over her shoulder on to her lap, where a black cat had made itself a bed in the soft, yellow strands. Baron ambled over to sit by Lucy and the cat, giving him an evil look, arched her back, leapt off Lucy's lap and disappeared. They all turned to look when Will entered. He stood in the middle of the room waiting for an answer to his question. No one chose to answer. There was an awkward silence as Wanley gazed at Will, his face a picture of disapproval and indignation. There seemed to be a dark cloud hovering over him throwing its shadow on to his face. The curate gave a self-effacing cough, but said nothing. It was Olivia who broke the silence.

"I am so glad you are here at last my dear. You are late and it is such a cold night. You look frozen. Now come and sit by the fire while I call Mary to fetch you something hot to drink."

"No don't bother to get up Mother. I do not want anything just yet. It seems that Sir Roger has some disturbing news and I want to hear it."

Will tossed his cloak onto a chair where the visitors' coats were spread. Flash parked himself comfortably against it and began cleaning his paws. Sir Roger's grey tweed cape, lined with lamb's wool, made a sorry thing out of the curate's overcoat lying beside it – dingy, clerical black, threadbare and skimped, as if when it was first made, many years ago, the tailor could have done with a yard more cloth and had thrown the thing together in a temper.

Will's attention moved from the overcoat to the curate himself, crushed into that wicker chair with his knees drawn up, looking as if his greatest wish was to be invisible. To most of the parishioners of Heddington he was as good as invisible. They vaguely acknowledged his existence, then forgot him. He was one of those small, inoffensive, unobtrusive individuals, who in the eyes of the majority do not matter at all. A man who spoke little and when he did stuttered, begged everyone's pardon and let his voice die away; who did anything that was asked of him and dared not ask favours of others in return.

He faltered his way through a sermon every other Sunday on behalf of the Rector, a sermon which he read from a book compiled by a previous minister. He was present at weddings, christenings and funerals- he hardly presided- always fearing that one day he would drop the ring or worse still, the baby in the font. He would visit the sick and sit helplessly by the bedside of the dying, twisting his thin hair around his fingers and weep with the relatives because he felt their grief deeply. The rest of his time was spent eking out a meagre existence on his piece of land growing vegetables and taking milk from his one cow.

There was no accommodation available on glebe land and the rector, Henry Rogers did not see fit to invite him to live in Heddington Rectory, although there was room enough. Instead he found him a one room cottage, just outside the Heddington parish boundary on Roger Wanley's land. He paid the rent from the parish stipend as a compensation for the curate's wages being shamefully meagre. Wanley treated Robert Seddon as if he was a personal chaplain at his beck and call, employing him to tutor his youngest child, Caroline in religious education. Employ was perhaps the wrong word seeing that Sir Roger saw no reason to pay him for these extra duties outside his parish, which he had the right to refuse, but lacked the courage to do so. He treated him to a good dinner once a month at Wanley Hall and considered that payment enough.

Will always pitied him when he saw how the squire bullied him and Rector Rogers ignored him. He went across to him now, holding out his hand.

"Good evening Reverend Seddon. I did not notice you for a moment all back there. Why don't you come up closer to the fire?"

He grasped the curate's hand. It was such a thin, narrow hand, all bones. Will felt that if he squeezed hard it would splinter like matchwood. The finger nails were broken and encrusted with dirt. Seddon was always sitting on his hands, shoving them into his pockets or delving them down between his legs as if he was ashamed of the state they were in. His face brightened at Will's attention, but he refused to move.

"No I thank you William, but I am very well here, very well indeed."

"Then perhaps," said Will, looking up at the squire, "Sir Roger would care to sit down and not block the fire. When he has made himself comfortable he might tell me the news."

Olivia Barry had taken up her embroidery once more. Her fingers stopped for an instant, but were soon at work again. Wanley looked astonished, but he sat down all the same.

"It's the Irish," he stated. "They have run wild, massacred their officials and the English settlers. Thousands may have been killed. It's a bad business."

Will was leaning against Robert Seddon's chair. He shook his head. Could this be the trigger for what he most feared, the time when men lost all control and debating turned to murder?

"I knew something would happen once Strafford's controlling hand was gone."

"You admit then that Strafford did well in Ireland?"

"Of course I do. He began to make Ireland economically sound. He improved the lot of the poor, revived trade, cleared the sea of pirates, cut monopolies, put new life into the Irish parliament- few men could have done as much.

The tragedy was that he did it all alone. It all depended on his personality, his presence. Even the improvement in trade depended on his funds. He had not built up a structure that could operate without him. Once he was gone the whole edifice fell to pieces."

"And who took him away? accused the squire, his voice carrying around the room. "Who took his head from his shoulders? Your precious Parliament."

"It is not my Parliament Sir, any more than it is yours." Will was partly distracted by Robert Seddon nervously twisting his hair around his fingers and trying to hide his other hand under the cushion. "I was very disturbed when they condemned Strafford. If you remember, I wrote a letter to our member of Parliament, asking him to plead for him, which he did very eloquently, though to no avail. Charles lost a very devoted servant when Tom Wentworth died, a servant he could ill afford to lose."

Sir Roger folded his arms, leaning back in his chair, as if he was taking a full view of Will. The way the young man stood vividly recalled to the squire his old friend Ralph Barry. Will was reckoned to resemble his mother, the structure of his face, his smile was like hers. Yet his walk, the way he held his head, a certain expression of wide-eyed indignation that sometimes passed across his face, in all these things he bore a strong resemblance to his father. Olivia Barry was thinking the very same thing as Wanley, as she watched her son then.

"Your mind my boy is as clear to me as a maze. You are a mass of contradictions," Sir Roger exclaimed.

"No Sir, I am perfectly consistent."

"Explain that to me."

"Perhaps you would like to explain to me why you are here first. You did not come here at this time of night, particularly bringing Reverend Seddon with you,"- the curate coughed his humble cough- "Just to tell us about the rebellion in Ireland."

Lucy had been toying with the curtains and gazing out into the darkness all this while, but now she left the window, rubbing Baron's great head as she passed and took a chair near her brother."I shall make the purpose of our visit very clear," Wanley was quick to answer. "I found out this evening why you left our race in such a hurry. I accompanied Cleverdon back to Lacock to collect our winnings, because Richard beat that damn professional fellow by a goodly margin-not that you care about that it seems.

Then I went into Chippenham on business and damn me if a group of fellows there knew all about this meeting with Hewer and your name was mentioned as providing literature for discussion. I rode straight back, collected Seddon and came here to talk some sense into you. We have been waiting hours for you."

Will took a deep breath, but said nothing.

"I won't have it Will, I will not have you fraternizing with these Puritan troublemakers and subverters of the social order. When a man denies his king and his church and delights in bringing dissention to the realm he ought to be horsewhipped. You do not want your name associated with men like these."

There was a pause, then Will replied with deliberate emphasis, "You mean that you do not want my name associated with them. Well frankly Sir, I don't think it is any of your business."

Looking beyond Wanley, he saw his mother had stopped sewing. Her hands, the calmest hands he had ever seen, even they were fluttering. He knew what a quarrel with Roger Wanley would mean to her, but the crisis must come. He expected Wanley to explode, but the squire, fixing him with an even stare, said quietly enough, "None of my business eh? I suppose you have forgotten how eight years ago I promised your father before he died that I would take care of his children. He was particularly worried about you. 'Will is at an impressionable age 'he said. 'He needs a father at this time' So I did my best to guide you. Do you deny that?"

"No Sir, you were very good to me when I was a boy and to Lucy."

"You always did have one or two strange notions, but I thought you would grow out of them. It was

Cambridge that did the damage. That infernal place is a hotbed of heresy and seditious nonsense. I always maintained that you should have gone to Oxford, but you would have your own way. William-I have watched you grow up, Richard thinks the world of you and you tell me this affair is none of my business. Man, you are paying court to my daughter. Do you think I would let her marry a man whose religion and loyalty is suspect?"

"What am I suspected of?" Will demanded. He felt a touch on his arm. His mother was standing beside him.

"Do not be so obstructive and argumentative my dear. Roger is genuine in his concern for you. You must not doubt that."

"But what does he want of me mother?"

"I will tell you what I want," Wanley cut in. "I want you to make your position clear. Tell me just what you believe in. Whose side are you on boy?"

Will began to laugh, but there was a note of desperation in it. The same old question prompted by that black and white view of the world.

"Make my position clear," he repeated. "Whose side am I on? The point is, I am trying not to take sides. I think I believe in what any man with sense and some kind of principles believes in, good government. I have never trusted extremes Sir Roger. Until the beginning of last year Charles had ruled England for eleven years without a Parliament- with society shifting as it is today, it is impossible for him to attempt absolutism."

"What do you mean impossible?" the squire fired back, "He's done it has he not, so it can't be impossible.

Why those eleven years have been full of peace and prosperity. I don't see much tyranny in it."

"On the surface there is peace and prosperity, but how deep does it go? If Charles had been truly successful, we would not be on the verge of civil strife. One man cannot speak for a nation, no matter how able and I doubt the King's ability. Oh he has some fine personal qualities, I don't deny that, but he is inconsistent, even deceitful and I cannot trust him. For instance, he crushes monopolies, only to use them for his own ends when he sees fit. He gives to his poorer subjects with one hand and takes it away again with the other.

Enclosure is a case in point. You know I have a great interest in the development of agriculture Sir. Agreed enclosure for the mutual benefit of all concerned is an excellent thing and probably the only way agriculture can progress, but these arbitrary enclosures, countenanced by the King, where the rights of the villagers are swept away without a second thought; deforestation at the King's whim, as it happened at Melksham just before I was born or later at Pewsham. We have seen it happen at Whetham and the creation of Bowood Park. Then there was Braydon, about ten years ago, where the compensation offered to the inhabitants was ludicrous. That is tyranny."

As he spoke he was expecting a host of interruptions, but the squire heard him out in silence. The only punctuation to Will's resonant voice was the curate's cough, which grew more and more frequent. Several times Robert Seddon had opened his mouth to say something, but he would look at Wanley's stony face and his nerve would fail him. He consoled himself by pushing his hands even farther down the sides of his chair.

"You are very fluent," the squire remarked in a voice that suggested he was holding himself on a very tight rein. "You can make everything sound so reasonable. So Charles cannot rule without his Parliament?"

"No Sir, he cannot. He has no money for one thing. If he and Archbishop Laud had not been fools enough to embroil themselves in a war with Scotland, he might have had a little more. He was forced to recall Parliament out of necessity."

"Have you considered that if His Majesty allows himself to be bullied about by the Commons, it is conceivable that we shall have a Parliament ruling without a king? Is that what you want?"

Will sat down on the arm of his sister's chair. Lucy stretched out her long fingers and stroked the back of his hand. He appreciated the gesture of sympathy and smiled at her before he answered the squire.

"No, I don't want that at all. I told you before I cannot accept extremes. The Parliamentarians have an hysterical streak amongst them which bothers me. If they push too far down the political beach, they will find themselves on very shifting sands. If you remember Pym, at the opening of Parliament, declared that the king's ministers had broken the fundamental laws of the kingdom, a very impressive phrase, but he did not define those laws. He could not because he was talking about customary law, approved by time. He has a very idealized view. He almost equates the laws of England with the laws of God, which is as bad as the King's insistence on Divine Right. Political philosophers often invent these conceptions to justify their notions of ideal government.

I have a great respect for John Pym, his sincerity and dedication, but I think he has misjudged this. He sees himself as a conservative reformer, upholding fundamental laws, but in fact he is preaching the subversion of the present constitution, stirring up the beginnings of something that could release a tidal wave of change that would wash through England, turning her upside down, quite beyond the control of Pym or anyone else."Wanley was looking at him hard, troubled lines creasing his forehead and the corners of his mouth.

"I'm not sure I understand you Will. Perhaps you are too clever for me, but you seem to have a foot in both camps."

Will sighed, looking across at his mother, so silent and anxious. Her doubts worried him, but the pressure of Lucy's hand on his, the knowledge that he had her support at least, gave him courage.

"I am not in both camps. I am in neither and pointing to a third way, the only reasonable way. You might call it constitutional monarchy if you were looking for a neat phrase. The monarchy and the Commons must come to terms. They need each other, but each must give up something so both can play their essential roles in ruling England."

Wanley shook his head. "So all these handsome words add up to a weak sort of compromise. Is that what your religion adds up to also?"

Robert Seddon's coughing increased as if he feared that he might be called upon to defend the Established Church, but there was little chance that the squire would ask his opinion.

"I do believe in God Sir, if that is what you are worried about," Will said, a touch of sarcasm in his voice. "And strange as it many seem to you, so does Isaac Hewer. What is more, it is the same God Archbishop Laud believes in. I feel a man should strive to lead a Christian life and find a right relationship with God. It is useless to attempt to force a particular form of belief or worship on the unwilling. A man must come to God in his own way and there are as many ways to God as there is diversity in mankind. I don't want to tear the Church of England apart, but I want to see much more of Christ in her. When she can stand by in complacency and condone a social order where a few own so much and so many own so little; when she uses 'Blessed are the poor for they shall inherit the earth' as an excuse to pass by on the other side like the Pharisee and the Levite, then I shudder. I am uneasy when I see administrators and politicians parading about in the guise of bishops and when I hear of ministers holding six livings. Mind you, now that the crown has battened on to so much episcopal property, pluralism has become a necessity for many ministers, else they would never survive. What can a man do on eight or ten pounds a year, except keep cattle in the churchyard and go farming? He cannot afford to stop long enough to write sermons."The flow of his righteous indignation was halted when he caught sight of Robert Seddon's face. An expression of painful shame was mirrored in the curate's faded blue eyes, such pain that Will felt an ache of misery in his throat.

"Oh Reverend Seddon, how can we blame you? How can you devote yourself entirely to the service of God and his children, when you are so poverty stricken you have to struggle to exist. When you are frightened to move until Sir Roger nods and Rector Henry Rogers, who has the right of tithe in his hands, allows you just enough to stop you starving and no more. Sir Roger knows this well enough and yet he uses you as an unpaid servant."

"By God!" Wanley was on his feet in an instant. Olivia Barry had also cried out a protest, but it was drowned by the squire's roar. "Young man, I am amazed at your impertinence. Your father would never have spoken to me in that fashion."

"I am not my father."

"Yes, that is very apparent when you insult me like this."

Will had also risen. He looked defiant and angry. He was so weary of the squire's insistent harping on his friendship with Ralph Barry, his continual expectation that Will would behave like his father.

"It was not an insult, it was a statement of the truth. Do you deny it Sir? I find it hard to accept your word when I see the Reverend Seddon's coat lying next to yours."

He flung his arm out in the direction of the chair and Wanley instinctively glanced at the coats. The contrast struck him perhaps for the first time and he stared at them in tense silence.

"William- I-uh- " Robert Seddon was bobbing up and down at Will's elbow, his face a strange mixture of gratitude and fear. "My dear boy- perhaps you- it is not exactly- you have been rather outspoken and although I realise that you- well- did not mean to hurt anyone-"

"Then he should not have spoken in that way Seddon."

Wanley's voice cut across the curate's faltering and Robert's attempt at amelioration trailed away.

"I have heard enough tonight William Barry to convince me that I was right to doubt you."

"Then issue your ultimatum. I know it will give you pleasure.""You mistake me. I take no pleasure in saying this to Ralph Barry's son, but say it I must. Renounce all your associations with Puritans, remove all heretical and subversive writings from your library, publicly confess your loyalty to the King and the Church – and I think after all you have said, an apology to me would be in order. If you do not, I must tell you that you are no longer welcome in Wanley Hall. Neither I nor my children will have any association with you. I will make certain my daughter never speaks with you again."

"That's a wicked thing to ask," Lucy spoke with fierce emotion to defend her brother. "Why can you not leave him alone? Why must you badger him continually? No matter what Will believes, he always tries to do what is right. Is that not worth all your protestations of loyalty?"

"Lucy," her mother rebuked. "Sir Roger has been insulted enough this evening."

Tears had begun to show on the high-ridged bones

of Lucy's cheeks. Will put his arm around her and kissed her forehead.

"Thank you for defending me."

"You must consider," Olivia Barry was saying, " Sir Roger means what he says. Think what our families have been to each other for so long. I cannot bear the thought of this breach Will."

"The quarrel is not of my making Mother. Sir Roger, you know what my answer must be. I can do none of the things you ask."

He tried to pretend that the little cry of anguish from his mother did not hurt him, but Lucy felt him wince as if he had been struck.

"Then, " replied Sir Roger, his face blank and immobile, " Do not approach my family until you can."

"I think I have the right to ask Maria what she feels. You cannot speak for her."

"She will think as I wish her to think."

"I do not believe that and I hope to prove you wrong." Will wished he felt as confident as he sounded. "Now it is late and I am very tired. I hope your determination to ostracize me does not mean you will penalise my mother. She is not responsible for my actions."

"I am well aware of that. Give me some credit at least. Olivia Barry will always be welcome under my roof."

"Thank you. Goodnight Sir."

The squire paused only for a moment before he strode out of the room. Robert Seddon hovered by the door, then shuffling over to Will with his short, hesitant steps, he seized his hand and pressed it as firmly as those bony fingers could.

"I know your heart is good," he murmured. "God Bless you."

Then he hurried after the squire. Will stood in the centre of the room, gazing bleakly at the far wall. He felt numb and cold. He was aware that his mother was crying. He sat down heavily in the chair the curate had vacated and covered his face with his hands in a weary gesture.

"I am sorry Mother, truly sorry, but it had to come. Please don't ask me to explain any more-I am too tired. Just try to accept me as I am. That is all I need just now."

"Should we condemn you for being honest?" Lucy comforted. "Mother is upset now, but she knows within herself that you must follow the dictates of your conscience, no matter how strange and repugnant they may appear to others. Sir Roger compares you to father so often, well I can promise you that father would never condemn you for your tolerance, even if he had not shared your views. He would have expected you to stand by your beliefs. Is that not so Mother?"

Olivia had turned her back to them in an effort to disguise that she was weeping. The heat of the fire lifted the ends of the muslin shawl she wore, so that it floated around her like a spider's web. She did not answer for some minutes, then without turning to face them she said, " Yes, Ralph would have been very proud of his son."

Will had to take what consolation he could from that.

CHAPTER THREE

The cattle were making a tremendous racket as they jostled their way through the narrow gateway out of the farmyard. They lowed and snorted in so many keys that with some rearrangement it might have harmonised. The mass of colour they made was certainly a harmony, patches of red, brown, white and black, changing position as the backs heaved and the heads pushed. Having been through their early milking, they were eager to get out into the pasture where some late autumn grass still remained. The cowherd, his thick gaiters streaked with the white of early morning frost, was singing in a full-throated bellow, the ballad of Mary Gray, a sad tale of unrequited love, which he punctuated with hoops of encouragement to the cows. Flash, the border collie was determined to assist him in his task, darting behind the cattle to nip at their back legs, skilfully avoiding retaliatory kicks.

A few moments before the horizon had glowed an orange yellow on the fringe of a grey sky. The house had stood in that yellow like a black shadow, but now there was a sudden brightness, a pale gold that touched everything. It accentuated the yellow leaves still left on the trees and reflected on the ice which had formed a thin layer over the pond. The air was winter cold, but the beauty of autumn still lingered.

"It's a fine herd Master Will, not the biggest, but one of the best in the county, I'll be bound. Those Chippenham cheese makers are falling over themselves to buy our milk. They know quality when they taste it," said Crispin Collington as he watched the cows being driven towards the pasture.

"Largely thanks to you Crispin. There have certainly been some beneficial changes since you have had your eye on the farm."

Will Barry and his bailiff were leaning against the fence of the oblong yard which led to the cow sheds. Crispin smiled.

"Thank you for saying so. I do my best. You giving me a free hand the way you do helps. Then of course there are all those books you make me read," he added with a mischievous expression in his eyes.

"You are not obliged to read them Crispin. I only try to suggest what might be helpful."

"No, I was only jesting. They often give me good ideas."

He patted Will on the shoulder in a familiar way. The evident ease in their relationship suggested friendship rather than just an employer with his employee.

"I finished "The Countryman's Instructor" last night. It didn't tell me much that I didn't know already, but it is full of good sense. I have also been dipping into the notions of that fellow Gabriel Plattes. He has some weird and wonderful ideas that one, but this business of steeping corn before sowing and setting it in regular rows instead of scattering, seems to me a valuable suggestion. If you have no objections, I might even take a gamble on this seed drill he has invented. It sounds expensive I know, but it will save labour and a good deal of seed too. They've no doubt started to manufacture them in Bath or Salisbury. I'll see if I can get someone up here to demonstrate one for us."

Will nodded approvingly. He was thinking how lucky he was to have a bailiff like Crispin Collington. He had no worries about the farm because Crispin was completely reliable. He had initiative, could organise and he took a comprehensive, long-term view of things. Sometimes he was a shade too sure of himself and could be over-bearing with the labourers, but even when Will was forced to deflate Crispin a little, he could understand his position.

Collington was better educated than the average farm bailiff and felt the gap between himself and the farmhands. He had received a grammar school education and it showed in his manner and speech. The strong west country accent had been modified into a mere intonation and the use of a hard letter 'r.'

His grammar was immaculate, his vocabulary extensive. He could read basic Latin, spoke a little French and took pleasure in poetry. His grasp of a logical argument sometimes astonished Will. He had intended to go on from grammar school to university and read law, but his father died and the family was involved in a legal struggle over their inheritance. This lawsuit swallowed up most of the money that was in dispute. Their final victory was pyrrhic and Crispin had to abandon all hopes of university and a career as a lawyer. Yet he showed few signs of frustration. He had an affable manner, a persuasive charm, which tended to mask his determination and drive. He talked fluently and had a quick wit.

He was explaining in more detail the economics of the seed drill as Will studied him. His physical appearance matched his personality. He was a big man, as tall as Will, and much broader. In his middle thirties, he had a youthful face, round and rather heavy, but as affable as his manner. When he laughed, which he often did, his whole face laughed. Yet open and communicative as he was, Will realised that he knew very little about Crispin. It was clear that he was eager to advance himself, but his deepest emotions, his true aspirations remained locked inside himself. He was willing to talk on a wide variety of subjects- he was always talking- but never about his inner self.

When Collington had finished his exposition on the uses of the seed drill Will said,

"Yes, I think we ought to try it. If it is successful we could buy several for communal use in the village."

" At the price they are likely to fetch, a man won't be buying them in batches." Crispin retorted.

" I cannot always worry about what is practical. You should know that by now Crispin. As heretical as this may sound to a good bailiff I can't allow myself to be ruled entirely by economics. Now I must go, I want to get over to Wanley Hall. I have left Lucy in charge of the school this morning because I have an important matter to clear up."

He had begun to climb through the rungs of the fence as he spoke, Crispin's face clouded. "Will you be welcome at Wanley Hall?" he asked.

"Has the word got around already?"

"Well, I was talking to the squire last night, before you came home. He was none too pleased about you attending that dissenters' meeting."

Will was interested to know what Crispin thought about it. There appeared to be genuine concern in his eyes. He had expressive eyes, large and wide-set, the colour of pale green crystal.

"And does it concern you that I may be straying from the fold of Mother Church?" Will challenged.

Crispin stared at him for a moment, then he laughed aloud.

"Master Will, a man's religion is his own affair, not mine. I bailiff farms not souls, but I am concerned that you and your family should be caused any discomfort or pain through strained relations with the Wanleys."

"Thanks for that anyway, but it is not for you to worry about. I shall be back before midday if you wish to discuss any business with me"- and Will was strolling down the valley with Flash in hot pursuit. Crispin watched him for a while, shaking his head, but there was no means of telling what the gesture signified.

Will Barry was off to Wanley Hall to see Maria. He had not slept that night, for his mind refused to stop churning over the events of the evening. He kept hearing his mother's cry of pain that stabbed his conscience, but what else could he have done? He had pondered over the various ways in which he might have avoided a break with the squire, but none of them were acceptable to him. He was sure now that he had been right to defend his principles, but he wished he could be as sure that Maria would agree with him. He would learn this morning the truth about Maria Wanley and he feared it would be a painful truth. This crisis should reveal whether she had any love for him, but what he feared more was the possible discovery that he had no love for her.

Walking fast, lost in thought, he was soon on Squire Wanley's land. The acres of arable, downland, pasture and woodland were all so neat and well-tended, separated by fences, ditches and hedges, no longer the patchwork quilt of open-field strips they had been less than ten years before. The sun was now gaining strength and freeing the land from its curtain of frost. The white melted away from the hedges revealing a variety of colours, finely blended.

There had not yet been frosts enough to sear the hedges, those cosmopolitan hedges with infinitely variegated leaves; yellow, faded greens, dark vivid greens, gold, brown with here and there bright splashes of red berries, clumps of thistles, stinging nettles and dock leaves. One such magnificent hedge stood in front of Will now in relief against a blue sky, broken only by a few smudgy clouds trailed across it. Momentarily all thoughts of the Wanleys faded. He could only wish he had his paints and a canvas.

As he stood there trying to imprint the colours on

his memory in the hope he might be able to reproduce them, he heard voices behind the hedge. A woman shouted in an angry tone, a man was laughing- a self-possessed laugh that was so familiar to Will. Flash ploughed through the hedge and climbing over a style at the side, Will was confronted with three beagle dogs yapping excitedly as they circled around Flash, who was bearing his teeth ready to pitch in if they got too close. A gun-metal grey horse was tethered close by.

Will looked around for the owners of the voices. The pasture ended here and a dry-stone wall separated it from a stretch of woodland. Over by the wall he saw Richard Wanley, his red hair gleaming fiercer than ever in the sunlight, struggling with a girl. She was brandishing a branch of dead wood, clearly intending to break it over Wanley's skull. It was as much as he could do hold her. As Will came closer he was surprised to find that the girl was Hannah Moss. They were intent on their struggle and both were startled when he spoke.

"What on earth is going on here?"

Wanley let go of Hannah's wrists and she spun round to face Will. Her cheeks were scarlet with anger, as she let the branch fall from her hand.

"Master Will, he killed it. I begged him not to, but he couldn't let bide. In his destructiveness and his viciousness he had to kill it. So we'll just see how he'd like a girt stick banged round his head."

She darted for the stick again, but Will stepped in front of her to restrain her, murmuring, " Hannah, Hannah."

She stood quite still for a moment, then she buried her face in his shoulder and cried. They were tears of angry frustration. It was only then that Will noticed the body of a badger lying at the edge of a clump of furze. The creature's teeth were still bared in defence, but the side of its head was crushed, blood staining the thick fur.

Richard Wanley let out a sigh of relief as he straightened his jacket, ruefully inspecting the hole where a button had been torn from it.

"God, am I glad you turned up Will- the little bitch had a good mind to kill me."

"And so I would if I'd had the chance," Hannah threw back at him. "Mercy won't be shown to them as knows no mercy."

"Your father crams your head with the Old Testament far too much."

"You got a blaspheming tongue as well as a murdering heart."

"The ten commandments don't mention badgers my girl," Richard mocked.

"Oh stop it Dick, don't torment the child. Why did you kill the badger anyway?"

"Now don't you start. I do not have to answer for every pest I kill on my father's land surely."

Hannah tossed her head. There was pride in the way she did that and Will admired it.

"There, he can't answer cos he'd no reason for doing it save for his pleasure. Tis all the same life, animal's and man's, life that God give. Just cos man thinks he's cleverer don't mean a badger's life isn't precious. No man has the right to kill anything for nothing. If he does so for food, cos he'll die else, that's different, but when he does so for sport and his own blood lust, then that's wicked."

Richard stood back surveying her with his eyebrows raised. He took pleasure in her anger, the way her body vibrated with emotion.

"Hark at her sound off. So I am a wicked man Hannah. You knew that already and you didn't seem to mind before. Let us forget about badgers and see how you kiss when you are so furious with me."

He grabbed her wrist and pulled her towards him. "I will not Richard Wanley," she hissed, straining her body back from him. "I'll never let you touch me again. I'd as soon stick a knife in your back as let you."

"Let her go Dick!" Will's voice was soft, but it was a command.

Wanley made some comment about Will's refined sensibilities and continued to struggle with Hannah.

"Dick, let her go or I will have to make you and neither of us would enjoy that."

Richard released the girl with a stylised flourish and she spat at him.

"You really mean that don't you. You really would make me. I know from past experience that you can whip the hide off me, so I won't risk it," he laughed. "I had no idea I was encroaching on your rights. Didn't realise there was anything between you two. She's worth having Will, a damn good fuck, but watch that temper."

Richard looked so sure of himself, standing there feet apart, shoulders squared, full of insolent humour that

Will felt a strong urge to hit him. It was not the first time. When they were boys they were always scrapping, but in later years Will had never let it come to blows. He had developed a control over himself which he exercised now. He turned on his heels and beckoning Hannah to him, walked away. The girl, snatching up a bundle of sticks that lay near the dead badger, ran after him.

"If you are going to see Maria," Richard called out, "You are wasting your time. They will not let you in. So when you've got over your moral indignation, come down to The Moorcock in Calne and have a drink with me. I know I am not supposed to associate with you, but frankly, I don't give a fart."

Will did not reply, he did not even look back, but kept on walking, taking long determined strides. Hannah doing her best to stop stray branches falling from her bundle, found it hard to keep up with him without running. Flash having seen off Wanley's beagles dashed on ahead of them and took a flying leap over the stone wall. Will jumped the wall himself, took Hannah's bundle from her and lifted her over with ease. When she reached out for the wood again, he picked it up himself.

"No. I will carry this."

"You mustn't carry wood for me Master Will," she protested with genuine astonishment. "It wouldn't be right."

"Why?"

"Well I be a cottager's daughter. I should do the fetching and carrying for you."

"This has nothing to do with degree. This bundle

is heavy and I can carry it more easily."

"No taint too heavy for me. I can carry loads three times the weight of that."

Will ignored her and walked on. She clutched her shawl around her in helpless acquiescence and followed him once more. The new experience of having her burden carried pleased her in one way, but she was proud of her physical strength and did not want it discounted. Besides any pleasure was counteracted by her fear that he was angry with her over what he had heard that morning. He had not smiled when he insisted on taking her bundle and now as he walked ahead, he was withdrawn, deep in thought.

"You aint angry with I over what he said are you?" Hannah asked suddenly.

Will looked down at her, a serious expression on his face.

"I did not heed what he said."

"But I don't deny it. I have lain with him once or twice. He did pester me so and besides he paid me for it. The money were useful along then, though father'd beat me if he knowed where it come from. I never did think much on him though and I'll never go near him again after what he done today. Twas no pleasure anyway. He has high notions of himself, but he's no great lover. He comes too quick."

Will raised his eyebrows, taken aback by her unabashed frankness. Not sure how to read his reaction, Hannah added hastily, "Tis only him. I don't go around offering myself to any man who takes a fancy to me. I'm no whore. Some of them who thought so were sore for days in places they don't want to mention."

She was looking anxiously at Will's face trying to gauge the effect of her words. She was not ashamed of her confession; she had no sense of guilt, but she feared losing his respect.

"I don't suppose you'll want me to help at the school no more now you know this."

" Hannah I can't presume to condemn you. Who am I to do that? I am sorry it is so because- well, because you should have saved the ultimate gift in your giving for someone whom you truly loved. If you give in that way too often without love, it may turn sour on you and you run the risk of never finding a true relationship."

He was immediately aware of how patronisingly wise and easy that sounded and wished he had not said it. It struck him then that he still saw Hannah as a child, a pupil. She was 18 and experienced in coping with a hard life and he had referred to her as a child when rebuking Richard. He had not meant to belittle her, but wondered now if she had regarded it that way. He resolved to see her with a clearer, more realistic vision.

Hannah's jade eyes had turned very grave. "I don't know how many folk come together out of real love. Fewer than we pretend I reckon, but if you say I must do it no more save with the one I wish to marry then I won't, I promise. Although there's no man I'd wish to marry at present, leastways not one who'd wish to marry me, only please don't be angry with me."

"I am not angry with you" and he smiled, thinking

how indignant Richard would be if he knew how she rated his performance. This was all the reassurance she needed. Will had closed his hand over hers and continued to hold it as they walked. He told himself that he did so to comfort her, but if he had been honest, he would have admitted that the feel of her hand was a comfort to him. Comfort was something that was fast becoming alienated from his life.

Hannah's confidence soon revived and she began to chatter about a host of things as they passed through the woodland. The trees grew thick here, crowded together with little space between the trunks, but it was not dark. The yellow brightness penetrated through the branches, painting the mosses and ferns at their feet. The wood was full of life. Pigeons' wings cracked as they barged their way out of the trees in a panic and the tips of rabbits' ears trembled just above the ferns.

Hannah was in her element here. As they stepped out of the ferns on to a track lined with blackberry brambles, a sleek, reddish brown body darted across their path.

"Did you see that?" Hannah called out.

"Yes, it was a weasel."

She looked at him for a moment as if she could not believe what she had heard.

"No tweren't, twere a stoat," Hannah corrected. "Don't you know the difference between a stoat and a weasel?"

Her astonishment amused him. "At that speed no, although I daresay I could tell which was which if I saw them both together. I don't know everything Hannah. There are many things you could teach me."

This was a new idea to her. She pondered on it as a strange new truth, then laughing, ran on to follow the tracks of the stoat. They were soon clear of the wood and stood on the edge of the common. Will could see the many chimney pots of Wanley Hall. Hannah held out her hands for the bundle of sticks.

"I'll take this now Master Will. If father's in the house, he could see us from the window and he'd be sure to go on at me for letting you carry my sticks. You go on wherever you be going."

She could see the apprehension in his face as he gazed at the array of chimney pots. He was going to see Maria Wanley. She knew that and could not help wishing he was going elsewhere. She stood watching him for a while as he walked away, dwelling on what he had said about saving herself for one she loved. She knew most men satisfied their needs when and where they could, like Richard Wanley and wondered if Will Barry believed that his advice applied only to women and that he too sought out those who could pleasure him. She was sure he would hold back from making love to Maria out of respect for her family, but might have other lovers. He was handsome, courteous, sympathetic and could converse with enthusiasm on so many interesting subjects. He would have no trouble attracting women from his own social level ready to offer themselves to him. He would have no need to resort to whores and she could never imagine he would force himself on a woman who was unwilling. Her thoughts irritated her and she turned towards the crumbling heap of stones she called home with a frown on her face.

The Moss family were squatters. Her father had been dispossessed of some land at Warminster due to an enclosure act and had wandered about Wiltshire looking for somewhere to settle. On the fringe of Sandy Barrow common he had come upon a deserted cottage and took possession of it. He had no deed or title to his land, but he reckoned that having lived there unmolested for ten years was security enough. He had no idea that in theory he was protected by an Act of Parliament which declared that "Certain necessary houses with ground under the quantity of three acres, which have been builded on commons or waste ground, which doeth no hurt and yet is much commodity to the owner thereof and to the others, should be secure to the occupant of such house or ground free from disturbance by the owner of the waste."

All that John Moss knew was that he would like to see anyone try to turn him off his land. Several more squatter dwellings had grown up around his house. Their walls were made of clay, strengthened with layers of straw, the roofs thatched, with rough holes cut in the centre for the smoke from the fire to rise. Hannah always felt her father was special amongst the squatter community because his house was made of stone. It did not matter to her that the walls were crumbling and now in this yellow light, the lime fillings between the stone blocks looked a dull, putrefying green. She did not care that the one window had no glass and was closed up with a piece of board at night or when the weather was bad. She was contented to sleep on a low, box bed, softened by straw, covered in a doubled up blanket. What really mattered was that her house had a chimney, a rambling rose bush trailed over one wall, the autumn light lending colour to even those stricken blossoms and her parents owned two pigs, a vegetable garden, two stools, a bed similar to hers but larger, a table- true it had a wobbly leg but stood well enough with one end against a wall – a bowl, three plates, a frying pan, a grid iron, two cooking pots and the thing that gave her most cause for pride, a brass flagon. She polished this assiduously every day. In times of trouble her father always threatened to sell it, but met with such opposition from his wife and daughter, that he relented.

Hannah felt no cause for complaint when she looked at her neighbours. Besides she could read and write. Her gratitude towards Will Barry for this was unending, but she was at a loss to know what she could give him in return. She could help others learn, but that was not enough. She wanted to give him so much more than that. As it was, all she could do was watch him walk towards Wanley Hall and Maria.

As he strode down the valley, Will could have no idea that Hannah was speculating about his sexual adventures. If he had known it might have brought to mind Kate O'Connell. He met her during his last year at Cambridge, when he paid a visit to the home of a fellow student in Winchester. She was the daughter of a horse breeder and trader, a girl with shining black hair and dark blue eyes full of mischief. Witty and energetic, she loved dancing and music and she made him laugh. She played the harp and had a singing voice of great beauty. Will never fancied that he was in love with her, but she fascinated him and he enjoyed her company. When he came back to live in Sandy Barrow, he would visit her for a few days several times a year, when his duties at the school and the farm would allow.

The morals at the O'Connell household were free and easy. Kate's father, a charming, hospitable Irishman was a widower and generous with his affections locally. However he had seen enough of the effects of syphilis on his travels to make him wary and he kept a supply of linen sheaths in his bedroom. He was happy for his daughter to entertain a lover whom he considered respectable, but insisted on her being careful. She knew Will Barry to be a serious, responsible young man, who held back for fear of getting her with child, so she introduced him to the sheath. He had heard fellow students at Cambridge talk of using them, complaining that they reduced the pleasure of intercourse, but the assurance of some degree of protection conquered his reserve and they became intimate.

This relationship continued for over two years while the idea of marrying Maria was still a vague and distant idea to him and he told no one about Kate, not even Lucy. His family believed that his visits to Winchester were to meet up with his university friend. He enjoyed having a secret and could smile when Richard Wanley teased him about his virtuous morals.

When it became more evident to him that he was expected to marry Maria, that his mother was taking it for granted, he felt a twinge of conscience and decided he must end the physical part of his link with Kate. He started to write her a letter, which took him several days because every time he read through it, he was dissatisfied with the way it was expressed and started all over again. He was on the fourth version when he received a letter from Kate. She told him in a light, merry way that she was returning to her father's family in Ireland to marry a distant cousin to whom she had been promised at the age of eight. He was relieved that he did not have to finish his troublesome letter, but wrote a different kind of missive instead, thanking her for all the times she had lifted his spirits and wishing her happiness in her future life. Theirs had been a relationship of pleasure not commitment and although he would miss their friendship, he felt no jealousy. He decided to be more committed to the idea of a marriage to Maria. However another eighteen months had gone by since then and he continued to put off making an actual proposal. Today as he approached Wanley Hall he was about to discover whether he would ever take that step.

There were few signs of activity around the hall when he passed through the ornamental gates emblazoned with the family crest and up the sanded drive to walk between the fluted pillars at the foot of the steps that led to the impressive front door. He hammered on the door and the resolute sound of his knock gave him courage. The door soon swung open, a servant appearing, a man with a face as grey and wasted as a cadaver and he limped badly on his left side. Flash could not resist the open door and slipped past the man into the hall, much to his irritation. Will whistled to the collie and Flash trotted back out receiving a malevolent look from the servant, who was often required to walk Maria's and Caroline's spoilt spaniels around the gardens when the weather was deemed unfit for the girls to venture out, a duty he deeply resented and fostered in him a dislike for all dogs. He turned an unblinking stare on Will, who said, "Good morning Cranston."

"Good morning Master Barry Sir and I perceive it is a good morning, very good for walking- a pleasure which alas I am now denied, at least for any great distance."

He indicated his lame leg to underline his statement.

"Yes it must be very frustrating for you." Will did not attempt to sound sincere. He had experienced Cranston's delaying tactics before. "I would like to see Mistress Maria if I may."

"Mistress Maria is not at home Sir."

"Oh, is it not rather early for Maria to be out?"

"I cannot say Sir. Perhaps the beauty of the morning was a temptation not to be resisted."

"Where did she go?"

"I have no idea Sir."

Will looked over the man's shoulder into the hall. A long flight of stairs spiralled up into the centre of the house. He was certain he saw a door on the first landing open a crack, then close abruptly. He felt an urge to push past Cranston and search the house for Maria, but the servant stood there cold and expressionless. The word reptilian came into Will's mind.

"Is there any message Master Barry?"

"No- no thank you. I will come back later."

"As you wish Sir."

Come back Will did, twice, but the answer was just the same. Mistress Maria was not at home, nor was there any sign of the rest of the family. After he had called the second time he walked around the gardens, finding their cold geometry depressing. He took some satisfaction in watching Flash pee against a statue of the goddess Diana. Once he caught a glimpse of Caroline Wanley playing with a ball and cup at the back of the house. He called out to her and ran in that direction, but when he reached the lawn there was no sign of anyone. Heavy brocade curtains covered the back windows and the door to the servant's quarters was bolted.

When Cranston answered his third enquiry in the same dead-pan manner, Will began to feel his temper rising."

"Is everyone out this morning?" he demanded.

"I fear I do not know Sir."

"You seem to know very little Cranston."

"I am a servant Sir, not a family confidant."

"How many times do I have to call before you have permission to start insulting me?"

"I am sure I do not understand you Master Barry."

"Well, I understand you. You do your job excellently. I hope Sir Roger rewards you in kind. I shall not call again. Good morning Cranston."

"Good morning Sir" and the door was closed on him with a heavy finality.

Will smacked his fist into the palm of his hand.

This was what Wanley had told him would happen, he even expected it, but he was frustrated by the way in which it was achieved. If Wanley had come storming down those stairs and ordered him out of the house, he might have felt some satisfaction in going, but to be blandly fobbed off by a servant, as if he was not worth bothering with, was something he had not bargained for.

He glanced up at the bedroom windows wondering if the whole family was up there somewhere laughing at him. As he did so, he saw a hand pull back the curtains at the window directly above his head. It was a woman's hand, small with perfect nails. There was Maria looking down at him without the least embarrassment. She was wearing the dress he had always admired the most, the dark green velvet. He had told her more than once how beautiful she looked in that dress. Under one arm she held a silky russet and white dog. She smiled at Will, a smile that answered all the questions he had been forming in his mind that morning, an insolent, mocking smile. Here was no girl forced by her father to snub the man she loved. She was not torn by conflicting emotions. Maria Wanley was enjoying herself. Will opened his mouth to speak, though he was not sure what to say, but the girl turned her attention to the dog, holding it up to look out of the window and became enrapt in something on the horizon far above Will's head. He did not understand why she would wish to taunt him, but it was so and that was answer enough.

"Come on Flash, " he said, " We are not welcome here, brushed away like dust from the floor. Let's go home."

He turned on his heels, just as he had turned his back on her brother earlier that morning and walked away. For years he had been pondering whether there could be a meaningful union between himself and Maria, whether there could be real love on either side. Now in one action, without a word being spoken, he knew the answer. He was not sure whether it was regret or relief that he felt. He hardly knew what he was thinking as he walked home, but he did know when he was told on reaching the house, that Crispin was waiting for him in the study, that he felt a surge of bad temper and irritation. He had no desire to communicate with anyone, just wanted time alone to comprehend his own emotions. Never-the-less he made his way to the study, struggling to present a calm demeanour. In the oak-panelled study with its simple furniture he found Crispin.

The bailiff was sitting at a desk, writing in an account book in a neat, curling hand. His long legs were stretched out full length under the desk and the room was permeated with the smell of tobacco, as clouds of smoke drifted up from the clay pipe, which he puffed on placidly.

"I hope you don't mind my smoke stack. I know she smells a bit foul and I shall no doubt dry up my lungs like smoked herring- at least my old mother thinks so. She keeps hinting that I read King James' blast against tobacco smoking and save both body and soul. Personally I think old Jamie ought to have worried a bit more about his own bad habits- the Duke of Buckingham for instance."

Will laughed in spite of himself. "James' pamphlet is in the school library."

"Yes, I've seen it. I might get around to it one day. Till then I'll go around with my face on fire."

Will sat down opposite the bailiff. "Well what can I do for you Crispin?" he said in a business-like tone. "I hope it will not take too long because I have other things to do."

His brusqueness did not escape Crispin, who could read a whole story into the slightest nuance or inflection. He put his pen down, folded his arms and replied with his pipe clenched in his teeth, "No it won't take long. I just want you to sign the monthly accounts for me."

He turned the book around to face Will and pushed it over towards him. Barry scanned it cursorily, then took up a pen to sign it.

"And I'd just like to mention Daniel Bray," Crispin continued, moving the ink well to within his master's reach.

"What about Daniel Bray?"

"He's fallen badly in arrears with his rent again." Crispin took the pipe from his mouth and rubbed the stem thoughtfully. " He usually sends one of his daughters up here with a tale of woe and tears in her eyes, but I went down to his cottage myself this morning and frightened the life out of him. But I still didn't get any money. He said you told him it didn't matter as long as he started paying it off when he could see his way clear. So I had to come and check with you."

"Well I did tell him that Crispin."

"Then it was a mistake, " Crispin returned in the complete conviction that he was right. "I don't want to sound disrespectful and I have a great deal of admiration for the just way you treat your tenants. It is a pity some of them weren't a bit more honest with you. Bray is an artful one. Give him an inch and he'll take a few miles. The longer you let him go on without paying, the less likely it is that he will ever pay. Other tenants, in circumstances little better than his, pay regularly. Why should he be an exception? Sir Roger's tenants don't get away with not paying their rent for very long, I can tell you."

Will's fingers had begun to tap on the desk in a rhythm of impatience. Crispin's self-assurance was starting to chafe on his sore nerves.

"I can't say I admire any aspect of Sir Roger's attitude to his tenants. I have given Bray some leeway because he is a very poor man with a big family to provide for. He cannot pay what he has not got and he has to live somewhere."

"I'd agree with your hypothesis if only the facts were correct." Crispin was lost in a film of smoke as he took another long draw on his pipe. "He has money right enough. I wouldn't mind betting he has that mattress he's so proud of stuffed with it. There aren't many desperately poor folk who can afford a mattress for that matter."

"Well what do you suggest I do?"

"Let me go down there and threaten him with eviction if he doesn't pay up. You'll soon see some money then and if he still won't pay, it wouldn't be a great loss to anyone if he was evicted now would it?"

The bailiff said this in such a reasonable, persuasive way, but Will was not impressed.

"You would like to prove him a liar and me a fool would you not? Why can you not trust in humanity for once, give them the benefit of the doubt? Does it matter so much if he is lying? If he wishes to think I am a fool, he is welcome."

Will was pacing about the room now with a restless impatience that he could not curb. Those pale green eyes of Crispin's followed his movements.

"I'm sorry if I often seem suspicious to you Master Will. I suppose I am suspicious- it's my job. I have to be or I could never do my job properly. I have to test, try and question everything. I'm not inhuman- at least I trust not."

Will shook his head. " No Crispin I am the one who should apologise. I am not in the best of humours."

"I gathered that. Things didn't go well at Wanley Hall I presume."

He was studying Will with a friendly sympathy for which the young man was grateful. He felt an urge to confide in Crispin. He sat there, solid, amiable, easy, the expression on his face encouraging Will to talk, but something held Will back. He smothered the urge. All he said was, "No they did not go well at all."

Crispin stood up, clearing the ash from the desk with his elbow.

"I won't try your patience any further then. I will get out of your way and tread gently for a while. Thank you for listening to me."

Will would have apologised again but the bailiff was gone, closing the door behind him. In the corridor outside the study, Crispin came face to face with Lucy,

who was anxious to know the outcome of her brother's visit to the Wanleys. She laughed when she saw his halo of smoke and counterfeited a coughing fit.

"Oh that dreadful pipe! You should be made to go right out into the middle of the common before you are allowed to smoke it. Whatever possessed Sir Walter Raleigh to bring that weed over here I will never understand. You will ruin your health Crispin."

"If I did, would you be concerned?"

His gaze was so direct that she looked away, but she answered quite clearly, "Yes, very concerned."

There was a pause as she saw the pleasure in Crispin's eyes, then she asked, "Have you been with Will?"

He nodded.

"Did he make any progress this morning?"

"I fear not. He is very perturbed, even to the point of losing his temper with me. I'm tempted to advise you to leave him on his own for a while. On the other hand your sympathy might be a comfort to him. I know it would to me."

She was so concerned about Will's state of mind that she did not register the significance with which he charged his last sentence.

"Can I say," Crispin murmured softly, "How sorry I am that this has happened. You are the last family on earth who should know unhappiness. You are all so thoughtful of others, they really should spare a thought for you. I hope you understand that if there is anything I can do for you Lucy, I will."

She was giving him her full attention now.

"You are surprised that I called you Lucy. Please don't consider me presumptuous. Ever since I came here you and your brother have treated me as an equal, a friend, not just a bailiff. I find it hard these days to say Master Will, not because my respect for him has lessened, but because it has grown."

Lucy smiled. "I am pleased you should wish to call me Lucy without the formality of saying Mistress. I have always called you Crispin."

"Now I suspect you are laughing at me."

"No, truly I'm not. Thank you for your offer of help, but I doubt there is anything you can do. If there is, I will not hesitate to call on you."

"That is all I need to hear."

He took her hand and kissed it gallantly, exaggerating the flourish in that way he had of making light of everything, but there was something in his eyes that made her start with surprise and a sudden excitement. Before she had time to judge further, to put into perspective the way he had looked at her, he was loping down the corridor with his long strides. She might have been more agitated if she had seen the enigmatic smile on his face as he stepped out of the side door into the autumn sun.

CHAPTER FOUR

The fist banged down on the table with such force that the glass ink bottle toppled from its stand and ink sprayed across the desk. John Dilke as so intent on his argument that he did not notice the damage he had done. Will Barry let the rasping voice flow over his head for a while, not making much effort to take in what he was saying, as he watched the black ink run into the cracks in the wood grain of the desk. He looked up at Sam Selfe, standing with his back against the window, one eyebrow raised until it touched that square, black fringe. Sam had not said much so far, but Will knew what was in his heart. He was as eager to go as the rest of them. His desire was deeper rooted, for Sam truly believed he would be fighting for his God.

Clem Draper, the blacksmith's assistant, always timid and deferential, astounded at John Dilke's presumption, snatched up his ragged, cloth cap and began to mop up the ink from Will's desk, whining at Dilke to apologise. But Dilke, red in the face and aggressive, was in no mood for apologies."

"Can't you see it's the only thing a man can do?" he bawled at Will, who sat motionless, wondering if Clem Draper had another cap. "If you can't see it then you're a fool Will Barry, for all that learning."

"John Dilke, what be thinking on!" said Clem, dabbing away at the ink splashes on the brass candlestick.

" He is thinking it is about time he told me what he really thinks of me," Will replied for him. "Mind you I have always suspected that he regards me as a foolish idealist."

"Then he be an ungrateful soul indeed," said Sam Selfe quietly. "For he bin glad enough for you to teach his children their letters and figures. Besides, all this shouting and going red in the face will take us no further on. You'll bust thee lungs one day John and few'll mourn if you go on behaving as you are now."

Sam had come over from the window and seated himself on a stool beside Will. He put his hand on the young man's arm.

"Will, you know why you must come with us in this. As God is my witness, I love you like a brother, not just as a brother in Christ, but as a brother in the flesh and it do torment me fearful to think you might be found wanting on the last day. Now the King have set up his standard in Nottingham, sides must be took. You must declare yourself for the true religion. We must pray that little blood is to be shed, but if we must fight for God's right, then so be it."

The room had fallen silent; even Dilke had given way to Sam's earnestness, but he could not contain himself for long.

"Not only for God's right," he declared, though not so loudly as before, "But for the people's right. The right of folk like us to be free from the oppressions of the King and his hangers-on."

Will paid no attention to Dilke. All he was aware of was the steady, penetrating gaze of Sam Selfe as he concentrated on Will's face.

"Sam, what show would you make of fighting, all of you? You're not soldiers. Look at you-"

He looked around at them, anxious brown faces in the light of the flickering candles, farmers, labourers, craftsmen gathered in the school house late on an August night to talk about war. Men that helped the earth to bring forth life should never trail a pike or level a musket in anger.

"How could a handful like you help?"

"Every man helps Master Will," Phillip Long suggested. "We may not know much about soldiering, but we knows how to fight. I've heard tell that the High Sheriff, Sir George Vaughan and his lieutenants lean our way. Feelings are running high in Salisbury and there are plenty of great folk been heard to speak for Parliament, men like Walter Long and Sir Edward Hungerford. My father have heard it from waggoners who come from all over the county and there's talk that Edward Baynton is to be made commander of the Parliamentary forces in Wiltshire."

He was afire with enthusiasm, his eyes bright with a fever that chilled Will Barry.

"If that is true," he murmured, " It is not the wisest choice. After a taste of his high-handed behaviour many people will consider the King's actions much less tyrannical. Edward Hungerford has his faults, but he might be a better bet than Baynton."

"I can tell thee though," Clem Draper's thin voice made itself heard. " There ain't no need for us to go fighting. If there's to be a war, it need not touch us ordinary folk. We can make our feelings plain, but let the armies fight. That's what soldiers be for."

He looked a pitiful sight with ink stains up to his elbows and still clutching his sodden cap. John Dilke snorted.

"You always did have a white liver Clem Draper. Where do you think soldiers come from? The militia that's where and who makes up the militia- folk like us. If a man believes in something he must fight for it, not leave it to others."

Sam Selfe nodded his approval and Will could see there was no budging them. The possibility of bettering their lot, breaking away from the humdrum life that bound them, filled some of them with excitement. The young ones like Phillip could hear the drums and trumpets, but not the screams of the dying. They felt that war was more noble than pushing the plough and how could he persuade them otherwise?

It was August 24th. The news had just reached the village that the King had set up his standard in Nottingham on the 22nd. What the moderates had feared had come to pass. Parliament had gone too far to withdraw and the King would not submit, so Englishman prepared to fight Englishman. Most of the inhabitants in Sandy Barrow and the surrounding villages shook their heads, prayed it would come out alright and left it at that. There was harvesting to be done. But this group of enthusiasts had come to Will Barry to convince him to lead them as Sandy Barrow's contribution to the Parliamentary forces in Wiltshire. The whole county was stirring and they did not wish to be left in the rear-guard. They needed Will to organise and direct them. They trusted him.

He had done nothing in the months following his break with the Wanleys to make his position clear. He had just lived from day-to-day pretending that the crisis might not come, but knowing in his heart that it must. Now it was here in the hot summer of 1642 and still he had no answer.

"I can't." he tried to explain to them. "I just cannot commit myself to the shedding of blood when I know that in many ways the Parliamentary cause is as mistaken as the King's."

He was going to enlarge on this when there was a mighty banging on the door. The villagers started and looked at each other nervously.

"Will, Will are you in there? If you are for God's sake open the damn door. What's going on in there?"

Richard Wanley had a habit of firing questions in rapid succession without waiting for answers.

"It's alright Richard, don't get frantic," Will replied. "Phillip, unbolt the door."

"You can't let Wanley's son in here." John Dilke jumped in front of Phillip as he went to the door. "I forbid it."

Will gave him a long, cool look that had amusement in it.

"I fear you have no right to stop me from letting him in John, but I would be interested to know how you would try. Phillip, go ahead."

The boy darted past Dilke and pulled back the heavy bolt. Richard Wanley burst into the room as if he had been about to break the door down. He stopped when he saw the assembled company, his mouth curling in contempt.

"I might have known the wise men had gathered. What's wrong Dilke, barley gone mildew?"

Dilke snarled and stepped back. He was afraid of Richard, afraid of his influence and hated him like poison because of it.

"Come and sit down," Will invited. "Join the wise men."

"I'm damned if I will. Look, clear them out, there's a good fellow. I have something urgent to tell you."

Richard looked as if he had been travelling in a hurry. The thick red hair was dishevelled and his clothes coated with dust. He was agitated, passing his riding whip from one hand to the other and rocking from toe to heel.

"At a time like this I think my friends should hear whatever you have to say." Will insisted.

"Oh yes, they make sure they are your friends when they need you. I bet they have been jackalling around you for your support."

"Well, are you not here to elicit my support Dick?"

"No, I am here to warn you. I suppose they might as well know. They will hear soon enough in the morning.

Father has heard rumours that the High Sheriff is inclined towards Parliament." -Phillip Long looked around the room with a smile of vindication- "He is going to make our move now, before Vaughan makes up his mind. Father wants the whole village to make an open declaration for the King."

"They won't all do it," Will said.

"They'll have to damn it. Father's demanding that his own tenants take up arms and follow him to join the nearest loyalist contingent. If they refuse, he will turn them off his land, even have them arrested."

The silence that settled on the room was audible. The eyes of the villagers widened and Will Barry stood up. He felt an angry despair surging inside him and he had turned pale.

"You can't mean that Richard. These people's beliefs are as passionate as his. They must be free to voice them, make their own choice."

"You think they are harmless, don't you? Look at them, sullen and vicious. They don't do anything because they have no power, but give them half a chance and they will trample all over us, burn down our houses, take everything for themselves."

"Now you sound just like your father."

"I am like my father."

"Then you support him in this iniquitous resolve of his?"

"Of course I do."

"Then God forgive you," murmured Sam Selfe.

He was sitting on the stool, watching Richard.

There was genuine compassion in his voice. Wanley turned on him angrily.

"I was not talking to you Holy Joe. Listen Will, I don't care what happens to them. I do not have your social conscience. I want you to use that fine brain of yours to some purpose. My father will not leave you alone. He will not let you sit on the fence. If you don't declare for the King he will do his damnedest to have you arrested."

" And you are convinced of the rightness of the King's cause are you?" Will was surprised by the calmness of his own voice. He was beginning to feel that great tension again, that pulling in opposite directions. The more he listened to Richard and thought of the squire's decision, the more he felt himself being drawn towards the villagers. He struggled to remain in the centre, but his footholds were slipping away from beneath him. Richard could sense this, but he was not sure which side was winning.

"You know I don't go around full of high motives," he said, lowering his voice to a more persuasive tone. "Cause is an emotive word, but I do know that when the King calls for men, we should answer it. I do believe in loyalty to him and to our families' traditions. There is no man I would rather have by my side than you Will, you know that. Would we be loyal to our caste if—" He stopped realising from the expression on Will's face that he had chosen the wrong word. " Well, loyal to our families then, if we stood by to give men like these the opportunity to run the country. A poor England that would turn out to be for sure."

Will could not argue anymore. There was no point.

"Richard I cannot declare for the King."

Not long past he had said the same about Parliament. Encouraged by this positive assertion, Phillip Long told Wanley that he was not afraid of his father's threats.

"When the High Sheriff declares for Parliament your father won't be able to arrest us."

"If the High Sheriff so declares my lad. He's wavering. The actions of men like my father may persuade him to remain loyal. Your families will spend tonight in the fields if you don't obey father and you will spend it in Devizes jail. There are no ifs or buts about that."

Richard's words struck home. The squire's power was immediate and real to them, the High Sheriff's vague and indefinite. Wanley was continuing to plead with Will, when Sam Selfe said quietly, " You must stop trying to divert him from the right path into your way of error."

Richard swore.

"You are a profane and misguided man Richard, with no notion of the danger in which your soul do lie. But that must rest with you, you mustn't imperil his also. Twere better that a millstone—"

Sam did not finish the quotation for Richard swung around so fast that no one had time to stop him from striking Sam across the face with his riding whip, a blow of brutal force. Selfe swayed a little, turning his head with the blow, but he did not cry out. The skin split from the edge of his eyebrow, across his cheek, down to the corner of his mouth and bright beads of blood were beginning to form, beads which swelled and burst like bubbles, until a thin stream of scarlet ran down his face. The steady brown eyes registered no pain. They just gazed at Richard, who was breathing hard, squeezing his whip in his fist as if he meant to crush it.

"Get out Richard!" Will's voice was as cold as Wanley had ever heard it. He did not need to repeat it, for pushing the villagers aside with a frustrated, choking cry, Richard ran out of the room. Will went to Sam who was staunching the blood from the cut with his sleeve.

"Oh Sam, I am so sorry."

"You bent responsible for his doings. Tis the only way he knows when he feels pain, to strike out. He can find no other answer. His love for you is strong, even though he would lead you astray. It hurts him that you can't put your conscience aside for friendship's sake."

The room was alive now with excited murmuring as the villagers discussed what they should do for the best. One thing was certain, they must leave the village. There was no acceptable alternative. Will felt both hot and cold at the same time and there was a stinging sensation in his throat like acid. Finally he had been drawn away from the centre. These men needed him and he must respond. All political and religious theory was irrelevant in the face of this personal need. He took a deep breath, steeling himself, then he told them, "You are right, you cannot stay here now. Far better you expend your energy in a cause that means something to you for whatever motive, then dissipate it frustratedly banging your fists against the walls of Devizes jail. Go home as fast as you can and get ready to leave. Tell your families that if the Squire's bailiff evicts them, they are to go to my house. I will leave instructions there. They will want for nothing. Bring horses if you have them and whatever weapons you can find and meet me in the south woods in two hours."

"Then you'll lead us to fight for Parliament Master Will?" Phillip Long's voice was full of expectation.

"As best as I can. I cannot predict what the outcome will be."

The room was suddenly full of cheering. They could not guess how sick he felt. Sam Selfe did not smile often. His was a sombre face, but when he smiled as he was smiling now, his face was irradiated. He gripped Will's hand.

"You bin blessed this night Will Barry."

"I truly hope so," Will returned. "Don't waste any more time. Go home now, all of you."

They scrambled out of the room and were gone, leaving Will in a strange, shadowy silence, as if all existence was suspended. He could hear his heart beating, his blood flowing, his thoughts forming, but he did not want to listen to those thoughts, to consider what he was about to do. He shook off the almost mystic state enveloping him and dashed for the door. He too must hurry home, perhaps for the last time.

The meeting in the school house had gone on through the night and into the morning. It was dawn when Will sprinted past the cattle pens on the north side of the house, a misty, shuddering dawn that spoke of a hot day to come. The cows had been milked and were being driven out to pasture. The ploughman, Jess Barnett, who had been up since four o'clock, was rubbing down his plough oxen as if they were his children and was probably thinking about his breakfast. He was astonished to see his master run past him shouting a greeting.

In the farthest cattle pen Will saw the large frame of Crispin Collington. The bailiff was driving a bull, a magnificent creature with a neck like a tree trunk and curving horns. It lumbered slowly and reluctantly out of the pen, encouraged by slaps on the rump with the flat of Crispin's hand. Will came to a halt by the fence and Crispin fastened the gate of the pen and trotted over to join him. He vaulted over the fence with the ease of a man half his weight.

"You see, I even have to drive the cattle myself," he said, smiling. "The cowherds are afraid of that old devil when he's in a bad mood. That's just what he wants. It's fatal to show fear in front of any bull. They'll turn on you. He has never attempted to turn on me because I make it clear that I'm not afraid of him. He knows who's master in this yard."

He bent down to pick up a book that was propped against the fence. It was a volume of French poetry. " I was trying to read some of this- recommended to me by your sister- when I had to go and rescue Mark Smart. Early in the morning and late at night are the only times I have for reading."

Will recognised the book as one of Lucy's. The green leather cover with the gold lettering seemed out of place in the cattle pens and Will could not help thinking

that his sister would not appreciate such a handsome book being trodden on by cows.

"You're a strange fellow Crispin," he murmured.

"So I've been told before," the bailiff was feeling in his pocket for his pipe. "But you're late in. Is anything wrong?"

He was not prepared for the answer that came in a hollow, unemotional tone.

"Yes, I think our world is beginning to roll off its axis."

Will explained briefly what had happened and what he planned to do while Crispin listened attentively, nodding his agreement now and then.

"The point is Crispin. I must know where you stand because you are going to play an important part in this."

He sensed rather than saw Crispin's body tense, a slight stiffening of his easy stance.

"If you mean am I going to rampage about the countryside behind a flag, the answer is no. I don't take sides, I just concentrate on my job. Like you, I can see the good and evil on both sides of this divide and I am going to stay well out of it. That would be my advice to you also Master Will."

Will did not comment on the advice but continued, "I am heartened because you feel that way, for I am going to give you full responsibility to run things in my absence, taking my mother's and Lucy's opinions and feelings into account of course. They will need someone to rely on, someone they know is trustworthy. I have no fears for their safety because I know Sir Roger will behave honourably towards Mother for my father's sake."

He did fear what his mother would think of his decision, not just the parting, but his taking up arms against his King. He did not share this thought with Crispin however. The bailiff was gazing reflectively at his pipe. The magnitude of Will's news had diverted him from filling it.

"I'm very flattered by your readiness to put your trust in me. It is a big responsibility and I shall do my very best to be worthy of the task."

"There is no one I would rather trust Crispin."

Will let his hand rest on Collington's arm for a moment, then he asked, "Is my mother up yet do you know?"

"I doubt it. She waited up very late for you and was likely very tired. Mistress Lucy is though."

Will was relieved that his mother was still in bed. He knew he would not have the courage to say goodbye to her. He convinced himself that it would be better for her not to see him go. He must see Lucy however. Asking Crispin to prepare Minstrel, his favourite horse, he ran into the house.

In half an hour, Will Barry was ready to leave the family house at Sandy Barrow. The sun had risen gloriously bright as the last male descendant of the Wiltshire Barrys, his father's sword and two handsome wheel-lock pistols at his waist, shook his bailiff's hand. He took one good look at the house, concentrating for a second longer on the window of his mother's bedroom. He dare not dwell on how beautiful the farmhouse looked, the rambling roses, the ivy and the busy yard beyond. Lucy held out her hands to him and he took her into his arms in a long embrace.

"Are you sure it is best to go without saying goodbye to Mother?" she queried doubtfully. "She will be so distressed."

"There is no good way to do it Lucy, but I believe she would be even more distressed to watch me go. Besides I fear my courage might fail me if I looked into her eyes. " He kissed his sister's forehead. "I know you will take good care of her. The school will keep you busy and Hannah Moss will help you there when she can I am sure. There is money enough left in the strongbox. I haven't taken much for myself. There are two more payments due next month anyway, for teasels and dye our agent supplied to the local fulling mills. Should the worst befall me contact Uncle Harper. Mother always was his favourite sister. He will know what to do."

Lucy was reluctant to let go of her brother. Only two years separated them in age and they had always been close. She had missed him so much when he went up to Cambridge and was relieved when he decided to dedicate his life to the school and the farm, rather than embarking on a career that would take him far from home. Now she dare not contemplate the possibility of losing him forever in some distant battle, never knowing where his body was buried. But she did know that it was her duty to keep her mother from dwelling too much on those same fears.

Will gently withdrew from the embrace as both Flash and Baron vied for his attention, the collie circling around him. excited by the prospect of a chase beside Will's horse. Baron just stood there, his head pushed up against his master's side.

"I might as well let Flash come with me. If you shut him in now, he will only follow the trail once he is let free again. He could be useful catching rabbits. Not you though old lad." He took Baron's head in his hands, stroking both sides of his face with his hands. "We will be travelling too fast for you. Besides, I need you to guard the house, protect Mother and Lucy. It's no good looking at me like that- you have to stay."

Baron sat down, but he continued to gaze at Will with his soft, amber eyes, as Barry swung himself into the saddle and urged his horse to turn. Flash was already racing on ahead, barking in sheer exuberance. Looking over his shoulder to wave to Lucy and call "I will send word to you as often as I can," Will noticed that Crispin was holding her hand. What he experienced at that moment he could only analyse as a dart of indignation. He did not like what he saw. Crispin was very swift to take up his role of comforter. A nagging uneasiness forced its way into Will's mind. He checked his horse in its stride and almost turned back. Then he was ashamed of his reaction. He trusted Crispin and he had never regarded him as inferior, so there was no reason why he should object to him holding Lucy's hand as if it was impertinent. She would be grateful for some reassurance at that moment. He put the feeling down to his disordered state of mind and let go of it.

He was hardly aware of what was around him as he rode towards the south woods. The drumming of Minstrel's hooves echoed in his head. A thousand thoughts raced through his mind, incoherent and disjointed with no thread of logic to hold them together. The quickest route to the south woods was past the school house, but he avoided that way. Some of the children might be on their way to school already and he did not want to see them. To leave what he had been so certain was his life's work in this summary fashion was so painful that he felt the sight of the stone school house would make him turn back.

When he reached the fringe of the woods, the men were waiting for him. They were quieter now, sobered by the experience of leaving behind all they loved. Will was surprised to find ten of them, all mounted. John Dilke for all his fire-eating, had not come. His possessions had too great a hold on him. His farm on the outer edge of the Squire's land, almost into Heddington was small, but prosperous. Unlike the rest of the men gathered there, he had a great deal to lose and was not willing to make the sacrifice. He had however provided horses for those who had none and divided his weapons among them. He also gave his chief cowherd, Abel Harding, permission to join them.

Will was greeted by Sam Selfe, seated on a grey mare, his beloved Elizabethan matchlock hanging in a holster from his saddle.

"Are you ready?" Will asked crisply.

"We'll never be readier," was the reply.

"Then we will make for Salisbury. That seems the most obvious rallying point."

At that moment a figure darted out between the horses and caught hold of Will's bridle. It was Hannah Moss, her hair loose and tangled, her face grubby as if she had just left her bed. She clutched a bundle in which she had packed her meagre possessions.

"I be coming with you," she declared. "As soon as I heard you were going, I said to myself they'll be needing someone to cook and mend for them on their travels to the wars and I knows how to load and clean a musket besides."

Some of the men laughed and she turned on them indignantly.

"I do then, as well as any of you."

"I am sure you do Hannah," Will ameliorated. "I am not surprised by anything you can do, but you cannot come with us. It is too dangerous."

"I'm not afraid, truly. I'll not get in the way, only be a help. Please Master Will."

"Now you must be sensible. Your mother and father need you at home and Lucy will want you help her at the school while I am away. You must make sure that the library is used properly."

She could see that he meant it. Throwing down her bundle, she caught hold of Will's stirrup, pressing her cheek against his knee. She wanted to cry, but suppressed it, too proud to do so in front of those smirking men, particularly Phillip Long.

"I don't want to help at school no more if you aint there. I only want to do things for you. Please let me come with you, please."

Will had not bargained for this. Lucy's dignity had helped him, but this was hard. The words caught in his throat.

"Hannah, if you want to do something for me, have some pity on me. God knows it is hard enough for me to leave you all as it is. I shall be back and then I shall want to find the school going along as well as when I left it."

"But five year since, our Noah just went into Calne and he never come back and I fear I won't never see you no more."

She had put into words the look that every man there had seen in the eyes of their loved ones that morning. Will leaned from the saddle and ran his hand very gently over her matted hair. Then Sam Selfe, who had dismounted, took her firmly by the shoulders and pulled her away from Will's horse.

"You pray for us all Hannah Moss. If you do it hard enough child, God grant we shall all come home safe."

The horses were growing restless, shaking their heads and setting the harness jingling. The men of Sandy Barrow and one black and white collie must be off to the wars. Soon the woods rang with the galloping hooves and Hannah Moss sat down on the small bundle, staring into the trees, their leaves still vibrating with the passing of horses.

She sat there for some time letting the tears come now she was alone. Then wiping her eyes with the back of her hand she said aloud, " What use be this Hannah Moss. Stop your weeping and do what he asked. Get down to that school" and taking up her bundle she set off at a determined pace.

❃

Two months passed and no word reached Sandy Barrow from any of the men who had left in August. Loyalties amongst the influential folk in the county were divided. Support for the King was strong in the West Country as a whole, but some of the squirarchy in the Calne area, the Ernles, Blakes and Bayntons were generally speaking pro-Parliament. Others thought it wise not to commit themselves too early. The Calne burgesses were clear in their Parliamentary sympathies. Walter Norborne, owner of one of the finest houses in Calne, had represented the Borough in Parliament in 1640, but was open about his loyalty to the King. The burgesses duly reported him to the Commons Chamber in the Palace of Westminster and it was rumoured that he was fined a large sum, as much as £380. Devizes, though only eight miles from Calne and despite both its M.Ps being pro-Parliament, remained a bastion of royal support, mainly due to the influence of the Mayor Richard Pierce and the presence of Devizes Castle, where the Welshman Charles Lloyd, the king's general-in-chief of engineers was governor. The crumbling castle was no longer the magnificent edifice of past centuries, but the keep remained and it still possessed formidable outer defences. Visitors reported seeing men labouring to repair and strengthen the outworks and barricades were being erected at the entrances to the town. Devizes was strategically placed between the King's HQ at Oxford and his potential support further west, so it was vital to maintain the castle garrison.

Only two days after Will Barry's departure from Sandy Barrow, Sir Roger, Richard and Edward Wanley had gone to join the Marquis of Hertford in Somerset. The King had appointed Hertford Lieutenant-General of the six south western counties and he had set up his headquarters in Wells.

Ellen Wanley had tried to persuade Edward to stay at home, but she received no support from her husband, who considered his younger son quite old enough at seventeen to serve his King. Caroline added her voice to her mother's protests, but Maria, when asked to back them up only remarked, "Oh let him go Mother. He will only sulk and make our lives a misery if he is made to stay."

This prompted Caroline to accuse her sister of having no heart. "Sometimes," she said tearfully, " I believe you are made of ice, not flesh and blood."

Ellen took comfort in Olivia Barry's company. Olivia welcomed it for Lucy was often occupied at the school and if she was too long alone she began to dwell too morbidly on the situation. The two mothers were united in their concern for their sons and refused to let politics get in the way.

Maria however avoided the Barrys when possible because she could sense their lingering, if unspoken, indignation over the way she had treated Will. She did not care much for Lucy anyway. She was too educated, too outspoken, too sympathetic towards the views of the villagers and too little interested in fashionable clothes for Maria's tastes.

She would have sneered no doubt at the simple blue dress with the lace collar and cuffs that Lucy Barry was wearing that morning when Hannah Moss arrived to lay out the books for the first lesson. Hannah thought how beautiful she looked, how well the blue suited her. Lucy was tall and slender with a long, elegant neck and moved with such grace. Hannah often wondered how it would feel to look like that in a dress that fitted perfectly, instead of being short and full-bosomed, wearing a garment that was bursting at the laces. In fact Hannah was not that short, just seemed so in comparison with Lucy and she would have been surprised to discover that the object of her admiration often sighed because she regarded her breasts too small.

It was early and no pupils had arrived yet, but there was a visitor, one that stirred Hannah's displeasure. Lucy was out in the yard talking to Crispin Collington. They were standing close together smiling and at one point he stroked her arm. Hannah snorted and walked out to the doorway, where she positioned herself so they could see her. Crispin bowed her a mocking acknowledgement- at least she judged it to be mockery and gave him a hard stare in return. He kissed Lucy's hand and walked away.

Hannah came out to join her and they both watched his figure disappear into the distance with very different thoughts in their heads. Lucy was thinking how strong and purposeful was his walk. Hannah however put her thoughts into words.

"He thinks too well of himself that one. He's setting his cap at you. Look at him striding along as if he owns the place now that Master Will's not here."

"You judge him too harshly," Lucy replied, her cheeks flushing slightly. " He has supported mother and I so whole-heartedly since Will left and my brother did ask him to run the farm in his absence. He is only carrying out Will's instructions. As for setting his cap at me, as you put it, I am sure he is only being protective. Why do you dislike him so Hannah?"

"'Tis not for me to like or dislike him. I own he knows much about farming and tis his job to make sure things are done proper, but he acts as if he is so much better than the rest of us, has no real respect for those who work for him, not like Master Will."

"You must remember that my brother is exceptionally enlightened," Lucy spoke with pride in her voice, feeling Will's absence sharply at that moment. "You should not compare everyone with Will. Crispin is much better educated than the farm hands, that is why he is a bailiff. He was sorely disappointed in his expectations when a young man. Financial constraints after his father's death prevented him from studying law. He envisaged a different life from his present one and perhaps feels the frustration of it at times. I am sure he has respect for the labourers and will help them when he can. He persuaded Francis Farrow not to evict the families of the men who went with Will in August, even though Sir Roger left instructions for him to do so before he went to Somerset."

Hannah gave her a direct look. "Collington told you that did he?"

"Yes, he was very pleased to be able to help them."

Hannah had heard a different story, that Crispin had advised Farrow that he would be wiser to carry out his master's instructions and it was Francis Farrow who had decided to be merciful in the squire's absence. She also knew for a fact that only a few days after Will Barry had left, Crispin had evicted Daniel Bray for not paying his rent, contrary to Will's instructions. She felt like telling Lucy, but decided against trying to score points over Crispin for fear of losing favour with her and besides, she had no desire to hurt Lucy. However she could not disguise the disappointment in her voice when she said, "So you're sweet on him then?"

Lucy's first instinct was to deny it, but she changed her mind. She had no reason to be ashamed of a connection with Crispin, She regarded Hannah as her friend and did not wish her to misunderstand the bailiff.

"I am very fond of him," she confessed, relieved to admit it. "We have many interests in common. We both love poetry and literature and can spend hours conversing about it. He has such a sense of humour and it is so good to laugh in these sad times. It cheers me. He is well-favoured too."

"He's well-made and handsome enough in his way," Hannah conceded, "But don't you feel sometimes that all his clever talk, his smiling and hand kissing when he is with you is just his route to bettering himself, to climb up the ladder?"

Lucy shook her head. "Oh Hannah, it is no crime to wish to better your lot in life, just as you have bettered yours by learning to read and write, which has enabled you to help others. Besides, our family is no better than Crispin's. We both come from yeoman stock. It is just that we were granted good fortune after our father died, whereas bad luck befell Crispin at his father's death."

She took hold of both Hannah's hands and looked earnestly into her face.

"Two weeks ago I was twenty three. Most women are married or at least promised to someone by that age. Mother is beginning to worry that I do not meet many suitable candidates for marriage, which is true because I avoid most of them. I would much rather give my heart to someone like Crispin, than agree to marry without love a mad-cap like Richard Wanley or a popinjay knight like

Gervaise Cleverdon, or even the son of some rich merchant who was a friend of Father's. Can you not understand that? I am certain that Crispin has a true regard for me."

As Hannah gazed into Lucy's clear blue eyes, she was convinced that all she wished for was her happiness.

"Course I understand. No one will ever force me to marry a man I didn't fancy. If you are sure of his feelings and he pleases you, then tis no business of mine."

Lucy hugged her, a spontaneous gesture that took Hannah by surprise. They were both silent for a while, returning to the task of putting out the relevant books. Then Lucy said, "It is Will's birthday next Tuesday. We were both born in October, two years apart. It is strange not to be able to give him a greeting and a gift on his twenty fifth birthday."

Hannah nodded. She knew the date of her birth although no one had ever marked it, just as her parents failed to mark their own. The only birthday that was ever celebrated in the Moss household was Noah's.

"I wish we could hear from them," she remarked, "Master Will and the others. I do worry about them all so- Sam Selfe, Phil Long, Clem Draper- all that lot."

"I am sure we will receive a letter or a message soon. The Wanleys have heard from Sir Roger, a letter arrived last week, but he is only in Somerset, not too far away. Crispin has discovered that most of the Wiltshire contingent that declared for Parliament have been sent down into Cornwall, which is many miles distant. I hear it is a very wild region, which may make regular communications difficult to send."

They both tried to find comfort in that. Children's voices could now be heard outside in the yard. Fewer pupils were attending the classes since August because the older children of the men who had gone to war were needed to do their fathers' work. Hannah, as she went outside to marshal them into the school room, was recalling the sensation of Will Barry's hand touching her hair so gently and was forced to admit to herself that her attitude towards Crispin was partly due to jealousy. Firstly, Lucy was her friend and she was sure it was a friendship Crispin would do his best to discourage. Secondly, she could find no valid reason to deny Crispin's right to court Lucy, whereas she could think of no possible way she herself could ever become the object of Will Barry's affections.

CHAPTER FIVE

The camp was settling down for the evening. The hum of voices was dying down and the blacksmith had finished his repair work, for the ring of his hammer had ceased. It had been a dreary, chilly day for mid-May and fires were crackling around the camp. Now and then a man laughed aloud or a horse whinnied and tugged at its hobble. The atmosphere was relaxed with little sign that these men expected a battle in the morning.

"Do you think they'll attack tomorrow?" Sam Selfe asked, as he unlaced his long-skirted leather jerkin and slipped it off his back. "I can't get into the way of sleeping in these yer things even now. The tails do dig into my backside,"

Will Barry was laying full length, his head resting against his helmet. His eyes were closed, but he was not asleep.

"Hopton must attack tomorrow," he murmured. "If these rumours are true about his officers having one dry biscuit each for their meals, he has no choice but to attack as soon as possible. Besides, he will want to do it before the rest of our cavalry get back from Bodmin."

"You never did think they should have gone did you Master Will Sir?" Phillip Long cut in. He was crouching beside them polishing the shell guard of his cheap infantry sword. Phillip could not bring himself to drop the 'Master Will' but now Will Barry was a Lieutenant in the fifth company of the 5th Infantry Regiment-the Five Fives they called themselves- he felt an additional 'Sir' was in order.

Back in August, when the men from Sandy Barrow first arrived at the rallying point in the water meadows lying in the shadow of the spire of Salisbury Cathedral, they were briefly assessed for their ability. It was clear that Will Barry's skill on horseback was far superior to that of his companions, most of whom were more familiar with driving a horse between the shafts of a cart than sitting on its back and had found the ride to Salisbury uncomfortable. It was suggested to Will that he should join a troop of cavalry, but he did not wish to be parted from the rest of the villagers, who had been assigned to the fifth company of the 5th Infantry Regiment, the four best marksmen, including Sam and Phillip as musketeers and the other six as pikemen.

The gnarled sergeant in charge of the assessment, a professional soldier with a keen eye, perceived that Barry was an educated man, respected by his companions and recommended him as officer material. So Will was given the rank of Lieutenant, regardless of the fact that he had no experience of warfare. When he protested that the little knowledge he had of military tactics came from reading accounts of past campaigns, the sergeant laughed and replied, " At least you can read. As for tactics, you will learn, if you live long enough."

As an officer Will was allowed to keep his horse, for junior officers of infantry regiments were often required to ride ahead as scouts or take communications between commanders and in battle an elevated position on horseback gave a clearer view of troop formations and made giving orders easier, the main disadvantage being it provided an obvious target for the enemy musketeers.

There were no objections to the presence of Flash. One of the captains had a pair of Italian greyhounds, who teamed up with the collie on rabbit hunting forays, bringing their prey back into camp.

When the army was on the march, Will would dismount and walk beside the men, leading Minstrel by the reins. This caused amusement amongst some of the other officers, most of whom were from the squirearchy or the families of minor aristocrats, who believed they were entitled to ride while the common soldier walked. The men however appreciated Will Barry's gesture.

It was customary when the army camped for the officers of the various companies to get together around a fire in the evenings. Will joined them occasionally, but he was not at ease in their presence and much preferred to sit and talk with Sam and Phillip as he was this evening. He considered Phillip's question before he opened his eyes and sat up, replying,

"No, it was a foolish move, born of Lord Stamford's over-confidence. We have got more men than Hopton and a good tactical position, but we all know how easily things can go wrong. If they should, two hundred horse won't help much, but 1500 could turn the tide."

"But we'll beat them," Phillip insisted. "They'll never get up this hill."

Lord Stamford, the commander of the Parliamentary forces in Devon and Cornwall, had chosen a strong position to offer battle to the enemy. He had disposed his men on a plateau, high above sea level, parallel with the coast. If Phillip Long looked behind him to the west he could follow the gentle slopes until far into the distance he could see the lights of the town of Bude. If he went to the eastern end of the plateau, he found himself gazing down a sheer drop, covered in trees. No enemy could possibly make his way up that slope.

Above his head he could see at the top of the plateau, the round mouths of thirteen cannon placed in a semi-circle on the western side of the hill. Phillip felt secure and eager.

"I only hope my sword don't snap off like the one I had at Sourton. You can't trust they damn things. Give I a good clubbed musket butt to rely on any day."

He was looking longingly at Will's sword lying on the ground beside him, a cavalry sword with a broad blade and a basket hilt. Will was looking at it too, but not longingly.

"Sam," he asked, "Have you bought yourself a new musket yet?"

An obstinate look came into Sam Selfe's eyes. "I don't need a new musket."

Phillip guffawed disrespectfully and Will smiled.

"I am only thinking of your own safety. I am willing to admit that your matchlock has done good service. I never imagined that it would last so long, but it's bound to give out soon. Don't risk it anymore."

"I can't afford up yer eighteen shillings for a musket. All my spare money is for going home for the wife and littluns. They tell me these new muskets can kill at four hundred yards. Well I haven't seen much evidence of that these past months. I don't believe there's accuracy above a hundred to a hundred and fifty yards and my old beauty can manage that well enough. Please God I shan't have to die in these wars, but if I do, I want to be holding my grandfather's gun."

Will left it at that; there was no more he could say.

Darkness had fallen very suddenly. A cold wind with a thin drizzle born on it was blowing across the crest of the hill. Phillip wrapped himself up in his blanket and soon his snores were carried along on the wind. Sam was pouring over his leather bound bible by the light of the fire. Will lay back and stared up at the solitary star in a sky that was thick and threatening. He hated the nights when he had time to think, time for tired, strained eyes that refused to close, to gaze into the dark and wonder if that blackness was really within his own soul. He had lost the knack of sleeping. He had packed his sketch pad and a few charcoals when he left home and for the first couple of months sketching the men and the activity of the camp in spare moments distracted him, but now even that had lost its appeal. He had not taken the pad out of his pack for weeks.

It was May 15th 1643. For almost nine months Will had been engaged in the struggle for the West Country.

The recruits had been sent from Salisbury to join General Ruthin's forces, continually skirmishing with Ralph Hopton's men in Devon and Cornwall. In the early days they had heard some news from Wiltshire, how the High Sheriff had indeed declared for Parliament and how that cause had prospered in the county until the Royalist commander, Lord Henry Wilmot took Marlborough early in December and changed the whole complexion of things. But as the fighting intensified, so the news became less.

Will had written several letters home, but had no idea if they had reached Sandy Barrow. He received no communications in return.

He had seen a good deal of fighting. He had been with Ruthin when he attempted to take the town of Saltash and had experienced the crashing defeat of Braddock Down in January, when soldiers in his regiment were clubbed and beaten in the streets of Liskeard by the loyalist citizens. Then he had distinguished himself in the victory at Sourton three weeks past, when a large Cornish army was taken unawares by Major General James Chudleigh and driven right back to Bridestowe. They had captured all Hopton's personal papers that day and amongst them was a letter from the King ordering Hopton to march into Somerset to join forces with the Marquis of Hertford. This was the reason why the Parliamentary troops were now ranged across the plateau. They must prevent Hopton from joining Hertford.

So here was Will on the eve of yet another battle. Of the ten men who had ridden out of Sandy Barrow with him last August, only Sam and Phillip remained. Two lay under the green turf of Braddock Down; two more were taken prisoner in Liskeard; one was sent home too badly wounded to fight; another died at Sourton and two had deserted as early as October.

Will did not bear one physical scar, but he feared that a great, ugly wound would tear his soul apart. Before every battle he prayed that he would revolt against it, this presumptuous extinguishing of life, that in the heat of battle he would have the courage to refuse to kill and so die for one principle that he truly believed in. Yet always in action he killed instinctively. He was an excellent swordsman, an accurate shot. The exultation of getting the better of an opponent, of slipping his blade beneath the guard of some sweating, smoke-blackened soldier and feeling it slice through leather and churn in the flesh was too much like pleasure. It was afterwards in the smoke and the desolation that a shuddering revulsion would take hold of him, a revulsion for himself, as if his whole being was cracking. Sometimes he would lay at night and tremble, feeling such a void within himself that he would wish away his existence, this dogged instinct for self-preservation, this resilient consciousness that lived and lived.

Sam understood. Will was sure he would have broken long ago without Sam's patient support. Selfe was certain that God could forgive this appalling waste of life for ultimately His ways would triumph. Will prayed that God could forgive him, but he doubted if he could ever forgive himself. There were those in the regiment who exulted with a fierce triumph in the death of the unbelievers, who gloried in their fiery sword of God. It was easy to call them fanatics and draw back from their hatred and intolerance, but they knew why they killed. They reached towards a purpose which they believed transcended death – and he- why did he kill? When he searched for his motives, he was too honest to maintain the spiritual and intellectual fraud that he fought for peace. His position had become similar to that of a professional soldier. He felt he was a licensed murderer and could not use God or a cause as an excuse.

This night on Stratton Hill was a long one for him and he was relieved when the dawn broke leaden and the camp began to stir. There would be little time for heart searching now. Around four o'clock Chudleigh had sent a party of dragoons with muskets to line the ditches and hedges at the bottom of the hill. Now half an hour later, shots were heard from the dragoon positions.

"Rabbits do ye think?" said Sam without smiling, as he fastened the latch of his helmet.

"Cornishmen more like." Phillip's musket was already in his hand. "We'll show 'em eh Sam? Damn lot of Catholics."

Selfe just blinked and made no attempt to reply.

"Well half of them be."

"That may be so, but Sir Ralph Hopton's beliefs are the same as our own. He had a good Puritan upbringing. Tis loyalty to his King as makes him stand on the side he does. He's an honest and courageous man and I wish he were for us instead of against us."

"Oh Sam you do get I down sometimes," and

Phillip was gone, scurrying with the rest of the men to fall in.

Will Barry was mounted, riding beside his captain, the pugnacious Elias Parker, organising the men into the agreed battle formation. Their regiment, together with the 15th Infantry formed the brigade that drew up on the south west side of the hill. In theory each company consisted of 100 men and ten companies formed a regiment, but it was very rare that companies were up to full strength. Will's company was now down to fifty five. He watched them falling into line, stumbling in their eagerness, a block of pikemen, flanked on either side by blocks of musketeers, six ranks deep.

The clatter of preparation went on for another fifteen minutes then all was strangely silent, as if the entire army was holding its breath. The rain had stopped, making it easier for musketeers to light the ends of their two feet long pieces of match cord from a linstock carried amongst them by a sergeant. The wind still blew across the plateau and the silence was broken by some of the men cursing because their match cords had been extinguished. Their oaths were joined by the snorts of horses and the shaking of harness as the mounts of Lord Stamford's cavalry, drawn up in reserve, began to sense the tension and grow restless.

Then another sound broke in, the sound of skirmishing intensifying down in the valley. It must have been nearing five o'clock when Will, straining his eyes in the grey light, saw the guidons of their own dragoons fluttering. The small party which had formed the outpost at the foot of the hill was making its way back up at a fast pace. The Cornish army was attacking. The weight of their steps made the hill shake and the wind set the powder flasks rattling as they swung from the bandoliers of the musket men.

It was soon clear to the defenders on the crest of the hill that Hopton's men were advancing in four columns, each column dragging two cannon. One moved directly from the south, another was heading for the position held by the 5th and 15th Infantry; a third was making good progress up the gentle western slopes and beyond them on the road farther west, the tips of cavalry and dragoon pennons were visible. It was hard to calculate the numbers of the enemy with any accuracy, but it appeared to be a smaller force than their own.

As Will watched the Cornishmen roll up the hill he felt a strong sense of foreboding. It was not just the half excited, half despairing feeling that always gripped him before battle, but something that he could not define. He wiped the sweat from the palms of his hands down the skirts of his leather jerkin and tightened the joints of his breastplate, before he pulled on his gauntlets.

The men were still and ready. They had great trust in their position and looked confident. Will however could not help remembering how Harold Godwinson, the last Saxon King of England, had chosen to give battle to the Norman invaders on a hill much like this one, where the cramped position caused bunching and jostling, restricting movement. He was also aware of the sheer eastern drop at the back of the Parliamentary forces. If Hopton did reach the top of the hill, there would be no room for Stamford's troops to give ground. He mentioned this to Captain Parker, who laughed. "They won't get to the top Lieutenant, never fear."

The enemy was gaining ground though. The men of the 5th Infantry could recognise amongst the blue, green and red jackets of the regiments, the distinctive personal colours of Sir Bevil Grenville at the centre of the column advancing on them.

"What's the betting I capture Sir Bevil myself," Phillip Long boasted.

Sam Selfe smoothed the barrel of Old Beauty as if the gun were a fretting horse.

"I aint a betting man," he returned.

The Cornishmen had been well within the range of the 32 pounder demi-cannon for some time and were now coming within range of the 16 pounder culverins. The order to commence artillery fire was given and the semi -circle of guns, mounted in the earthworks on the very summit of the hill, belched out their iron shot. Some confusion was caused in the enemy ranks, but the gaps were closed up as the advance continued. As the echoes of the first artillery rounds died away, the cry of 'Make Ready' sounded from each regiment. 'Present'- the musketeers brought the three and a half feet of their gun barrels into position on their rests, the match cord burning in the gun cocks, at the same time trying to stop the pinch of fine gunpowder from being blown away by the wind. There were some colourful oaths as the men tried to hold steady. 'Give Fire'- they fired by rank, so that when the sixth rank had loosed its fusillade, the first rank was waiting to fire again, pieces primed and ready.

The first volley was devastating. Will Barry watched the entire front line of the south western column fall. A howl rang through his head. Perhaps it was the scream of a wounded man, but it sounded to him like the howl his collie, Flash always made when firing first began. He knew it could not be Flash, for the dog was speared by a royalist pikeman during a skirmish last winter. He remembered that well for it was the first time he had killed in anger; the first time the sight of a man's blood coursing down his side had given him satisfaction. The pikeman had paid for Flash's life. The collie had died months past, yet Will was often aware of his presence, as if his spirit still lingered. At night he would wake from a light doze and swear he could feel Flash's warm fur pressing against his side. The sleek black and white coat seemed to be brushing against his stirrup even now.

He shook his head, coughing as the acrid smell of burnt gunpowder penetrated to the back of his throat. The enemy was returning fire. The battle of Stratton was on in earnest.

At first the confidence of Lord Stamford's men seemed to be well placed. Throughout the course of the morning the Cornishmen charged up the hill a dozen times, only to be beaten back. Those who reached the crest were engulfed and overwhelmed by the defenders. Their musket fire was not as accurate as Stamford's because they were moving up hill; their artillery, mostly light field pieces, had a shorter range. Will found in the lulls between charges, when he could check on casualties and regroup the men, that most of the damage in his regiment had been caused by accidents. A spark from a gun had dropped into a powder cask and five men were killed in the explosion. Then one of the cannons up on the western earthworks overheated and cracked, showering hot case shot over the men below, causing one fatality and some bad mutilations.

The troops defending the western slope were harder pressed for access was less arduous and the Royalist commanders, Sir Nicholas Slanning and Colonel Trevanion were pushing with great vigour. Yet as the day wore on the effect of the Cornishmen's attacks waned. They were exhausted by the relentless toil up hill. It was nearing three o'clock. The stocky captain of the 5th Infantry looked at his lieutenant and grinned.

"Very quiet down there. I wouldn't be surprised if Hopton's running short of gunpowder. Still, he won't give up yet, not if I know Ralph Hopton. I wish I could see something. Some damned fool trod on my perspective glass in the last scuffle."

Will followed his gaze down towards the bottom of the valley. He could see plenty. A hill green with early May grass, littered with corpses and wounded men crawling like big lizards along the slopes. Out of the corner of his eye he saw a horse, its back legs smashed, trying to get up. Each time it tried, it fell again and lay kicking with its front legs like a beetle. The sun was shining now, although a grey pall of smoke hung over everything. Men and animals moved in a shuddering haze, as if in a dream, some hideous nightmare. Will could almost believe that he might wake in the school room with a pile of essays in front of him.

Then through the smoke came bright flashes from the bottom of the hill- the sun on steel. The Cornish were attacking again, all columns pounding up the slopes, drawn swords and pikes protruding like the spines on a porcupine. They were shouting and cheering wildly, making no attempt to fire on the defenders, concentrating only on gaining the crest of the hill. Will glanced at his men priming their muskets and saw their apprehension. They had believed the spirit of the enemy to be broken. The sight of this courageous charge disheartened them.

"Now lads," Captain Parker called, "Don't let them worry you. This what is known as the desperation charge. If this fails they are done for, so let us break them now."

The Parliamentary muskets blazed once more, but the enemy came on. They had gathered such momentum that the volley hardly checked them. There was a mighty thud as the western column smacked into the first line of defenders and the valleys of Stratton rang with the sound of steel on steel. There in the south west position, the 5th Infantry, stationed in front of the 15th, took the impact of the first few ranks of Royalist pikemen. They staggered back a few paces, but instinctively aware that they had little room to manoeuvre, held their ground a yard in the rear. Elias Parker let out a long explosive breath as if he had been punched in the stomach.

"I don't believe this," he shouted to Will above the din. "How in God's name did they do it?"

He broke off abruptly to defend himself from the clubbing butts of two Cornish musketeers who were bent on bringing him down from his horse. Will did his best to keep the men in a rough formation, but they were breaking under the ferocity of the attack. The very thing he had feared was happening. They were being bunched up together in the centre of the hill until there was hardly room to swing a sword freely.

"Good God Barry, this is nonsense."

At Will's side, his green silken sash torn, blood seeping from a wound across his forehead was Major General James Chudleigh. The noise was deafening now and Will strained to hear him.

"You can see what is happening. We are being rolled up like a map. We will either crush each other to death or be pushed over the eastern slope. I don't fancy either do you? We must counter attack and regain some of the lost ground."

Will's horse, Minstrel was pivoting on its toes and he had to work hard to keep it reined in,

"Well Sir, we could try their tactics. A really fierce charge of pikes down on Sir Bevil Grenville's regiment there in the centre could knock a hole right through them."

"We'll try it. Get me a good stand of pikes with a sprinkling of musketeers and you and I shall lead them." He tapped Will's boot with his sword and smiled wryly. "Death or glory William, that's what they say."

He jerked his horse's head around and began to call the men to him. In the moment before he followed suit, Will had time to tell himself how much he liked and admired Chudleigh. The Major General was only in his mid-twenties and was full of dash and verve. Everything he did, he did with panache, but he was not shallow. He showed a genuine concern for the welfare of his men and they in turn gave their best for him.

It was difficult to extract enough men from the turmoil on the slopes to form an effective stand of pikes, but between them Will and Chudleigh pulled men out individually and formed them up. Will saw Sam Selfe slipping into formation, shouldering his smoke-blackened matchlock.

"God be with you Will," he called out.

"And with you Sam. Where's Phillip?"

A shadow darkened Sam's already sombre face. "His spirit's free," was all he said.

Will did not reply; there was nothing he could say. He must concentrate on the charge now. He was wet with sweat and strangely cold, although his face felt hot and swollen. His helmet seemed to be growing tighter and more restricting with every moment that passed and he longed to tear it from his head and shake his hair free. Through the smoke he could see Grenville's centre column half way up the hill, so they must make the counter attack now. Chudleigh was shouting and he could hear himself encouraging the men as he urged his horse into a trot. He was aware of the pikemen's feet pounding as they gathered speed down the slope. Someone on his right was cursing violently, beyond that he heard prayers. He tried to empty his mind of all distracting thoughts, deaden sensation and feeling so his body would react with rigid efficiency.

Shot was falling amongst them. He swerved his mount to avoid a man writhing on the ground ahead of him and saw to his dismay that he was riding into the firing line of a piece of light field artillery that was primed and ready to fire. He could see the gunners' eyes, white and round in their soot blackened faces and dug his heels into the horse's flanks to reach them before they fired. He was not fast enough. There was a roar and the air around him was full of burning case shot. It struck Minstrel full in the chest and the horse stumbled, throwing Will right over its head. He landed on his back with a force that jarred his whole body. The tail of his helmet hit him across the back of the neck like a club and a pain ran the length of his spine.

He lay there half conscious, wondering if his back was broken. Then a soldier stumbled past him, kicking into his legs, somebody screaming and sobbing.

He rolled over on to his side with an effort, trying to clear his head. The earth on this Cornish hill was hot and smoking. He tried to push himself up, but the ground was slippery with blood, so he lay with his cheek against the grass speculating on whether it was his own blood. The smell of it permeated everything, the salty taste of it coated his tongue. There was a searing pain in his right arm as if it were on fire, but he was afraid to look at it. All he wanted to do was lay there. Then he felt hands on his shoulders. Someone was unlatching his helmet. The relief when that helmet was removed was so great that he almost let go of his tenuous hold on consciousness, but those hands were shaking him now.

"Will, Will take hold of yourself lad. We've got to move or you'll be trampled on."

Those earnest brown eyes- Sam was always so calm, no matter what was happening.

"I rode right into a cannon," Will murmured, not sure whether he was laughing or crying. "There's tactics for you. Minstrel, poor damn horse, good, brave creature. He deserved something better."

He tried to look around for the willing animal that had borne him so well for months, but he could see little through the smoke and was too dazed to focus clearly. First Flash and now Minstrel- his conscience revolted against the way humanity in its arrogance dragged the rest of creation into the carnage of war and he was part of it, as guilty as the next man. But this was not the time for introspection.

"There's nothing can be done for that horse now lad." Sam was easing him on to his feet and he found he was not hurt as badly as he had imagined. His right forearm was a mass of blood, badly ripped by case shot and he could not close his fingers around the pistol that was still tucked in his belt, but otherwise he appeared to be whole.

Just ahead of them was a heaving confusion of men, but the colours of the Parliamentary pikemen appeared to be predominant. Grenville's men were giving ground, stumbling back down the hill.

"Is it going to work do you think?" Will asked Sam as they headed for the struggling morass of soldiers.

"It's hard to tell. We hit them pretty hard, made

them stagger like drunks. If we keep on at this rate, we'll soon be at the bottom of the hill."

It seemed the only course to take, to keep pushing on down, slashing, heaving, bludgeoning down. Very little skill was involved, mainly strength and luck.

Will wielded his sword with his left hand and Sam fought on the right of him to protect his wounded arm. They soon found themselves amongst the broken stone walls and ditches at the foot of the hill. The ditches were half filled with water from the rainy days of the previous month and mud began to cling to their boots.

Will was looking round for Chudleigh when he saw a block of musketeers advancing across a flat, open field to their left. They were moving in good order, six ranks deep and wore the field sign of Sir John Berkeley, Grenville's fellow commander.

"They appear to have reserves."

"And we don't," returned Sam grimly, taking a long look at the musketeers.

Farther down their own line, which was now strung out, they could hear Chudleigh telling his men to take cover behind the walls. Will and Sam splashing through a shallow ditch, found a thicket of furze bushes, edging a part of the wall that was untouched by cannon fire. Here they decided to make a stand.

"Have you much powder and shot?" Will asked, struggling to load his pistol.

"Precious little, but it might hold them up awhiles. There's no alternative I 'spose?"

"Not as I see it Sam."

"Then in God's hands be it."

The musketeers were moving on towards the main section of the wall. They looked fresh, as if they had been held in reserve throughout the battle. The defenders' only chance was to catch them in a crossfire.

"Shall we fire yet?"

"No Sam, give them another two yards. Hold it- now!"

Both shots dropped a man. Sam began the arduous task of reloading his matchlock, whilst Will cursed his useless right arm that made it so hard to handle his pistol. A small party of musketeers detached from the main group and began to dodge from cover to cover in the direction of the thicket.

"It's to be cat and mouse," Sam observed, "But they'll be dead uns if they don't keep their heads down."

He drew a bead on the head which showed above a furrowed ridge, fired and a man started up like a rabbit, threw his arms outwards and fell back into the furrow. There was silence for a moment, then the musketeers were over the wall in the centre and there was hand to hand fighting. Two musket balls passed through the furze bushes. A man broke cover and began to run towards their position.

"Thinks I load that slow do he," said Sam, levelling Old Beauty. He squeezed the trigger again, but this time there was a deafening explosion, which threw Will sideways. The man running across the open space stopped in his tracks and dropped for cover. Through the billows of black smoke Will saw Sam Selfe sliding to the floor clutching his face. Will was paralysed. He could not force his feet to move. Sam was curled up on the floor, his knees drawn up to his chin, his hands still over his face and around him lay the shattered pieces of metal that once made up his matchlock. He was groaning, but he lay quite still. Forcing himself free from his paralysis, Will knelt down beside him. He tried to pull the hands away from Sam's face, gently at first, but when Selfe resisted, he forced them away. The first sight of that face made him rock back on his heels with a cry of pain and desperation. It was burned black, but beneath the powder burns, the flesh was torn and raw, more like a hideous mask than a face. Will slid to the floor beside him and lifted him forward in his arms.

"Sam- Oh God- that damn gun, that damn gun."

He was half aware of feet pounding over the fields and musket balls falling close by, but he did not care anymore. The only reality was Sam's shattered face. He felt an ache which began somewhere in the pit of his stomach, spreading across his chest and tightening in his throat until he thought he would choke. Suddenly Sam took hold of his arm.

"Get away. They'm coming I know." His speech was slow and thick for his blistered tongue was swelling in his mouth.

"I am not going anywhere Sam."

"I can't see. There's no shapes, nothing." He said this calmly, but his grip on Will's arm tightened.

Men were crashing through the bushes. Four of them broke through simultaneously and Will saw the ugly muzzle of a musket pointing at his head. As he looked at Sam's eyes. the pupils shrunk to tiny points, the whites scorched yellow, he wished that sweaty, panting Cornishman in front of him would fire his musket. Nothing but oblivion could smother the ache and weariness that overwhelmed him.

"Throw down that pistol now Sir," the Cornishman demanded with the respect he would accord any officer. Will hardly knew the pistol was still in his hand. He just opened his fingers and let it drop to the ground. "I'm afraid you must consider yourself my prisoner. Will you get to your feet Sir?"

Will lay Sam down gently, murmuring. " You will be alright. They will take you to a physician soon." Then he brised himself to his feet. "I presume Ralph Hopton has won the day."

"Yes Sir, he has. What's left of your forces are in retreat."

Will could hear Sam muttering. It was not clear, but sounded like a prayer. He felt ridiculously weak and his arm was throbbing.

"My friend needs attention urgently. I trust you intend to care for your prisoners."

The Cornish corporal gave an indignant cough.

"Our officers are honourable men Sir." He peered over at Sam and crossed himself. "Poor devil. Cannon?"

"No, his own gun."

The soldier whistled through his teeth at the irony of it all, then he said briskly,

"All will be done that can be done. We have plenty of our own wounded to attend to, but we will take him over to that barn back beyond the field with the rest of the wounded."

He signalled to two of his companions to lift Sam.

"Will, where are they taking me?"

"With the rest of the wounded for attention. It is not far. You will be more comfortable there."

"Are you coming?"

Will looked at the corporal, who shook his head.

"No it seems they have other plans for me. I will be safe enough. Perhaps I will be able to join you later."

"Can you tell me what's left of Old Beauty?"

On the floor at his feet Will saw the butt of the gun, scorched, but whole. He picked it up, running his fingers over the inlaid bone carving.

"The butt is here."

"Can I hold it? I shan't feel so alone if I've got something familiar to hold." Will pressed the piece of wood into his hands and he drew it in close to his body.

"She didn't let me down, not really. Kept on as long as she could."

Impatient to be gone, the soldiers hauled Sam to his feet and began to move towards the barn, supporting him between them. Will wanted to call out 'God be with you,' Sam's own favourite farewell, but the words stuck in his throat.

The corporal was watching him with a sympathetic expression. He understood the pain of losing a close comrade.

"Well," said Will, straightening his back, "I am ready to go wherever you want to take me."

The wall of the cellar was damp and cold. Will pressed his arm against the stone in the hope that the coolness would alleviate the burning. His whole arm was swelling, the skin tight and hot. His captors had bandaged the wound to check the bleeding, but pieces of shot were still embedded in the flesh and it was beginning to fester.

There was no light in the cellar. The whiteness of stone glimmered faintly but did not alleviate the darkness enough for the prisoners to see each other. Someone had knocked against the single candle, extinguishing its flame. Will could hear the drip of water as it trickled down the wall, hitting the floor close by him,

Colour Sergeant Mason of the 15th Infantry had fallen asleep. His breathing was regular and contented. Will wished he could sleep like that. He had tried, but the pain kept him awake, pain of body and spirit. At last, after months of inflicting it on others, physical suffering had come to him too. He was disappointed that it gave no comfort to his raw conscience, no salve for his guilt. If he closed his eyes he could see a writhing montage of destruction burning its way through his brain and always at the end of it was Sam Selfe's wrecked face and those words, "I shan't feel so alone if I've got something familiar to hold."

The prisoners had been kept in separate groups. He had been given no chance to look for Sam; he could be dead for all Will knew. They were all gone, all the men from Sandy Barrow, all the men he had led into war and here he was in the cellar of a crumbling Cornish mansion house with no notion of what might happen to him.

Hopton's men had treated them with civility at first, dressed their wounds, fed them, given them as much freedom of movement as possible. One of the prisoners however, a young captain of artillery, had taken advantage of this, killing one of the guards and escaping. Since then the prisoners had been kept under strict surveillance. They had travelled around five miles, reaching this house by nightfall, where some were locked in the attic, the rest in the cellar.

From what Will could gather, the house was a makeshift headquarters for the coordination of local military operations. There was much coming and going upstairs, feet tramping, doors slamming, which echoed down to the cellar. He leaned his head back against the wall, listening. Someone was coming down the flight of steps leading to the cellar. There was a springing of bolts, the door groaned open and the naked flame of a torch stabbed through the darkness. In the shadows behind the flame, a broad, hairy face peered at the men lying around on the floor.

"Is anyone one of you here the officer who led the troop that captured Hopton's papers at Sourton?"

The man had a guttural snarling voice. His accent suggested he was a Londoner. Will sat forward. He and a detachment of twenty men had taken Hopton's baggage train against heavy odds, He debated whether it would be best to keep silent, but the possibility of being taken out of the cellar prompted him to risk replying, "Yes, I am."

"Then you can come with me. The Major wants a word with you."

Will stumbled across to the door and was pushed on up the steps. They were slippery with fungus and he found it hard to keep his balance. Each time he slipped he was prodded in the back with the barrel of a pistol.

"Get on there. We don't hang about here. No respect for airs and graces in this place. You may get to see a lot of me, so I'll introduce myself. I'm Sergeant Dan Leech and I'm as persistent as one. Keep your mouth shut until you're asked to speak and you'll be alright. But rub me up the wrong way and you'll be for it my lad, officer or no officer. I hope that puts things clear."

"Crystal clear," Will thought, but he did not bother to reply.

They passed through the kitchen, where a conglomeration of rusty pots and pans hanging from a beam clanged against Will's head as he failed to dodge them in the dim light. A series of passageways led them to the centre of the house, to a room where two soldiers sat outside the door playing cards. They scrambled to their feet when they saw the scowl on Leech's face- it was a permanent scowl- and moved aside for him to pass. He hammered on the door and without waiting for an answer, hustled Will inside.

The young lieutenant was instantly struck by the fact that it was a library he had entered. The shelves were almost empty and thick with dust, but the atmosphere was so familiar. It felt like years since he had watched the folk of Sandy Barrow gazing at the books on his own library shelves in the school, saw Sam Selfe sitting in a corner pouring over some doctrinal tract and shaking his head in puzzlement.

The room was lit by six oil lamps and he had to accustom his eyes to the brightness before he could take a clear look at the man sitting at the desk over by the window. When he did, he took an instinctive step back in his astonishment.

The man had not looked up when they entered. He was writing on a sheet of vellum. His head was bent over the desk and his face half obscured, but there was no mistaking the shock of red hair or the thick fingers that laboured over the parchment.

"This appears to be the lieutenant who captured Sir Ralph's papers." Leech announced without ceremony.

Still the major did not raise his eyes from his task.

"Good evening Lieutenant, I will be with you directly when I have finished this dispatch."

Will was struggling with a faintness spreading over him.

"I have all the time in the world Richard," he said gently, "But do you mind if I sit down and wait? I am not feeling at my best."

Major Richard Wanley banged his pen down on the desk and snapped his head up as if he had been struck. He sat motionless for a moment, just staring, then he noticed that Will was swaying.

"Leech, get the man a chair, quick."

The sergeant raised his eyebrows, but he dragged over a chair and helped Will into it. Will shook his head to clear the mist that had begun to form over everything. He could hear Richard asking, "Are you alright Will?"

"Yes, I am now."

"I thought you were going to faint then. Here, drink this. It will do you good."

He could hardly believe that this was Richard, speaking in his old, friendly tone. He took the cup and drank. It was brandy.

"Oh Dick – in the middle of a war and you are still drinking your favourite brandy."

"I'm damned if I can see why I should go without it. I bet the King doesn't go without his."

Still the same ebullient Richard. It seemed that the war had not changed him, but if it had, Will did not want to find out just then.

"But you're wounded."

"It's my arm, case shot. There are some splinters left in it and it's festering a bit."

"More than a bit by God. Why hasn't someone let a surgeon take a look at it?" Richard roared. "If I had known you were here I would have had you out of that cellar ages ago."

He looked blackly at Leech who was not perturbed.

"Well, we wasn't to know he was a friend of yours Major Wanley."

"We come from the same village. We grew up together."

"Oh I see Sir," Leech returned with an enigmatic emphasis on the word 'see' that Richard did not like. He pulled himself up sharply as he realised the full implications of the situation. He was not talking to the best friend he had ever known, but a captured enemy officer, a potential danger to the Royalist cause.

"No you do not see Sergeant," he snapped, turning away from Will and walking back to his desk. "I have not lost sight of my reason for calling Lieutenant Barry here."

Will tried to ignore the changing note in Richard's voice.

"Have you been home at all? Have you seen Mother and Lucy?"

"I was back there two months ago and they were well enough then. But to the business in hand- were you indeed the officer who took Sir Ralph's baggage train at Sourton?"

Will nodded his assent.

"We have captured Chudleigh by the way, almost in one piece- a few flesh wounds, but nothing serious. I would venture that his pride is the worst wounded. It was rumoured that the man who had captured the papers might be among this group of prisoners. I fought at Sourton. By all accounts it was a damn brave thing you did there."

"You haven't done so badly- major already."

"Rank means nothing in wartime, rapid promotion inevitable." Richard brushed aside this attempt at a broader conversation. He feared being diverted from his duty. "The point is, most of Sir Ralph's papers were taken back with our victory this afternoon, but one satchel is missing, one very important satchel, which Sir Ralph is anxious to get back. These papers are not only military, they include personal letters."

"What has this to do with me?" Will asked wearily.

"One of the prisoners told us that Chudleigh entrusted the papers to you after Sourton, but he could not remember your name. Is that correct?"

"Yes that is correct. It was an honour accorded to me for capturing them. They were in three large satchels with my own belongings in one of the company's baggage carts. But you know that if you have recovered them. They were altogether, I didn't separate one satchel and take it into battle with me, if that is what you are getting at. Why ever would I do that? If I had, you would have found it on my person anyway."

"Not necessarily, you could have given instructions for the satchel to be hidden when things began to look desperate. You must have searched out an extra special place for it with the hope of recovering it later. Just tell us where it is Will."

Will sighed. He felt that now, at last, he could sleep. The chair was comfortable, he had not eaten since the previous day and the brandy made him feel lightheaded and drowsy. He could almost ignore the pain in his arm.

"I cannot tell you because I did not hide it."

"I'm afraid I can't take your word for it."

"I am too tired to lie Dick."

He looked so very tired, so pale and haggard that Richard felt to bully him would be a sin, yet all the time Leech was watching him, that damn Sergeant Leech.

Wanley was coordinator of operations behind Hopton's line of advance. He was in charge of intelligence and supply systems. It was a key position. One or two words in the wrong place, any shadow of doubt on his loyalty in this hysterical atmosphere of war and his life could be in jeopardy. He was aware of that and knew that Leech was too.

"Do not rely on our friendship," he warned Will. "The last time we were together, so told me to get out remember. You made your position very clear. Well let me elucidate mine. My job is to get that information out of you and by God, I'll do it."

" You won't, because I have nothing to tell you."

"Well, do you think any of your men would tell after a bit of pressure? I have some snivelling little Gloucester potboys out in the yard. One of them tells me he carried the flag of the 5th Infantry this afternoon and that you spoke to him during the conflict. Perhaps he knows where you hid it. We've a rack in the outhouse. If we stretch him a bit, he will soon tell us."

Will had a mental image of fourteen year old Charlie Horn, snatching up the company flag when the ensign had fallen and carrying it with such care, as if it had been a bar of gold.

"No, you can't do that. He does not know."

"We will soon find out. Leech, see to it will you."

"No wait, Richard, for God's sake. He is only a boy. He does not know. I am the only one who knows."

Richard held up his hand to stop Leech, who was making for the door. Will had lied. He had no idea what had become of the missing papers, but it was all he could think of on the spur of the moment to save Charlie. Wanley was smiling, not in triumph, more in relief. His frustration was mounting, for he had begun to pace the room, clenching his fists, signs that Will knew so well.

"I thought that would make you see sense. The war hasn't beaten that high-mindedness out of you. Now we have established the truth, you might as well tell me where it is."

"You have chosen to play the role of the dedicated major with me, so I will try playing the heroic lieutenant. I refuse to tell you."

"Oh that's unreasonable," Richard shouted. " What will it achieve? It's not like you. You are no fanatic."

"Everyone is unreasonable in this war. If your father had been reasonable last August perhaps I would be marking the children's spring spelling test tonight, not sitting here and perhaps the bodies of men from Sandy Barrow would not be lying all across the West Country and Sam Selfe would not have had his face burnt raw. He would still be potting the occasional pheasant in my woods and his gun would have lasted another fifty years. Do not accuse me of being unreasonable Richard."

"You know what I told you about your mouth," Sergeant Leech reminded with a vicious kick at Will's chair. "I'll have that tongue out before you can blink. Likes to talk this one does he?"

"Oh yes, Lieutenant Barry has always been a good talker- prodigiously well educated, Cambridge graduate you know."

"Is he now, fancy that! Well let me make him say the right things. Leave him to me for a bit and I'll soon find out what he's done with them papers. The rack's all set up. Don't waste it Major, you'll spoil my evening."

Will's eyes were intent on Wanley's face. Richard wanted to plead with him not to force the issue because he did not want to hurt him, but the more he realised he could not do this, the more angry he became.

"What is wrong?" Will challenged. "Are you hesitating because you don't wish to cause me physical pain? If so, don't be afraid to admit it. It is no shame to show compassion, not even for a dedicated major."

"Don't try to be clever Will, I'm warning you."

"Rack him," Leech insisted. "If you let him get away with this a few people will be wondering why and they just might get the wrong impression about you."

Richard was cornered. He smacked his fist into the palm of his other hand.

"We will not use the rack, it's too extreme. We might need him again later. Try ducking his head in the water barrel out in the barn for half an hour, but don't overdo it. Don't drown him. I know how zealous you can be."

"I know what to do Major."

He jerked Will to his feet, his fingers pressing so hard on the swollen flesh of his arm that Will gasped with pain.

"Don't care for much pain, you delicately bred ones, do you? Certificates from Cambridge don't help you much with that. Tonight will be quite an experience for you. Coming down Major Wanley?"

"No, I have too much work to do."

"Have you not the courage to watch Richard?" Will inquired calmly.

"Take him out of here."

Wanley refused to look up any more as Will was hustled from the room. He put quill to paper and began to scribble furiously for a few moments. Then he poured himself a drink and wandered restlessly around the room, staring into the cup. Times innumerable Will Barry had shielded him when they were children. They had shared the same tutor, an eccentric, old pedant, who had no tolerance for high spirits and more than once Will had taken responsibility for crimes organised by Richard and been soundly thrashed for them. Whenever Dick needed anyone, he had always turned to Will. He remembered then how alone he had felt when Will first went up to Cambridge and he was left to amuse himself.

The night when he came back on his first vacation, they had gone to a tavern in Lacock, drunk too much and embarked on a dangerous tree climbing competition all the way home. He could see Will now, at the top of a massive oak tree, leaning back against the branches and laughing loudly because Richard kept sliding down the trunk. The laughter rang in his ears.

" Hell and damnation!" He hurled his cup at the far wall, snatched up his cloak and ran from the room.

He was through the house, across the yard and exploding through the barn doorway in moments. By the light of a lantern he saw Leech and another soldier holding Will Barry's head down into a hooped rain water barrel. They let him up when they saw Wanley, but had to support him to keep him on his feet

"How any times has he been under?" Richard

demanded.

"About a dozen. I thought he'd crack much quicker than this."

Richard took Will by the shoulders and shook him.

"Will," he hissed in a fierce whisper, "You fool. What good is this doing?"

Barry did not register that it was Richard. "I cannot tell you." This was what he said every time he was brought back out of the barrel. It had taken on a strange rhythm – head plunging down into the water, eyes and mouth closed tightly as possible, gasping for breath as he came up, then repeating that phrase. When he was out of the water he could not make any sense of anything. Sights, sounds, colours were all a synthesis in a weird kaleidoscope, dancing to the sound of rushing water. Somewhere in the depths of it all was mocking laughter and he knew it was his own.

"Oh, you can't tell us eh?"

Before Richard could intervene, Leech shoved Will's head down again with a vengeance. Wanley did nothing at first, but then he noticed Will's muscles relax, his whole body going suddenly limp. He tore Leech away from him, shouting,

"Let him up damn you. Can't you see he has had enough? He has lost consciousness, you will drown him."

Leech gave him a stony look, but he said nothing, just stepped back and let Will's body fall into Richard's arms. Wanley dragged him across the barn and lay him down on a pile of straw.

"Bring that lantern over here."

Leech did not move, but the other soldier scrambled to obey the major.

"Put it on that horse stall over there and then clear out, both of you."

Sergeant Leech lingered in the doorway.

"Don't do anything you may regret Major Wanley."

"I could say the same to you Sergeant-" but Leech was gone, closing the barn door behind him.

Richard folded up his cloak and put it under Will's head. Barry's face was colourless, his wet hair clinging to it in long strands. Richard smoothed it back from his forehead in a gesture that was unusually gentle for those broad hands. The lantern was burning low. In its dim light Major Richard Wanley sat in the barn holding his friend's hand, muttering, " Damn, stubborn fool. Rotten, pox-ridden war. We're all bastards."

✻

He had been looking at the sky for some time, a clear, wide sky with a sharp horizon. He was stiff and there was pain, but the straw was warm and sweet smelling. He knew that he was moving somehow, just as he was certain he was lying on his back, but he did not want to make the effort to draw any logical conclusions to solve this mystery. Then the smoothness of the movement was broken by a thud and a jar that made him hurt all over.

"You alright boy?"

He could see a face upside-down, peering at him from above.

"That April rain made a fine mess out of these cart tracks."

It was a leathery face, the pale brown colour of old parchment. At the corner of the eyes the skin puckered into a myriad wrinkles and beneath the heavy lids the eyes were grey. The head was adorned with an incredible hat, the brim tattered and bent in all directions, as if it had been stolen from the nearest scarecrow. Coarse hair, the colour of mud long dried in the sun, bristled out from under the hat and rambled down to meet his beard, so that the face was framed in a halo of hair. Will sat forward, eager for things to start making sense.

"Hey steady there, you want to take things slow for a bit."

The strange head was on the shoulders of a Cornish farmer, who sat on the seat of a waggon, coaxing on a bony cart horse. The rest of the man's clothes matched his hat. The cloth of his jacket was in several different stages of wear, a mosaic of variegated shades. His breeches resembled a patchwork quilt and were frayed at the knees where they joined his gaiters. He smiled at Will, displaying six decaying teeth, two stumps and a great deal of gum.

"Bewildered young feller?" he asked

Will nodded. He was riding in a farm waggon that had seen many years hard service for it was loose at the joints and the wheel axles squealed like angry pigs. Tied to the tailboard was another horse, a handsome creature, lifting its feet with the disciplined rhythm of a cavalry mount.

"You were like a dead man when we put you in the cart. He was main worried about you, but I said you'd come to yourself in time. Here, have some breakfast."

He tossed a bundle down on the straw beside his passenger. "'Tis only rye bread and a bit of cheese, but you need something inside you. Helps keep the fever back, with that arm you'll be lucky not to have the fever."

Will glanced at his arm. It was swollen to twice its normal size and was an ominous, fiery red. He tried to move it, but it weighed too much and the pain was intense. "My old Uncle Seth had an arm like that once after an horse bit him- went poison and he died."

"Thank you for the reassurance."

The man laughed. "No harm meant lad."

Will was surprised how readily he could eat the bread and cheese, washing it down with some ale from a leather bottle. As he ate, the Cornishman explained in his cheerful voice what had happened the night before. He was a farmer from the Cornwall side of the River Tamar, who had been taking supplies into the Royalist headquarters for some weeks. He had been camping overnight in the front yard of the mansion when Major Wanley called him to the back of the barn.

"He told me that if I wanted to earn a bit of extra money I must help him get you out of there with no one knowing. I was willing enough and asked no questions. I brought the waggon around to the back, we covered you up with straw and I was off about dawn, the same as always."

"Where are we now?" Will asked, looking around

at the green, wooded countryside. In the far distance there was the sound of a woodman at work, an axe striking a tree trunk echoing across to them, but there was no sign of human habitation.

"We be in Devon now, just west of Oakhampton. I'll take you a mile or so farther on, just to let you find yourself a touch more and then I must leave you." He jerked his thumb out towards the back of the waggon. "That horse there is for you. Tis the Major's own. He said if anyone was to question me I was to say I was taking it for shoeing. He says you are to ride back home on it."

Home was the only place Will wanted to go. Things would never be the same, because he doubted if he was the same man who had left it, but he must get home. He sat in silence for a while thinking about what Richard had done. Wanley had taken a grave risk. It gave Will strength to know that the indefinable bond which had always held them together was not yet broken. He was so encouraged that when he eased himself out of the waggon ready to take leave of Jonathan Haxby, the farmer, he was confident that he could make it back to Wiltshire.

"Wiltshire's a fair way," Haxby warned. "Don't ride yourself too hard. Your best way will be to pass between Tiverton and Crediton, then on up the Taunton Vale heading for Warminster. Tis a quiet road, but if your heart's not for the King, you'd best not talk about it till you leave these parts. The Major said I was to give you this cloak, pistol and purse. I haven't looked to see what's in it, but I guess it will take you home." Will turned the purse over in the palm of his hand. He could remember the very afternoon Richard had commissioned Alfred Tanner to make that purse, Alfred who had lost both his legs at the siege of Saltash.

"Tell Major Wanley that I hope to be able to pay it back in person one day."

Haxby was fastening the cloak around Will's shoulders.

"This will protect your arm. When you come to a good, clean stream bathe the arm a while. Twill help to keep down the swelling."

It was not easy to mount, but once he was in the saddle Will felt secure enough. The horse inspired confidence. It was powerful, but patient and well-trained. Dick had always been a good judge of a horse. Haxby was already clambering back on to the seat of his waggon. He held out his hand and Will shook it, struck by the rough, horniness of his fingers.

"Well I wish you good fortune lad. The Major says when you get home, you're to stay there."

"I do not know how to thank you for what you have done."

"Don't you worry about that, I'm being paid well for it," and he coaxed his horse into its steady plod, heading back towards the River Tamar and Cornwall. Will watched the bizarre, scarecrow figure until he was just a speck on the horizon, then he turned his horse's head and set off in the opposite direction.

The ride back into Wiltshire was much harder than he had anticipated. He began by driving himself hard, hoping to get home in the shortest possible time, but he found he could not keep up the pace and by the afternoon he was forced to stop regularly to rest. Each time he stopped he found it more difficult to remount. He tried to avoid people, but by evening, when he was nowhere near Taunton, he decided he must stop for food and drink.

He chose a quiet village tavern where a few locals drank cider and talked about their crops. He intended to stop for a short while only, but exhausted, he fell asleep by the open fire. The hostess, concerned because he looked so ill, did not have the heart to disturb him and consequently it was morning before he woke.

He cursed himself for wasting time. Every moment was urgent now for he could feel the fever rising in his blood and for the first time he began to fear that he would never reach Sandy Barrow.

The journey from Taunton to Warminster was agony. His arm was on fire and the slightest jar set off a chain reaction of pain all over his body, so that his head reeled and he vomited. He could not think clearly, but hung on to the goal of reaching home. He repeated this to himself over and over again, chanting it like a magic incantation to hypnotise his body into obeying him.

An Irish tinker, travelling to Lacock Fair, was his salvation, for he found Will lying shivering on the banks of a stream on the outskirts of Warminster, trying to bathe his arm. The tinker lanced the wound and dressed it using a noxious smelling herbal salve that he carried in his pack. He persuaded Will to rest for most of the day and then offered to accompany him to Sandy Barrow. The company of the swarthy tinker, his wares jangling like untuned bells, made those last few miles bearable.

It had taken him four days, but here he was at Sandy Barrow. The tinker was bidding him farewell, saying that he hoped the Puritans had not cracked down on Lacock Fair. His pots and pans were clattering away into the distance, but none of this registered on Will. Sandy Barrow, sprawling untidily down the valley was all he wished to see. He wanted to ride down amongst the cottages, shouting, but he felt so faint and useless that all he could do was bury his face in his horse's mane and weep. This would never take him home. Making what he hoped would be his final effort he urged his mount in the direction of his house.

In his relief to have made it back, he failed to notice that Sandy Barrow was full of people shouting and jostling; that every now and then a roaring cheer echoed up. Just beyond the trees he would see the school; a little farther on he would reach the farm house. But as he rode through the trees the people thickened around him. There was the school, but it was surrounded by a crowd surging around a group of soldiers in uniform- lobster tail helmets.

A man was standing on the low wall around the school, raving like a maniac, calling for the destruction of idolatry, all wickedness dressed up in the guise of learning. The eyes stood out in his head and the veins in his temples throbbed. As he whipped himself into a frenzy, so he drew the crowd along with him until they snarled when he snarled, screamed when he screamed. Stones began to fly at the shutters of the school house windows and some of the soldiers were breaking down the door.

For a moment Will could not grasp what was happening. His horse was circling around, frightened by the excitement and noise. He slid out of the saddle and clung to the reins to steady himself. A boy clutching a heavy stave brushed close to him and Will grabbed hold of his coat. The lad turned angrily, but his shout of 'Let go' died on his lips when he saw who held his coat. Job Dilke, the boy who had so much trouble with his arithmetic, let out a yelp. "Master Will, where did you come from? We didn't know you was back. Why you look like a ghost Sir."

He squirmed in Will's grasp, his eyes round, as if he really did entertain the possibility that this might be a ghost. There was a ghastly pallor to Will's face.

"Job, tell me what's happening. Who are they? What are they doing?"

"It's the soldiers for Parliament Sir, going to join up with Waller. They bin camped around Lacock. Some of them have been preaching the word of God and now they're going to destroy what's evil."

"You mean the school house?"

"Mainly the library I think Sir," the boy faltered. "They've heard tell there's Papist books in there. Please let me go Sir. I be scared."

There was a feverish glow in Will's eyes. He seemed to be staring right through Job and the boy was genuinely frightened.

"Please Sir, please Sir."

He jerked himself away and ran, leaving the tail of his jacket in Will's hand. He crushed the fabric in his fist as if he was trying to squeeze the life out of it and he was trembling all over. The soldiers were heaving armfuls of books out through the door. One fellow staggered out with a pile of paintings, works of art that Will had been collecting for years, not only because they gave him pleasure, but he hoped it would help the children to be surrounded by them. He had often based lessons around them. This trooper, with his sleeves rolled up, was tearing them out of their frames and smashing them against the wall.

His companions were heaping up books. There was a crackle, a spurt of flame and the bonfire began.

"Oh God- oh no-" Will began to push through the crowd, desperately heaving forward, oblivious of the pressure on his arm. "You must not do that. You can't. You do not understand. You cannot serve God by such destruction. You need those books, this school. You mustn't destroy them."

But his voice was lost in the din, only one more cry in the general babel. Everything Will had ever worked for, all he truly believed in was here. It was not just a school house and a pile of books. It was an ideal, a symbol of the inroads he had made into the ignorance and poverty of ideas that held the villagers in thrall and those very people were helping the soldiers to destroy it in the name of God. He had carried arms under the same flag as these soldiers, killed in the name of Parliament, helped to soak England's fields with her own children's blood. Was it to lay the country open to such outbreaks of Philistinism as this that he had become a murderer, imperilling his soul and his sanity? Before the last nine months of blood -letting he had never contemplated the notion of destruction. It was always build, cultivate, teach, develop. The only thing that had held him together throughout the fighting was the thought that someday he might go back to work again. He could not give back life to those who had died, those men of Sandy Barrow who had trusted him, or those Royalist soldiers who had perished so easily on the edge of his skilful sword, but he could help to open up the way to a new quality of life for their children through education.

Now this noisy, frantic day in Sandy Barrow shattered everything. It was worse than any battle. It was like the end of the world. He lunged through the inner ring of spectators, the impetus nearly throwing him into the fire.

"Hey, careful there!" A soldier reached out and took hold of his arm. "Don't get too near, you'll burn yourself."

"Don't touch me, damn you," Will screamed at him. All his self-control was gone. He was too weak to fight the hysteria rising inside him. He stared into the flames, watching them eat away the leather bindings, watching the pages curl and crisp into ash. In the school room they were smashing up the benches, scattering all the papers and slates about the floor. More books were brought out, the folios, some of them unique, irreplaceable. A whole load of treatises were committed to the flames. Will recognised every one of them. Leonard Maskell's 'Book of Cattle', Gervaise Markham's 'Discourse on Horsemanship,' John

Crawshey's 'Countryman's Instructor.' What had these to do with God's anger?

Will hurled himself at the nearest offender, but the soldiers forced him back through the crowd until he found himself up against the wall. At his feet, half trodden into the ground was a book. He picked it up. It was his school register, the covers stained with ink. It was open in his hands at a page which began' Phillip Long- absent. Says he had the toothache'. Will felt his legs giving way. The writing on the page began to fade. He was falling into a long, hollow nothingness that echoed and echoed and ended in darkness.

Chapter Six

Will Barry opened his eyes and stared at the ceiling. His vision was blurred and out of focus and he could not fathom where he might be. He felt stiff, although the support behind his head was soft and warm. He wondered if he was a prisoner again, locked in some barn or outhouse. Pulling himself up into a sitting position, he realised that he was lying on a narrow, slatted bed covered with straw. As his sight gradually cleared, he could see a girl sitting on a stool with her back to him, tearing the tangles from her curly hair with a teasel. It was a painful process and she dug the toes of her bare feet into the floor to help her concentration. Beyond her was an older woman, sewing and singing to herself.

Will could not think clearly, but he recognised Hannah Moss and was about to speak to her when a large paw, decorated with a woolly fringe, was laid across him, pressing down on his thigh.

"Baron," he said aloud, "Baron old boy." Then he saw a wound across the dog's forehead, healing now but still red at the edges. "You've hurt yourself. How did you do that?"

At the sound of his voice Hannah Moss dropped her teasel and ran over to him. When her father had assured her that the fever had left Will she was relieved, but he remained in a deep sleep and she hated to see him lie so still. She would sit and study his face, the face that had been imprinted on her memory for nine long months. It was such a clear cut face, with its long, angular jaw. She loved to trace with the tip of her finger, the lines that ran from beneath his cheek bones to the edge of his wide mouth. She had always liked to see the way those lines deepened when he laughed. It was wonderful to hear him speak rationally again.

He gazed at her, engulphed in a vast tangle of silver blonde hair, as she took hold of his right hand, holding it to her lips and kissing it. He ran the back of his other hand across his forehead. It was a puzzled gesture.

"Hannah, who hurt Baron?" he asked, fixing on the one thing that was clear in his mind.

Hannah did not answer his question but gave vent to her relief.

"Oh Will Barry, at one time I never thought to hear you speak my name again. Those few days after we brought you in, I was sure you must die. Your arm was the size of Marley's oak and the fever was burning you so that you were hot to touch." His feeling of comfort began to give way to unease, as memories began to filter through-the smell of smoke, book pages taking on odd shapes as they turned to ash. Hannah was talking excitedly, dodging from one topic to another, but he let her continue, piecing it together as best he could.

"Twas lucky father and I found you lying down there by the wall and that you hadn't been trampled on by that mad crowd. They didn't know what they were doing. Father says the folks round yer would follow a cow if it bellowed loud enough. 'Father forgive them for they know not what they do' that's what Parson Seddon said we must remember. He was truly scared inside, I could see for his face was like chalk and his legs did tremble, but he stood up to them and told them they were doing the work of the devil, not God. They knocked him about a bit for saying so and he had a job to crawl home afterwards so I were told. He's been here often while you bin sick, sitting and praying for you. Twas him who helped me to persuade Father not to try to take your arm off."

" Take my arm off?" Will echoed, sick at the thought of that gentle man Robert Seddon being beaten up with no one willing to help him.

"Well, twere so bad Father said the poison would touch your heart and kill you. He had picked out all the bits of metal left in it, but the swelling didn't go down, so he said the only way was to take the arm off below the elbow."

Will felt a tingling sensation in his arm and instinctively glanced at it, but Hannah was holding his hand in her lap; the arm was intact and he sank back on the pillow with an intense sigh of relief.

"I cried and carried on. I didn't want him to do it. Tis your right hand. You wouldn't be able to draw or write no more. I couldn't bear the thought of that."

She stroked the hand. It was cold.

"You have such skilful hands. There's magic in the fingers that can capture the face of a being or the shape of a creature with a stroke or two of charcoal. I don't believe I could ever have forgiven Father if he had destroyed that magic.

The Reverend Seddon came that morning, with his black eye and his swollen jaw and he thought it wrong to take the arm off. He said you might die anyway from loss of blood and the shock of the pain. A surgeon would be needed to do a job like that properly he said and twere mighty different from jointing pigs, which was all Father could claim to have done.

He said what we must do was pray for you and trust in God to heal you if twere His wish- and here you are. Your fingers may be stiff for a bit cos Father says the tendons in your hand be damaged and you mayn't grip so well, but it'll come right in time."

He tried to make a fist and found that the fingers of his right hand were inflexible. His forearm ached, but the swelling had gone. He did not feel like talking, but just lay there, absently stroking Baron's head with his left hand and watching the animation in Hannah's face, the way her jade eyes sparkled. The words were pouring from her like a shower of rain. He was more aware of his surroundings now, the bare room and Annie Moss sitting by the curtain half-drawn across the bed she shared with her husband. She was still sewing and singing, lost in a world of her own.

Will saw the table with the short leg wedged up with a chip of wood, the sooted-up fireplace, the stew pot on the hearth covered in white ash. When he looked up at the ceiling, the rotting beams were evident. Two black beetles emerged from the woodwork and began to circle around each other in slow motion, a ritual dance either of courtship or war. Outside he could hear the scoop of a shovel and the sound of distant voices. He was puzzled over why he was here in the Moss' crumbling cottage.

"How long have I been so ill?" he inquired.

"Tis two weeks to the very day since we brought you here."

"Two weeks, but why was I not taken home? Was I too ill to be moved? You have told my mother and Lucy that I am here?"

The smile faded from Hannah's face. She looked down at her feet. In her excitement at his recovering his senses, she had almost forgotten that there was another part of the story to tell. Her father had said it must wait until he had regained some strength, but she never could lie to Will Barry and her consternation had given her away already.

"Hannah, is anything wrong at home?"

"Perhaps twere best we waited a bit to talk of such things. You've no strength to bear-"

"Bear what? Do you think I could rest if you did not tell me now?"

"I don't know how to tell it. Well, you couldn't be taken home cos like the school, taint there anymore. They burned it that day, Wanley Hall too, burned it all in their wickedness and foolishness, drove off the stock, though the soldiers took some of it for their wants. It was that preacher they had with them, he worked them all up, soldiers and villagers alike- that preacher and- " she stopped abruptly, afraid to finish the sentence.

"But my family and the Wanleys, what happened to them?"

Beads of sweat had broken out on Will's forehead. Hannah wiped them away with her fingers pleading, "Don't upset yourself. You'll bring the fever back for sure. They weren't harmed, they nor the Wanley womenfolk-leastways they weren't killed I mean. The soldiers took them away when they left here. Father reckons they was took for hostages to exchange for prisoners taken by the other side, so they will be safe. Mark Smart saw them sitting in a cart with the baggage train so they weren't forced to walk."

She had let it come out in a rush because it was the only way she could say it. He was silent and she dare not look at his face, so she began talking again, just as rapidly.

"That's how Baron got cut. He tried to protect them and a soldier struck him with a sword. I had run down to your house to see if I could help Mistress Lucy and your mother, but I were too late, they were already taking them away. I saw what happened to Baron though and I made him come with me. Jess Barnett resisted them so tis said when they come to the farm. He went for them with a pitchfork cos they were trying to take the oxen. He loved them beasts as much as if they were his children. They stabbed him in the shoulder, but it didn't go deep and tis mostly healed already."

"Crispin, what about Crispin? Was he hurt? He must have tried to defend Mother and Lucy."

Hannah jumped up from the stool and went over to the glassless window, looking out as if she hoped someone might come and rescue her from what she must say next.

"You won't believe me," she warned. "You'll say I'm lying and be angry with me I know, but I can't say more than the truth. As God is my witness, that bailiff of yourn were in on it. He and the preacher whipped the crowd up between them.

All of a sudden he come out strong for Parliament, though beforehand, just after you left for the wars and the Wanley men were going off to join the King, he good as told Squire Wanley he was for the King. Jess Barnett heard him say it. Twas Collington who told them to burn the houses, though he made sure all that were worthwhile were took out first. Francis Farrow told them they had no right to ransack Wanley Hall or take the livestock- said as he were the squire's bailiff, it were his duty to stop them. They just mocked him and took him prisoner too."

Will sat forward. "That cannot be true Hannah. It is nonsense. You must be mistaken. Crispin would not do that."

"Oh I wish twere a lie, for your sake I wish it, but it's true, all of it. There were witnesses enough. They say in the village he just saw his chance and took it."

Will was shattered by this revelation. He could believe that Crispin might put himself on the right side of whoever he was speaking to, for safety's sake, but the thought of him encouraging troopers and villagers to loot and burn was incredible, particularly as it could endanger the very people Will had left in his care. So this was what that enigmatic streak added up to, that little bit of Crispin that he had never fully penetrated. This was what had almost persuaded him to turn back that August day he left Sandy Barrow.

He could see him now with that affable smile on his face, filling his pipe and hear him say, 'I am flattered by your by your readiness to put your trust in me------ I shall do my very best to be worthy of the task'

What had Will Barry said in reply? 'There's no one I would rather trust Crispin.' The phrase ran through his head. He had gone to war because of his concern for the villagers of Sandy Barrow and in return they had helped to destroy his life's work. He had trusted Crispin and he was betrayed.

He remembered Richard Wanley's warning, 'You're a fool about these people Will. Give them half a chance and they will trample all over us.' Images and voices began to crowd in on him. John Dilke was bawling,' You're a fool Will Barry for all that learning.' Sam Selfe was clutching a raw, powder-burned face. There was Clem Draper screwing his ink-stained cap in his hands, or was he writhing on Braddock Down with a musket ball through his liver. Phillip Long was chanting poetry in his monotonous voice and beyond it all stood Lucy, waving goodbye to him as she held Crispin Collington's hand.

"Fool!" Will shouted, struggling to shut out that kaleidoscope of image and sound. " You are the biggest fool in creation."

Hannah knew he was accusing himself. He turned his face from her, and burying it in the soft fur of Baron's back, began to sob. The note of rejection and desperation in his grief touched her deeply.

"Oh don't do that," she begged. "Please, I can't bear you to do that. I feel as if my heart will crack with yourn."

She sat down beside him and taking his head in her hands, pulled it gently away from Baron and hugged it to her breast. All the reserve created by their relative positions in the social order that had always caused her to suppress the more obvious signs of her love for him, she abandoned now.

"Don't Will love, don't. We can make it right somehow, I know we can. You must get strong and well first, then we'll find them, your mother and Mistress Lucy. I'll help in any way I can. I'll give you anything you want. There's never been a man in this whole world as have filled my mind, eyes and heart like you. Let me show my love and don't despise me as a child. I may not have airs and graces, but I'm no child. I grew up long ago and I do love you so."

She lay down beside him on the bed, easing her body close to his.

"I'll sooth the pain as best I can. Let me love you Will Barry."

Just as she spoke these words her father came into the room. The sight of his daughter holding Will in her arms took him by surprise and he was ashamed of her forwardness, the way she was lying beside him so intimately.

"What be you doing? Mind your place girl," he barked.

Before Hannah could answer, Annie Moss who had been sitting so quietly mending a smock, threw down her mending and rounded on her husband.

"Leave them be. The boy needs comfort. We all need some comfort. I have got more comfort from that great kindly dog over there than I have ever got from you since our Noah was took from us. Yes we all need comfort, even you John Moss, though you won't own to it in your man's pride."

He was astonished by her fierceness and the words struck home. He could find nothing to say in his defence and turning on his heels walked out of the cottage.

Baron seeming to sense Annie's distress ambled over to her and put his chin on her knees. She began to stroke his small, triangular ears murmuring,

"Ah my sweet, you understand, I know you do. You shall have some pottage soon with bits of rabbit in it and a bone to chew on."

When the soldiers had embarked on their orgy of destruction, Hannah had run up to the Barry farmhouse, worried about the womenfolk. She had arrived just in time to see Olivia and Lucy Barry pushed roughly along by four soldiers. Mary Lipton, the house maid, was screaming and trying to reach them, but one of the villagers pulled her away. Baron was barking in agitation and bewilderment. He launched himself at one of the attackers, knocking the man to the ground. A soldier slashed out at him with his sword, opening a cut across the dog's brow, which caused him to yelp and back off, as the blood began to run into his eye.

Hannah had now lost sight of Lucy and her mother in the confusion, but she dodged in between the noisy crowd ransacking the house of anything valuable and took hold of Baron's collar. Talking soothingly to him, she encouraged him to follow her away and looking back saw lighted branches being thrown into the house and barns, the hayloft already ablaze.

She heard someone shouting that the school was on fire. Most of the crowd were heading for Wanley Hall now, but she did not care about the Wanleys. She led Baron in the direction of the school and ran into her father, who was searching for her, worried about her safety. They went together towards the school, Baron walking close to Hannah, shaking his head to clear the blood trickling into his eye

They found the school and the bonfire of books still burning, deserted now except for two figures by the wall beyond the bonfire.

Job Dilke was bending over a man lying on the ground. He straightened up and jumped back, eyes wide with fear as Baron loped over towards him. Recognising Hannah and her father, he blurted out, "I'm sorry, I'm sorry. I reckon he's dead Hannah. Tweren't me, I never hurt him. I never burned nothing neither, God's truth I never."

He was pale and shaking, genuinely terrified by the violence he had witnessed. When Hannah realised the identity of the man lying on the grass, she felt as if all her blood had ceased flowing. She was frozen to the spot, unable to move forward. John Moss, seeing the look on his daughter's face, knelt down beside Will and put an ear to his chest.

"He's not dead you lackwit," he snapped at Job. "But by the look of that arm he soon will be if something aint done. I hope your father had nothing to do with all this destruction Job Dilke," he added, gesturing back towards the gutted school building.

"No, Father's in Warminster on business- won't be back till tomorrow. He wouldn't want to see no burning. The sight of this will anger him for sure."

The three of them carried Will to the Moss cottage and laid him on Hannah's bed. Then Job Dilke ran back home as fast as he had ever run. He was grateful to find that the looters had come nowhere near the Dilke farm. Taking the goose feather pillows and three blankets from his own bed, he put them in a dog cart and wheeled them back to the cottage. Job was used to being mocked for his slow wits, criticised and set at no account by his impatient father. Apart from his mother, Will Barry was one of the few people who listened to him and did not set him aside as a fool. Will had spent many hours helping him with his reading and writing and trying to find ways to make him understand arithmetic more easily. Job hoped that offering up his own pillows and blankets to make Will more comfortable would show in small part, his gratitude for all those patient hours. He was sure his mother would not chide him for an act of kindness and with luck she would not mention it to his father.

John Moss had been willing enough to take Will Barry into his cottage and do all he could to restore him to health. He was not so keen however to give house room to that giant dog. He complained that they would not be able to feed him, but Hannah was adamant that he should stay. Her father knew full well that food was more plentiful than usual right then because the soldiers had not been able to round up all the livestock from the Barry and Wanley estates. There were plenty of chickens, geese and ducks still ranging free, with no bailiff on either estate to keep an eye on them, so the villagers helped themselves. Baron would eat most things and was fond of porridge and milksops.

Annie Moss took to him instantly, impressed by his gentle nature. She fussed over him and when her melancholy came upon her, she would put her arms around his broad chest and hug him tight. He responded readily to her affection and although John continued to grumble about him, he accepted that Baron was there to stay.

The dog was sitting down now beside Annie, as she looked across to her daughter and said, "You comfort him as much as you can Hannah. Pay no heed to your father. Comfort's hard to come by. Don't you ever stint it." Hannah was rocking Will gently. He had stopped weeping now and was passive in her arms. Through the threadbare dress he could feel the warmth of her skin on his cheek. She was throbbing with life and strength.

"I'll always be here. I shan't let you down like the rest. You will be safe with me."

It was a hot June. Now, as the midday sun dominated everything, it seemed as if beads of perspiration lay on the thick foliage and the blades of grass. Will Barry was struck by the startling black and white clarity of a magpie's plumage as it rose up through the trees and flashed across the sun. He did not know how long he had been wandering about there, turning over the ashes with his feet and picking up bits of rubble as if he expected to find something underneath them.

The mob had burned everything, even the cowsheds, had rooted up fencing and smashed down the gates. Only the malthouse had escaped destruction. All that remained of the farmhouse was a gutted shell, raw and sore looking in the hot sun.

The first time he had ventured out to the ruins, Hannah had come with him, worried that he would over-tire himself and what his emotional reaction would be to the sight of the house that had been in his family for generations, destroyed. They had both been struck by the strange view of the stone steps to the cellar still standing like a piece of sculpture, leading down to the lower level, now full of charred roof beams and blackened wall plaster. Several barrels of ale had been stored in the cellar, but there was no sign of burned barrels or the metal hoops, so the soldiers must have taken them. Searching amongst the rubble Will found the flagstone covering a secret that had eluded the looters. He brised it up to reveal the family strong box, untouched by the fire, safe in its hollowed out, earthen hiding place.

No one but the Barry family members knew the

where-abouts of that strong box, not even Crispin, which was fortunate in the circumstances. There was no knowing what had happened to the key to the padlock. Will had always kept it in a drawer in his bedroom cabinet, but he managed to spring the lock by striking it with a heavy stone. Besides family documents, it was full of gold and silver coins. It was ironical- his house was in ruins, all the livestock from the farm gone, yet he was still a prosperous man. He would need some of that money when he started to search for his mother and sister. He knew he should have begun that search already, but he could not summon up the strength just yet. His mental exhaustion was a greater barrier to action than his physical weakness.

He sat down on a heap of rubble, plucking at the ivy which still clung to the stones, although it was beginning to grow sear and die. A mosquito droned, hanging in the heavy air, then flitting away in a heat haze. It was still beautiful here. The roses in the garden were particularly abundant this year, their fragrance intoxicating.

Hannah was happy to let him walk around alone now. She understood that he needed some time alone. He had been astonished at the depth of comprehension and sensitivity which Hannah Moss had revealed in the past weeks. Her presence was always a comfort to him. Her natural common-sense, her reasonable view of life, her harmony with the environment, contrasted so sharply with the bigotry, fanaticism and greed that had shattered his world.

The feel of her hair, springy to the touch like fresh grass, was such a pleasure. She smelled of potato peelings, freshly turned earth, mown hay and sometimes less fragrant scents- everything that was comfortable and real.

They did not lie together in John Moss' house out of respect for his feelings because they knew he was not happy about the relationship. John did not believe there was any future in it for Hannah and feared that his daughter would be left sorrowing for a man whose social status was too far above hers for any permanent union. Besides that, the cottage was too small for any privacy, so Will and Hannah made love in the malthouse on these warm June evenings, before walking back to the Moss dwelling.

He felt no guilt during sex. Her total surrender to the act of love, almost as if it was sacred, made it seem pure somehow. But afterwards, if he allowed himself to dwell on it, he felt uneasy. Although he was only six years her senior, he had been her teacher and he had not yet rid himself completely of the feeling that she was a child, a pupil who should be protected, rather than being used to satisfy his desires. But she gave him strength, revived his spirit and he needed her. If he was apart from her too long, the desolation, that emptiness and despair pressed in on him. That need prompted him to push away his doubts too easily.

As he sat there twisting a stem of ivy around his fingers, he began to feel the heat of the sun on his head and decided he should find some shade. He could not bring himself to visit the school house and felt uncomfortable when he met any of the villagers. Men who had been involved in the burning and looting were embarrassed in his presence and could not look him in the eye. He was not sure that he could conceal the rawness of his feelings when he spoke to them.

He had made the effort to visit Sam Selfe's wife and tell her what had happened to Sam as soon as he was strong enough to walk. It was his duty, no matter how painful. Keziah Selfe had the same deep faith as her husband and her reaction was stoical. If it was God's will that she should see her husband again, she would be grateful, but if Sam had died of his wounds then she could take comfort in the fact that he had died doing what he believed was right. She had been supporting herself and the children basket weaving and tending the vegetable patch beside their cottage, but she did not refuse the bag of silver coins that Will left on the table.

Earlier that morning as he was wandering up to his ruined house, Will had been overtaken by Jess Barnett. The ploughman had played no part in the riot and was still grieving for his oxen. He felt no personal guilt regarding Will, but he was mightily ashamed of the behaviour of his fellow villagers.

"Aint done them no good," he declared, "Cos half of them aint found no other work- lived on what they pilfered and sold for a bit, then they were in trouble. Two families took into Calne poorhouse this week. I be lucky. John Dilke took I on as a ploughman in place of Abel Harding- at least till he comes back."

"Your job is safe Jess," Will confirmed. "Abel will not be back. He is buried in Cornwall."

"God rest him," murmured Jess. "Tis a strange, fearful world we live in now Master Will. We were warned, but didn't see it. First the plague and then the Calne Church tower falling down the very next year. Reverend Mortimer told I that the sound of them bells crashing down into the nave sounded as if the end of the world were nigh, it were so loud. Omens they were, the plague and the tower, warnings of this evil time now come upon us. But I never thought to see Sandy Barrow folk burn and destroy like they did, nor believe they would heed the words of that ranting preacher that come with the soldiers.

Twas an evil thing they did. I tried to stop them taking Shadrach and Meshach. I have tended them oxen since I were a lad. It aint so bad if they use them as draft animals, but I was feared they wanted them for meat."

Will had been touched by Jess' genuine love and concern for the oxen. It made him wish he had been more thoughtful for the safety of Flash and Minstrel before he had dragged them into a war. That thought came into his mind again now and he considered whether to walk to John Dilke's farm to see Richard's grey horse that had carried him home from Cornwall.

Job Dilke had found it in the woods near the school, contentedly grazing and as it was saddled and harnessed, with a pistol in a holster slung from the saddle, the boy guessed it was Will's. He took it back to the Dilke farm and stabled it with his father's horses. He was reluctant to come to John Moss' cottage to tell Master Will what he had done because he was afraid of John's sharp tongue. At that time Will was in the throes of fever anyway and the whereabouts of his horse was hardly significant. Job however waylaid Hannah and told her. Since he had brought the pillows and blankets for Will, she had begun to see Job in a more favourable light and she praised him for his care of the horse. Her praise gave him a glow of pleasure.

Will was thinking that he should offer John Dilke some payment for stabling and feeding the horse and reward Job for finding it. He started off with the intention of walking over to the farm, but he tired easily still and by the time he had reached the woodland near the school, he changed his mind and decided to go back to the village instead.

As he turned back in that direction, he saw a figure walking towards him and as it drew closer, he realised the man was waving to attract his attention. He soon recognised the shuffling gait of the Reverend Robert Seddon and stepped forward to meet him.

"William- I am so glad to meet up with you. I first called at the Moss' cottage and Hannah said you were out walking. So good to see you able to come so far. You are looking much better than when I saw you last."

There was so much Will wanted to say to Seddon, but he did not know how to begin.

"Thank you, yes I am improving- not fast enough for my liking, but I feel more myself now I have some clean clothes and have had a shave and look less like a man recently rescued from years on a desert island."

After they had found the money in the strong box, Will had despatched Hannah to Calne, to buy him two suits of clothes at Ezra Parfitt's, the tailor's shop in

Cousin Street. Like his father before him, Will had always bought his clothes from Parfitt and was confident that Ezra, knowing his size and taste, would find Hannah something suitable off the peg.

He also instructed her to buy herself two pairs of shoes from the shoemaker in Church Street. The clopping sound of her ill-fitting shoes, which had never bothered him before, now grated on his frayed nerves. His instructions did not end there, for from the shoemaker, she was to go to the dressmaker in the High Street for two dresses and a shawl for herself and a bolt of cloth for her mother.

Hannah had never carried so much money on her person and she pushed the bag right down inside her bodice for safety.

She took Ezra Parfitt's advice regarding Will's clothes and bought wisely for herself- a pair of sturdy boots and a lighter pair of shoes and two plain serge dresses, one russet, the other grey. Her only flight of fancy was the worsted shawl, smooth, soft and multicoloured. She had never owned anything so beautiful before. She showed it to the Reverend Seddon that morning and pointed out her new shoes that were so comfortable. The curate was smiling as he recalled it.

"Hannah told me she had been shopping for you and for herself it seems. She showed me her new clothes and shoes- very sensible, appropriate garments and very bonny she looked in them too. She has grown into a most pretty, healthy girl and full of common sense."

Will nodded, knowing that Seddon was aware of how much he depended on her common sense.

"I called because I wished to tell you that I made some inquiries in Chippenham yesterday- about the soldiers who did so much damage here." He paused for a moment, a shudder passing through him as he recalled the events and Will realised what an effort it must have been for him to stand up to that mob.

"They passed through Chippenham heading for somewhere in the Mendips to meet up with other forces, but I gleaned nothing regarding your mother and Lucy or Lady Wanley and her daughters. We have had no news from Sir Roger for some months and I doubt if he has any knowledge of what has happened."

"I should be out looking for them," Will interrupted," Not relying on others to do what is my duty, but to my shame I cannot seem to push myself into action. I have no energy, my mind seems paralysed. I am an empty vessel."

"William, my dear boy, you have been very ill and your spirits are very depressed by what you have witnessed- the death and destruction you have seen- the fear for your family. You need time to heal. You are not strong enough yet to cope with the world. I- I am sure that your family and the Wanleys are safe. Once that party of soldiers met up with the rest of the army, responsible officers- gentlemen-will have taken them into their custody and housed them somewhere safe. Once Sir William Waller hears of their plight I don't doubt they will be released and escorted home."

"What home?" Will asked. "They have no homes left."

"Perhaps -uh- an unfortunate choice of words, but I am sure they will be treated honourably. I have Caroline's spaniels, Toby and Tessa at my house you know. They were wandering about the village quite lost. None of the villagers seemed to care about them. The foolish little things had no notion how to care for themselves, having been petted and spoiled all their lives. Their accommodation with me is far from the luxury they were accustomed to, but they are fed and sheltered and to speak true, I find I enjoy their company in the evenings. Caroline loved those dogs so. It will be such a pleasure to see her dear face when they are reunited."

Will took hold of Robert Seddon's hand. "Oh Reverend Seddon. I owe you an apology."

"An apology William- to me. I- I am sure you owe me no apology."

"I do Sir. I have underestimated you for so long. When I saw how Rector Rogers treated you and Sir Roger bullied you, I pitied you and that was unworthy of me for you do not need my pity. You are a far stronger, braver man than I and a true Christian."

He felt tears welling up in his eyes as he spoke. At present the smallest thing reduced him to tears, much to his aggravation. "No, no William- no, no. I- I do my best in a small way- a very small way."

"Much more significant than you imagine Sir, I assure you."

The curate coughed to cover his embarrassment over such unexpected praise, then murmured, " I realise dear boy that you struggle to-" he hesitated, searching for the right words. " To forgive- yes- forgive the villagers who took part in the destruction, after all you have done for them."

"My intellect has done so already, but my emotions, my heart cannot obey my head. It hurts too much and what they did to you appals me."

"It was the soldiers who were rough with me, not the village folk."

"But they did nothing to help you."

"They would have stood little chance against armed troopers had they tried. No- I hold nothing against them. When your life is hard and you possess so little, it is easy to be led into temptation. We must not expect gratitude for acts of charity."

Will shook his head. "I was not dispensing charity or looking for gratitude. The men who laboured on the farm did a good day's work for fair wages and as for the school, what I was offering them was a way for their children to better themselves through education, to enrich their lives, but I never belittled them for what they were."

Seddon coughed again. "Indeed, indeed, but for some, any act by a benefactor, no matter how well intentioned, only serves to remind them of the – uh- the gap that exists between them and they store up- resentment- yes- resentment, almost without realising that they do so. Then when something happens, as it did here, that enables them to- to- uh- assert some vestige of independence, they are led astray."

Will was grateful that Seddon did not touch on the behaviour of Crispin Collington. That he could not discuss yet.

"I must go now," the curate said. "I have been invited to dine at the rectory- a rare occurrence and I must not be late." He patted Will's arm. "You will win through in the end William. You will conquer your- your- despair, with God's help. I know it is hard to fathom God's role in all this, but we must have faith that all will be revealed in time. I will call on you again soon and should you wish to- uh- unburden yourself, although I have no solutions, I have always been a good listener."

One final touch on Will's arm and Robert Seddon was off towards Heddington Rectory. Will stood for some time contemplating what the curate had said about charity. He could hardly believe that the villagers had regarded him as dispensing charity from a position of lofty superiority, but perhaps Seddon was right and the very fact of his prosperity and education made him appear patronising despite his good intentions. He had always struggled hard not to give that impression and it was painful now to think that some of the folk of Sandy Barrow put him in the same category as Sir Roger Wanley.

As he began to walk slowly down to the village he heard the sound of hooves thudding on the turf. He looked towards the cottages and caught sight of a black horse, flanks gleaming, galloping past the dwellings and across the Common towards the ruins of Will Barry's house. The rider spurred his mount on with the ardour of someone in a hurry. His bush of red hair stood out angrily beneath a plumed hat and his whole body was straining forward, as if his spirit was travelling much faster than his horse. Will was filled with a surge of something close to hope as he watched Richard Wanley mad-capping across the paddocks.

Wanley was bawling his name long before he was in comfortable earshot. Will stood still and waited. Richard screeched to a halt, leaped from his saddle and was embracing him with all his old vigour. Barry could only marvel that nothing seemed to impair Dick's strength and energy.

"Will, by God am I pleased to see you. When I put you in that cart last month and watched old Haxby drive away, I never thought you would make it. I could only hope. Hannah Moss tells me you were lucky not to lose your arm. How is it?"

"Healing, but it would probably feel better if you were not so affectionate with it Dick."

Wanley let go with an oath and an apology. He was agitated and tense, unable to stand still. Now that he could study him more closely, Will could see some suffering in his face, suffering that vented itself in an explosive anger.

"I sent you home for security," he said," And you came home to this barbarity. It was enough to kill you."

"It almost did," Will murmured, but Richard did not hear him as he ranted on.

"I have just been down to the Hall- completely gutted- ruined like your house and the school. I knew it had to happen. I always feared the worm would turn.

There's your good, honest, industrious villagers for you Will. They turn into a pack of wolves slavering at your throat. I warned you, but you wouldn't have it- always taking from you, but never giving anything back to you in return. That they dared to lay their hands on my mother and sisters, to humiliate and degrade them as they did, as if they were local whores and little Caroline-God above- what must it have been like for her?"

He was shaking with rage. Will wanted to help him, but he felt so useless. He could only say, "I am so sorry Dick."

"You have your own sorrows- your mother and Lucy. That bastard of a bailiff, he was the cause of it all they told me, he was the one who egged them on. Worming his way into your confidence, just waiting for his chance."

"Don't," Will pleaded wearily, "You might as well bang my head against a stone. It would hurt less."

He thought of Robert Seddon, facing that brutal crowd, saying, 'Father forgive them for they know not what they do' and wished he could feel some forgiveness inside him.

"Well, I will get him for it," Richard vowed, "the deceitful, conniving bastard. I will catch up with him and he will answer with his life. For my fathers' sake I will avenge this outrage. If I don't stick a sword through his guts myself, I will see him hang."

"Does your father know about this?"

Richard stopped his pacing, stopped throwing his arms around in an histrionic manner that would have been comic if the grief behind his anger was not so apparent and looked into Will's face.

"No, he will never know. At least he has been spared this. My father and Edward died fighting side by side in April. Their cavalry regiment was with a force led by Prince Rupert trying to recapture Lincoln. Half a dozen troopers led by father had penetrated right into the cathedral close, but they got trapped in a narrow alley by the defenders and shot down. It is a small comfort that he and Edward were together when it happened. I received the news a few days after I had smuggled you out of our Cornwall Headquarters. Wrote to mother straightway, but letters don't always reach their destination these days, so I came myself as soon as I was free to do so."

A greyness had crept into his voice. It was as if someone had stuck a pin in the swell of his anger and he was deflating like a balloon.

"Oh God, I'm tired," he confessed, before Will could speak. "I have ridden non-stop from Cornwall. I went with Hopton's advance up country in the hope of getting a few days at home to support mother. We joined the Marquis of Hertford and Prince Maurice near Taunton, where I hived off and headed for home. I rode like the very devil, but when I came through Calne, I was stopped by Jackson, the parish constable. He told me what had happened here. He had heard that you were back, but very sick and being nursed in that hovel belonging to John Moss, so I went there first. It is a marvel that you were not poisoned even more in that place."

"Hannah and her parents have tended me with great care and patience, kept me comfortable even in those conditions."

Richard shrugged, then he fumbled in his pockets and produced three badly wrapped parcels.

"Look, presents for the family. Caroline always wanted a necklace of shells- thought it might cheer her a trifle after the bad news about father and Edward. She was very close to Edward you know. Then there was the thought of my favourite chair and a glass of good-" The words caught in his throat and he turned away, muttering savagely, "Damn me, I haven't cried since I fell in that blasted briar pit near Lacock Abbey, when we were running away from that pockmarked old verger with a face like a stewed prune. God that must be fifteen years ago. Do you remember that?"

"Yes, I remember it Dick."

He put his arm around Wanley's shoulder with all the friendliness of those days which had just flickered across Richard's memory.

"I grieve with you for your father and Edward. I will always be grateful for the way Sir Roger protected us after my father died and Edward was so young, not yet fully grown into a man. I know I parted from Sir Roger on bad terms, but it hurt me more than you can imagine to break with him so completely."

Richard nodded, murmuring, "I'm sorry I let that ruffian Leech try to drown you."

"It does not matter much. What does matter is that you stopped him before he did. How did you explain my absence to him by the way?"

"Didn't need to. I knew his regiment was due to pull out in the morning to join Hopton's main force, so he would have no time to poke around looking for you."

"Still it was a risky thing to do Dick and I am

grateful."

"Well damn it all, friendship ought to count for something, war or no war."

Will could certainly second that. "Look," he suggested, " Come back to the Moss cottage with me. You can rest there and we can have a drink together. We can go into Bromham, to The Pewter Tankard and buy a couple of bottles of brandy, bring them back to the cottage and have a drink in peace- if there is any brandy to be found in Wiltshire these days that has not been requisitioned by army officers."

"What like me you mean? Yes, I would like that. You know Will, it's a funny thing, but I never enjoy a drink so much as when I am drinking with you."

Will smiled. "Strange phenomenon that, I suffer from it too."

He had never imagined he would see Richard so vulnerable. Wanley was not a man to indulge in introspection and soul searching. He would never truly understand his own loneliness and sense of loss. Now his anger had faded, he was bewildered and irritated by this nagging ache inside him. Will was touched to see him sniff and wipe his eyes with his sleeve with an air of embarrassment, like a schoolboy ashamed to be caught weeping.

They began to walk down to the village, Richard leading his horse by the reins. Then he said in a quiet voice, but in a tone that conveyed more determination than any of his earlier ranting, "I do mean to get him Will. The men who passed through here were on their way to join

Waller in Somerset. Collington and his bunch must have been travelling with them when they left here. He may have slunk off on his own since, but someone must know what has happened to our womenfolk. They may have been handed over to William Waller. He would treat them with respect surely. I can follow the route the soldiers took, picking up scraps of information as I go. I will not rest until I find them."

"The Reverend Seddon has been making inquiries for me around Chippenham," Will offered, not wanting Richard to know that he had not been able to stir himself into action.

Wanley snorted scornfully. "And much good he'll do with his stuttering and apologising."

Will knew that Dick would never come to understand or appreciate the qualities hidden beneath the curate's timid surface, so he did not argue. He just asked, "Do you truly think there is a chance we will find them?"

"There has to be a chance, a good chance."

"When are you going?"

"As soon as I have had a rest, a meal and that brandy."

"Well at least I have not much luggage to pack," said Will, feeling that this was perhaps the hour when the world would start turning again and he would be pushed into some action.

"You can't come," was Richard's abrupt reaction. " You are not fit enough. Damn it man, you nearly died a few weeks ago and it shows. You have no colour and you are as thin as a rake- and that hand doesn't grip properly."

Will flexed his fingers as much as he could. "It is improving gradually every day. I cannot write or draw yet, but I can just about hold a piece of charcoal now and I can certainly control a horse. Dick, if our roles were reversed, I would not even consider trying to stop you from joining me. I doubt if I could anyway."

Wanley nodded. "You are right of course. Let's hope the brandy inspires us both."

✶‖✶

Hannah Moss sang so softly it was hardly distinguishable from the buzz of insects hovering around in swarms, drawn to the flames of the fire. She stroked Will's hair with the tips of her fingers and watched the dragonfly's blue whirl as it threaded its way through the very tongues of the flames. The meadow turf was like a quilt. Will forgot his weariness as he lay there with his head in Hannah's lap. The air was redolent with the smell of wild hyacinth and grass freshly dampened by rain. It was a balmy night, drowsy, dream-like. The reflection of an orange moon shuddered in the pool behind them.

"What cursed luck though," Richard Wanley declared, "For such a thing to happen when Sir Ralph might easily have pressed home his advantage. Then the loss of Sir Bevil Grenville just when those brave Cornishmen of his had reached the top of the hill, that was a double blow."

"Oh peace Richard Wanley," Hannah shot him a reproachful look. "Must you talk all the while? Can't you

see Will's tired? Let him sleep some. I think your tongue
do run on wheels."

Will laughed. "You mustn't talk to my friends like
that. They are in short supply as it is."

"Ah well, I'm not sure you'd be worse off without
this one."

Will's eyes apologised to Richard, who shrugged.
He had objected to the idea of Hannah accompanying
them at first, fearing she would slow them down, but when
he discovered she could manage a horse with competence
he withdrew his objection. They bought a sturdy, roan
cob from John Dilke that carried their saddle bags as well
as Hannah.

She had learned to ride with confidence when she
was twelve. Noah's friend Henry Stringer had acquired
a horse and brought it up to the woods in the evenings
for Noah and Hannah to take turns riding. They had
no saddle but slung a blanket across its back. Sometimes
all three of them rode on the horse together, galloping
through the woods, laughing and shouting. Hannah
suspected that Henry had stolen the mare because he did
not have the means to buy the animal. Her instinct proved
correct for Stringer was arrested at the end of the year for
stealing four piglets from a farm in Bremhill and the theft
of the horse was also revealed. They never saw Henry
Stringer or the horse again.

After Richard's objection to Hannah's presence was
removed, there was her father to satisfy. He complained
bitterly about being left in the lurch. Will Barry solved
that one by riding over to Westbrook to speak to Mary

Lipton, his mother's house maid. Mary had found no other work since the riot and was struggling to support herself and her grandmother. Will gave her a generous sum of money to visit the Moss cottage every day and do some of Hannah's chores. It was John's opinion that such a dainty, skinny female as Mary would never be able to work as hard as his daughter, but he did not refuse the help.

Mary considered it a come-down in life to be associated with squatters, but she squared it with her dignity by making it clear to everyone that she was working for Master Will while he searched for his family, not for John Moss. She also declared that she was keeping an eye on Baron to make sure he was properly cared for. She need have no fears for Baron, who was perfectly contented with the attention he received from Annie Moss and treated the occasional volley of oaths thrown at him by her husband with supreme indifference.

So Hannah Moss was free to go on the search and despite the tense situation and her concern for Will's health, she took pleasure in the freedom from the village, travelling to places she had never seen before.

Richard Wanley was watching her now as she stroked Will's hair. He was not offended by her hostility. He knew that their past relationship made it impossible for her to feel at ease in his presence. She hated the thought that she had once given herself to Wanley. He had accepted this new relationship with Will Barry without comment, but sometimes she would catch him watching her with an ironical smile in his eyes, as he was then and she despised him for it.

"How did Hopton's accident happen?" Will asked to draw Richard's attention away from Hannah.

"Well that trooper was saying that a spark from some prisoner's pipe dropped into a powder magazine. Half a dozen men were injured. It's easily done. Hopton was partially blinded they say and had to travel in a litter. Magnificent fellow Hopton. It's a damn shame!"

Will had grown to respect Sir Ralph Hopton during his campaigns in Devon and Cornwall. He had heard no report of him that did not speak of his generous nature, courage and the genuine care he had for his men. He was sorry to hear of the accident at Lansdowne Hill.

They were camping now in the meadows that skirted the Devizes Road with a group of refugees from the skirmishing that had continued all along the road from Chippenham to Devizes, when Waller's advance guard caught up with the rear of the retreating Royalist army. Prince Maurice had managed to rally some of the Royalist cavalry and there had been a fierce rear-guard action fought at Rowde that very day, allowing the majority of Hopton's force to get into Devizes and the temporary safety of the castle.

Along the road Will, Richard and Hannah had met exhausted men, some of them wounded, intent only on getting home. Stray cavalry troopers sometimes skittered past them on jaded, lathered horses. No side commanded their allegiance now. It was over for them. They had taken enough and were in search of safety.

There were several camp fires burning in the hollow where Richard had chosen to camp that night. He had been strolling amongst the refugees asking questions about the fighting, hoping perhaps to pick up information by the way about their families or Collington. He continued to search with a remorseless energy.

When they first set out from Sandy Barrow they had followed the trail of the soldiers who had captured their womenfolk, through Chippenham and on into Somerset. Richard was convinced that once Sir William Waller became aware that there were women hostages, ladies of some status, with the army, he would order them to be released and sent to the Royalist Headquarters in Wells. So they headed in that direction. If they met Royalist scouting parties, Richard did the talking, but if the troops were Parliamentarian, Will stepped to the fore.

They discovered before they reached Wells that there had been an inconclusive clash between the two armies at Chewton Mendip on June 12th. Both sides had regrouped and were now attempting to manoeuvre into a favourable position to prevent the other from taking possession of Bath.

The first piece of information they gleaned concerning the hostages came when Will spoke to a young cavalry captain, who was hurrying to join Waller with a small detachment of troopers. The captain recalled that Waller's attention had been drawn to the hostages and he had indeed ordered their release, but protected by four troopers, they were taken to a house in Marshfield to rest, before being escorted to any destination they chose. He did not know the name of the man who offered them sanctuary, but remembered that he was a physician.

Richard fumed and cursed because they had passed through Marshfield some days before, when the women might still have been lodged in that house. Turning back they hurried to Marshfield and after prolonged searching found the house. It was locked up and deserted. A neighbour told them that the visitors had only stayed one night and then drove away in a carriage with two troopers on either side of it. He had no idea where, but they appeared to be going towards Chippenham.

Will thought his mother might have asked to be taken to her brother's house in Bratton. Richard on the other hand was sure his mother would wish to go to Devizes where she had cousins and surely both mothers would wish to be near Sandy Barrow in case their sons came looking for them. They decided to try Devizes first, but because Will was exhausted, rested the night in a tavern before travelling on. They started back, unknown to them, on the day the battle was fought at Lansdowne Hill. Richard had suggested a short cut across country by various lanes, avoiding the main road, so they did not get caught up in Waller's pursuit of Hopton after the battle and were not aware of it until they hit the road the far side of Bromham. It was clear then that it would be hard to get into Devizes and they camped for the night, agreeing to decide on their next move in the morning.

Will had been over-optimistic about his reserves of strength. At the end of each day he was on the point of exhaustion. He had developed a dry cough and had no appetite. Richard was so intent on his quest that he did not notice how badly Will was flagging at the end of a long day. This singlemindedness in Wanley encouraged Will to hang on and try to disguise his weakness.

Wanley was leaning back against a rock, uncorking a flask of brandy. He drank as remorselessly as he searched, but he was always sober and clear-headed.

"If only Hopton had won a clear cut victory at Lansdowne. It was damnably close. When the battle was stalemate, Waller lost his nerve and withdrew into Bath-had no idea our forces were in a worse state than his own, so those fellows up there were saying. If Sir Ralph could have pressed home his advantage then, Waller would have been caught like a rat in a trap, but this damnable explosion ruined all that. The men lost heart. Waller could call on reinforcements from Bristol and Hopton knew they could never make it to Oxford with Waller's advance guard attacking their rear columns. Their only hope was to retreat into Devizes. If only we had found out about Marshfield earlier, we might have got into the town before all this happened."

"Ifs wear away your soul," Hannah told him. She felt Will's lips brush her fingers as they rested against his cheek. "You go to sleep love, don't you bother about his ifs and buts."

Will closed his eyes to mollify her, but like Richard, he could not help speculating. There was silence for a while as both men pondered on their situation, a silence broken fitfully by the cries of pain coming from one of the refugees camping on the opposite side of the pool. They were the sounds of a man in delirium.

"Poor little devil," Richard glanced across at the group of figures huddled around the tossing, struggling heap of blankets. "He's got as many holes in his belly as a cullender. I swear to God, his insides are oozing out. Why they bothered to drag him all the way from Bath I will never understand. Far kinder to have put a bullet through his brain than let him suffer like that."

"Perhaps he wants to die in his own house with those as means most to him gathered around," Hannah flashed at him. "Not on some lonesome hill, to be buried in a pit with many others like him and no name put above his grave." She was thinking of Noah in the plague pit, his bones mixed with the other victims, while Will was reminded of those young men from Sandy Barrow lying in such nameless graves, Phillip Long, Clem Draper, perhaps even- but just as the image of Sam Selfe was forming in his mind, he heard a voice singing. It was not a tuneful voice, but the strength and conviction of it made it good to hear. The voice was singing a psalm so familiar to Will Barry. At first he told himself it must be his imagination, all the old associations coming back to him when he thought about Sam, but the voice began the second verse. It was coming from the camp fire the other side of the pool. Will scrambled to his feet.

"What's wrong love?" Hannah asked, surprised by the suddenness of the action.

"Where are you going?" Richard stood up too, but he received no answer from Will, who had already passed into the shadows beyond the fire.

The other camp fire was guttering low and only the shafts of orange moonlight brightened the faces of the people sitting there. The wounded man had stopped tossing and lay in rigid stillness. A woman was bending over him, the folds of her shawl and her long, straight hair covering him like a blanket. Two men sat at his feet, talking in low voices and the hymn singer, perched on a rock beyond them had begun the third verse.

The two men started as Will dashed past them, but the woman neither saw or heard him. She was keening, the thin, high wail of the Celtic peoples. The sound accompanied the psalm like a reed pipe, blending as if they were two parts of a whole. Will had reached the singer now. Sam Selfe was swaying with the rhythm of his song, his hands clasped around his knees. He was sitting full in the moon's rays, his face upturned as if he was bathing in it. The face was not so blackened now; in places the burnt skin had peeled away, leaving red, sore areas, but there were still blisters and some skin that was brown and wizened like dried apples. One side of his hair, including half of that square fringe had been burned away, stubble beginning to appear now, promising new growth.

His clothes were threadbare and his toes pushing through his boots, yet there was still that air of untroubled serenity about him.

"I hope you have thought about me now and again when you have been singing that," Will said.

Sam stopped singing and his hands reached out instantly.

"William Barry?"

Will gripped the hands and held them tight. He could hear the others coming up behind them.

"I've remembered you in my prayers every day since we parted," Sam assured him. He showed no signs of surprise at this chance meeting. He accepted it in the calm way he accepted everything.

"I tried to reach you Sam, tried to find out what had happened to you, but they would not let me."

"That's what I thought. I fared well enough. They tended me kindly- I've no complaints."

Will looked at the sightless eyes, one of which suppurated puss that dribbled down his cheek and wondered how Sam could say that with such conviction.

"Who is it?" Richard Wanley was at Will's elbow. "Anybody I know?"

Sam tilted his head in an effort to pick up the voice more clearly. It was difficult to recognise Sam's face, but before Will could explain, Hannah cried out,

"Why tis Sam Selfe. What have they done to your poor face Sam?" She knelt on the rock beside him and stroked his face, a spontaneous, compassionate gesture. "Tis wicked to have done this to you."

"Is that Hannah Moss?"

"Yes, tis Hannah," she confirmed. She had not expected to find him like this. Will had never spoken to her in detail about his experiences during those months of fighting. Sometimes she had watched him when he sat brooding and felt that if she stared into the dark depths of his eyes, she would see all that had happened mirrored there, just as the moon was mirrored in the pool beside them.

" I be so pleased to see you again Sam. Sandy Barrow has missed you all these months."

"Tis good to be on my way back there child. I consider myself lucky to have the chance- not like that poor lad lying dead amongst us."He inclined his head towards the sound of the lament.

"I'd rather be dead than like that," Richard murmured to himself, but Sam's ears, already sharpened by his lack of sight, picked up the words. The identity of the speaker registered with him.

"That's a selfish and ungodly thing to say Richard Wanley. A man's sight is precious and tis a great trial to lose it. I shall find it hard to present myself to Keziah and the children in such a lame condition with them fearing how I be going to provide for them. But life is the most precious gift of all and to wish it away is more than foolishness, tis close on sin. If it has pleased God to take my sight, then perhaps He has another gift to bestow, which will be more use to me in the end."

Richard tossed his head. "It hasn't taught you any sense has it? You can still preach that canting Puritan nonsense of yours. What about the lives you have taken so far in this war? Have you considered that your condition might be a punishment from God for your revolt against His anointed King? I wager that hasn't crossed your narrow, little mind."

"Richard, why must you talk to him like that?" There was genuine pain in Will's voice. Wanley felt the rebuke. He backed down with an ill-grace and moved away as if he was no longer interested in the proceedings.

Will suggested to Sam that he move over to their camp. He was sharply aware of the mourning woman and felt they were intruding on her privacy as he watched her swaying over the body in rhythm with her chant. Sam agreed and after exchanging a few words with the two men, he allowed himself to be led across to the other camp. Richard lingered behind, scuffing his feet moodily on the stones and feeling for the brandy flask in his pocket.

Far into the night, long after the fire had dulled into a dim glow beneath grey ash, Will and Hannah sat talking with Sam Selfe as he recounted all that had happened to him since Stratton. The prisoners had been taken up country with Hopton's forces when they moved to join Hertford. In the confusion after the Battle of Lansdowne, he had escaped in the company of the two men from the camp across the pool. The wounded man and his Welsh wife they had encountered on their flight and promised to accompany them to Potterne where the lad's parents lived. They cut down some tree branches and tied a blanket across them to make a litter to carry him. Their intention was to guide Sam to Sandy Barrow first, then travel on to Potterne. Sam was full of praise for their kindness.

"This war is a terrible thing," he mused, as he dabbed the matter from his infected eye with his sleeve, "And we must pray it won't have to go on much longer-that the right will prevail. But many, many acts of brotherliness and kindness have been done to me, which makes me feel there is hope for England yet."

Listening to Sam, Will could almost believe it, but when he looked at Richard huddled against the rocks, nursing his brandy, absorbed in his desire for revenge and saw once again the pages of his books withering away in that orgy of fate-filled iconoclasm, he doubted everything.

"I visited Keziah, Sam and told her what had happened to you," he said. "She bore it so bravely and was content to leave it in God's hands whether you returned or not. She has been supporting the family basket weaving."

"Ah she's a constant and hardy woman my Keziah, capable of dealing with anything. Perhaps she can teach me to make baskets by the feel of it. My left eye is not wholly dark- a little light breaks in and I can see shapes in it, but not enough to make out what or who they be. Better than nothing though. I was hoping to meet someone who could tell me how my family fared and tis good to know they are forewarned about the state of me.

Tis strange because only yesterday I was certain that someone I knew passed by me on the road. A whole gang of them come rattling past us and my companions struck up conversation with some of them. I heard one of them say how good the crops looked in these parts and what a shame it would be if the main army came this way trampling it all down.

I said to myself 'Sam you know that voice' but I couldn't bring it to mind. Long after they had gone I was puzzling over it, till all of a sudden I heard that very same voice say in my head 'Well open the sack up Sam and we'll just be sure it's wood you've got in there and not a brace of pheasant' and then I knew twere your bailiff, Crispin Collington."

Richard, who had wandered over to join them, started forward as if he had been pushed from behind without warning. Will felt Hannah grip his hand.

"Are you sure?" he asked, running his tongue over his lips, for his mouth had gone dry.

"Did you hear any of the conversation, get any idea where he was heading?" Richard demanded before Sam had time to answer the first question. He grabbed Selfe's arm fiercely below the elbow and Sam could feel the heat in his touch.

"I can't tell you that- didn't speak to him myself and I doubt if he would have known me even if he had looked. Ask my two friends yonder. They conversed with him for some time and could best tell you."

Richard was gone in an instant, stumbling in the darkness, for the moon was paled by a rampart of grey cloud. Will tried to explain the situation to Sam. He did so in a controlled, unemotional way to disguise the fact that he was trembling inwardly. Sam digested the story in silence, dabbing away at that eye. When he was sure that Will had finished he said, "It must have been a great temptation for him, placed as he was. I hope he can find it in his heart to forgive himself or he is damned for sure."

Hannah's jade green eyes searched Will's face. She did not understand what Sam had said and hoped to find the answer in Will's reaction, but his face remained impassive. All she could read were the signs of illness. The skin stretched across the fine bones of his cheeks had a pale translucency. It reminded her of the white porcelain figure that used to stand in the window of the school library and the comparison scared her.

"Damnation!" Richard was cursing his way back again, calling out before he reached them. "Why is our timing always destined to be wrong? He told those fellows he was going to take the ancient track along the downs towards Marlborough. Didn't you tell me once his mother lived the other side of Marlborough?"

Will nodded.

"He had a woman with him, a tall, fair woman they said- didn't look or speak like a doxy. Sounded damnably like Lucy."

"No, it could not be Lucy," Will was quick to contradict him. " She would never leave Mother."

Hannah touched his arm. "Will, it might be her. She was sweet on Collington."

"What?"

"She told me herself that she was very fond of him and would much sooner marry a man like him than someone she didn't love. After you'd gone, he was openly courting her- waiting for her after school and they'd walk home together holding hands. If I passed by the farm of an evening, I would see them sitting on that seat amongst the rose bushes. She often had her head on his shoulder or they'd be gazing into each other's eyes like something out of a story book. Folk in the village were beginning to gossip about it."

"Even if that were true," Will countered, "She would not have gone off with him after what he did, after that betrayal."

"Ah but she may not have seen him stirring things up and he would have told her some story to put himself in the right. He's good at that and if she was sure your mother were safe in Devizes with the Wanleys, she may well have agreed to go with him."

Will would not accept the possibility. "No- no she would not have deserted Mother, I'm sure of it."

"If I had known he was only a day ahead of us, I would never have bothered to stop tonight," Richard was muttering. "We'll get after him now. If that is Lucy with him, it is even more urgent. They may have camped somewhere for the night on the old trackway. As it looks unlikely that we can get into Devizes yet, at least we can catch up with him and settle the score."

He was scrambling his things together and pushing them haphazardly into his saddlebags. Will stood there watching him, wondering just how this was going to end.

"Come on then," Richard hustled. "What are you waiting for? Hannah, make yourself useful, roll up those blankets."

Hannah did not move.

"You can't go now," she told Will. "You've had no rest. We bin talking instead of sleeping. Anyways it's too dark yet."

"Don't interfere." Richard was already mounted. His horse had picked up his agitation and was wheeling around, snorting. He wrenched hard on the reins to check it, pulling the bit into the soft flesh of the horse's mouth causing a trickle of blood to run over its teeth,

"Do as you are told my girl. You are getting above yourself- asking for a slapping."

"I'll not do as you tell me. You got no reins round my head Wanley. Go on then, slap me and I'll hit you back just as hard."

Richard spurred his horse towards her, but she stood her ground, hands defiantly planted on her hips.

"Nor can you frighten me with your bullying and roaring. I know you of old. What are you trying to do to Will? Sam Selfe may have lost his sight, but he'll never be as blind as you. Can't you see how Will's strength drains day by day? But you rant on looking neither to the left nor the right, wrapped in your own self. If you be determined to kill Crispin Collington, go away and do it, but don't you kill Will Barry as well."

"I told him not to come," Richard shouted back at her. "It was his own choice. Speak up for me Will. Tell her that at least."

Will put his arm around Hannah's shoulder and drew her back from the skittish horse.

"He's right. You know that well enough. I could have stayed behind, but I was sure I could manage the journey if you were with me and so I have. I could not sleep tonight anyway, not after hearing this news and it will be dawn soon, so we might as well go."

She tried to pull away from him to show her displeasure, but he held her by the shoulders.

"Look at me now and listen- dear Hannah, please listen." She turned to face him, the stubborn set of her mouth relaxing. "That's better. You have understood me so well this past month. I think you have always understood me, so go on trying just this short while longer. This thing must come to a conclusion one way or another. Until it does I shall never have any true rest because I shall not have any peace of mind. So the sooner it is concluded, the better. Please don't mutiny like this Hannah, even though you believe it is for my well-being. It is thanks to you that I have any strength left. Your support at this stage is vital."

He was so earnest and when his hands caressed her shoulders as they did then, she lost all power to resist him.

"Now if I saddle the horses, will you gather up the blankets?"

She nodded and began her work in silence. Richard was circling his horse with growing impatience, cursing under his breath, but Will had one more concern. He turned to Sam Selfe.

"Sam, what are you going to do? Do you wish to travel with us?"

Selfe shook his head. "No, my horse is a poor, broken-winded creature- only slow you down. Besides I've not got used to this living in perpetual murk as yet and would hold you back that way. My friends promised to see me back to Sandy Barrow and they'll be as good as their word. I be truly eager to see my family again, even more so now I know they are prepared for the man I am now. But take my hand Will. My blessing goes with you as always. Make sure you come back to the old village."

"I doubt if I would be much use there anymore."

"I will not contradict that- only you know the truth of it. Just come back and see what use you can be to us."

"Take care of yourself Sam."

Five minutes later Samuel Selfe was left in darkness not sure if he felt a sense of loss or reunion.

CHAPTER SEVEN

It was all laid out before them like models arranged on a board for a general to work out his strategy. From the heights on which they stood, they could see across to where Sir William Waller had made camp. Below them Devizes looked small and vulnerable. Only the dark hump of the castle with its turreted keep seemed at all truculent. But the little market town was not sleeping this July day. Through his perspective glass Richard Wanley could see that the streets were full of armed men. He might have laughed even in his grim frame of mind, if he had known that the staff of the General of Ordinance was scouting the houses for bed cords to soak in resin and convert into matches and stripping the roofs of lead to make musket balls.

As he moved the perspective glass over the area Richard could see that the outer approaches were barricaded and manned by troops, whilst the hedges on the outskirts were lined with musketeers, hoping to prevent the Parliamentary cavalry from breaking through into the centre of the town. They had been under heavy fire from Waller's gun batteries positioned around the hills. Great gaps had been torn in the hedges. Sparks had caught the half ripe corn, starting a blaze that destroyed most of the crop and an oak tree on the edge of the field had been shattered, so that it stood horribly disfigured, black and jagged. "What's he doing?" asked Hannah Moss, as she watched a horseman ride out of the encampment and urge his horse down towards the town. He was resplendently dressed in a green coat with a matching cockade in his hat. The polish on his leather boots was dazzling in the sunlight. Fluttering from the staff he held in his right hand was a white pennon and slung over his shoulder on a tasselled, golden cord, a trumpet.

William Waller had sent his regimental trumpeter to ask Ralph Hopton to surrender. He was to inform the Royalist commander that five waggons of ammunition sent by the king from Oxford, under the convoy of the Earl of Crawford, had been captured and there was no hope of immediate relief.

"Is that a flag of peace he's carrying?"

"Well, a flag of truce." It was Will Barry who answered. " The two words don't quite mean the same thing. He has probably been sent to offer Hopton terms of surrender."

"And will he surrender?"

"No he will not." Richard was emphatic. "It'd take more than a charge of gunpowder to break Sir Ralph's resolution. If he's fit enough to keep command in his own hands, he will do it, even from his bed. I've served with the man. I know what courage and determination he possesses."

"I don't doubt that Dick." Will held out his hand for the perspective glass which Richard was reluctant to relinquish and trained it on the trumpeter as he reached the bottom of the hill. "But what I cannot understand is why Waller does not go full out to storm the town while everything is still in his favour. With all the determination in the world, Hopton could not hold it for long with the resources at his command. On the other hand, if he has managed to send to Oxford for reinforcements, that could change the situation. When they arrive, the defenders could advance out of Devizes and Waller could be caught between the two forces. Besides that it looks as if we are in for some heavy rain."

He looked around at the sky. The sun was bright now, but banks of thunder clouds were building up. "That will lessen the effectiveness of Waller's artillery and make progress more difficult. If Hopton refuses those terms, Waller's best bet would be to attack as soon as possible."

"You sound as if you want him to." There was irritation in Richard's voice.

"You know better than that. I lost interest in who wins or loses a long time ago. I am just puzzled by Waller's tactics that's all."

"Well the man never was much of a soldier," Wanley retorted dismissively. Will could have taken issue with that remark, but he could not be bothered. He had let the perspective glass stray from Waller's emissary and was following the line of the hills around them, with their soft, curving contours. Sheep were scattered across them and the outline of a small farmhouse was just visible in the distance, tucked in the fold of the downs. He was tracing the sweep of a long, barrow-shaped ridge, when he saw something that made his pulse race.

Two figures were toiling up towards the crest of that ridge, leading laden pack-horses. At that distance, the image in the glass was not in clear focus, but Will could not mistake them. The big frame of the man, the angle of his body as he clambered up the hill, the lithe grace of the woman who walked beside him made Will sure of their identity.

"Richard," he said in a low voice. "Take a look over there."

Wanley took the glass. "Why, what's up then? I can't see- my God, it's Collington isn't it and it is Lucy after all- I can tell by your face. I would never have recognised them from here, but you are certain."

Will nodded. He felt cold and began to shiver.

"Well what are we waiting for? Let us get hold of the bastard."

Richard spurred his horse into a headlong dash in that direction. The ridge over which Crispin and Lucy were now disappearing was beyond Waller's sprawling camp and they were forced to skirt around the edge of it. They were half way around, when a young soldier with a musket stepped out in front of them. Richard screeched to a halt inches from him, cursing wildly, but the soldier did not flinch.

"You damned fool," Richard yelled. "Are you trying to get yourself into an early grave? Get out of my way."

More soldiers were now lining up and they looked in obstinate mood.

"Can I ask what your business may be?" demanded the first soldier, a clean-shaven, immaculately turned out youth with close-cropped hair.

"No you may not. This is a matter of life and death. You have no cause to hinder us."

"It might well be as you say- life or death for us," replied the young corporal coolly. "You could be spies sent up by Hopton."Wanley exploded into another stream of abuse. He was frantic now; his quarry had disappeared from view and every minute was precious.

"Do you think I have got the time to bother with a pack of roundhead hounds."

The line of the corporal's mouth hardened.

"You idiot Dick," Will hissed through his teeth. "Sometimes I wonder if you have an ounce of brain in your head."

The corporal told them they would have to go before Captain Blaine for his decision. Richard would have struck him in the face with his whip and made a break past them, but Will would have none of it.

"You will only make things worse. I do not fancy being shot in the back. Our best course is to be reasonable and talk our way out of this." He turned to the corporal." We will be pleased to see Captain Blaine and clear things up."

They were escorted into the camp. It was fifteen minutes before Blaine could be found. The sweat stood out on Richard's forehead in great drops. He had compressed his anger into a sullen silence, but his face was flushed with the effort. Will was agitated too, but he was aware that they needed to be calm in this situation, to appear relaxed and he smiled at Hannah when he saw the corporal returning with his officer.

Captain Andrew Blaine was an affable man, ready to listen to reason. Will outlined their problem. praying that Richard would have the sense to keep his mouth shut and talked about his association with the Parliamentary forces in Devon and Cornwall. Blaine had fought at the siege of Saltash and Will's intimate knowledge of the campaign was enough to convince the captain that he was genuine. He was willing to send a detachment of men after Crispin, an offer that was brusquely turned down by Richard and more courteously refused by Will.

They were on their way again, but they had lost almost an hour. Thunder was now bouncing between the hills and the heavy cloud had settled in low. A flash of lightning snaked down behind the ridge beyond them and the rain began to fall. The gigantic drops seemed to be falling slowly at first, then gained momentum until rain was cascading across their vision in blinding, flagellating sheets. It slowed their progress down to a snail's pace.

The storm lasted for half an hour, then the thunder was just a distant grumble once more and the rain ceased as suddenly as it had come. The soft turf yielded to the horses' hooves and they soon struck a trail. Richard let out a triumphant yelp. "The prints of two horses. It must be them. It must be."

Will said nothing. The storm had been yet another trial of his ebbing strength. Although the atmosphere was warm and heavy, he was shivering in his wet clothes, but he maintained a grim silence and kept pace with Richard. He was aware of Hannah's anxious eyes on him and struggled to look in control.

After the noisy melodrama of the storm, the silence was impressive. Waller's artillery had ceased firing, so a truce must have been arranged. Small sounds echoed up to them in the stillness. Right down in the valley a woodpecker had begun to attack the trunk of an elm tree and the knocking of his tiny beak drifted up to them like the ringing of a hammer.

There was another sound too, the crackle of burning wood. In front of them the land rolled away in a series of shallow depressions, then flattened out into a broad plain where sheep grazed. Beyond them, in a copse of stunted trees, rubbing his haunches against the bark was a shaggy, brown bull. They were not far now from the farm that Will had seen through the perspective glass. To the right of the trees was a sheep fold and a shelter for a shepherd. It was little more than a windbreak, four upright poles supporting a thatched roof. One side was blocked in with wattle and daub to form a wall, but the three remaining sides were open to the elements.

A fire was burning in the shelter and around it were Crispin and Lucy. Crispin was stripped to the waist, spreading out his shirt on a hurdle to dry in front of the fire. Lucy's clothes were already drying. She sat wrapped in a blanket and was combing through her wet hair. Crispin's body was tanned copper by the days of summer sun. He fetched another blanket from one of the packs he had unloaded from his horse's back and began to rub

Lucy's hair dry. They were laughing and looked at ease.

Richard unsheathed his sword with deliberate ceremony.

"Perhaps I haven't thanked God enough in the past, but I swear now Will, I am thanking him for bringing me to this moment."

"Dick," Will lay his hand on Richard's arm. He struggled to put what he felt into words and failed. There was a silence as he let his fingers rest on Wanley's sleeve and Richard demanded impatiently, "Well what is it?"

"I am afraid," Will replied.

"Afraid? Afraid of what? Good God not of Collington surely?"

"No, I am afraid of what is going to happen. Somebody is going to die today and I have seen enough death. Everything is being destroyed. We must try to start building up again, not tear down and we cannot wait until this war is over. We must start now somehow."

"I don't know what you are talking about." Richard's grip was so tight around the hilt of his sword that his knuckles were turning white. "I think you are feverish again. Somebody is going to die right enough. I can confirm that. Collington won't tread this earth much longer."

"Dick, let me talk to him, please. Don't just lunge in there like a madman. I must talk to him. I want to know why he did it, give him the chance to explain himself, grant him that much justice at least."

"Justice!" the word came out of Richard's mouth in a long gush of hot breath, "He is past everything but the justice of the sword. You know why he did it- because he is greedy vicious scum, like the all the rest of those vermin you have wasted your life on Will Barry. Why can you not accept the truth? Always struggling to be tolerant and understanding when there is nothing to understand. The fact is, a fact that every farm boy knows, that vermin must be destroyed. My God, if he cut your throat you'd waste your last breath asking why he did it. You must always talk and reason. You would never have gone to war if my father had not forced your hand."

"Do you think I am grateful for it? What good has it done me? Almost drove me insane- that is what it did for me your damn war. We are blindmen and fools fighting in a sack for a prize that none of us can name. Tell me what we are fighting for Richard. What is this precious prize that makes us count life so cheap? Don't tell me it is freedom- I shall never stop laughing."

His voice was unsteady, but his eyes were fixed unwaveringly on Richard's face. Wanley hesitated. For the first time he saw a connection between what he was about to do and what Will was saying, but the glimmer of light was soon extinguished by the darkness of his desire for revenge. He threw back his head, spurred his horse around and set off for the sheep fold, shouting a battle cry that seemed to fill the whole sky.

"Dick! " but Will knew his shout was useless.

"I ain't sure about the one who's going to die," murmured Hannah Moss. "If ever I saw a man set on dying it be Richard Wanley today."

Will did not reply, but she had voiced his own fear.

Crispin Collington was pouring out a pot of warmed ale when Richard's battle cry hit the air. He straightened up and took a puzzled look around him. Wanley was bearing down on him from the left like a thunderbolt, the flanks of his horse throwing off clouds of steam. Will urged on his mount in an effort to catch him, but everything happened so quickly.

Crispin, unaware as yet of the identity of his assailant and whose first thought was of bandits, ordered Lucy to take cover behind the wattle and daub wall. She leapt to her feet, clutching the blanket around her, but she saw the other riders and stopped in her tracks. The first rider was almost upon Crispin now, but Lucy's attention was caught by the young man who rode so urgently behind him. She hardly dare believe it was her brother. Since Will had left Sandy Barrow the previous August, they had received no word from him and although she continued to encourage her mother with optimistic words, Lucy had begun to fear the worst. She had tried to train herself not to expect or hope for a happy outcome and now she was even doubting the evidence of her own eyes, as she stood there as if turned to stone.

Crispin, yelling at her once more to run for cover, snatched up the musket that lay at his feet. He had no time to load it. The rider hurtling towards him was just a blur of speed with splashes of colour in it. He could feel the hot breath from the horse's nostrils and saw the winking of a sword blade in the beams of the weak sun struggling through the clouds. He hoiked the musket around and struck out with all his strength at the rider, jumping forward as he did so. Richard Wanley's sword missed his head by a whisker and the butt of the gun caught the rider a great crack across the ribs. The impact unseated Richard. He turned a neat somersault, ending up on his knees, with his sword still in his hand, whilst his frightened horse thundered on.

Will had reached the scene now. The first thing he saw was that familiar, affable smile spreading across Collington's face.

"Well, if it isn't Richard Wanley." There was no surprise or agitation on Crispin's face. The pale green eyes registered only amusement. "I had heard rumours of you posting after me like some avenging angel and knowing you I could well believe it, but I didn't think you'd have the wit to find me. I never did think much of your ability."

He was edging back as he spoke, to stand where he could see both Richard and the riders behind him. He was now parallel with his saddle on which his pistol rested, fully primed.

"Good morning Master Will," he said, as if he had just strolled in with the accounts to be checked. "I must admit that I didn't really expect you- thought you had probably come to a bad end down in the wilds of Cornwall." He nodded to Hannah, his fingers playing all the while along the pommel of his saddle. "You don't look as if your recent experiences have done you much good."

"I wish I could say the same for you Crispin, but you look remarkably well."

Crispin laughed. "You find that ironical? I always knew you'd run into trouble with your approach to life."

Will could see Richard's face contorting with hate, although he made no attempt to rush Collington. The fall had dazed him and he was gathering himself together before his onslaught. Will knew he must prevent it somehow. He slid from his horse, staggering slightly with the effort, feeling so inadequate for the task that faced him. His apparent physical weakness broke Lucy's frozen immobility. She had been standing like some marble goddess in a Grecian temple, the folds of the blanket falling around her with classical perfection, but now she became Will Barry's sister. She darted past Crispin and took her brother in her arms. She did not speak or weep, but Will could feel so many emotions in the body pressed so closely against him.

He ran his hand over her hair, praying for some kind of strength, so that he might gain control of the situation instead of being carried along helplessly in its wake. He had always relied on reason and understanding as weapons, but all the events of the past year screamed at him to doubt their efficacy now. He had spent months killing without reason. Nothing was coherent any more. Perhaps there was only a physical solution to this situation- Richard's solution.

"Where is my family you swine?" Wanley snarled like a hungry tiger. He was on his feet now, legs apart, all his muscles drawn tight, ready to spring.

"Down in Devizes I should imagine with Hopton, being shelled by Waller's artillery. Not the safe haven they were hoping for. They asked to be escorted back to Devizes. It was their choice. I had slipped away from the soldiers before then, kept my distance until Marshfield. I came to Lucy while the women were in that house and persuaded her to come away with me, so we could carry out our plan to get married. I assume you trailed those soldiers all the way into Somerset on your search. The irony of it is that your womenfolk were right under your noses in Marshfield. Lucy and I doubled back homeward. We stayed for two nights on the Melksham side of Bromham with an old friend of mine- one of Edward Baynton's gamekeepers- under your noses yet again."

That was enough for Richard, he launched himself forward, whirling his sword around his head. Will saw Crispin's hand close on the pistol. He tried to disentangle himself from Lucy and cried out, " Dick- the pistol!" but it was too late. The ball hit Richard in the middle of the forehead, a perfect circle, ringed with scarlet. His head rocked back, but he came on several feet more towards Crispin, his face rigid and blank, before he crashed forward face down and lay still.

Will Barry knelt down beside him. He was too weary for a display of emotion. That desolate gulf of emptiness had opened up before him again and he did not care if he fell in or not.

"He's dead alright," Crispin confirmed. "At that range I couldn't fail to kill him. He should have known I wouldn't be sitting about here without a loaded weapon. The odd thing is, it is a Wanley wheel- lock pistol. I took it from the Hall before I put a torch to the gun room. 'The times are out of joint' I believe Prince Hamlet said in one of those plays you encouraged me to read. Oh cursed spite that you were ever born to set it right eh Will?"

Barry did not reply; he was trying to take the sword from Richard's hand. Wanley's fingers held the hilt in an iron grip and he had to brise them apart. When he succeeded he lay the sword on the ground at Richard's side.

"It is a shame I had to do that," the bailiff continued. "But you must agree that it was necessary. He would never have been satisfied until one of us was dead and I'd rather it was him than me. I have always been a practical man, as you have often remarked yourself."

"Is that why you chose to betray my trust?"

"I suppose you could put it that way. I was a good bailiff to you, although if things had gone my way, I could have been a lawyer and an excellent one too, instead of a farm bailiff. I doubt if I would have come down from Cambridge with so much glory on my head as you did, but I should have done well enough. I would have been respected and recognised as your equal."

"Did I ever treat you as anything but an equal Crispin?"

Collington smiled, but it was a bitter smile.

"I think you truly did not intend to be condescending, but no one else considered me your equal. Ploughmen, cowherds and dairymaids all respected me for the trouble I could cause them, but not for what I was. I was only the bailiff after all, you were the master and they knew they could always get you to believe some hard luck story when they needed to and overturn my instructions. It didn't occur to them that without me you would have most likely let the farm fall into chaos, while you carried on your love affair with learning, truth and beauty. I despise the people of Sandy Barrow as much as he did."

He pointed at Richard's body, stiffening on the damp earth.

"You thought your idealism had won them over. Wanley knew better than that and he was hardly insightful. I showed them up for what they are, greedy and ignorant, ready to be blown along in any wind. Your influence wasn't as strong as mine in the end."

"Does that not prompt you to pity them?" Will asked.

"Pity them- why should I? Pity is an insult. Loathing is far more healthy. I knew I would never shake off the stigma of having been a bailiff, but I saw the opportunity to run rings around the Sandy Barrowites and grow richer in the bargain. Besides, I wanted Lucy and she wanted me. She loves me and she is carrying my child. What do you say to that Will Barry? When we get to my mother's house we are going to be married. It will all be legal."

Lucy had been listening to Crispin's flow of words with wide, astonished eyes. She was shocked by Richard's death, but reasoned that Crispin had no choice other than to defend himself. However, she found it hard to comprehend what she had just heard Crispin confess. It was so unlike the care and gentleness he had shown her all these months.

He stepped over to her now and pulled the blanket from her, revealing her nakedness, smoothing his hands beneath her breast and down across her belly. "Look- if you were me, would you not say this was worth having? Few men from any station could boast of a wife comparable to Lucy."

She reached out for the blanket, pleading, "Crispin please let me cover myself. Whatever are you saying? I don't understand you."

Will had taken Lucy's dress from the hurdle by the fire and now he held it out to her. She gazed at it in his hands in a bewildered way, but Hannah Moss stepped forward and began to help her put on the garment, persuasive, but firm. The look she gave Collington was full of disgust.

Lucy was eager to justify her actions to her brother. "I would never have left Mother if I did not believe she was safe and she was not alone. She was with Ellen Wanley and her daughters. I had agreed to marry Crispin back in May, but had not told Mother, even when I realised I was carrying his child. We both thought it would be easier if we slipped away and got married first, then come back to find Mother."

"It would not have been easy to persuade Olivia Barry that I was good enough to marry her daughter. So we thought we would present her with a fait accompli," Crispin added, "Besides, we did not know if you were still in the land of the living, so Lucy needed me."

Will ignored him, saying to Lucy, "Mother must have been frantic wondering what had happened to you."

"No, I left her a long, loving letter explaining everything, even about the child and promised to join her as soon as we could."

"I still find it hard to credit that you would abandon Mother in such desperate circumstances to go with a man who had orchestrated the destruction of our homes and the school- if you had seen all those books turning to ashes- all we had both worked for so diligently."

"But Crispin did not take part in the burning and looting," she protested. "He thought it was wise for all our sakes not to resist the soldiers, so he could stay with us to support and protect us. Tell him Crispin!"

Collington stood there smiling, but he did not reply. It was Hannah Moss who said, " Oh he did take part in it right enough Mistress Lucy. I was there- I know the truth of it. He stirred them up, encouraged the burning. Didn't you hear him say he put a torch to the gun room at Wanley Hall after he took that pistol?

He took plenty of stuff from the houses for himself. There are folk who can testify to it. Have you looked in his pack? I wager you'd find things in there you'd recognise."

"Crispin is this true?" Lucy's eyes appealed to him to deny it, but he saw no point now.

"Oh Lucy, Lucy you are as innocent as that brother of yours. We can talk about this, resolve it all later. Right now we must be on the move, get as far away from this fighting as we can before it spreads all over the downs."

Those luminous green eyes were on Lucy's face, willing her away. He always drew her like a hypnotist when he concentrated on her so intently. She looked at Will, who was shaking his head.

"So you still wish to go with him, after all he has done, after he put you, Mother and the Wanleys- damn it

Lucy, Caroline is still only a child- in such potential danger for his own ends."

"But I love him Will." She could find no other words to justify herself.

"That should be good enough for you," Crispin took Lucy's hand to draw her away, but her brother caught hold of her other arm.

"No, I refuse to let you go with him. I can't trust him anymore. You will never be happy with a man like him. It is my duty to protect you- father would have expected it and mother will not want you to marry the man who destroyed the house she loved so much- all the associations it had with father."

Crispin laughed aloud. "Just how do you intend to stop us from leaving?"

Will was attempting to draw his sword. He had little physical strength left and no desire for anymore killing. It was not even about revenge. If he was the one to die here on these Wiltshire downs, defending his sister with his father's sword, it would be a solution of a kind. He could see no sense in it, but maybe he had been wrong to search for a meaning in life. Once he thought he had found it, but now he doubted everything. Perhaps it was fitting that his life should end in an act of violence.

He managed to get the sword out of its scabbard, but he found that he could not grasp it fully. The sinews in his injured right hand had stiffened with the effort of controlling a horse's reins every day and the hilt was wet from the heavy downpour. He tried to transfer it to his left hand, but it slipped from his grasp and fell at his feet. "Look at you," Crispin mocked. "What chance would you stand in a fight with me? You can't even grip your sword and can hardly stay on your feet. One big shove would send you flying. I could beat you to a pulp."

Will had to acknowledge the truth of it. He was powerless to prevent Lucy's departure. He hung his head in despair. Both Lucy and Hannah came to his side, interposing themselves between him and Crispin, urging him to accept the situation and not to risk getting hurt.

"You don't need to protect Lucy," Crispin stated with triumphant contempt. " She has made up her mind to come with me. You are the one who needs protecting it seems- protected by women. They need not worry, I don't want to hurt you physically. Why should I? I have got what I want. Lucy is coming with me of her own free will. I am in control here. My child will be brought up as a Collington, not a Barry. You are a broken man William Barry. The body will heal I trust, but I have doubts about your mind. Your idealism wasn't strong enough to cope with the real world. I'll leave you now to contemplate the lessons I have taught you. Come on Lucy."

Lucy stroked Will's hair, whispering, "Don't fear for me. Find mother. It will cheer her so much to know you are safe. We will meet again soon."

She went to Crispin and Will sat down on the floor, exhausted, powerless. He had always believed that ideas were the strongest, most permanent things and that he was mentally strong, but aggression and brute strength had shattered his world. He was helpless and Crispin Collington radiated confidence and power. Hannah sat down beside him, but could find nothing to say that might help.

Crispin had turned his back on them and was gathering up bits and pieces from around the camp fire having directed Lucy to pack her things on to the horses.

"Are you ready?" he asked. When there was no reply, he looked across towards the horses. Lucy had not reached her destination, for planted firmly over the nearest bundle of belongings, turning it over curiously with his nose, was the massive brown bull that an hour before had been scratching his back in the copse. The noise and activity at the sheepfold had attracted his attention and he had edged closer to satisfy his curiosity. He seemed to have picked up the hostility and tension in the atmosphere. He was nervous and tetchy. When Lucy took another step towards him, he swung his head around and fixed her with a baleful look. She was afraid to move again, but a smile spread over Crispin's face. "Nosey old devil," he said. "I've never known a bull yet that could mind his own business."

He strolled up to the bull and cracked it resolutely on the haunches with the flat of his hand.

"Go on, get out of it. You don't scare me. You couldn't fool a rabbit."

He half turned as if he expected the bull to lumber away, but the animal spread his front legs in defiance, the great head jerking up and down.

"Stubborn eh? Now get your great bulk off those bundles."

This time he wrapped him sharply on the nose. He was not expecting what followed, for the bull swung his head and hooked at him with a yellow, curving horn. This creature would not acknowledge Crispin Collington as his better. Crispin reacted swiftly. Shouting at Lucy to get behind the wall, he launched himself on to the bull's back, where he clung on to the horns and tugged with all his strength. Snorting and pawing, the bull began to twist his head and buck like a wild horse to unseat the rider.

"You'll grow tired before I do old fellow," Crispin advised, wrenching the horns harder. "You might as well give in and calm down. You don't impress me in the least."

Despite Crispin's confidence, the bull did not lessen his efforts to break free. He intensified his careering and stamping until Collington's grip on his back was weakened, then with a mighty heave hurled him right over his head.

"Will, Will for the love of God," Lucy was shaking her brother by the shoulders. "You must get on your feet. He will be crushed. Help him."

She was frightened by his cataleptic state and in her desperation slapped him across the face. He looked at her with vague recognition, then his gaze moved beyond her. He wondered if it was an illusion, if his sanity was really disintegrating at last – Crispin Collington clinging beneath the head of a bull, clawing into the rolls of flesh on the animal's neck to keep hold, as the horns angled to gore him.

"He cannot hold on much longer," Lucy was pleading. "That bull is in a fury. It will tear him to bits."

He had never heard such desperation in his sister's voice before. Hannah was also urging him to get up. He struggled to think. At that moment the bull shook Crispin off. As he hit the ground he rolled himself into a ball and stretched his arms over his head to protect it. The bull drove his horns at his quarry, trying to lift him into the air, rolling him along the ground like a football. Will's brain began to function. He looked around for his horse. It was lurking at the back of the sheep fold, well out of the bull's range. Snatching up his sword in his left hand, Will stumbled across to the horse. He did not know how he managed to swing himself into the saddle, but as he did so he saw Crispin raised in the air on the horns, a bright gush of blood spurting from his side.

"Hannah, take Crispin's pistol, load it, then you and Lucy get behind the wall."

He forced his frightened mount towards the bull. Crispin had hit the floor with a crack and lay flat on his back, too dazed now to try to protect himself as his adversary, sure of victory, knelt on his chest, pinning him down. Will rode headlong at the animal, yelling at him and struck him a blow on the head with his sword. The bull bellowed in surprise and pain, heaving his bulk off Crispin and hooking at the horse. Will pulled his mount back, drawing the bull away. He was still in a murderous temper and Will knew he must go in for the kill to be safe. Jerking his horse sideways, he drove his sword down between the bull's shoulder blades. The bull shuddered to a halt and stood, legs planted wide apart, the steel quivering in his back.

Will rode back to the wall. "Give me the pistol Hannah."

She handed it to him and he returned to the bull, still standing there, jerking his head, snorting with frustration. He made no attempt to turn on Will when he aimed the pistol at his head. The shot passed straight through the brain and the impact as the animal sank to the floor made the ground tremble.

Will dismounted, joining Lucy and Hannah who were already beside Crispin. His body was badly broken. There was a red froth on his lips but he was talking calmly to Lucy. She would not look at the mangled flesh, but concentrated on the pale green eyes. As Will knelt down beside him, Crispin turned his head towards him.

"That was a gallant effort Will," he said, struggling for breath, "After I had taken so much pleasure in humiliating you. Not a bit logical, but just like you."

"I am not sure what we can do for you Crispin."

Will took off his jacket and placed it under Collington's head. Crispin was coughing and more blood tinged his mouth.

"Can't do anything for me. That bull has done all there is to be done for me. He was a mean one- strong though, first bull ever to get the better of me- admire him for it." Another bout of coughing brought up clots of blood. Lucy wiped them away from his chin with the sleeve of her dress. "Feel in my pocket- my pipe- never forgive that devil if it's broken."

Lucy slipped her hand into his pocket and drew out the white clay pipe intact.

"Take it Will," Crispin urged. "You should take up smoking-settle your nerves a bit after this." It was becoming harder for him to talk as more blood filled his throat. Lucy put her face close to him, whispering, "I love you Crispin, no matter what you did at Sandy Barrow. I will always regard you as my husband. I promise your child will bear the name of Collington."

"Sorry it didn't work out. Perhaps that brother of yours is right to trust in the essential goodness of humanity." He was digging his nails into the ground in an effort to resist the pain. "But my experience didn't school me that way. But I am damned if I thought I'd ever be beaten by a bull."

They sat with Crispin Collington on the wet turf until he died. It was only a matter of half an hour. Will left Lucy to grieve in private for a while as she held Crispin's hand in her lap, He walked over to Richard's body and sitting down beside him, he took his friend in his arms and began to rock him gently.

"Oh Dick, why did you throw your life away? Has your family not suffered enough already?"

Hannah Moss stood between two people she loved very much, not knowing how to help either of them in their grief- Lucy sitting so still, her feet tucked under her as she held Crispin's hand and Will rocking Richard Wanley as tenderly as he might rock a child to sleep. She did not feel much sorrow for either of the deceased, but her heart went out to both brother and sister. She decided to be practical and try to initiate some action. They had to move forward somehow.

"Will love, we can't sit about here much longer. What Collington said was right, the fighting might spread all over the downs. We need to try to get into Devizes and find your mother."

"I don't have any strength left."

"Yes you do. Look how you tackled that bull. You've got me to help you."

"I do not know what I would do without you Hannah Moss."

"Oh once you become yourself again you will be able to do without me well enough."

"I fear I have no knowledge of what my true self is anymore."

"Never mind that now. Let's comfort Mistress Lucy a moment or two, then get going."

There was determination in Hannah's voice. Will lay Richard's body down with care, kissing his forehead, heedless of the blood from the wound smearing across his own face. He brised himself to his feet and went to Lucy. He took her by the shoulders, raised her up and held her close in his arms.

"I knew he was bitter about his lost opportunities," she murmured. "But I had no idea it ran so deep- the cruel things he said to you, when to me he has only ever spoken well of you. I am sure once things were settled, he would have come to regret what he did and said."

Will did not believe Crispin would ever have come to regret it. His silence prompted Lucy to continue, "I am so sorry about Richard. My earliest memories are of you two playing together. I know how close were the ties that bound you, despite your differences. He may not have realised it fully and could never articulate it, but he loved you more than anyone else in the world. Ellen Wanley had received his letter with the news of Sir Roger's and Edward's deaths only a day before the soldiers came to Sandy Barrow and now she has lost Richard too. Oh Will, what are we going to do?"

Will did not want to dwell on the extent of Richard's love for him. The emotional numbness he had experienced earlier was now giving way to a stabbing grief. He and Richard Wanley had played, laughed, rode, argued, fought and drank together for as long as he could remember. It did not seem possible that they would never do so again. Selfish, infuriating and profane he may have been, but Will had always admired his zest for life and taken strength from it.

"I think what we must do," he replied to his sister's question, "Is listen to Hannah. She is the wise one here, talking common sense while we lose all perspective in our distress. She has just reminded me that we must endeavour to get into Devizes to find mother and take the news to Lady Wanley that she has another sorrow to bear."

Lucy looked over to where Hannah was stamping out the fire.

"But what about Crispin and Richard? We cannot leave them lying out here in the open."

Will had been considering that problem.

"I would like to take them into Devizes for a proper burial and let Ellen see her son for the last time, but if we are prevented from getting into the town, in this hot weather, the bodies will soon start to corrupt. That farm down there- the bull must belong to the farmer- a heavy loss for a small farmer. We must go to the farm, tell him what happened and pay him compensation for the bull. We can give him Richard's and Crispin's horses. They are worth a good sum between them. Then we can ask permission to bury the bodies in that stand of trees beside the farm on the understanding that once the fighting is over we can disinter them and rebury them elsewhere, if that is what Ellen and Crispin's mother wish. I promise we will get word to his mother."

He was relieved that his mind was working with some clarity now. After consulting with Hannah, this was agreed on as the best plan. They wrapped the bodies in large woollen blankets from Crispin's considerable store of belongings and bound them with twine. Hannah, packing up the rest of the bundle to transfer to her horse, found a leather satchel that was full of money- almost as much as the stash they had found in the strong box at the Barry farmhouse. This confirmed to her that Collington had been selling articles looted from the houses and she nodded to herself in satisfaction.

She gave the satchel to Will, who strapped it on to his saddle. He had brought money with him, but half of it had been spent during the weeks of searching, so this would prove a welcome addition.

Richard's horse had galloped some distance before it came to a halt, but now it had wandered back towards the other horses. The stallion's last duty for his master was to carry Richard's body down to the farm in the valley.

Will noticed as they approached the pens that held a dozen bony cows, an empty pen where the railings were broken down. This no doubt had once held the bull, who may have broken through it, perhaps disturbed by the artillery fire. This assumption proved to be correct, for the farmer had been higher up the downs with his sheep earlier in the morning and had no idea that his bull had escaped.

As the story unfolded he grew more and more dismayed, but was mollified by the offer of the two horses and twenty pounds. Will assured him that no charge of negligence would be brought against him for his bull killing Crispin and he was only too willing to allow the burials on his land. He fetched shovels and did most of the digging himself, then stood back respectfully while Will broke branches from a tree, tying them with twine to form two irregular shaped crosses to mark the graves.

Hannah suggested that Will should say a prayer. It did not seem right to her to leave those newly buried without a prayer. He looked doubtful.

"I'm not a worthy enough man to do so."

"Why do you need to be worthy?" Hannah retorted. "If we all waited till we were worthy, nothing would ever get done."

He could see that Lucy was also expecting him to say something over the graves. She took hold of his hand and Hannah did the same on his other side. Clearing his throat, Will said, " Lord, accept these troubled souls. Wipe away the rancour and bitterness created by flawed mortals like us with your redeeming love and receive them into your eternal kingdom. Amen."

As a final tribute Lucy scattered some leaves over the two mounds so they did not look so bare and lonely.

"See," Hannah murmured softly to Will. "Words come when they're needed."

He did not reply, but he smiled at her.

They led their horses away from the farm down towards the remains of the linear bank and ditch known as The Wansdyke. It was still impressive in places where it was not worn down, the bank twelve to fourteen feet high and the ditch eight feet deep. The section that faced them now was less forbidding, the ditch shallower and the bank about four feet only.

Will Barry had always been fascinated by this defensive earthwork. When he was about thirteen he had ridden the twelve miles along it to where it ended in the ancient forest behind the town of Marlborough. He had repeated the journey many times since then, taking pleasure in the striking views it afforded him. The landscape dotted with tumuli and barrows stirred in him a strong sense of oneness with the past. The presence of the ancestors seemed to be all around him. He was aware that the earthwork extended westwards into Somerset and intended to explore that section too, but had never gotten around to it. When he was at Cambridge he had frequent discussions with antiquarians about the origin and purpose of The Wansdyke. The name had become current many centuries past and was thought to derive from Woden's dyke, in honour of the chief Saxon god. Some scholars believed it was constructed by the Romans, others insisted it was built by the native population, faced after the Romans had left Britain, by a wave of Saxon invasions from the Thames Valley. The ditch was on the north side, suggesting invasion was expected from that direction. Will favoured the theory that it was the defensive system of the West Saxons against a neighbouring kingdom. Whichever was true, it was certainly ancient and had been used throughout the Middle Ages by drovers herding their animals to stock fairs along the route.

Before crossing the ditch and mounting the bank, Will decided to stop and try to plan how they were going to get into Devizes. Beyond them they could see in the distance the tower and spire of St Mary's Church in Bishops Cannings. He calculated that all the main routes into Devizes would be blocked by Parliamentary troops. They had been told by Captain Blaine in Waller's camp that there were two companies occupying Potterne.

Hannah then recalled that her brother Noah used to visit a friend in Bishops Cannings and often went into Devizes along byways through Horton and Coate, emerging on the eastern side of the castle. She had only been that way once herself. Noah's friend Alfred Appleyard had taken a fancy to Hannah. She was only twelve then, but well-developed for her age and Alfred was hopeful of a fumble or two in the hay at the very least. He persuaded Noah to bring his sister along one spring. He and Noah drank some powerful strength cider for an hour before Alfred made a grab for Hannah. He did not expect Noah to transform into a protective older brother, despite being very drunk. Alfred ended up in a horse trough and Noah took Hannah home along the tracks she had just described to Will Barry.

"Can you still remember the route?" Will asked.

"Pretty much," was her reply.

It seemed worth a try. Lucy was quiet and submissive, willing to agree to any suggestion. Her heart and mind were still back in that copse beside the farm. As they led the horses up over the bank, they heard a mewing cry.

Looking up, Will saw two buzzards, gliding on the currents of warm air, their wings fully extended, revealing the white feathers on the undersides. They circled around each other in a smooth sweep, majestic, elegant. Will envied their freedom and ease which contrasted so sharply with the despondency and weariness that weighed him down.

"If only we could take wing and fly into Devizes," he said. " But as we cannot, we must rely on you Hannah to lead us along the byways."

Taking a deep breath, he jumped down from the bank and headed for Bishops Cannings. They passed the break in the Wansdyke known locally as the Shore where the old track cut through the bank and then they skirted around Bishops Cannings. Although Hannah had walked this route only once, she recalled it accurately. Any memory that involved Noah was clear and vivid in her mind. He had been so drunk on that walk, she had been amazed how he managed to remain upright, let alone take her home. He did fall into a couple of ditches on the way and now as they led their horses around the edge of a barley field, Hannah stopped short for a moment at the sight of one of those ditches. She recognised it by a small cairn of stones laid beside it, as if perhaps some animal had been buried there. She could see Noah struggling out of it, covered in mud, but laughing loudly at his misfortune. The laugh echoed through her head and she realised just how much she missed hearing her brother laugh.

"Is anything wrong?" Will asked, wondering why she had stopped.

"No, just getting my bearings."

She did not feel like sharing her memories of Noah right then. They were precious, one of the few things that belonged only to her. In the present circumstances she judged that neither Will nor Lucy were in the frame of mind to appreciate her memories fully, so she kept them to herself. Their sorrow was more recent than hers.

They met few folk as they walked through Horton, stopping at a ford to let the horses drink, before mounting and riding on to Coate. But here, passing a small farm, they were accosted by two hostile lurchers, barking wildly and snapping at the horses' legs. Two men ran out of the farmyard carrying pitch forks. They shouted at the dogs to back off, but blocked the progress of the travellers in a threatening manner, demanding to know their business. Will appreciated that all the military activity must be making the villagers nervous and suspicious of strangers. Soldiers had a habit of commandeering supplies from villages and farms without offering any payment and there were plenty of unscrupulous locals ready to take advantage of the situation.

He dismounted and apologised if they were trespassing, but explained that they were trying to follow byways into Devizes in an attempt to avoid any soldiers and had no intention of damaging or stealing any property. The fact that two of these strangers were women who looked respectable and this young man was courteous and soft spoken, despite the smear of blood across his face, reassured the men that they meant no harm.

"We have to be careful see," the elder of the two men said in a gruff voice. "Lot of strange folk about these days- taking advantage of the fighting. We've lost five chickens and three ducks this week- stole by somebody- no doubt thinking the soldiers will be blamed- but they aint been round yer this fortnight, so twern't they."

Will sympathised and suggested if they judged it appropriate, that he pay a fee for crossing their property, which would compensate for the loss of their poultry.

The two men looked at each other for a moment as if trying to decide if this was something they were justified in accepting. Will held out some silver coins, which decided the matter. The older man took them, nodding as he did so.

"Seems very fair lad, very fair seeing as you are passing across the land I rent- can't afford to turn down money fairly offered. You pass on through. Keep to the edge of the fields. Don't let your horses trample on anything mind. Bout four mile I reckon if you loop round towards the castle. Probably guarded though near the town. Soldiers everywhere, some of them foreigners. You keep them girls away from the foreigners. They don't know how to behave with women."

Will thanked him for his advice and they rode on, the lurchers chasing behind them for half a mile before giving up and turning for home. He was relieved that his offer of payment had not backfired and insulted the farmer. What Reverend Seddon had said about how charity was perceived by labourers had made an impression on him. It kept coming back into his mind and made him less confident that generous gestures, no matter how kindly meant, might not be received as such.

As advised, they avoided the main route into Devizes from Coate and circled around towards the castle. The outline of the keep soon loomed into view. Although it was an early evening in summer, the skies were clouding over again and steady rain began to fall, impeding visibility. They were grateful not to have run into any Parliamentary troops by the time they came within range of the castle outworks.

Three tiers of embankment surrounded the keep and inner bailey with an additional wooden palisade around the lowest level. Leading their horses and using a hedge and dilapidated barn for cover, they moved closer to the palisade. Several soaked and discontented sentries were patrolling both inside and outside the fence, their conversation audible to the watchers behind the barn. Hannah looked puzzled.

"I can't understand a word they be saying," she whispered. "Perhaps tis they foreigners the farmer spoke of- the ones who don't respect women."

Will, straining hard to hear more clearly, recognised the lilting rhythm of the speech. "They are Welsh," he told her. "There are a number of companies from Wales amongst the King's troops. Charles Lloyd, the castle governor is a Welshman. I have never heard stories of them behaving licentiously. I think the farmer was referring to some of the Dutch and German mercenaries who were recruited by Prince Rupert. I have heard tales about them, but stories are often exaggerated as they are passed on."

Lucy had hardly spoken a word throughout their journey, but now she came close to her brother asking, "Do you think they understand English? If not, how are we to explain to them that we need to speak to someone in authority in the castle?"

"They must have bi-lingual officers. I'll approach them and say I must speak to Charles Lloyd. If Mother and the Wanleys were escorted into Devizes, they would have been formally handed over to him, so he must know where they are. Sir Roger dined with Lloyd on several occasions. I remember him visiting Wanley Hall just after he had been appointed governor- so he would take some responsibility for the welfare of Ellen and the girls."

He began unbuckling his sword belt. "I will go first and lay down my sword as a gesture of friendship. You follow behind, but keep well back."

He stepped from behind the barn, holding out his sword in front of him. He was challenged by the nearest sentry and two more came running to stand either side of him, as he lay the sword on the ground and held his hands palm outwards to indicate that his intentions were peaceful. He tried to explain that they had urgent business with Charles Lloyd and must speak to him. The sentries consulted together. One of them spoke some English and decided to alert his officer while his companions kept Will under close guard.

Their officer was an Englishman, a stocky Midlander to whom Will related a fuller version of their story. The man admitted that a group of women had been given refuge in the castle, housed in a building in the inner bailey. He refused to let them within the palisade however until he had spoken to Charles Lloyd. The sentries beckoned Lucy and Hannah to come closer and they all stood like a tableau as the rain came down harder, soaking them through to the skin.

One of the sentries began to stare intently at Lucy, which bothered Hannah until she realised that he was looking at the front of Lucy's dress. It was covered in the dark stains of Crispin's blood and the rain dripping from her clothes was turned to liquid pink.

More than ten minutes went by before the captain returned to inform them, "Governor Lloyd has instructed me to admit you. You're fortunate to have arrived during this temporary cease fire. If Waller's artillery was still operating you would have been unlikely to get this far and even if you had, we would not have been able to assist you. Follow me- and you can retrieve your sword Master Barry."

Will picked up his sword, but had trouble buckling on the belt with his stiff right hand. Hannah fastened it for him with discreet efficiency and they followed the captain farther around the outworks to a gateway cut in the bank. Here they were instructed to unload their saddle bags and the horses were led away by one of the sentries to be stabled in the outer bailey with the cavalry mounts.

Their guide, who had introduced himself as Captain David Ashley, continued to lead them towards the eastern end of the castle where another gateway and ramp gave them access to the inner bailey. Finally they reached the area behind the Market Place and were let into the main entrance to the keep, where the hall and a few outbuildings sat on the motte with a curtain wall around them. Ashley took them to largest of the outbuildings.

"Your women folk are quartered in here. Governor Lloyd is in conference with Sir Ralph Hopton and his officers at present but he will want to see you tomorrow. Right now you had best get dried off, change your clothes and rest. There is both food and drink in the house."

"Sir Ralph is recovering from his accident then?"

"He is improving rapidly thank God. His sight is returning and although his wounds still need attention, it is less painful for him to move around. His faculties were never affected and he is impatient because he is not healed enough yet to leave the castle. Now I must bid you good evening. I shall call for you in the morning."

He saluted and walked off without further ceremony leaving them standing outside the entrance to the oblong building. Will pushed open the door and they dragged their sodden saddle bags inside.

"He might at least have got one of them Welshmen to help carry the bags," Hannah grumbled, the palm of her hand red from the strap of the heavy bag. Will was not listening. It was a different voice that had captured his attention. The building was divided into five rooms, one large and four smaller ones, once the living quarters for orderlies who had been turned out in favour of the refugee women. The door to the largest room was ajar and Will could hear his mother in conversation with someone with a light toned voice, probably Caroline Wanley.

Pushing the door open wider, he saw his mother, Caroline, Maria and Ellen Wanley all sitting close to a blazing fire. Even on this summer evening the room was damp and chilly and the fire was clearly a great comfort to them. The small windows at each end of the room did not admit maximum light and as the shadows lengthened outside, it became very dingy in the corners. A six stemmed candelabra on a table near the women brightened the area where they sat.

"We are so relieved to see such a welcome fire," Will announced from the doorway.

All four women turned towards the door to look at the three figures dripping water onto the rush matting. Caroline gave a little scream of pleasure. Olivia Barry ran to her children and pressed both of them to her, unable to speak until Will said, "You will get very wet Mother."

"Oh my dears, what does that matter? To see you both safe is all that counts for me. William, when we did not hear from you all those months we began to fear the worst."

"I did write to you- several letters. They must have gone astray. I didn't receive any from you either."

"Richard's letter reached us," Ellen Wanley spoke with a gentle sadness as she contemplated the contents of that letter. "I wish it had been better news. He said he would try to get leave to visit us soon. He will wonder what has happened to us. Have you heard from him at all?"

Will disengaged himself from his mother's embrace and walked over to Ellen's chair.

"Lady Wanley, I fear I have more grave news. It is hard for me to say this but –"

He had no need to finish his sentence because Ellen knew the import of his news from his manner.

"Not Richard too- not both my boys." She covered her face with her hands. Caroline burst into tears and flinging herself down on the floor, put her head in her mother's lap. Ellen began to stroke her daughter's hair and asked Will, "Do you know when it happened?"

"Today. He was buried with respect, more than that, with love, for I helped to bury him myself. I know this is little comfort, but his grave is very near. When we can move freely again, I can take you there and should you want him to be reburied elsewhere, I will arrange it. I only wish I could do the same for Sir Roger and Edward."

Although her grief was evident, she thanked Will for his care with great dignity. She did not wish to hear about the circumstances of Richard's death at that point and asked no more questions. Olivia Barry's arm was still around her daughter's shoulder and she felt her shudder. Lucy was dreading the moment when the Wanleys learned how Richard died. She had forgiven Crispin, but she doubted if the Wanley family would do so. She even wondered about Will. The joy at seeing her children had put thoughts about Lucy's letter and Crispin Collington out of Olivia's head, but now his absence struck her.

"Where is Crispin? Is he not with you?" she murmured in a voice too low for the others to hear.

Lucy instinctively looked down at the front of her dress before replying, "No Mother, he is buried beside Richard."

Olivia was bewildered by this answer, but knew it was not the time for an interrogation and Lucy was grateful. Will was looking at Maria, who was standing by the fire. He had almost forgotten how beautiful she was – so dainty, yet perfectly proportioned, immaculately dressed even in these circumstances. She hardly seemed real. Those dark blue eyes, almost the colour of violets, showed little emotion over the news he had brought. He could not prevent himself from challenging her.

"No tears for your brother, Maria?"

"What use are tears?" she gave a slight shrug of her shoulders. "They will not bring anyone back. We were relying on Richard to rescue us from this dreadful, draughty place, take us somewhere safe and civilised. I might have known he would regard his wretched war more important than us."

"You do your brother a great injustice. He began searching for you the day after he got back to Sandy Barrow. He searched with relentless determination, complete devotion to his purpose. I know because I was with him all the while. He died because he was searching for you."

She turned her head away, gazing down into the fire to deflect his earnestness.

"I will explain everything later, but now Lucy, Hannah and I need to get out of these wet clothes." Will was beginning to feel dizzy. The outline of a cupboard in the far corner of the room kept changing its position and he could not hold it in focus. "Besides, I am exceeding weary and desperate for rest."

Maria gave an impatient sigh, which Hannah would not let pass.

"What be you sighing about?" she demanded. "Will was wounded down in Cornwall. When he come home he had a poison arm and a fever that near killed him. He was getting stronger when Richard came back, but not strong enough to go searching for you, but he did go out of love and duty. He has had no rest nor sleep for days. Tis nothing for you to sigh about."

"Will, are you going to let this creature talk to me like that?" Maria responded in an outraged tone.

"Hannah speaks as she feels. You will have to accustom yourself to that. I am sorry if I don't appear before you as a dashing rescuer, but she is right, I am exhausted. Perhaps you should be comforting your mother." He was swaying and Hannah put her arm around his back to support him. Olivia ushered the three of them into one of the side rooms where there was a bed and a smaller fireplace.

"This is where I have been sleeping. You must change your clothes in here. I will fetch some more blankets to dry you all. Then William you must lay down and sleep. I can rest in the big chair in the other room."

Hannah went out to fetch the saddle bags,

defiantly marching past Maria, almost knocking into her when she returned with the bags.

"That vulgar girl." Maria complained. "I won't share this house with her. She must be sent elsewhere."

"Oh Maria," her mother chided sadly. "Can you think of nobody but yourself?"

Hannah found that the garments in the saddle bags were damp, but not so wet as the ones they were wearing. She and Lucy laid out the drier clothes in front of the fire and stripped off their sodden dresses, wrapping themselves in blankets. Will had dropped into a chair, every ounce of energy drained away, incapable of undressing himself. His mother began the task of peeling off his drenched clothes. Hannah stood back, not sure if her help would be welcome. She was happy to butt heads with Maria, but feared offending Olivia Barry, aware of the strength of Will's affection for his mother and the possibility that she might object to their relationship.

Seeing Hannah hesitate Olivia suggested, "Perhaps you might care to wait outside the room for a while. We must remove all his clothes and dry him all over."

Hannah looked across to Lucy. Neither she nor Will had spoken to Lucy about what they had become to each other, but she had sensed it during their journey to Devizes that day- the way they spoke and touched each other, the fact that Hannah had dropped the prefix ' master' from his name- these things reminded her of Crispin. She recalled the day when he had first used her name without the respectful prefix and ached for his touch. It prompted her to support Hannah.

"Mother there is no need to consider either Hannah's or Will's modesty here. They keep no secrets from each other in that regard. Let her help you."

Lucy's meaning was plain enough. Olivia had wondered why Hannah was accompanying her children, but not yet knowing the details of their story, she assumed all would be revealed in due course. She knew Hannah Moss helped Lucy at the school and thought she might have offered herself as a servant to her daughter. It had not crossed her mind that she was Will's lover. Lucy's relationship with Crispin had been revelation enough; this was an even greater one. She stared at Hannah for several moments before asking, "Could you please pull off his boots for me?"

Will was barely conscious when they helped him into bed, covering him with several blankets. In minutes he had fallen into a deep sleep. Hannah volunteered to stay in the room and keep the fire burning up to make sure he was warm.

Ironically Will Barry, who had found sleep so elusive for months, was the only one in the building who slept soundly that night. Hannah was anxious to prevent him catching a chill, which could lead to another bout of fever and feared falling asleep in case the fire went out. Ellen and Caroline Wanley consoled each other over their loss as best they could, whilst Maria wriggled irritably on the bed she considered too hard and uncomfortable, convinced that no one understood the humiliation she suffered. Olivia and Lucy sat side by side in front of the fire in the largest room, holding hands, while a tearful

Lucy confessed the truth about how Richard and Crispin died. Olivia did not find it hard to sympathise with her daughter's grief, but she was bewildered by the paths both her children had taken and wondered how their father would have viewed it.

Maria Wanley paced around just outside the door to the room where Will Barry was sleeping, not sure whether to go straight in. She had arranged her hair in the style that he used to admire, with ringlets falling down over her shoulders. There were no mirrors in this Spartan accommodation, so she could only hope it was perfect. She wished she had a finer dress to wear. When they had been hustled out of Wanley Hall they were allowed to take nothing with them. The physician who had granted them hospitality in Marshfield was a widower and some of his wife's clothes were still folded in a camphor wood chest. He generously offered them to his guests if they felt in need of fresh garments. Maria took four dresses, two petticoats and a shawl, all the while complaining that they were fit only for merchants' wives. She was wearing one of the dresses that morning. It still smelled vaguely of camphor and she longed for some rose water to sprinkle over it. Maria had been thinking things over during her uncomfortable night. She had been contented enough to reject Will Barry at her father's behest when times seemed good and she envisaged a golden future. But her situation had changed and she did not enjoy the thought that he was now rejecting her. At least that was how it had seemed the previous evening. She found it hard to believe that he was no longer attracted to her. She convinced herself that his weariness had clouded his judgement and once he was rested and refreshed he would respond to her if she made an effort to charm him. He might still be her best chance of re-entering society at a level high enough to be noticed.

Deciding to enter the room, her hand was on the door knob when the door came open and Hannah Moss emerged.

"What do you want?" was her blunt query to Maria, who replied in her most imperious tone, "Is your master awake yet girl?"

"No he ain't. He's still sound asleep."

"But surely he must have been awakened by this hateful noise."

The noise to which she referred was the roar of Waller's artillery, which had begun to batter Devizes again from very early that morning. It was intended as a softening up exercise before the infantry made a determined assault on the town's outer defences. She put her hands over her ears as a cannon ball thumped into some masonry in the outer bailey below them.

"How can anybody sleep through this?"

"'Tis not an ordinary sleep he's in," Hannah retorted. "'Tis deeper than that, the sleep of someone worn right down. He'll wake in his own good time, but it may be hours yet."

"Well I will go and sit beside him anyway."

"Suit yourself."

"I most certainly shall." Maria swept past in what she considered a regal manner designed to impress Hannah with her superiority. She was not confident that it had produced the desired effect however when she heard the girl laughing as she walked away.

Will appeared to be sound asleep still. He was lying on his back, the blankets fallen away from his bare shoulders. Maria sat on the side of the bed, gazing at his face. He was pale and unshaven, his thick brown hair dishevelled, but she told herself this could soon be put right. He was handsome, cultured, respected and had done enough service in the war to be considered brave. Despite the loss of his farm, she was sure that the import business built up by his father was thriving. He was still a good prospect for a husband. He stirred, sighing. The sound of the guns had begun to penetrate his consciousness. He was in that state between sleeping and waking when it would be easy to slip back into a deeper sleep, but a stimulus might force him to wake. Maria smoothed his hair back and kissed his forehead, then his cheek, speaking his name close to his ear, softly at first. When he stirred again, she repeated his name much louder and was pleased when his eyes flickered open.

Another cannon ball thudded into the outer bailey defences, the noise reverberating in Will's head, as he wondered if he was dreaming about Braddock Down or Stratton. He was confused for a moment when he saw Maria smiling at him, but then he remembered where he was and knew the gunfire was real.

"Oh Will," she exclaimed, affecting concern. "I did not mean to wake you. I was worried about you because you looked so unwell last night. That girl said you might not wake for hours, so I thought I would just sit beside you for a while, but I couldn't resist kissing you."

He sat up, studying her face, her beguiling smile, that creamy skin with just a blush of pink on her cheeks. She reached out and placed the flat of her hands on both his shoulders, caressing them gently. The strength of the repulsion he experienced surprised him. She felt his muscles tense and drew back, standing up and walking over to the fire.

"You are so thin. I suppose your wound and the fever affected your appetite. You must have suffered. I also know what it is to suffer now. It was terrible being handled by those rough soldiers, given no respect, leered at, fearing any moment we might be raped."

She wished Will would say something, give some small sign of sympathy, but he remained silent, watching her with an expression in his eyes that she could not interpret.

"I wanted to speak to you so much because last night we did not understand each other. You were so weary, it was impossible for you to think straight. Of course I was shocked and upset by Richard's death, as I was by father's and Edward's.

Just because I do not weep and wail, that does not mean I do not feel. Caroline is so emotional, the slightest thing sets her weeping and I am sure that does not help mother. Someone needs to keep a clear head and plan for the future. You cannot imagine how pleased I am to see you, to know that you are safe."

Will started to get out of bed, but realising he was naked, managed to wrap a blanket around his lower half before standing up.

"Forgive me Maria if I am unconvinced by your expressions of concern for me when I look back to that day when I was forbade entry into Wanley Hall."

"But I was only obeying father," she protested. "You know how domineering he could be- quite frightening when he was angry. It was different for Richard. Father was always more lenient with him than with Edward and us girls. I couldn't go against his wishes."

Will shook his head. "No I cannot accept that excuse. Don't forget that I saw you at your bedroom window mocking me with such distain and taking pleasure in it. I had come to suspect by then that you were shallow, but I never thought you cruel until that day. It convinced me that you had no love for me and also that I had none for you, that is why I did not come back. During the months between that day and when I left Sandy Barrow, I heard that you entertained several potential suitors for your hand, one of whom apparently owned half of Berkshire. I am surprised you did not marry one of them. Did they not measure up to Sir Roger's standards?"

She was playing with her ringlets in a manner that was almost coquettish, relying on the effect of her beauty, which often worked with him in the past. She had no idea how much he had changed.

"I rejected them myself because they did not measure up to you. No don't laugh at me Will, I mean it. Can we not forget that unfortunate time and start over again? Mother intends to live in our town house in Warminster. It is a very fine house, not so big as Wanley Hall of course, but capacious and well placed right in the centre of the town. Now you have rested, you could hire a carriage and escort us there, away from this terrible, damp, noisy place."

"You mean today?" Will asked wryly.

"As soon as possible. I do not think I can stand another night on that lumpy, hard bed and I am sure I have been bitten by bugs."

"Maria, you live in a world of your own. We are under siege, surrounded by Parliamentary troops. There will be hand-to hand fighting in the streets. Do you truly imagine that we could hire a carriage and sweep unhindered out of town? I suppose you think Waller's men will doff their helmets and stand aside, impressed by your majestic bearing. There is no way we can leave Devizes at present."

"But you got in yesterday," she insisted, ignoring the scorn in his voice.

"Only by the skin of our teeth because a truce had been called. We would not have made it today."

Maria was not yet ready to give up. She moved close to him, her hands hovering around his waist where he had knotted the ends of the blanket. She seemed to be suggesting he might let her untie the knot.

"Please Will, you could try. You could ask Governor Lloyd. He is quite a gentleman, even though he comes from Wales. Your mother and Lucy could come as well of course. They could live with us for a while, so could you. But not that vulgar peasant girl, Lucy's servant, who doesn't know how to hold her tongue in the presence of her betters. She can be packed off back to wherever she came from. I cannot think what possessed Lucy to take her on as a servant. Is she related to that bailiff of yours that Lucy is so enamoured with? I was surprised to see Lucy with you. I thought she had run off to get married to him."

"Crispin Collington is dead and Lucy is heart-broken," Will replied, not intending to give her any further explanation. Clearly his mother had said nothing to the Wanleys about Lucy being with child. "And Hannah Moss is no one's servant. She and her parents live in Sandy Barrow. They saved my life, nursing me through fever and she loyally supported Richard and I as we searched for you. I should not be here today without Hannah's strength and ingenuity. She will not be packed off anywhere. She pleases herself where she goes."

The light dawned on Maria.

"Will Barry," she exclaimed in disgust. "You are not sleeping with her surely, not that village slut? I understand a man has needs, but I credited you with better taste than that. I could have believed it of Richard, but not you. I am disappointed."

He had a strong urge to push her out of the room and slam the door on her.

"I fear your disappointment has little effect on me. Hannah is not a slut and I have no intention of casting her off like some old garment."

"What is your intention then?" Maria goaded. "To marry her? Visitors would receive a fine welcome in your house then, with her quaint peasant burr and common ways. Oh it's too ridiculous to imagine."

"My intentions are no business of yours." He had not forced himself to formulate a plan for his future relationship with Hannah, but he was ready to defend her from insults.

"I declare you Barrys are determined to go back to the ways of your labouring forebears instead of continuing to improve your status. I thought when the bailiff wasn't with you that you had talked some sense into your sister and persuaded her to leave him, but it seems I was mistaken as you are behaving with even less sense. You need me to rescue you."

Will had reached the limit of his patience.

"Maria, I see no point in continuing this conversation. You and I have nothing in common except our childhood and are completely unsuited to each other. We would make one another very miserable. I am sorry that I procrastinated so long over our relationship when I knew years ago that we should never marry. I was lazy and too respectful of the ties between our families to be forthright and say so."

She tried to interrupt him, but he held up his hand to stop her.

"I apologise for my lack of courage in that respect because you could have been looking elsewhere for a husband much sooner. I am sure once you are established in Warminster society you will have a choice of eligible, rich, young men from good families that you can charm into marriage with your undeniable beauty. Some at least will survive this carnage around us."

She could see that there was no moving him and was offended by the harshness of his attitude.

"I do not recognise you anymore William Barry. You are a stranger," she said in an aggrieved tone. "Perhaps you are not sufficiently rested. We will speak again when you are in a kinder frame of mind."

Feeling she had taken the high ground she left the room with a swish of her skirts and Will breathed an audible sigh of relief.

As Maria glided down the passageway, pondering her next move in her assault on Will's affections, Caroline emerged from the room she shared with her mother. Her eyes were red-rimmed from weeping and lack of sleep.

"Aren't you going to ask after mother?" she demanded of Maria.

"Probably much worse with you weeping all over her most of the night," her sister snapped back.

Caroline ignored the barb. "I suppose you have been trying to get round Will."

"I don't know what you mean."

"Of course you do and had no luck by the sour look on your face."

"Will Barry is a very different man from the one we grew up with," Maria announced. "He has changed and not for the better."

"The world has changed," Caroline replied. "And we have all changed with it- except you Maria. I don't think you will ever change."

"So my little sister has become a philosopher now.

Please spare me your tedious reflections."

She pushed past Caroline with a haughty tilt of her head. Her younger sister was wondering just how far Maria had gone with Will Barry. She was embarrassed that she would even try. Caroline had always been fond of Will, who was like another brother to her. It was a comfort to know that he was with Richard when he died. She knocked on the door of his room, a hesitant knock.

"Will, it is Caroline. Can I come in?"

"Of course, but wait a moment while I finish dressing."

He pulled on a pair of breeches and a full-sleeved lawn shirt that felt pleasingly warm after a night in front of the fire, before he went to the door and welcomed Caroline into the room. She asked after his health, shy and formal at first, worried that Maria may have upset him, but she could not hold back her concern for long. It all came out in a rush.

"I am sorry if Maria troubled you. I knew she would try to get around you for her own ends. She thinks she can twist any man around her little finger by smiling, pouting and playing with her hair. She can't help it. She truly believes she is irresistible. She is determined to go back to how life was before all these bad things happened. But we can't can we? She is sure that you will marry her eventually. But you won't marry her will you? Please don't."

He smiled at her earnestness. "Don't worry, I have no intention of marrying her. I told her very plainly that we would make each other miserable."

"No," Caroline contradicted. "She would not be miserable, no matter who she married, if she could live in style and be the centre of attention in a social circle chosen by her. You would be miserable though and I would hate that, even though you would be a kind brother-in-law. Oh I do miss my brothers so."

"I can be your brother Caroline. We shall always be friends regardless of Maria's machinations, which will have no effect on me whatever."

He sat down on the side of the bed and invited the girl to join him by patting the blanket. She sat beside him and could not resist leaning against his shoulder. It was comforting.

"Are you afraid of the fighting?" he asked, aware of her need for reassurance.

"A little- when I hear the cannon balls make that whizzing noise and then the thump when they hit something, I want to duck down, even though I know they are nowhere near me."

He put his arm around her and she rested her head on his shoulder.

"What will happen? How will it end?"

"There are several ways for it to end. Waller's troops may break into the town and force Charles Lloyd to surrender the castle. Even if they do not break through the defences, Hopton's men cannot hold out much longer because supplies will run out and they will be obliged to surrender. On the other hand, if Royalist reinforcements arrive there could be a pitch battle that could go either way. Whatever happens, you will be safe enough and able to leave for Warminster in due course."

"When we were taken by the soldiers in May, although they were rough at first, once their officers took over we were treated kindly, with respect and allowed to ride in the baggage cart because our indoor shoes weren't fit for walking. One young officer picked me a bunch of wild flowers. I wasn't afraid of them. I am sure Maria told you a different story. She is forever complaining about suffering violence and foul language. It isn't at all true."

Will was struck by how much Caroline had matured since they last met. She was always a thoughtful, generous hearted child and now she was growing into a woman with insight and compassion. She snuggled up close to him, making the most of that feeling of security. "I am comforted to know that you were with Richard when he died," she said. "Did he suffer much pain?"

"No it was instant- one shot." He felt he must consult with Lucy before revealing the truth about Richard's death to his mother and the Wanley family. He had not guessed that Lucy had told Olivia already. "I was fortunate to have the time to hold him in my arms a while- to say goodbye and to bury him with dignity."

"I am so glad you did so – that you loved him. He didn't have many real friends, but he truly loved you."

"Dick was more affectionate than he would ever own to. He put himself in danger to arrange my escape when I was taken prisoner in Cornwall. I wish I could have saved him yesterday. He was devastated by the loss of your father and Edward. He was worried about you all, you were always in his thoughts."

Will remembered then that one of the saddle bags contained Richard's possessions, including those presents he had brought back for his family.

"The few possessions Dick brought with him when we set out to look for you are in our baggage," he told her. "I am sure your mother would wish to keep them. He bought presents for all three of you- a shell necklace for you because he recalled that you always wished for one."

"Oh fancy his remembering that," Caroline was genuinely surprised and tears started up in her eyes. "But is there nothing of his that you wish to keep?"

"I have his leather purse, the one Alfred Tanner made years ago. I will attach it to my belt and make good use of it."

There was a loud but disciplined knock on the outer front door, three sharp raps that made Caroline jump up nervously. A few minutes later Hannah put her head around the door. "That Captain Ashley has come to take you to see Charles Lloyd."

"Tell him I shall be there shortly."

Hannah disappeared and Will tucked his shirt into his breeches and began to put on his jacket. "There is something I must tell you Caroline. I almost forgot. A small thing perhaps but one that may cheer you. Reverend Seddon has your two little spaniels at his house."

He was pleased to see how her face brightened.

"Toby and Tessa- oh I was so worried about what had happened to them. I thought I would never see them again."

"He found them wandering about the village and took them home. I believe he has grown rather fond of them, but he is eager to reunite them with you. When we are free to do so, I will bring them to you. Something for you to look forward to at least."

"Can you bring Flash to see me as well? I love playing with him. He takes such pleasure in games."

Will shook his head. "No, Flash is another casualty of this war alas. Baron is still thriving, but Flash is buried in Cornwall beside many other good fellows who should never have gone to war."

"I am so sorry to hear it. He was such a young dog."

"Only just three. It was my fault. I should never have taken him with me. But I must go Caroline- mustn't keep Governor Lloyd waiting. Go and see Hannah. She will find Richard's things for you."

He kissed her cheek before heading for the front door where Captain Ashley was waiting. The artillery had stopped its onslaught but out in the open courtyard between the outbuildings and the hall the sounds of hand-to-hand fighting drifted up to them, steel on steel and musket fusillades. Ashley paused and pointed beyond the Market Place to the myriad of lanes and alleys that led to the outer defences. From their elevated position they could see Hopton's valiant Cornishmen manning the barricades, hard pressed by Waller's infantry with cavalry waiting in the rear.

"They are getting too damn close for my liking," Captain Ashley commented. "If their cavalry break through into the Market Place we are done for."

Will did not reply, but he was thinking that the best way to save lives on both sides was for the town to surrender. Ashley led him through the imposing doorway of the Hall. Although much neglected, it was clear that the Hall had once been a magnificent building, worthy of entertaining the kings and great men of ages past. Six bays stood either side of a central aisle under a high, oak-beamed ceiling. Several faded tapestries, which must have been spectacular when new and bright, still hung on the walls. The candle brackets with their gilded sconces also spoke of better days.

In one of the bays, gathered around a long table, was a group of officers pouring over maps spread out before them. The Captain told Will to wait where he stood, while he approached the group. He returned accompanied by a slender man in his early forties, wearing on the shoulder of his jacket a badge signifying his rank as Governor of Devizes Castle.

"Good morning Master Barry," Charles Lloyd had a light, pleasant voice with the lilting rhythm of his Welsh ancestry. "I am sorry that I could not greet you last night, but as you can appreciate we are somewhat occupied with the present situation."

"Governor Lloyd, I think I must surrender myself as your prisoner because only a few months since I was a lieutenant in the Parliamentary 5th Infantry, fighting under Lord Stamford in Devon and Cornwall."

Lloyd smiled. "Most honourable of you to own up to it, but I understand your only motive in coming here was to reunite with your mother and the Wanley family. That I can fully understand and consider you a guest, just as they are. When they were handed over to me, I intended to find them comfortable accommodation in the town, but events overtook me and it was safer for them to stay here. I knew Sir Roger Wanley well. He and Lady Ellen entertained me several times at Wanley Hall. Her story is a tragic one. Captain Ashley tells me you brought news that her eldest son Richard was killed also."

Will confirmed it and Lloyd shook his head sadly.

"Sir Ralph Hopton was sorry to hear that. He would like a quick word with you."

He motioned Will towards the table where the officers were gathered and he realised that they were grouped around a man sitting in a commodious armchair, bolstered up with pillows. He was swathed in bandages around his head, neck, forearms and hands. A sheepskin rug was wrapped around his legs. Despite being so incapacitated he was conversing animatedly with the men around him. Will felt a pulse of excitement. He had fought in several battles in opposition to this man, who was fast becoming a legend, but he had never seen him up close. Charles Lloyd moved in beside the bandaged commander and spoke quietly. Ralph Hopton peered in Will's direction, struggling to focus his impaired vision.

"So you are the young man who came looking for your mother and her companions. Come closer so I can see you properly. My eyes are still clouded."

Two of the officers stood aside to enable Will to

approach Hopton. He thought about Sam Selfe and how fortunate Sir Ralph was to be recovering his sight.

"I was saddened to hear of Richard Wanley's death." Hopton's voice was strong but croaky, as if his throat was still affected by the smoke and heat from the explosion. "He came up from Cornwall in June and I gave him permission to go home to comfort his mother regarding Sir Roger and young Edward. Charles has told me about the vandalism and arson at your village, what the women folk had to suffer. It must have been a shock to Richard when he arrived home. How did he die- run into some of Waller's scouts?"

"No Sir. We were searching for our families, unaware that they were here in Devizes. We came upon one of the men responsible for what happened at Sandy Barrow. Richard intended to administer justice with his sword, but the man was too quick for him- shot him in the head. I tried to prevent it, but failed. Richard was always hot tempered and impulsive."

"Your friendship was a strong one?"

"We grew up together."

Hopton was too firmly bandaged to nod or shake his head.

"Have you served in any of the recent fighting?"

"I was an officer in the 5th Infantry under the command of Sir James Chudleigh during Lord Stamford's campaign in the west Sir. I fought at Braddock down, Sourton and Stratton."

The man standing next to Will swore under his breath, but Hopton was unperturbed by this information.

"Hard fought engagements all of them," he conceded. "Particularly Stratton- could have gone either way. Do you wish you were out there now with Waller?"

"No Sir, I have had my fill of slaughter. All I wish is for this conflict to be over. I was propelled into fighting by a particular circumstance when I had no great zeal for either side and only advocated a sensible compromise."

"I fear we have gone too far for compromise now young man. Few of us relish the position we are in. William Waller and I have been friends for many years. We fought in the German wars together and were part of the force that rescued the King's sister Elizabeth from Prague after her husband was deposed. Sharing such dangers forms a strong bond. Before the battle at Lansdowne I wrote to him, suggesting we meet to try to talk through the situation, perhaps look for a compromise. He sent back a most affecting, sincere reply confirming his affection for me and how much he detested what he described as 'this war without an enemy.' But he felt obliged to be true to his conscience and the cause he believed in. Whatever the outcome of this current clash we shall remain friends."

"And meanwhile," Will could not prevent himself from saying, "Hundreds of men will die or be maimed, many of whom do not believe in any cause, but have been pressed into service."

Charles Lloyd touched his arm as if to suggest he had gone too far and it was time to withdraw, but Sir Ralph wished to pursue the conversation further.

"You are very disillusioned. What do you suggest we do to reduce the casualties?"

"Surrender the town Sir. If Waller does not break through today, he will tomorrow. You have no hope of holding out for more than a couple of days more."

Several of the officers protested angrily, accusing Will of Parliamentary sympathies still and asked Charles Lloyd to remove him from the room, but Hopton silenced them.

"No Lieutenant Barry is quite correct. If we do not receive reinforcements soon, we will be obliged to surrender, but he is not aware that we may be saved yet."

He turned to Will, irritated by the way the heavy bandaging hindered his movements. "Yesterday Prince Maurice and the Marquis of Hertford with what was left of our cavalry made a break for Oxford. If they made it safely, a relief force should be here the day after next at the very most."

"Then I understand why you continue to resist," Will said, ignoring the hostile looks directed at him by the officers. "I have experienced the courage and hardiness of your Cornish regiments. They will hold out to the limit of their endurance."

"True. I was born and raised in Somerset, but am proud to be considered an honorary Cornishman these days."

There was a bustle in the entrance and a breathless trooper ran across the room to report that the situation in one section of the outer defences was desperate. Some of Waller's infantry had broken through and were only two lanes away from the Market Place. Someone pointed out the location to Hopton on the map, but he had difficulty seeing it and cursed his incapacity. He ordered Charles Lloyd to dispatch the majority of the castle's garrison to reinforce the area in danger. Lloyd hurried to do so, taking Will Barry with him and instructing him to return to his lodging house. "Your task is to comfort and support those women," were his parting words as he left to marshal the garrison.

Will stood in the courtyard watching the garrison's Welsh troops run across the outer bailey and into the Market Place. The sounds of conflict grew louder now as Waller's infantry pushed closer. He wanted to shut it out – to ensconce himself in that small room where he had slept and cover his ears- at least part of him did. But there was a contradictory emotion stirring within him. He had been assigned to protect the women, but Crispin Collington's taunt was in his head, that he was the one being protected. That still applied. The women's presence protected him from further action. There were men in Waller's force no doubt, whom he had fought beside in Cornwall, still risking their lives while he was safe. He felt a confusing mixture of relief and guilt. None of his emotions were simple and straightforward anymore- always so complicated and ambivalent.

Looking across to their lodging house, he saw Hannah Moss standing in the doorway, anxiously waiting for him and he hurried towards her.

"What's happening?" she asked.

He ushered her inside and closed the door, explaining that the castle garrison had been sent out to reinforce the defenders.

"You can stay with us though? They won't lock you up for fighting for Parliament?"

He realised why she had been looking so anxious.

" No, no," he assured. "Charles Lloyd regards me as a guest, but some of Sir Ralph Hopton's officers are not too keen on my being party to their deliberations, so I had best keep out of the way."

"Did you see Hopton?"

"Yes, the poor fellow is wrapped up in bandages like an Egyptian mummy, but his mind is still keen and he was very courteous to me."

He was about to go farther into the house when Hannah put her hand on his arm.

"Before you go in you'd best know that Mistress Lucy told your mother the truth about Collington last night and that he shot Richard. Both of them went to Lady Wanley while you were out and told her too."

"Oh but they should have waited for me!" Will felt he had no control over anything.

"Well Mistress Lucy was so tormented by the thought of it, she could hold back no longer. They told Ellen Wanley on her own, so she could decide whether to tell her daughters or no."

"What was her reaction?"

"I don't know. Twas not my place to be there. I come outside to watch for you. You know full well that I don't grieve for either of those two who died. Tis Mistress Lucy's and your grief that touches me. I feel sorrow for Lady Wanley cos I know what it is for a mother to lose a son. My mother was never the same after Noah died. Twas as if half of her had gone with him and Ellen Wanley has lost two sons and her husband. I never liked Collington much, but Mistress Lucy's love for him was strong and I know how I'd feel if twas you."

Will found his mother and sister sitting in the small room where he had spent the night. They wished to give Ellen some time alone to consider what they had revealed and how best to proceed. Lucy was pale and distressed. It had been so painful to confess what Crispin had done at Sandy Barrow. She wanted to defend him, but could find no valid reason for doing so. Ellen was willing to accept that he had shot Richard in self- defence. She was well aware of her son's hot temper and could imagine him rushing Collington without regard for his own safety. She was shocked however to learn of the part Crispin had played in the destruction of Wanley Hall and the Barry farmhouse and could not understand why Lucy was willing to marry such a perfidious character once she had discovered the truth about him. In her opinion Richard had every right to bring him to justice and made that very clear to Lucy.

When Will said he wished they had waited for his support, his mother replied, "We decided that you have had so much stress to bear of late that we could spare you that confrontation at least William dear."

He could hear that voice in his head again- protected by women. He wanted to shout in frustration, but built up the fire instead and brooded on it.

Hannah, practical as ever, warmed some ale above the fire, fetched tankards from a cupboard in the corridor and served them all with drinks.

Later that morning Ellen Wanley knocked on the door and informed them that she had decided not to tell her daughters the full circumstances of Richard's death yet, but would wait until they were no longer all living together.

She did not wish to upset Caroline further and also wanted to avoid the inevitable sarcastic remarks from Maria regarding Lucy's choice of lover. Her manner towards Olivia was unchanged but Lucy fancied that Ellen was more formal, less warm towards her than before the revelation.

They all shared a frugal meal together in the main room, bread, cheese and apples from the larder. There was a mutton pie on the top shelf, but as they could not be sure how long it had been there, they were reluctant to chance it.

The afternoon was a long and uneasy one. Maria carped about the food and the boredom. In normal circumstances there would be tapestry and embroidery to work on or books to read, but here there was nothing to entertain them. Conversation might have filled the gap, but none of the others were inclined to talk. Eventually Maria stamped her foot, declaring, "Oh it's like a graveyard in here" – a tasteless remark considering the circumstances and she received some stony looks.

Oppressed by the atmosphere, Will went out into the courtyard several times during the afternoon, only to find he was equally oppressed by the noise of the continuing struggle for the town. No Parliamentary cavalry appeared in the Market Place, so the vulnerable section of the defences must have been shored up successfully by the soldiers from the garrison. A heavy rain storm and the late evening darkness put a halt to the hostilities for the day.

Will insisted that his mother and Lucy share the room where he had slept the previous night. He and Hannah made themselves comfortable in the chairs in the main room, but even though he was still weary, he did not sleep soundly this time. Vivid, troubling dreams caused him to wake numerous times during the night. Awaking with a start after one particularly confusing dream, he saw Hannah sitting on the floor by his chair. She put her head in his lap and he found that stroking her hair soothed his jangling nerves. She did not need to speak. She was aware that her presence alone had the power to calm him.

Just before retiring to bed, Maria had sashayed over to Will to wish him goodnight. She held out her hand as if she expected him to kiss it gallantly. He was too polite to refuse, but Hannah could see that he took no pleasure in it. The gesture was meaningless. Hannah made sure that Maria knew she would be keeping Will company and hoped she would assume they intended to be intimate. She knew he would never make love to her in that house, but putting the notion in Maria's head was good enough.

Early the next morning the artillery barrage began again, the overture to another assault on the defences. Will had not bothered to undress overnight and now he strolled outside just as the sun was coming up. He was in time to see a cannon ball strike the side of the Bear Tavern, splintering wood from the gate that led to the stable yard. He walked up towards the Hall and met Captain Ashley coming from the outer bailey. The soldier greeted him cordially enough, although his flat, midland intonation could never sound enthusiastic. He expressed his relief that the range of the guns fell short of the inner bailey and the keep.

"The outer bailey is getting a peppering though. Bits of masonry are flying off St. John's church. I've just been talking to the sexton. He's worried about the safety of his little cottage down in the churchyard. Nothing we can do about that. He will just have to rely on prayer."

Will asked how long Ashley thought the town could hold out.

"Another day, maybe two," was his honest reply. "Ammunition and supplies are running very low. Soon there won't be any lead or cord left in the town for us to requisition and folk don't take too kindly to having their roofs stripped and their guttering dismantled." He looked across to the Hall which was his intended destination. "I would not come too near the Hall if I were you. Some of Sir Ralph's adjutants are suspicious of your intentions."

"I gathered that yesterday, but it doesn't seem to bother you."

"If Governor Lloyd and Sir Ralph trust you, that's good enough for me. Besides you can't do much harm shut up in here."

"Well, I still have my sword, although I can't use my sword hand properly due to a light field gun at Stratton, so I doubt if I would attempt assassination. But there are candles in our lodgings with a tinder box. I could set light to the castle."

Ashley stared at him evenly. "I'd advise you not to jest in front of any of them," he jerked his thumb towards the Hall. "Not in the mood for humour at present."

Will thanked him for his advice, assuring him he was not that foolish and Ashley walked on to the Hall. The sound of fighting ceased in the afternoon and Will marvelled at the resilience of the defenders. He reckoned that Waller's troops must be tired too. They had pursued the retreating Royalists all the way from Bath, engaging in several fierce skirmishes on the way. Even though they had received reinforcements from Bristol after Lansdowne, they had suffered casualties during the last few days.

At the very moment Will was thinking this over, William Waller had ordered that his men be issued with supplies of beer, sack and brandy for the officers to keep up morale and inspire confidence. He was aware that Prince Maurice, the Marquis of Hertford and the Earl of Carnarvon had escaped the net with about three hundred cavalry and headed for Oxford. His scouts had killed or captured eighteen cavalrymen from Maurice's unit. It did not worry him that the rest had got away. Robert Devereux, the third Earl of Essex, Commander-in-Chief of the Parliamentary army was near Oxford with a large body of troops and Waller was confident he would prevent any reinforcements reaching Devizes. He disliked Essex personally. He believed that although his commander planned his campaigns in meticulous detail, he did not carry them through with enough energy and determination. Devereux was true to Parliament's cause, but he had no desire to be regarded as a traitor to the King. He did not wish Charles to be utterly defeated in battle, but to be brought to a position where he was ready to compromise. In Waller's eyes, this limited his effectiveness as a leader.

However, he trusted him with the ability to keep a small force of cavalry trapped in Oxford, while he gave his own troops a well-deserved respite.

The morning of the 13th July dawned clear and bright with no sign of rain. The usual artillery bombardment began, but ceased in less than half an hour. Puzzled by its sudden cessation, Will went out into the courtyard, followed by Hannah and Lucy. He expected to see Waller's infantry advancing in full array on the defences all around the town, but instead he had a view of them in the distance pulling back in good order towards Roundway Down.

As the three of them stood watching, they heard artillery fire, two blasts from a field gun, with a few minutes between them.

"That sounds like a signal of some kind," Will said. "Appears to have come from the direction of Bishops Cannings."

He ran across to the far side of the courtyard. Just below him, soldiers were manning the cannon mounted at the edge of the inner bailey. They fired two shots in answer, confirming Will's guess that it was a pre-arranged signal. "Reinforcements must have come from Oxford," he told Hannah who had joined him. "The gun fire was to let the castle know they had arrived. They probably came through the Shore and on to Rough Ridge Hill. Waller's scouts will have spotted them and reported back. That's why he has withdrawn the troops from Devizes."

"What is he going to do?" Hannah asked.

"Form up in position on Roundway Down I should imagine, ready to give battle."

"Will there be many casualties?" Lucy was beside them now, peering down at the mounted cannon below them. She did not wish to contemplate the consequences, even as she asked the question.

"In a hard fought contest there is bound to be," her brother replied, wishing he had a perspective glass in his hand. Despite his avowal that he had his fill of slaughter, he could not prevent his desire to know what formation Waller had drawn up.

"Oh please, let's go inside," Lucy begged. "I do not wish to hear it, all that waste of life. I am so thankful that you are not out there with them. Come inside."

She took hold of Will's arm and pulled him towards their lodging house.

As they went inside, up at the Hall Ralph Hopton was urging his subordinates to form the defenders into their regiments and march them up to Roundway to support the relief force. They were reluctant to commit however, preferring to wait until they were sure battle was joined in case the signal had been a trap laid by Waller to lure them out of Devizes. Confined as he was to his chair, Sir Ralph chafed with frustration because he could not get out there and control the response. If he had been his normal, active self they would not have dared to defy him. When one over-confident young major suggested Sir Ralph's state of health might be affecting his judgement, Hopton nearly exploded and the major beat a hasty retreat.

Will Barry had escorted Lucy and Hannah into the main room of the house to join the other women. He explained the situation to them and assured them that whatever the outcome, they had nothing to fear. He was too restless however to sit with them for long. He remembered Richard's perspective glass and wondered if Caroline had taken all his possessions to her mother. Hannah found him searching through the baggage in the hallway.

"What be you looking for?"

"Did Caroline come to you for Richard's things yesterday?"

"Yes, she took the gifts, his gloves, sword, some papers and money. She's wearing that necklace today. Didn't you notice?"

"What about the perspective glass?"

"She left that for you- thought you could make use of it. Tis here look."

She deftly extracted the instrument from inside a cooking pot and without another word Will dashed outside with it in his hand. Hannah wondered why he was so eager to watch the fighting when the memory of it troubled him so. She found his moods and reactions often difficult to interpret because they were not consistent. He appeared to contradict himself frequently. When he was her teacher and mentor at the Sandy Barrow school he was always so sure, so confident in his vision for the future. Now he seemed unsure of everything.

In the upper area of the courtyard Will trained the perspective glass on the broad expanse of Roundway Down. It was too far to see in great detail, but a company of cavalry was moving at great speed from the direction of Rough Ridge Hill, bearing down on another cavalry unit drawn up in order, six ranks deep. They remained stationary and the opposition coming down hill with velocity, smashed into them, pushing them back. What he had witnessed was Lord Wilmot, Lieutenant-General of the King's Horse, piledriving into Arthur Haselrigg's cuirassiers on the right flank of Waller's formation. The battle of Roundway had begun in earnest.

After that the melee was too confusing for Will to follow the progress of the conflict. What was clear however was that Hopton's officers had finally decided that the signal was not a trap and the relief force had arrived in truth. The Market Place became the rallying point for Hopton's troops. It was a whirl of trumpet calls, barked out orders, flying banners and running footsteps. It took some time to recall around two thousand five hundred men from their positions all around the outer defences and form them into companies ready to march.

Will once again felt admiration for those doughty Cornishmen, who had been hard pressed for days defending the town and must have been weary, yet were ready to toil up to Roundway Hill and attack. He watched them march away, drums beating out a steady rhythm.

On the down itself he could see smoke drifting as

artillery fired, hear muskets discharged and the cries of men and horses. He closed his eyes and saw himself riding towards that cannon at Stratton. He heard a strange sound, half grunt, half sigh, which at the time had been lost in the noise and confusion, but now he realised it was the last exhalation of breath from his favourite horse, Minstrel, as the case shot tore into its chest.

"Why do you stand out here listening when it distresses you so?"

Hannah Moss was standing beside him, hands on hips, a puzzled expression in her eyes. "Why torment yourself?"

"I don't know. Some contradictory spirit within me compels me to do so."

"Well I am compelling you now to come indoors."

She took hold of his hand and he allowed her to lead him back into the house.

The contest on the downs was fierce, but it lasted only a few hours. The first hint of the result came when cheering broke out in both the inner and outer baileys.

"Does that mean the King's side have won?" Hannah asked.

"Not necessarily. The result of a battle is often more like a draw than a win for either side, but both sides claim victory for the sake of morale," Will replied.

Through the narrow window at the far end of the room, they could see four men emerge from the keep, laughing jubilantly. They paused by the window and among them Will recognised the officer who had been most aggressive towards him when he was questioned by

Hopton. He was a tall, thin man with a pock-marked face and a mouth that turned down at the corners sardonically.

Stepping forward, he hammered on the window, shouting, "Hey, Parliament man, that traitorous dog Waller is on the run with his tail between his legs like the cowardly cur he is. Think yourself fortunate that true servants of his Majesty the King have been generous enough to offer you hospitality or you would have been on the run with him instead of hiding behind women's skirts."

Will felt the mocking keenly as it touched that sore nerve and he also had a desire to defend Sir William Waller.

"Pay them no mind." Hannah tossed her head at the jeering officers and turned her back on them in a deliberate gesture. They walked off, guffawing loudly.

"Waller is no coward," Will declared. "Nor is he a traitor. He wishes no harm to the person of the King and neither do I."

He addressed this remark to Ellen Wanley, wondering how she really felt about his break with her husband.

"I know that William," she replied. "There is no need to justify yourself. I may not be in tune with your political reasoning, but what matters most to me is your friendship and care for Richard. I shall always be grateful for that."

"Yes, yes that is taken for granted," Maria cut in. "But does this mean we can go to Warminster tomorrow? That is what is truly important."

Will turned away with a sigh.

He discovered what had transpired on Roundway Down the following morning. The outer bailey had become a dressing station for wounded men to be stitched up and bandaged. Accompanied by Lucy and Hannah, Will filled a bucket with fresh water and they walked amongst the wounded, offering much needed refreshment, scooping up the water with ladles. Lucy marvelled at her own composure presented with such ugly wounds and the pain and fear of the casualties. She was sure that prior to previous events, her courage would have failed, but nothing could be worse than the loss of Crispin. If she could bear that, she could bear anything.

Captain David Ashley was in charge of organising the dressing station. He assessed the severity of the wounds and directed towards the cases in most need, the two local physicians, who had been persuaded away from their usual patients by armed troopers. He thanked the water bearers for their assistance and from him Will learned how Sir William Waller, with superior numbers and a favourable position, lost the previous day's engagement.

By the time Waller had withdrawn his army away from Devizes and formed them in the traditional manner with infantry and two light guns in the centre and cavalry on the wings, Lord Wilmot's relief column was just over a mile away. Prince Maurice was disappointed that he could muster only eighteen hundred cavalry in Oxford, for the rest of the men were with his brother Rupert in the Midlands, trying to insure a safe passage through the country for Queen Henrietta Maria. Despite his exhausting ride from Devizes to Oxford on the night of the tenth of July, the twenty two year old Maurice, full of the enthusiasm and energy of youth, was determined to accompany Wilmot.

Sir Arthur Haselrigg had drawn up his formidable cuirassiers, known as the Lobsters because of their overlapping plates of armour, six ranks deep on the left flank of Waller's battle array. The approaching Royalist cavalry were divided into four units. Major Paul Smyth's unit had an initial skirmish with the Lobsters and was repulsed, but Wilmot's own unit followed up at speed. Their formation was only three ranks deep, outflanking Haselrigg on both sides. Instead of moving forward to meet them, Sir Arthur chose to remain stationary and was driven back by the momentum of Wilmot's charge. After a brief rally, the cuirassiers were routed.

On the other flank Waller advanced his own brigade of cavalry towards Sir John Byron, hesitating momentarily to allow the infantry in the centre to fire their artillery and muskets. But Byron's cavalry charged regardless of the fusillade. Taken off guard by such daring, Waller's troopers fired their pistols too early before the enemy was in range and caused little damage. Despite this, they managed to force the Royalists back initially, but after continued pressure they broke and fled westwards towards the Iron Age hill fortification, pursued by Byron. Here a number of men and horses fell to their deaths down a deep gulley.

Byron's men returned to the fray, capturing the Parliamentary artillery.

Meanwhile the infantry was pinned down by the Earl of Crawford's cavalry. Waller had placed a reserve cavalry unit behind the infantry, whose job was to back them up, but instead of supporting their hard-pressed comrades -in-arms, they fled the field. It seems that the infantry acquitted themselves with more courage, repulsing several cavalry charges. They began to withdraw in good order, still fighting, but caught between fire from their own captured guns and Hopton's Cornishmen, now arriving on the downs, they were in an impossible position. They threw down their arms and scattered.

"Overwhelming victory," Ashley said. "Parliament's forces crushed and dispersed- lost everything. We took thirty six standards, all the artillery, ammunition and baggage- more prisoners than we can adequately deal with. They are housed in two barns on the outskirts of the town, being fed on the livestock of the unfortunate fellow who owns the barns. In theory, he will be compensated, but I wouldn't bet on it. That's war for you."

Will could imagine that the man would receive a letter written in high-flown language, thanking him for loyally supporting His Majesty's cause and be left to deal with his financial loss as best he could.

"Was Sir William Waller captured?" he asked Ashley.

"No, he and Haselrigg managed to escape, probably in the company of that cavalry brigade that ran away. We think Haselrigg may have been wounded, despite his armour plate. I expect they will head for Bristol."

Will nodded, thinking that Waller's military reputation would be sullied after this defeat, particularly if he escaped in the company of a brigade whose actions were less than honourable. He was indignant on behalf of the abandoned infantry, who were always held in less regard than cavalry. Minor poets and balladeers would be composing verses about it for months.

"It appears that two tactical errors were key to the defeat," he suggested.

"That and the boldness of Wilmot, attacking straightaway," Ashley reminded him. He turned to Lucy and Hannah. " At least in a couple of days, when things have settled down, you ladies will be free to leave for somewhere more suitable. The Governor regrets that circumstances prevented him from paying you more attention. He will be visiting you today and will be more than willing I'm sure to give you an escort to see you safely to any new destination."

"Lady Ellen and her daughters will be very relieved," Will said. "They are eager to go to their house in Warminster."

"And will you be going with them?"

"No, I don't think so." Will looked at Lucy, knowing it was the last place she wished to go. "We must begin to search for a new home."

CHAPTER EIGHT

Heddington Rectory stood at the end of a lane, branching off from the main road through the village that led to Beckhampton and on towards London. Another lane meandered past the rectory into Heddington Wick. It was an imposing building, fifteenth century in origin with a part tiled, part thatched roof. A large hall, two rooms and a separate kitchen took up the ground floor. The three rooms on the first floor were topped by a loft. A gravel drive with lawns and shrubs on either side led up to the front entrance. At the back were vegetable plots and an apple orchard with a row of pear trees at the far end.

The Rogers family owned a considerable amount of land in the local area and other parts of Wiltshire. The glebe land alone, the acreage attached to the rectory, was ample- eight acres of enclosed pasture, ten acres in the open fields and five plots in the commonable meadows. Although this land was not owned by the rector personally, he enjoyed the benefits of it. Henry Rogers lived a life of comfort and ease. In 1639 he had bought the advowson for Heddington, the right to appoint a candidate to the benefice, to make sure that his son, another Henry, would inherit the post of rector. There was a Rogers in the rectory before him and he envisaged a whole dynasty of rectors called Rogers.

Olivia and Lucy Barry sat in the rectory's handsome parlour. They were dressed for outdoors, both wearing light capes and walking shoes. Will strolled in from the hall, a broad smile on his face. He was carrying a sketch pad and a stick of charcoal. Lucy demanded to know what was so amusing.

"The deer are in the rector's apple orchard again, feasting on the fallers and anything they can reach on the lower branches. He will be apoplectic if he spots them."

"Rather than laughing, perhaps you should have driven them away," his mother suggested.

"Why should I? There is a bumper crop this year, plenty for man and beast alike. Henry Rogers is too grudging, too possessive."

"That is hardly a fair judgement when we have been benefitting from his hospitality for a month," Olivia chided. "I wish you would be more cordial towards him."

"I am perfectly courteous and proper in conversation and behaviour, but that is as far as I will go. I have never liked the man. His treatment of Robert Seddon speaks volumes regarding his character. I keep out of his way as much as possible."

"True enough my dear. You are rarely in the house. You wander off early in the morning and often don't return until late evening- never in for meals."

Lucy could see that her brother was not in the mood to be worried over by their mother and intervened to change the subject.

"Have you been attempting to sketch?" she asked.

"Attempting is the right word. I can grip the charcoal much firmer now and manage outlines well enough, but detail defeats me."

He held out the pad to Lucy to reveal loosely drawn shapes of deer reaching up into the branches of an apple tree.

"But it is much finer than the drawings you did last week," she encouraged. "There is no reason why you should not regain all your skill in time."

It was the beginning of the second week in September. The Barry family had been lodging in Heddington Rectory for the whole of August, but Will was hoping to change that soon. Two days after the Battle of Roundway Down, Ellen, Maria and Caroline had been escorted to Warminster by six troopers from the garrison. Ellen Wanley had urged Olivia to join them, but mindful of Lucy and Will's reluctance to do so, she refused. She wished to stay close to Sandy Barrow in the hope that her son would choose to rebuild the Barry farmhouse and take up his inheritance again. He however had made up his mind that his mother and sister should move in with Uncle Harper in Bratton.

In the meanwhile he set about searching for accommodation in Devizes. It was hard to come by because soldiers were billeted all over the town, making demands on their hosts that many of them could ill afford. In the Market Place he happened to run into Henry Rogers and his wife Margaret. The couple's children were grown and no longer resident in the rectory. They had plenty of space and offered two rooms on the first floor to the Barrys on a temporary basis until a more permanent solution was available. Ellen was more than willing and Lucy had no objection. Will had to bite his tongue to prevent himself from asking why Reverend Seddon had never been offered such hospitality, but he conceded to his mother's wishes and they moved into the rectory while Harper West made the necessary changes to his house in Bratton to accommodate them.

Hannah went back to her parents, but she met Will every evening in the malthouse. Sometimes he went back to the rectory late at night, but at others not until the next morning. The rector locked the doors at eleven o'clock.

Will walked miles on his own trying to come to a decision about his future. He had lost all confidence in his ability to teach or to run an estate and knew he could not face starting over again in Sandy Barrow. The import business was a possible answer. He had never involved himself in the details of running the business,

leaving that to his factor, the efficient James Marsh. Sir Roger Wanley had certainly displayed sound judgement when he had employed Marsh on the Barry family's behalf after Ralph Barry's death. Will did not wish to step on the man's toes and try to take over, but perhaps he could travel to Portsmouth, Weymouth, Dover and London with the factor to observe how things worked. He sent him a letter asking if they could meet in Calne in the near future and was awaiting a reply.

He visited Robert Seddon and Sam Selfe every

week. Sam was already able to make a fair job of weaving a basket with some help from his daughter Ruth. He was disappointed by the result of the battle on the downs, but still optimistic that God's will would prevail and tried to lift his friend's spirits. But Will found that neither Sam's burning conviction, nor the Reverend Seddon's gentle faith were any solace to him. He was irritated by his own self-pity.

One day he walked out of Heddington, past the long barrow and on to Roundway Down. It was serenely quiet now, but crows and rooks circled above him. Those birds must have had quite a feast before all the corpses were cleared away. The turf was imprinted with the marks of horses' hooves and scorched brown in patches by artillery fire. He walked towards the ancient earthworks, built up in terraces by a long forgotten tribe of people centuries ago to protect them from their enemies. Scattered around were tattered bits of banner, broken weapons, a trumpet trampled into the earth with just the mouth-piece projecting upwards. He found himself staring down into the deep gulley, where a number of men and horses fell to their deaths. They were buried where they lay, man and horse together. Locals were already referring to it as Bloody Ditch and talking about ghostly sightings,

Will sat down on the edge of the gulley, gazing into its depths for some time. Then suddenly the souls of the dead called out to him. They seemed to rise up towards him and he was overwhelmed by grief. He struggled to shake it off, angry with himself for indulging his melancholy and hurried back to the rectory at a rapid pace.

He had bursts of activity where he tried to do something useful to keep his mind more positive. Ellen Wanley wished Richard's body to be disinterred and reburied in the graveyard of Warminster Parish Church, where she intended to place a

memorial to her husband and sons. Will fulfilled his promise to oversee the removal of the body from its resting place near the farm on the downs and escort it to Warminster.

A few days later he hired a pony and trap from John Dilke and drove Robert Seddon, with the spaniels Toby and Tessa bedded down in a large wicker basket, to the Wanley house. He was relieved to find that Maria was out visiting with her mother, but Caroline was at home reading, grateful to be free of Maria's company for a while. The dogs greeted her, jumping at her skirts, yapping and dancing. She hugged and kissed them, then much to his embarrassment, did the same to the curate, showering him with praises for looking after them so well.

"Well, I-I was no substitute for you, as we can see by their joy at meeting you again, but I did my best to keep them content and to tell you the truth, I have grown rather fond of their funny little ways," Robert confessed. Will knew that the curate would miss their company, despite the pleasure he took in reuniting them with Caroline. When she invited Robert to visit as often as he liked, he suggested that perhaps she should ask her mother first.

"But you will be my special visitor," she replied. "Come to see me, Toby and Tessa, not Mother."

Seddon smiled and promised to come when he could, but he would not have been surprised if he had heard Maria's comment on her sister's open invitation.

"Well, I hope he won't come too often," she said, pushing Toby away from the skirts of her silk dress. "Hardly an adornment to a parlour is he, with his shabby coat and broken nails? And I do hate the ridiculous way he bobs up and down."

It was meeting Francis Farrow again and hearing Ellen Wanley's plans for her husband's estate that brought Will to a decision. Half of the cottages in Sandy Barrow were empty now and Farrow had been instructed to sell the entire estate. Edward Baynton was eager to buy it to extend his already considerable land holdings in the area. He intended to demolish all the cottages and turn the land into pasture. Although Roger Wanley and Baynton had often been at odds, he was offering a good price and Ellen decided to accept it. Francis Farrow was given the task of negotiating compensation for the remaining tenants, who would be turned off the land. Baynton was inclined to be reasonable because he wanted the deal settled quickly.

He had been removed from his command as leader of the Parliamentary forces in Wiltshire in January and replaced by Sir Edward Hungerford. This prompted him to try to win favour with some of the King's chief supporters. Suspicious of his intentions, Parliament had him arrested and he had spent a month cooling his heels in the Tower. Now he was free again and eager to rebuild his reputation.

It made sense to Will Barry to offer Baynton the chance to buy his one hundred acres also. He knew he was never going to rebuild the farmhouse, even though his mother still clung to that hope. It was this hope that made her reluctant to agree to live permanently with Harper and Elizabeth West.

That morning Olivia and Lucy were waiting in the parlour of Heddington Rectory for Harper to pick them up in his carriage and take them to Bratton, to view the way he had rearranged his house to accommodate them. This was the right time for Will to reveal what he had decided. After he had shown Lucy his sketches, he sat down in front of his mother and took hold of both her hands.

"Mother, today you must tell Uncle Harper and Aunt Elizabeth that you intend to accept their offer to live with them on a permanent basis. They have gone to so much trouble to prepare the house for you both. You will enjoy living in Bratton again; you were born there and your family is well-known and respected. There will be plenty of social life. You will dine with the Whitakers at the Court House for instance and on Sundays you can worship in that quaint church tucked under the downs. It will be a good place for Lucy's child to grow up. It has always been a sorrow to Aunt Elizabeth that she and Uncle Harper had no children. She will take such pleasure in having a child in the house."

Lucy had insisted that her baby should bear the name Collington and she herself would be known as Mistress Collington, for she considered Crispin her husband. She did not want him painted out of his child's life by the West or Barry families. There would be plenty of widows in England by the time this war was over and no one would be asking to see marriage licences. She had written a long letter to Crispin's mother, explaining the circumstances of his death, as an accident while they were on their way to her house to get married and promising to visit her with the baby as soon as she was able. She assured her that she would have a proper share in the upbringing of her grandchild. Lucy also promised to attend

Crispin's grave regularly and erect a headstone with whatever words his mother felt appropriate. The letter was taken by carrier three weeks past to the small village of Axford, the other side of Marlborough, close to the River Kennet and Lucy was anxious for a reply.

"William," Olivia replied, " I may have been born in Bratton, but you were born in Sandy Barrow. Your father, grandfather and great-grandfather put so much hard work and love into the house and farm. We can afford to rebuild the house. You told me only the other day that some of the cows that had escaped the soldiers had joined with John Dilke's cattle. I am sure he would be willing to return them as a basis for a new herd- enough to start cheese-making again perhaps."

Will shook his head. "No Mother. I have already told him to keep them. I have no intention of rebuilding the house. It won't be the house Father knew- all the things associated with him have gone- destroyed in the fire. Anyway, who can guarantee that another band of soldiers won't come along and burn it down, perhaps Royalists this time."

After the courteous treatment she had received at the castle, Olivia found it hard to believe that supporters of the King would do such a thing.

"Oh both sides are capable of cruel things in a war," Will assured her. "You ask some of the folk in Devizes what they think about His Majesty's army billeted there."

"But now Parliament's army has been defeated and the King is in control, the war will end soon." Olivia had taken that for granted.

Her son laughed, but there was no humour in it.

"Granted the King is in the ascendant in the West Country now, particularly since Prince Rupert took Bristol, but that is not the case in other parts of the country. In fact there are still pockets of resistance here in Wiltshire. The Blakes up at Pinhills are openly pro-Parliament. When I was in Calne the other day I heard that Henry Blake was strengthening the defences of his manor house, creating a moat around it with the help of some soldiers from Gloucester. It is being turned into a miniature fortress. I can't see the garrison at Devizes putting up with that for very long, so there is bound to be trouble soon.

There are two High Sheriffs. Sir James Long for the King and Edmund Ludlow for Parliament. They are continually skirmishing and trying to ambush each other. Fortunes ebb and flow like the tides. This conflict has a long way to run yet. I have made up my mind to sell the land. Ellen Wanley has already agreed to sell their estate to Edward Baynton. Francis Farrow has been negotiating with the remaining tenants to move out."

"Move out? Why?"

"Because Baynton intends to demolish the cottages and turn it over to grazing. The only exception will be John Dilke's farm."

"But surely you would not sell to such a quarrelsome, unpleasant man as Edward Baynton. What will happen to our tenants?"

"We don't have any tenants now Mother. Daniel Bray was evicted by Crispin Collington as soon as my back was turned last year." He glanced at Lucy as he said this, but she did not return his gaze. "Mark Smart and his family moved to Chippenham where he has found work, two weeks ago. Jess Barnett is a single man with no ties and because he values his work, John Dilke has offered him accommodation on the farm. Knowing Jess, as long as he has oxen to care for, he would be willing to sleep in their stall. That just leaves Sam Selfe and fortunately his son Micah has been taken on as an apprentice by the candlemakers on the Green in Calne. I have spoken to Master Bridger and he has an unused workshop behind his premises. It overlooks the River Marden, is bigger than Sam's present cottage, in reasonable repair and he has agreed to allow the Selfe family to live there. Job Dilke and I will bring over one of his father's carts on Friday and we are going to help them move. So don't you see Mother, there will be no one living in Sandy Barrow anymore. It will cease to exist as a village."

Olivia was bewildered. She had not realised that the situation was that far advanced and wondered why her children had not made this clear to her before. Neither the rector nor his wife had mentioned any of this to her.

They seemed to have no interest in Sandy Barrow.

"What will happen to the Wanley tenants if their compensation is insufficient?" she asked.

"That is the concern of Francis Farrow, not my responsibility. He is a fair man. He will do his best for them. I did what I could for Sandy Barrow and it was thrown back in my face. I have no regrets leaving it."

His mother knew he struggled to come to terms with what had happened, but she did not expect to hear him say something so bitter.

"I do have responsibility for Hannah Moss and her parents though," he continued. "And I have a plan, although John Moss might take some persuading. He is a very stubborn man."

"Do you intend to continue your association with Hannah?"

Olivia Barry was grateful for all Hannah had done for her son, but she was hoping that the relationship would fade as Will moved on to other things. She was worried about his happiness.

"Do you want me to abandon her Mother? Hardly an honourable thing to do. I am willing to maintain the fiction that Lucy and Crispin were married because that is what she wants and it will make life easier for her, the child and for you too. I may even get used to hearing Lucy addressed as Mistress Collington in time."

Lucy did meet his gaze now. Nagging at the back of her mind was a worry that her brother would never be able to love Crispin Collington's child. She tried to dismiss the thought because she knew his nature was essentially a generous one, but every time he made a hostile reference to Crispin, she wondered just how much his recent experiences had changed him. The troubled expression in her eyes caused him to look away before continuing, "But I will not hide Hannah away as if she is something to be ashamed of. She deserves a decent home of her own and as she would never accept anything that did not include her parents, I must settle them too. That's why I want to talk to Uncle harper about those two cottages in Edington."

"You intend to live with her rather than us?"

"Yes."

"Are you going to marry her?"

"That depends on what Hannah wants. Would it bother you Mother if I did? Isn't she good enough for the Barrys?"

"I did not mean that my dear. I worry about your future happiness. If you tie yourself to Hannah, what will happen if you fall in love with a beautiful young woman from a good family?"

"Someone more suitable you mean. I honestly believe that I am incapable of feeling that passionate, all-consuming type of love that the poets write about. I love and respect Hannah. We understand each other and her company is a pleasure and a solace to me. That is good enough for now. I do not believe in making plans far into the future anymore."

She could see that her arguments were making no impression on him and wished that Lucy would support her, but her daughter sympathised with Hannah and kept silent.

"If you refuse to teach or farm, what are you going to do with yourself?" Olivia tried a different approach.

Will was pacing around the room, flexing his damaged hand, a picture of restlessness. He stopped to look out of the window and saw Henry Rogers urging on his gardener, who was waving a spade as he chased three deer out of the orchard, their white rumps disappearing behind the trees.

"The rector has put a stop to the deer's free meal I see," he murmured before answering his mother. "I have a fancy to become better acquainted with the import business. After all it is our only source of income now and we may be able to expand it- as long as the war does not cause the ports to be blockaded-then we could be in trouble. I have written to James Marsh asking if he will meet me to discuss it. I should receive a reply soon."

The sound of horses hooves and the rattle of a carriage caused them all to look towards the window to see Harper West rein in his sandy coloured cob, Bessie near the front entrance. Bessie began eating one of the ornamental shrubs in planters that flanked the rectory door and was shooed away from it by Henry Rogers as he came to greet his guest. As soon as he turned away, Bessie resumed her nibbling on the bush.

"I'll just have a word with Uncle Harper before you go." Will was half way out into the hall.

"Are you not coming with us?" Olivia queried.

"No Mother, I have errands to run."

His mother sighed. "You have not been much help to me this morning Lucy," she accused. "You have spoken hardly a word. Surely you think as I do that William will regret selling the land."

"No, I do not think he will regret it at all. You underestimate the effect on him of what has happened here. He is quite lost at present."

"But it affected us all. It pains me to see all that your dear father worked for abandoned. You and Ellen Wanley have been bereaved, have just as much sorrow to bear as William."

"Yes, but bereavement is something we all share at some time in our lives and at least I have the child to look forward to and cherish. Will feels that everything he believed in and achieved was pointless. His conscience is wracked because he killed his fellow men, something that would have been inconceivable to him but a short while ago. He feels guilty also about the men from Sandy Barrow who died. He does not know who he is and it may take him some time to find himself again, but to do so he must start afresh. I know father would have understood that."

They were walking through the front door together as they spoke, Olivia shaking her head in a regretful way. Lucy squeezed her hand, murmuring, " And don't worry about Hannah. Will needs her. She can comfort him far more than we can just now. She is quite remarkable in her own way. I value her friendship."

Outside Will was in conversation with his uncle, while the rector had placed himself between Bessie and the shrubs. Harper West had just agreed to rent two adjoining cottages in the village of Edington to his nephew with the option for him to buy them later if he wished. They shook hands on it.

Harper was in his early fifties, a man of middle height, trim and strong. He had an air of confidence and purpose, emphasised by his direct way of speaking. He did not believe in wasting words with needless courtesies. He patted Will on the back and climbed up on the driving seat, while Will helped his mother and Lucy into the carriage. Olivia leaned forward and kissed him on the cheek. He returned the kiss, saying softly, "Remember you are going to accept the offer of a permanent home."

As they drove away he was sorry that his mother was unhappy with his decision to sell the land, but she would have to accept it. He turned to Henry Rogers who was fussing over the damaged shrub.

"Old Bessie has taken a good chunk out of your ornamental bush I see," he commented, repressing a smile. "Quite spoiled the shape of it."

"Yes indeed," Rogers fretted. "Your uncle did not seem the least concerned. These shrubs were cultivated expressly for me at great expense. I do not know what my wife will say when she returns from visiting the Ernles. Master West could have made more effort to restrain his horse."

"Ah but my Uncle Harper has little experience of fancy shrubs Rector. To him one bush is much like another and natural fodder for horses."

Will strolled away to prevent his satisfaction becoming too obvious. He had decided to tackle John Moss about moving to Edington, now he had made a firm deal with Harper. The September air was soft and gentle, the sun, low in the sky, touching everything with a muted gold. Will stopped to look across to the downs and thought, "Is this what I have come to- taking such pleasure in another's discomfort just because he doesn't suit me?"

The varied greens of the downland, the rich brown of the freshly ploughed fields, the edge of each sillion shining as the sun caught it, held a timeless beauty. He could acknowledge it, but did not feel it warm his soul as once it did and experienced a bitter sense of loss. He glanced briefly towards the ruins of the farmhouse as he walked towards John Moss' cottage, blocking from his mind any image of how it used to look.

He could see John out in his small patch of garden, carrying a bucket over to the pig stye. Baron was standing in the doorway of the cottage and came ambling forward to meet Will. There was stiffness in his gait now and Will was reminded that the dog was almost ten. He had known lurchers and collies that lived to sixteen or more, but was not sure about the life span of so large a dog as Baron. He seemed well enough. His eyesight and hearing were good, as was his appetite, but he had slowed down noticeably. Will hugged him around the neck and they walked to the cottage together.

As he had expected, he found John Moss in combative mood regarding Edward Baynton. "Why should I move for the likes of him? I had little love for Wanley, but Baynton's even worse. Seduced his wife's maid when she was scarce fifteen year old, fathered children on her, stuffed her head with false promises, then cast her aside without a qualm. That's the sort of man he is. Let him try to shift me."

"But he will John. I don't admire him any more than you do, but I have come to see things in a more realistic light these days. You are in a difficult position. In theory you have rights if you built on waste land where there was no building before and this strip of land between the pasture and the common has never been cultivated, so qualifies as waste land. But your cottage was already there, empty and dilapidated I grant you, but was lived in by a tenant of the Wanleys once. Baynton goes to law so often, he has several slick lawyers in his pocket, who will argue that you are therefore a tenant and what is more, a tenant who has never paid any rent, so can be evicted without compensation. He won't hesitate to use violence if you resist and if you fight back, you will be the one that ends up in prison."

"But taint right. Thinks he can lord it over everybody just cos he lives in that monstrosity of a house in Bromham. Half of it was built with stone his father robbed from Devizes Castle. Bullies and thieves that family, like half the rich men in the kingdom."

John was seething with resentment, his grey eyes narrowed and his chin thrust out.

"I understand your frustration, but you cannot win this one."

"What am I to do then, take to the road and ask my wife and daughter to sleep in ditches?"

"Of course not. I have a proposition and don't

fly off the handle before I have fully explained. I am not dispensing charity. I owe you a debt, rather than the other way round."

John Moss made a huffing, uncomfortable sound in the back of his throat, but allowed Will to continue.

"There are a pair of conjoined cottages in the village of Edington, near Westbury. They stand near the old priory and belong to my uncle, Harper West. My mother and sister are going to live with him and his wife in Bratton. He has agreed to rent both these cottages to me, with the option to buy later. They are small, but in reasonable repair, as the previous tenants left only recently. There are about four acres of land attached to them, which has never been cultivated. Plenty of room for your pigs and a few chickens." He paused, expecting an interruption, but John was interested. "My plan is that Hannah and I should live in one cottage, you and Annie in the other. I will pay the rent, but ask you in exchange to create and maintain a vegetable garden, help me plant and tend an orchard and build up a broken down shed into a stable for my horse. I intend to become involved in my father's business, supplying teasels and dyes to the local mills, so I might be away for several days now and then. You could keep an eye on Hannah while I was away and she can continue to help you and her mother."

"You mean to marry our Hannah?" There was a doubtful note in his voice.

"If she will have me. Whether she does or not, I will never hide her away or pretend she is only my housekeeper."

"No one else will do for Hannah save you, but I tell you now, she has her own pride. She don't worry about being looked down on by others- I brought her up tough- but she would rather never see you again, than think that others laughed at and scorned you because of her. She told her mother that."

"I will bear that in mind and whatever happens I will always respect her wishes and treat her honourably, I swear it."

"Don't swear to anything. It will only make me madder than ever if things take a wrong turn. You truly mean to try to make a go of it over in Edington?"

"I do. There is nothing here for me now. Sandy Barrow is already like a ghost village and in a few months' time it will have vanished off the face of the earth."

John Moss nodded. "True enough. Bugger Edward Baynton, let him have the land. We'll try them cottages in Edington- see how it works out."

"Good." Will patted his shoulder, relieved that he had agreed without too much resistance. "But what about Annie, will it upset her to leave?"

"Go so far from Noah's grave you mean? She has never been near that plague pit on the Alders, not once in these six years. She don't like to think of him being in there with all those other plague victims. No she'll come along quiet enough as long as that girt dog comes too."

He glanced over to where Baron had his head in the empty pig-swill bucket in the hope of finding something worth eating.

"Look at him- never satisfied. Get your girt head

out of that bucket. Don't Annie spoil you enough, you lummox?"

Baron finished his inspection of the bucket before obeying John's instructions. It was clear that he was not the least concerned by the shouting. Will began to laugh.

"Oh I yell at him when he gets in my way, but he pays no heed," John admitted. "He's gentle enough and Annie dotes on him. Tis as if she is giving him all the love she was prevented from bestowing on our Noah. I don't mean it in a witchcraft kind of way, as if he's Noah's soul come back in the form of the dog mind. She acts a mite strange sometimes, but she's not that troubled in the head."

Will assured him he did not think that for one moment.

"If you want to tell Hannah about this, she is down by the stream doing the washing," John continued. "Tis good to have her back. Put Mary Lipton's nose out of joint though. Come round here whining to Annie about being out of work. I told her there was nothing I could do about it."

"Yes, she came to the rectory begging Mother to take her on again as a maid, but Mother has no need of a house maid now. She did write her a glowing testimony though to show any prospective employer. I think she was going to inquire at Whetham House."

"Ah, that would suit her better than trying to help me. Far too dainty for hard labour. More in her line, curtseying and cow-towing to the gentry."

Will was thinking that John had no idea how demanding the life of a house maid could be in a large country mansion or town house.

"I won't interrupt Hannah's work now," he said. "You can tell her about the cottages. I must get back to the rectory to see if the carrier has brought any letters. I will see Hannah this evening."

"The floor will break through in that damn malthouse one of these days," John Moss muttered to himself as Will walked away.

Baron was tempted to follow his master, but the aroma of meat stewing in the cooking pot inside the cottage proved the greater temptation and he wandered towards the savoury smell.

❈

Jacob Chard's carrier service, based in Calne, visited all the surrounding villages, his three employees delivering and collecting letters and parcels in their pony carts. One driver called at the rectory every day, usually around twelve o'clock.

When Will Barry returned to the rectory he found amongst a pile of letters for the rector on the hall table, the one he had been waiting for, with James Marsh's name and Portsmouth address on the back of the envelope.On his way in, Will had noticed the bush that had so attracted Bessie had been trimmed into a neat shape, but it was now half the size of its companion on the other side of the doorway. The lack of symmetry would aggravate Henry

Rogers every time he looked at it.

Will was sorry that there was no letter yet for Lucy from Crispin Collington's mother for he knew it was worrying her. When Crispin first took the job as bailiff on the Barry farm, he chose to lodge with a distant relative of his father in Chittoe. It was only a short walk from the farm and he was comfortable there. After he and Lucy travelled back from Marshfield, before lying low with the gamekeeper in Bromham, he had called at his lodging and collected his personal belongings. Lucy still had his saddle bag in her possession, stowed away under her bed at the rectory. The remaining objects looted from Wanley Hall she had returned to Ellen. The few things she recognised as belonging to her own family she gave to Olivia, but all the rest she wished to offer to Crispin's mother and was eager to take them to her. The only thing she intended to hold back was his pipe. She could not bear to part with that.

Will was thinking that perhaps he should offer to drive her over to Axford and find the house. However, he knew little about what was safe for expectant mothers, only that childbirth was beset with potential dangers even in the best of situations. Travelling that far on poor roads could prove harmful for both Lucy and the baby. He decided to consult with his mother before making such an offer.

As he went upstairs to his room on the first floor to read his letter, he considered that another reason for his reluctance to suggest the journey, lay in the knowledge that he would find it hard to face Crispin's mother and pretend that her son was the perfect, loyal bailiff. He knew that when Lucy wrote to her, she chose not to reveal Crispin's actions on that day of destruction at Sandy Barrow. She would expect her brother to conceal it as well and hand over the money from the saddle bag, as if it was wages due to Collington. He was uncertain that he could carry that off with conviction.

James Marsh's letter informed him that consignments of teasels were due to be delivered to several mills in and around Calne the following Wednesday and Marsh would be happy to meet him at the Town Mill in the early afternoon.

He was re-reading the letter when he heard a noise downstairs – a scream and a crash like a tray being dropped and crockery breaking. There was a strange scratching sound on the staircase and an enormous, shaggy wolfhound bounded into his room, knocking the door open wide. It sniffed at Will's boots and then began to inspect every corner of the room. The aggrieved tones of the rector could be heard below demanding that the dog must be kept outside. This was followed by a shrill whistle and the wolfhound disappeared as quickly as it had come. More footsteps on the stairs – this time human ones belonging to Henry Rogers and another man not familiar to Will Barry.

"A visitor for you William," Rogers announced. "Now you must both excuse me while I sort out that disturbance in the parlour. There are broken plates everywhere and that silly child Eliza is in floods of tears."

He withdrew, coughing irritably. The visitor

stood in the doorway, smiling and said, "I trust Achilles did not scare you. He is a very sociable dog, curious about everything and can't resist exploring. He terrified that poor lass downstairs. She dropped her tray. I believe she mistook him for a wolf. I will of course offer to compensate the rector for his broken crockery." He had a mellifluous, educated voice, his tone full of good humour.

"No indeed, he did not frighten me in the least," Will replied. "I could see he was amiable enough. I have a large dog of my own, as tall as your Wolfhound, but heavier, a shepherd dog from the Pyrennes."

"Ah yes, I saw some of those up in the mountains when I was in Switzerland, many, many years ago."

"Baron is not here," Will explained. "He is boarded out in Sandy Barrow. The rector does not allow dogs inside the house. The only ones that meet his approval are beagles and foxhounds and even they must be kept firmly in kennels."

"My dogs are allowed to roam everywhere. Perhaps I should remember that it is not always so with others," the stranger replied. "But forgive my lack of manners. I have not introduced myself. I am Thomas Mountfield."

Will jumped to his feet, an astonished expression on his face and held out his hand, which Sir Thomas shook warmly.

"Sir Thomas, I scarcely know what to say. It is an honour to meet you."

"Hardly that" was the wry response.

Will invited him to sit down and he eased himself into a chair. It was clear that he was an elderly man and

Will calculated that he must be past eighty years old, but he did not look it. His back was straight and although his face was weathered and lined, he was still handsome, with a wealth of white hair, traces of brown remaining in his beard and eyebrows. His sight appeared to be good, for his dark eyes were bright and piercing. He had a calm, dignified presence that impressed Will.

"In fact I owe you an apology," Sir Thomas said. "Some years ago you came looking for my house and were deflected from your purpose by the villagers."

Will confirmed that it was six years ago when he first planned to build the school in Sandy Barrow.

"I believe Amos Carter told you that no one in the village knew the way to my house. It was a deliberate untruth. Amos often works with my son felling timber. His grandfather worked for me for many years with his cousin Toby Aycliffe- both passed on now of course"

Will remembered the man's wary suspicion well.

"He took me to see the cottages that used to be the school, but said he was not sure if you were still alive. I searched for your house myself, but failed to find it."

"You must forgive Amos. He is always over protective of my privacy- I think for his grandfather's sake. There is no need. I do not ruffle the feathers of the authorities these days- too old to be considered a danger to orthodoxy. Anyway I am sure many people do believe that I was put under the turf long ago."

He laughed and Will was surprised to see that he had what appeared to be a full set of teeth in excellent condition.

"The last time I got involved in national politics was when I managed to extract a young friend from the mess he had become entangled in when he let his mistaken admiration for the Earl of Essex draw him into that hare-brained plot against Queen Elizabeth. That must be more than forty years ago, long before you were born."

"But I have read accounts of it Sir. He was executed, but his son, the present Earl, the commander of the Parliamentary army, has restored his family's reputation."

"Yes, the current Robert Devereux looks very much like his father, but thankfully has much more sense. But I did not come here to maunder on about the past like some old dotard. Amos told me at the time that you came in search of me. I liked the sound of your plans and truly meant to return the visit, but to my discredit I never made the effort. That was very remiss of me and when I heard the full story of what happened at Sandy Barrow a few months ago, I determined to do what I should have done six years ago- come to see if I can help in any way."

Sir Thomas was leaning back in his chair, toying with a gold hoop earring in his right ear. The habit of men wearing earrings had gone out of fashion and indeed Mountfield was like someone stepped out of the past, redolent of the Elizabethan age. His white shirt, beneath a close-fitting black jacket, was open at the neck and at his throat he wore a piece of rough, unfaceted turquoise strung on a strip of leather. Will could imagine what an impressive figure he would have been as a young man.

Even now his presence dominated the room. He radiated humour, wisdom and experience.

"May I ask Sir, how you came to hear about it?"

"Call me Tom please- I don't stand on ceremony. My son took a consignment of timber to the lumber yard in Chippenham and an employee there who recently worked for you, told him the whole doleful story. His name is Mark Smart I believe. He said Edward Baynton is buying up all the land previously owned by you and Roger Wanley."

Will affirmed all that Mark Smart had told Mountfield's son. Sir Thomas gave him a searching look, as if he was calculating Will's state of mind, then said quietly,

"Baynton is a hollow-minded, self-important fellow, who cares for no one but himself. His recent sojourn in the Tower will have taught him little. His chief hobby is dragging people into the law courts, so if you sell to him make sure there are no loopholes in the contract. But I can see from your expression that you are well aware of that and need no advice from me."

Will nodded. "But it makes sense to sell to him, as Lady Wanley has already agreed to sell him her husband's estate and I have no intention of staying here. My mother and sister will live with relations in Bratton."

"I can see you were deeply affected by the loss of your house and school, by your experience of war too perhaps. The original reason that fires you up to join a cause is often lost in the reality of it. I know that from experience."

Will had a sudden dart of panic that this man who had done so many courageous and exciting things, would consider his depression weak and morbid. During his long life he must have faced adversities just as severe as the Barry family and here he was offering to support a stranger.

"I find it wonderful to think that I am speaking to someone who saw Queen Elizabeth when she was still a young woman."

It was the first thing that came into his head to divert Sir Thomas' intent. A curl of amusement played around the corners of Mountfield's mouth. Will's tactics were so obvious.

"I was born the year of her accession, 1558. She was 25 then, so I never saw her as a very young woman. She was in her mid-thirties when I first set eyes on her- in her prime and every inch a ruler, the equal of any man. I met her in her middle-age when she knighted me after my return from the Low Countries war-camouflaged with face powder and the trappings of magnificence- but still a force to be reckoned with. I shall never forget those demanding eyes."

"You respect her memory?"

"I do indeed. It was a brave and lonely path she chose, not to marry because she believed it was best for her country. She was astute in her judgements and chose able councillors."

Will was considering what to say next, when Sir Thomas stood up and walked over to the fireplace, leaning against the mantle shelf and flexing his knee to relieve the stiffness.

"Forgive me if you considered it ill-mannered of me to mention your suffering. I am well aware that you are trying to head me off from further questions. But sometimes talking to a stranger comes easier than to loved ones. Now I will be blunt. What holds you back is that you are ashamed of your own self-pity. That is a feeling with which I am well acquainted."

Will looked up at him, his pain mirrored in his eyes and Thomas knew he had hit the mark.

"When I came back from the Low Countries, accompanying the body of my dearest friend, I was so sorry for myself- mired in grief. Our attempt to form a colony at Roanoke had failed, I believed the war in which several good friends died, was pointless, estranged from my father because he refused to accept Dawn

Light as my wife- I indulged my melancholy. I disowned the world and its false values and tried to hide myself in the depths of the forest, hoping to find some purpose in life by writing, studying and philosophising. Oh I convinced myself that I did this for my wife's sake, to provide a home for her where she was free to be herself, but it was just as much for my own sake. I felt truly empty, an utter failure. But the world would not leave me be. It broke in on me in various ways and forced me to realise I could still be of use to my fellow men. Starting the school was my first step in that direction."

"But they closed it down." Will could not see how this could encourage him.

"Yes, but they did not burn it down and destroy all my books. That must have been a terrible sight to endure.

My school was open for ten years, longer than I expected. I always knew that one day some parent would take exception to my efforts to widen my pupils' outlook on the world, open their eyes to the many wonderful things happening around us. And that was what happened- one man complained to the religious and civil authorities, who questioned the pupils and that was that."

"You must have been devastated though."

"Saddened, but not devastated. I still had my personal library at home, which I continued to extend. Some of the older pupils risked coming to my house in secret so we could continue our discussions. I was also fortunate enough to be invited by my former tutor at Oxford to join regular symposiums at the University. You see I never did the hard work at the school, the task of teaching reading, writing and arithmetic. I employed a teacher to do that. I just breezed in twice a week and told them exciting stories to fire their imaginations. The unfortunate Seb Braddon was the one who suffered most from the closure, not me. He went back to Salisbury and it was more than a year before he found work again and his wife left him. But I am wandering off the point again. I hear that you, with your sister's help, did both the routine hard work and the firing of imaginations. Some achievement."

"Much good it did me." Will got up and began pacing the room. "The school clearly meant little to them when they were so eager to join the soldiers in burning it down."

"But they were coerced somewhat. The average labourer is far too wise to argue with a company of fully armed, combat trained soldiers, especially when they are stirred up by religious fervour. Such things happen all too easily in the febrile atmosphere of war."

"I know that Sir, but I cannot feel it." There was a desperate note in Will's voice. "All I feel is that my whole life's work is destroyed and there is no point in anything."

"Of course it is still raw," Thomas replied patiently. "But what you see is the destruction of the outward manifestation of your work, the physical symbols of it- buildings and books, not the essential core of it. What about all those children over four years who have learned to read, write, multiply and divide because of you? Their skills remain, not destroyed in the flames and may stand them in good stead one day. Whether they grant you credit for it or not, you gave them those skills and would do well to remember it. Good teachers are hard to find."

"But it is not for me anymore. I intend to pursue a business set up by my father which I have much neglected in the past."

Will tried to sound definite and purposeful. Mountfield nodded.

"Perhaps a change will be beneficial. I hope you are not offended by my opinions."

"Not at all Sir Thomas. I am flattered you should consider me at all."

"Oh come now, the pontifications of an elderly man are seldom welcomed by the young. Why I really came to see you was to invite you to visit my house whenever you wished. You may enjoy browsing in my library since you have lost your own. My tastes are very eclectic. I am sure you would find something of interest. I will inform Amos Carter that you are not a government or clerical sneak and instruct him to guide you to my house should you choose to come."

"I should like that very much. Is your wife still alive or do you live alone?"

A smile of great pleasure spread across Mountfield's face as he contemplated his wife. "Dawn Light, my wife, is very much alive. She is five years younger than I. We will celebrate her eightieth birthday in November - but she is still as spirited, active and remarkable as she ever was. I doubt if I would still be in the land of the living without her determination to keep me healthy." He rubbed the knee he had been flexing. " She keeps these stiffening joints moving with her herbal lotions and magic fingers.

I think she believes she can keep us both alive for ever. Her energy is so fierce, she may well be able to perform that particular miracle."

"I have never met anyone from the Americas. I have never travelled beyond this island."

"You may be taken off guard at first. She is a force of nature. My daughter, my youngest child, Willow, still lives with us. She never wished to leave the forest and the animals. She has much of her mother's spirit in her and loves to be free of formal convention. There is one more resident, our housekeeper Sarah Bushy. She is a simple soul, devoted to the family. Her mother, Joan was our much loved housekeeper for many years. But we have room for two or three guests. You and your family are most welcome."

The warmth of his offer was very genuine. Will had taken a strong liking to this dignified man with his penetrating dark green eyes that so readily filled with humour or understanding. He had a great desire to see the house and Mountfield's Indian wife and was also eager to hear more of Sir Thomas' intriguing life story.

"You mentioned that you had a son."

"I have two. My eldest, Harry, lives in the family house in Salisbury, in the close near the cathedral. He and his wife have four children. When my brother-in-law Godfrey Roper died, Harry took over the running of his cloth factory on behalf of my little sister Cecily." He laughed. "Hard for me to believe she is seventy two. Godfrey was twice mayor of Salisbury. He was much older than her, but their marriage was very happy, if a short one- only eight years. He died of the sweating sickness. They had no children so Harry became a cloth merchant and seems to enjoy it well enough. My younger son Philip manages my timber business. I am still the titular head, but Philip does all the work now. I just fiddle about now and then giving my advice, which he tolerates in good spirit- in the main. He lives with his family in Lacock- five children- so plenty of grandchildren growing up around us- most of them already grown in fact. At our age few of our contemporaries remain, so my wife and I must look to the younger generation for our social pleasures and be grateful that we still have each other."

He gave Will a direct look.

"You are unmarried I believe. Is there no woman in your life?"

Will hesitated before replying, " There is someone dear to me, who has supported me with courage and affection over these last few months. I have known her since she was fourteen and she grows in my estimation every day."

"Is she here in the rectory?"

"No, we are intimate and could hardly be under the rector's roof in such circumstances. Besides she is not someone he would consider appropriate. She is too plain-spoken and although she is literate and eager for knowledge, her speech is not cultivated. She lives with her parents in a cottage in Sandy Barrow."

"Ah, so there is a disparity in degree. Do your family perceive this as a problem?"

"Not my family. My sister loves her as a friend and my mother, although she has reservations, will overcome them soon enough. But what passes for polite society may ridicule our relationship."

Sir Thomas sighed, fingering the turquoise pendant at his throat.

"Another situation very familiar to me. My wife, because of her distinctive appearance and complete disregard for the niceties of conventional behaviour and conversation was called all manner of names from whore to witch and everything in between. I used to bridle at it far too readily. It took me a long time to realise that she could deal with it and was more concerned with my hurt than her own. Our love was too profound for the relationship ever to be broken. Are you in love with this girl?"

"I am not sure. I love her and she calms my restlessness. When I am with her I find peace for a while and there is great satisfaction for both of us in our physical union."

Will felt at ease revealing personal thoughts and details to this man whom he had known for such a short time. It was a relief.

"Sounds like a good foundation to build on" Thomas said.

"Whether we marry or not- she is more undecided than I- we will live together and I will regard her as my wife."

"Is she comely?"

"She is not beautiful, not in the classical definition of beauty fashionable now. She has a fine, firm figure, wild, untameable curly hair and bright green eyes, like emerald or jade. She is full of health and life, but can be surprisingly gentle and perceptive. My friend, Reverend Seddon, the curate here at Heddington, described her once as bonny. Yes, comely and bonny are both good words to describe her."

He had never spoken about Hannah in this way before and was surprised by the pleasure it gave him to do so. Mountfield's reply was interrupted by another commotion downstairs. Eliza Atkins, the housemaid was calling in a shrill voice, "Keep it out Rector. Don't let the creature in. Shall I hit it with my brush?" accompanied by Henry Rogers' stentorian shout, "Shoo, shoo you tiresome creature. Away with you! You are not allowed in my house."

Sir Thomas raised his eyebrows. "It sounds as if Achilles has tired of waiting for me and decided to fetch me out. I had best leave, but I have a fancy to meet your bonny lover and your mountain shepherd dog on my way home. Would you ride with me and introduce me to them?"

"With pleasure," Will answered as they both hurried downstairs to find Rector Rogers in his open doorway trying to close the door on Achilles, who refused to budge. Eliza stood behind him clutching a rough-bristled broom.

"He will not hurt you child," Thomas assured, smiling at her kindly. "He thinks I have been in here too long and is anxious for my welfare. There is no need to wield that fearsome weapon at him."

He held her with his gaze and she seemed hypnotised as he gently took the broom out of her hand and rested it against the wall. Achilles celebrated his relief at seeing his master by lifting his leg and spraying a jet of urine all over the shrub attacked earlier by Harper West's horse. Seeing the look on Henry Rogers' face, Thomas said with a mischievous smile, "Not the kind of christening you would welcome Rector. But you must understand it is nigh on impossible to direct where a dog chooses to piss. It may encourage the plant to flourish. It seems stunted compared with its fellow on the other side."

Rogers could scarcely hold back his indignation and Will sprinting down to the rectory stables to collect his horse, was laughing aloud before he was out of earshot. He walked his horse back to join his visitor, wondering if

Sir Thomas might need assistance getting into the saddle, but although he mounted with care, it posed him no difficulty. Riding had always come as easily as breathing to Thomas and even at eighty five he was still master of his horse.

They rode across to Sandy Barrow, in the mild September air, Achilles keeping pace with the horses and reminding Will yet again of the absence of Flash. The Moss family were astonished when they learned the identity of Will's companion.

Hannah blurted out, much to the amusement of Sir Thomas, "You'm real then, not a legend made up by folk. However old must you be?"

Baron and Achilles sniffed around each other warily at first, but both decided that the other posed no threat and ignored each other from then on. Thomas made a great fuss of Baron, putting him immediately in Annie's good books. When John Moss said to his wife, pointing to the wolfhound, "There look, that's how a dog should be, lean and fit, not heavy like that great lump of a Baron, because of your overfeeding," Thomas defended the mountain dog.

"Not entirely fair Master Moss. They have very different physiques. Wolfhounds are by nature bony, whereas Baron here was bred more heavy set and his thick coat makes him appear even heavier. I am sure your wife does not overfeed him. I have had wolfhounds as my companions since my boyhood. They have enormous appetites, yet remain lean."

This put the seal on Annie Moss' approval and

marked out Sir Thomas as a wise and courteous man in her eyes. After he had taken his leave and stepped outside the house, she murmured to Baron, "Now that's a true gentleman my sweet, a true, handsome, old gentleman. Rare these days."

Before he rode away, Mountfield reminded Will that he was welcome at his house any time and urged him to bring Hannah. "I am sure she will get on famously with my wife."

During the course of that brief visit Hannah had told him all about Will's damaged hand. She showed him the sketch Will had made of her in the schoolroom, almost two years ago and expressed her hope that one day he would be able to draw that well again. "'Twas like magic, the skill he had in his fingers, captured the very life of things."

Now Thomas leaned out of the saddle and told her, "By the way, I am sure my wife has a lotion that will help William's hand to grow more supple. She will make one up for you if you visit. I hope to see you both soon."

As they stood and watched him ride into the distance, Achilles loping alongside him, Will felt he had gained a friend and sensed a tiny spark of optimism for the first time in what seemed an age.

❈❈❈

It was dark in the malthouse now except for the patches of light cast by the lanterns standing on two upturned buckets. Hannah lay with her head resting against Will

Barry's chest as she watched the moths. Even the more common brown variety were intricately patterned in different shades of brown with cream fringes on their wing tips. Earlier a huge moth, olive green banded with pink and a wingspan almost the size of Hannah's hand, was beating against the lantern glass with enough force to cripple itself. Will caught it and put it outside through the malthouse hatch, pulling the wooden shutters across the opening.

A number of moths remained trapped inside, not just brown ones. Some were a diaphanous, pale yellow, light and insubstantial – ghost moths. Another had bold black and white markings with a central splash of red. They all flittered around the lanterns, magnetised towards the candle flames inside the protective glass.

"It was kind of that Thomas Mountfield to visit us," Hannah mused. "I liked him. He weren't full of himself like Sir Roger Wanley used to be, nor go around with his nose in the air like some others around here I might mention. Mother were fair taken with him and even father were pleased when he admired the pigs and you know how grudging father can be about well-to-do folks."

"Yes I found him to be very sincere and courteous, but with a ready wit. He soon laid bare Rector Rogers' pretensions."

"I find it hard to believe he's eighty five though, being so spry. The only other person I know that old is Charity Bunce down in Bromham. Tis said she's nigh on ninety, but she is all bent and twisted- can hardly walk and don't have a tooth left in her head. But then she has borne ten children and had a hard life, not had any comforts or such nourishing food as Sir Thomas. Do you think he minded me asking him how he had kept all his teeth?"

Will laughed. "No he did not mind in the least. He is accustomed to directness and appreciates it. He was charmed by your openness."

"Fancy cleaning your teeth every day with a special paste mixed up from herbs and stuff though!" she continued. "I never heard of such a thing before. He also said to stay away from sugar, but that's no problem. We've never been able to afford any sugar in our house- too dear for the likes of us. Perhaps if we do visit his house his wife might show me how to make that paste. I'd like to have clean teeth that didn't rot too soon- the same for you. Father says there were tales that his wife were a witch. Perhaps magic helps to keep them young."

"Superstitious nonsense." Will dismissed the idea with conviction. "Clearly she has a profound knowledge of the properties of plants and herbs and has skill in healing. It's a rare gift, but it is not magic."

Despite her practical nature, Hannah was not yet ready to dismiss magic, but she did not argue.

"I would like to see her though and his house in the forest. Do you mean to visit?"

"I fully intend to do so soon and of course you shall come with me. I am eager to hear more of Sir Thomas' adventurous life."

"And there's that library he spoke of," she reminded him. "It's about time you did some reading again. You've not touched a book in ages. I miss seeing you with your head stuck in a book and reading bits out aloud to me like you used to at the school."

He did not respond to her comment, saying instead, "Mother and Lucy will be moving to Bratton next week. Then we will need a week or two to find some furniture for the cottages and get your parents settled in. After that we should be able to visit Sir Thomas for a few days."

She snuggled in closer to him. The temperature had dropped outside, but it was still mild and she always felt warm and safe in the malthouse. Their sexual activity had been prolonged and intense that evening, but now she could feel that he was calm and relaxed. Neither of them spoke for a while, just taking pleasure in their closeness, until Will asked, "Do you think you will miss Sandy Barrow?"

"No, tis only a place. I loved helping at the school, but that's not there anymore. Tis people that count, not places and I shall have all the people I love most close to me."

"We will come back to see Sam Selfe sometimes and the Reverend Seddon. No doubt if I need any new clothes I shall still use Ezra Parfitt in Calne because he has my measurements and knows my tastes."

Hannah had not spent much time dwelling on what her new home would be like, but now she asked, "Are you pleased with them cottages in Edington? Funny-it sounds like I be saying Heddington every time I use the name."

"They are hardly palatial, but much better than the house you live in now. Two rooms and a wood-framed extension at the side for a kitchen downstairs and one room upstairs. Both cottages are exactly the same. There is a well with a pump outside. Enough land for a pig stye and chicken coups and to create a garden, plant some fruit trees. There will be plenty to keep you occupied."

"I mean to be busy." One thing was bothering her though. "This business bringing in goods for the mills, does it mean you will go away for long stretches of time, travelling down to the sea and big towns?"

"Only for two or three days at a time. You will hardly notice I have gone and you will have your parents and Baron for company. When I was walking through Heddington Wick the other day, I saw in a farmyard a pair of grown collies and four young ones, five or six months old. I have a fancy to ask the farmer to sell me two of the young ones. They will be extra companions for you and some competition for old Baron. Would you like that?"

She was delighted at the prospect, but had not finished voicing her concerns over the import business.

"But what happens if you don't get on with working in that trade your father set up? You might dislike it and feel discontented."

"I shall have to bear my discontent," he replied, stroking her hair lightly with his finger tips. "There are hosts of folk who are far from contented in the work they do and bear it all their lives because they have no choice. Men are presently forced into becoming soldiers against their will. Nothing could seem worse to me than what I was doing a few months past, killing my fellow countrymen against whom I had no personal grudge and they had none against me. I will never do that again. I would rather languish in prison than agree to it."

The suggestion startled her. "They won't try to make you fight again surely?"

"I doubt it. I can plead disability with this injured hand anyway. In war no one and no place is completely safe. Edington is a small village, off the beaten track. Our cottages are not visible from the road because they are shielded by the remains of the priory walls. The priory is a ruin now, but the church still stands and is a magnificent building. But most towns, villages, farms and cottages fall prey to soldiers demands at some time or another now. If they need food or equipment, they just take it. If they come to the cottages we must convince your father to give them what they want and not try to resist. We can always restock."

Hannah put the image of such dangers out of her mind with haste. She did not wish to contemplate the possibility. Instead she queried, "I know Mistress Lucy will come to see us, but will your mother?"

"Of course she will. So will Uncle Harper and Aunt Elizabeth and we will visit them in Bratton. I shall invite others to visit the cottage, Sam, Reverend Seddon, Caroline Wanley too."

Hannah wrinkled her nose. "Sam Selfe and the Reverend are welcome, but I aint so sure about the Wanley girl. She is sweet enough, but so excitable and she might bring her sister. I aint having her in no house of mine."

Will smiled at her determination. "Caroline will be only too pleased to be free of Maria now and then. Anyway such a humble abode would be beneath Maria's dignity to visit and she is far too busy hunting for a wealthy husband in Warminster."

"I pity any man fool enough to marry her," Hannah said with feeling.

Will agreed, marvelling at the thought that he had once contemplated doing that very thing himself. He was pleased to hear Hannah taking mental possession of her prospective new home. He wished her to regard it as her house to govern as she pleased. It prompted him to say, "Hannah, when we do have visitors I shall introduce you as my wife regardless of whether we marry or not. You may have to tolerate being called Mistress Barry."

"Well if you can put up with hearing your sister addressed as Mistress Collington, I dare say I can bear being called Barry."

"But don't you think we might as well marry. Your father told me why you are so reluctant and I understand that to a point."

"Well he had no business talking to you about that," she scolded, sitting up. "But tis true I'd rather leave you be than become a tie and have you despise me."

"I could never do that Hannah, whatever happens in the future. You are far prouder than I am it seems."

"Why shouldn't I be? Pride aint the preserve of rich or educated folk."

Will could not help laughing. "You have no idea how much you sounded like your father then."

"Oh don't say that," she pleaded, laughing with him. "But as for marrying, I'd rather let that alone for the time being."

She resumed her previous position beside him with her head resting on his chest and he leaned across to kiss her cheek, but was surprised when she said suddenly,

"If a child should be conceived, then I would want to marry. I'm having no child of mine called a bastard."

"Neither would I Hannah, neither would I," he confirmed.

"But," she continued in a similarly truculent tone, "I won't be married at some fancy ceremony in a big church with high-flown words spoken by a vicar who would turn his nose up at me if he saw me working in the fields."

"That is your father talking again. You are echoing his anti-clerical sentiments, always freely aired. Not that I blame him. There are plenty of ordained ministers both orthodox and reform whose behaviour is less than Christian. When I told Sir Thomas that we would be moving to Edington, near the old priory, he informed me that almost two hundred years ago, during Jack Cade's rebellion against King Henry VI, Cade's supporters in Wiltshire turned on the Bishop of Salisbury, who was the King's personal confessor. He fled to find sanctuary in the priory, but they dragged him out and murdered him in the fields near our cottages. I must tell your father that. It will make him immediately fond of his new abode."

She had to admit that the story would tickle John Moss' fancy, before Will assured her that there was no necessity for anyone to marry in church.

" A spousal, a signed marriage contract, is legal if done before a minister. We could ask the Reverend Seddon to marry us in that way at the cottage, or out in the fields if you want with only Lucy, Mother and your parents there. Perhaps Uncle Harper and Aunt Elizabeth could come too."

Hannah considered for a moment, then agreed she would be willing to accept that, adding, "if we do get married" just to underline her earlier statement.

"Are you going back to the rectory tonight?" she asked.

"No, by the time I get over there Rogers will have locked the doors. I am very comfortable here and this is where I'll stay."

"Good, I'll put out the candles then." She paused before she did so, saying, " There is one thing about Sandy Barrow I shall miss."

"What's that?"

"This malthouse. Twas where we first come together and I should hate for it to be broke up and cast aside."

"Well we can take it with us. Raised up on these staddle stones as it is, it should be easy enough to lift on to the back of a cart. Four of us could do it, you, me, your father and perhaps Job Dilke. He's a strong lad. He has been very helpful to me ever since the day of the fire.

He wishes to help us turn the derelict shed besides the cottages into a decent stable for my horse."

Will had become very fond of the grey horse that was once Richard Wanley's favourite mount. Beside its beauty, strength and amiable temperament, the horse was a constant reminder of how Dick had put their friendship before his own safety when arranging Will's escape from the Royalist headquarters in Cornwall.

Hannah was dubious about Job. "He won't stick that out for long. He's too scared of my father."

"You may be surprised. Job is beginning to stand on his own two feet and he is smitten with you. He will risk your father's tongue if he can please you."

Hannah snorted. "And a lot of good that will do him."

"I was hoping Hannah that if Job spent some time at the cottages you could work with him on his reading and writing. He may be growing in confidence, but his progress in that direction has come to a full halt."

She looked him square in the face. "Tis not my task to do, tis yourn. You can teach him far better than I ever can."

"You could do it very well and it would be good for you too- widen your interests."

She protested again, declaring that she still had much to learn herself.

"You are quite literate enough to help Job, I assure you. I am determined that teaching is something I will never attempt again."

After that pronouncement he lay back on the

blanket as if discussion on the subject was finished.

"We'll see about that," Hannah Moss murmured to herself as she extinguished the candles in the lanterns.

THE END

Author's Note

I feel obliged to warn any local history buffs reading this book, who might be prompted to search the archives for the lost village of Sandy Barrow, that they will not find it, because like the Barry and Wanley families, it is purely fictional. Its location however is easy to pinpoint. Travelling on the A342 from Devizes to Chippenham, passing all the left hand turnings into Bromham, you will reach the relatively new entrance and driveway to A J B Farming Ltd. on the right. Just past here my imagination placed Wanley Hall. From there onwards all the land on the right, where a Roman villa once stood, up the hill to the A3102 turning to Calne and across to Heddington Wick and Heddington, including part of the remnant of Chippenham Forest at Whetham Bottom, made up the estates of Sir Roger Wanley and William Barry. The village of Sandy Barrow stood on that land.

I saw the Barry farmhouse as being at the top of the hill, with its back to the Calne road, just past the turning to the road leading to Heddington.

I drive from Poulshot to Calne regularly because of my involvement with Calne Heritage Centre and one bright, spring day my mind's eye saw with great clarity those cottages of Sandy Barrow scattered down the valley and I was determined to bring them to life.

Much of the history of the local area depicted in this book is factual and many of the characters surrounding the fictional ones did exist. Calne did suffer from a serious outbreak of plague in 1637 and the Parish Church tower came crashing down in 1638.

The current houses in Mill Street, Calne are 18th and 19th Century, but as Calne Mill was recorded as early as mid-14th Century, I have taken the liberty in assuming that there were earlier houses in Mill Street, superseded by newer builds. The two 16th Century houses opposite the Mill that were demolished to make way for the new vicarage, suggest that my assumption is credible.

Heddington Rectory was standing at this period and a dynasty of rectors from the Rogers family did develop. I found no clues to the true character of Henry Rogers and he may well have been a more generous man than the one I have painted in my story. My apologies to his descendants if it is so.

All contemporary records agree that Sir Edward Baynton was arrogant, quarrelsome and generally disliked. His pretentious mansion, Bromham House was burnt down by the Royalists in 1645 to prevent it becoming a Parliamentary stronghold. Baynton bought Avebury Manor and lived there while he built Spye Park, using some of the remaining fabric from Bromham House.

I have tried to give a flavour of the military aspects of the early stages of the Civil War in the West Country and also underline how the local population was pressurized by both sides to provide them with supplies without payment, depleting their often meagre resources.

The effects of the Battle of Roundway Down must have been evident in the local area for days after the event itself, as men, some of them wounded, straggled through nearby villages and towns trying to escape capture. I was struck by a brief entry in the Calne Burial Register for July 1643 " *Buried three soldiers wounded to death upon the Vizes Down the 13th July.* "

The clash at Roundway was the most complete Royalist victory of the whole war. Most engagements at this early stage were inconclusive, with little advantage to either side. Roundway, followed by the taking of Bristol, put most of the West Country under the King's control. Charles Lloyd dispatched a raiding party from Devizes Castle to Pinhills Manor and the small garrison was forced to surrender. Prince Rupert ordered the house to be destroyed and on 8th January 1644, Lloyd reported that he had "*made Blake's house uninhabitable and drained the moat.*"

However, Henry Blake's successor, Ambrose Blake, built a fine farmhouse out of the ruins, where the family continued to live for some years.

Despite the Royalist domination in the West, pockets of resistance remained. The King failed to take Gloucester and during 1644/45 the tide gradually turned.

Sir William Waller's reputation had been dented by the defeat at Roundway, but not destroyed. He won an important victory against Ralph Hopton at Cheriton near Winchester in March 1644 which proved to be a turning point.

When Sir Thomas Fairfax became the new Lord General of Parliament's forces, he and Oliver Cromwell set about the task of training the army to a professional standard, creating what was called the New Model Army.

Fairfax took retook Bristol in September 1645. It was Cromwell's task to mop up the Royalists in Wiltshire with 5,000 troops and a train of heavy artillery.

Faced with these guns stationed in the Market Place, Charles Lloyd surrendered Devizes Castle on 23rd September. Orders were issued to demolish the castle fortifications and work began the following year. It proved a handy source of building materials for local people for many years afterwards. The antiquarian William Stukeley wrote in 1723, *"The castle is ignobly mangled and every day destroyed by persons who care not to leave a stone standing, though for a wall to their gardens."*

Cromwell went on from Devizes to force the surrender of Lacock Abbey and then on into Hampshire to take Winchester. By April 1646 the whole of Wessex was in Parliamentary hands and King Charles surrendered on 5th May.

But that was not the end of the story. I will leave those readers interested enough to follow the progress of the conflict through to its conclusion for themselves.

Readers who read my first novel "Fathoming the Universe" may have been surprised to find Sir Thomas Mountfield appearing in "Fatal August." I had a number of requests for a sequel to "Fathoming the Universe," but although I have some ideas, I have never got around to forming them into a complete narrative. I am very fond of Sir Thomas. He is one of my favourite creations. His magnetism took on a life of its own and I sometimes find it hard to believe he is not real. So it gave me great pleasure to imagine that he and his formidable wife, Dawn Light, were still alive and active fifty years on from the ending of that first book. His conversation with Will Barry gives some hints to those of you who already know him, of what happened in his life during the intervening years. I like to think of him helping Will to come to terms with his shattered life.

Perhaps one day I will embark on that sequel.

Sue Boddington
March 2022